The Solaris Book of New
Science Fiction
Volume Two

The Solaris Book of New
Science Fiction
Volume Two

Edited by George Mann

Including stories by

Dan Abnett
Neal Asher
Eric Brown
Brenda Cooper
David Louis Edelman
Paul Di Filippo
Dominic Green
Kay Kenyon
Mary Robinette Kowal
Michael Moorcock
Robert Reed
Chris Roberson
Karl Schroeder
Peter Watts

SOLARIS

First published 2008 by Solaris
an imprint of BL Publishing
Games Workshop Ltd, Willow Road
Nottingham NG7 2WS
UK

www.solarisbooks.com

ISBN-13: 978 1 84416 542 1
ISBN-10: 1 84416 542 6

Contents

Introduction

George Mann

*The return of the original
science fiction anthology?*

IN THE PAGES of the September 2007 issue of *The Magazine of Fantasy & Science Fiction*, James Sallis reviewed the first volume of *The Solaris Book of New Science Fiction* alongside *Fast Forward #1* (edited by the estimable Lou Anders), pointing to the similarities between the two new anthology series and wondering whether there was any relevance to be read into the timing of their appearance on the market. He talked about "windows that open from time to time" and whether the two books represented "a new breed of original anthologies," having already discussed at some length the science fiction anthology series of old: *Orbit, Star Science Fiction, Nova,* and others.

It's an interesting question, and one I don't think I'm in a position to answer, at least not directly (perhaps things like this are better judged by critics, readers, and posterity). But I think it *is* worth exploring the reasons behind why I'm sitting here writing this introduction to a second volume of new science fiction stories and why, shortly, I'll be doing the same again for volume three. If the original anthology is returning, what is it returning from? Was there really a golden age of SF anthologies in the first place? And what is it that Solaris is trying to achieve by offering this new series of short story anthologies to the market?

I think the answers to all of those questions are intertwined.

It's my particular view that short fiction is the lifeblood of the SF genre, a fundamental testbed of ideas, a breeding ground for new writers and a perfect form for the genre in all its aspects: punchy character pieces, concept-driven tales full of sense-of-wonder, instalments in a larger future history. Many writers first come to the attention of editors through their short fiction and go on to become novelists in the wider field. Many others continue to write nothing but short stories, yet the impact they have on the genre is still immense, still *vital*. Not only that, but the whole experience of reading short fiction is also markedly different than the experience of reading a novel—a good story punches you in the gut, makes you sit up immediately and pay attention, whilst a novel can toy with you for longer, playing the long game.

Having said all that, though, I think it is clear that the short story market has come under intense pressure in recent years. Markets have dwindled. Writers have found it increasingly difficult to find new venues for their stories. Publishers have found it even harder to make the economics of publishing original anthologies work. Whilst there is a core readership who remain steadfastly glued to the monthly digests (and receive a little thrill each and every time that packet arrives in the post), it's fair to say that there is a much wider audience of readers—casual book buyers—who never come into contact with these periodicals. They may stroll into their nearest bookstore on a weekend, browse the shelves, and leave with an armful of books, blissfully unaware that their favourite author has a new short story in one of that month's new magazines. In fact, the first time they may even become *aware* of that story may be years later, when it's finally collected by the author into a book.

In the past, this wasn't as much of an issue. The SF genre grew out of the American pulps and short stories *were* the genre. If people wanted to read an SF story, it was usually a short one. Commercially, however, the genre has changed. Novels are the order of the day. Casual readers want the perceived 'value for money'; they want to buy books by the inch, want their experience to last longer. Of course, that's just a sweeping generalisation, but it's certainly true that the days of the aforementioned *Orbit, Star Science Fiction, Nova,* and *New Worlds* have gone. It's harder than ever before to get books on shelves in bookstores, and harder still to get readers to buy them.

So, knowing this, what madness drove us to launch a new series of anthologies into this marketplace? Faced with a climate where the only original anthologies having any real mass-market success were themed anthologies, what made us decide to go down the route of a book of non-themed stories?

There's an obvious place to start: *because no one else was doing it*. When we first sat around the table to plan our new imprint, we looked long and hard at the markets in both the US and the UK. And we saw a gap. More than that, we saw a *need*. While a number of important annual reprint anthologies (typified by Gardner Dozois's *Year's Best Science Fiction* and David Hartwell & Kathryn Cramer's *Year's Best SF*) were finding a home in the mass market each year, no one appeared to be developing a series of *original* annual anthologies. We decided to step into the breach. Of course, we were driven by a certain amount of nostalgia for the anthology series of old, a desire to publish the type of books that inspired us in our youth. But it was more than that, too. We wanted to rise to the challenge and make it work in the modern market. We made no claims to knowing differently to anyone else—we simply set out our stall in the best way we knew how, and crossed our fingers.

The original brief was simple: we wanted to reach a wider, book-buying public with great new science fiction stories from a range of talented authors. We wanted to appeal to fans and new readers alike, the people who would search out our books in their local stores, and the people who would pick them up at random because they saw them for the first time sitting on a shelf in that same store. We also wanted to appeal to authors, as a venue to get their stories into people's hands and allow them to reach a wider audience with their work. We aimed to take some of the very best short science fiction stories we could find, and provide them with a showcase. I'd like to think, in some small measure, we succeeded in this.

With *The Solaris Book of New Science Fiction: Volume Two*, our original brief remains the same, and we present it to you in that spirit. For me, the fifteen stories in this collection are true to that original brief: vibrant, sparkling, dark, bitter, exciting— the spectrum of human experience played out against a background of stars, or standing in line at an airport, nervously waiting for a security check.

So, THE RETURN of the original science fiction anthology? In my opinion, it's far too early to tell. But one thing's for sure—it is clear there were others with similar thoughts to our own, and with a number of other new original anthology series now hitting the shelves, *The Solaris Book of New Science Fiction* is in excellent company. When all is said and done, today's science fiction reader has a remarkable array of new stories with which to feed their addiction—and that is the most important thing of all. As James Sallis says at the end of his review, let's hope that it's the start of something great.

George Mann
Nottingham, England
August 2007

iCity

Paul Di Filippo

I LOST A whole neighborhood last night to that bitch Holly Grale. The Floradora Heights. Renamed this morning, after its overnight reformation and subsequent QuikPoll accreditation. Now the district was officially "WesBes," as in "West of Bester." I *hate* those faddish abbreviated portmanteau names. Where's the dignity? Where's the sense of tradition? Where's the romance? Plus, once Bester Street disappears, as it's bound to do soon, where's that leave your trendy designation?

But my tastes were obviously in the minority, since 67.9 percent of the residents of the quondam Floradora Heights had voted to accept Grale's reformation over my established plan which they had been living in for some time.

Still, I shouldn't have been so down. Floradora Heights had lasted 2063 hours until suffering the diminishment in popularity that had triggered the reformation. The average duration stats for all iCity sensate neighborhood plans were not quite 1600 hours. So my plan had performed over twenty percent better than average. That result, along with my ten extant accreditations, would certainly allow me to maintain my place in the planner rankings—and maybe even jump up a notch or two.

So round about noon of the day I lost to Grale, after moping and enjoying my loser's morning sulk, I began to cheer up. I figured I deserved a drink, either as solace for the loss or affirmation of my genius. So I headed out in search of the Desire Path.

I was living then on Dictionary Hill, a district created by my friend Virgule Partch. A very pleasant plan, although I would have oriented the main entrances of Hastings Park north-south rather than east-west. My condo, an older model which I had opted to carry over with me during every reformation over the past five years, was currently incorporated into a building dubbed the Rogue Mandala. Very conveniently situated right next to a Starbucks. (God bless Partch's thoughtful plans!) So after exiting the Mandala, I stepped inside the Starbucks to grab a tall guarana and a teff cake. No sense imbibing booze on an empty stomach, especially this early.

It was such a nice blue-sky day outside—the faithful faraway pico-satellite swarm had moderated the August sunlight and the ambient temperature to very comfortable levels—that I took my drink and food outside and let the peristaltic sensate sidewalk carry me along while I ate.

I arbitrarily headed toward the Konkoville district. Or at least what had been the Konkoville district last night; I confess I hadn't scanned the reformation postings for all of iCity yet, checking only on my eleven accreditations (now ten, damn it, thanks to Grale!). Konkoville was where the Desire Path, my favorite bar, had resided the last time I had visited, a couple of days ago.

But as I approached the edges of the district, I could see that it was unlikely I would find the Desire Path here any longer.

Konkoville was now an extensive tivoli named Little Sleazy, full of wild amusement rides and fast-food booths, bursting with the noise of screaming kids.

I took out my phone and got a map of iCity as of this very moment. I queried for the Desire Path and found it halfway across town, in the Coal Sack. Oh, well, I had plenty of time and nothing better to do. So rather than dive underground for a quick subway ride, I continued on the relatively slow sidewalk toward my goal.

I used the time to study the stats on my ten remaining districts.

Resident satisfaction was holding steady in six: Cyprian Fields, Bayside, Crowmarsh, East Plum, Borogroves and Lower Uppercrust. My figures had taken a hit in two: Tangerang and Bekaski. And the remaining two showed an uptick: Disco Biscuits and Nuala's Back Forty.

I immediately scheduled an interim charrette for Tangerang and Bekaski. No sense letting things get bad enough to open up these two districts to a competitive reformation. That'd be just what I needed, the loss of two more of my fiefs to someone like Grale. In Disco Biscuits and Nuala's Back Forty I initiated proxy polling to try to determine what the residents found so newly appealing about life there.

Finished with that, I looked to see if any new postings for competitive reformations elsewhere had come up. I sure didn't want any of my fiefs to be the subject of such a contest. But if some other unlucky planner let his district slide, prompting such a referendum—well, that's just how the system worked. I wasn't going to hold back out of pity. Competitive urban planning was not a game for the weak-spined. And I needed to pick up a new district to make up for my loss of Floradora Heights.

Yes! Bloorvoor Estates, currently accredited to Mode O'Day, was up for reformation! I liked Mode, but I couldn't afford any weepy sentimentality. My mind already churning with plans, I set my sights on Bloorvoor Estates and vowed not to look back.

I was just hoping Mode wouldn't be present at the Desire Path. If I didn't have to see her and commiserate, my life would be a lot easier.

I crossed over the district line separating Bollingwood from the Coal Sack, and within another minute had dismounted the sidewalk to stand at the door of the Desire Path.

The interior of the bar had changed since my last visit two days prior, a complete makeover. A gallery of taxidermied animal heads—and some human ones—filled one whole wall. All utterly realistic fakes, of course, composed of sensate putty. Beneath the glassy-eyed heads, a bunch of my peers sat at a variety of tables. I moved to join them.

"Hey, look, it's Moses!"

"Moses proposes, and the populace disposes!"

"Fred Law!"

I dropped down into a seat and soon had a drink in hand. After a polite interval of small talk, the expressions of pity for my recent loss came. Some were genuine; some were thinly stretched over glee.

"I always thought Floradora Heights was one of your best districts, Moze," said Yvonne Lestrange. Yvonne and I had lived together some years ago for almost 5000 hours, and retained genuine feelings for each other.

"Thanks," I responded. "I particularly liked how Sparkle Pond reflected the spire of Bindloss Church."

Cristo Rivadavia said, "Yes, quite a pleasant sentimental effect. But really, Moses, whatever were you thinking with that plaza?"

"Which one?"

"The one where the fountain placement created absolutely chaotic traffic flows."

"That placement was determined by the best shared-space models!"

"Nonetheless—"

Laguna Diamante intervened before our argument could escalate. "Hey, boys, that's enough head-butting. We all know that Moses has done plenty of good work. He couldn't help it that the

Floradora citizens eventually tired of his plan. We all know how fickle populaces are."

A general round of "Amens" arose, and glasses were refilled for a toast.

"To Diaspar!"

"To Diaspar!"

"Diaspar forever!"

With genuine conviviality restored, the talk naturally turned to the Bloorvoor competition.

"Well, I'm out of this one," said Tartan Vartan. "Unless I get randomly seeded. My stats don't put me in the top ten any longer."

Hoagy Spreckles put a comradely arm around Vartan's shoulders. "Don't worry. Just run a few more phantom zones like your last one, and you'll get an invitation from one populace or another. After that, you'll be in like Unwyn."

Everyone began to talk at once then, tossing out hints of how they would approach this competition.

And then in walked Mode O'Day herself.

If I had been dragging earlier, then Mode was positively flatlining. Her pretty face resembled a bulldog with dyspepsia. She carried a lump of sensate putty with her that she continually kneaded like a paranoid ship's captain angry about his missing strawberries.

To massed silence, Mode dropped into a seat like a sack of doorknobs. She plopped the putty in the middle of the table and took out her phone. Still no one spoke. She sent the plans for the Bloorvoor district to the putty and the shapeless lump instantly snapped into the configuration of that neighborhood, a perfectly detailed miniature we all recognized.

Mode studied the tiny sculpture for nearly a full minute. No one dared offer a word. Then with the swipe of a thumbnail across her phone's screen, she rendered the putty into the semblance of a human hand with middle finger outthrust and the others bent back.

"That's what I think of my populace!" she said.

And we all cheered.

So I DOVE right into the work of reifying my plan for the reformation of the Bloorvoor district. After so many years as both an amateur and competitive urban planner in iCity, the whole procedure possessed an intimate familiarity.

First, of course, came the dissatisfied populace. Registering their accumulating displeasure or simple boredom with their district, the continuously polled voice of the populace eventually triggered a Request for Reformation.

At that point the top ten urban planners (barring the one who had designed the failed district), along with a handful of randomly seeded contestants, were invited to enter their designs.

Any district plan arose from a planner's innate creativity, experience, inspiration, and skills, of course. But the charrette process also held importance. Citizens got to weigh in with suggestions and criticisms.

At some prearranged point all the plans were locked down. At that stage they were instantiated as both phantom zone walk-thru models and physical tabletop versions. (The phantom zone was littered with thousands of other amateur walk-thrus compiled on a freelance basis.) A period of inspection by the populace lasted a week or so. Then came the first and most important vote. The winning plan would govern the overnight reformation of the district. A final pro forma poll on the morning after the reformation, once the populace had a short time to verify the details of the full scale instantiation, would award final accreditation to the planner.

Simple, right?

If you think so, you've never been a competitive urban planner.

I spent several nerve-stretched weeks subsisting on a diet of daffy-doze and TVP bars, trying to design the best, most exciting district I had ever designed, a brilliant mix of utilitarianism, excitement, surprise, grandeur, and comfort. What governed me? Well of course I wanted to please the populace. But I was working just as hard to please myself. The esthetics of my plan were actually uppermost in my instinctive choices and refinements and calculations.

Urban planning was my artform, iCity my medium.

I sought advice from a couple of my compatriots whom I trusted and who also weren't involved in this competition. (I trusted any of my peers just so far.) Virgule and Yvonne saw my roughs and offered suggestions.

"You really think the tensile parms of the senstrate will support a pylon that high?"

"You used that same skin last year in Marple Cheshire, remember?"

"Siting the Jedi Temple within a hundred yards of the Zionist Charismatics? What were you thinking!"

The long hard slog to a final plan took all my concentration and energy. But still, I spared a little attention pinging the grapevine and trying to learn what the other contestants were doing.

That included Holly Grale of course. That stinker ranked two spots below me, but still within the top ten. Right this minute, as I struggled to balance greenspace with mall footage, taverns with schools, she was doing the same.

But her security was tight, and no news filtered out about her design.

Not even when I bumped into her at the reformation of Las Ramblas.

BACK WHEN THE announcement that Bloorvoor was up for reformation appeared, the Las Ramblas remodeling was already in the populace-inspection period. The eventual popular vote awarded the honors to Lafferty Fisk and his plan, and tonight Lafferty was throwing the usual party to witness and celebrate his triumph.

The venue was a restaurant named Myxomycota that cantilevered out from the side of Mount Excess. Mount Excess held all the extra mass of sensate substrate not currently in use by any neighborhood. It was in effect a solid vertical reservoir which could be drawn down or added to, and thus its elevation and bulk was constantly changing. Tonight Mount Excess was pretty substantial—minimalist designs were hip just then—affording us a good panoramic view of iCity and Las Ramblas, the neighborhood lit up all red as a sign of the impending transformation.

The food and drink and music were splendid—I seem to recall a band named the Tiny Identities was playing—the company was stimulating, and I was just beginning to relax for the first time in ages. My plan for the competition was almost finalized, with a day or two to spare till the deadline. As midnight approached, a wave of pleasant tension and anticipation enveloped the room. Everyone clustered against the big windows that looked out over the brilliant city.

I turned to the person at my elbow to make some innane comment, and there stood Holly Grale.

Her black hair was buzzed short, she had six cometary cinder studs in each earlobe, and she wore a cat suit made out of glistening kelp cloth, accessorized with a small animated cape. Her broad, wry, painted mouth was ironically quirked.

"Well, well, well," she said in a voice whose sensuous allure I found distractingly at odds with my professional repugnance for this woman. "If it isn't Frederick Law Moses, once the baron of Floradora Heights."

My name sounded so pretentious coming from her lips. I suppose "Robert Olmsted" might have been a less dramatic alternative to honor my heroes, but when I had chosen my name I had been much younger and dreamier.

"Oh, Holly, it's you. I didn't recognize you for a moment without your copy of *Urban Planning for Dummies* in your hand. Shouldn't you be home trying to master that ancient emulation of *SimCity*?"

My jibes had no effect. "I have plenty of down time now, Moses. I've just locked in my design for the Bloorvoor competition."

This news unnerved me. Only a very confident or foolish planner wouldn't be making changes right up till the last minute. I tried to dissemble my anxiety with a quip, but then events outside precluded all conversation.

The reformation of Bloorvoor had begun.

The entire red-lit district began to dissolve in syrupy slow-mo fashion, structures flowing downward into the sensate motherboard like a taffy pull. The varied cityscape, the topography of streets and buildings and all the district's "vegetation," was losing its stock of unique identities as all constructions were subsumed back into the senstrate from which they had once arisen.

Of course, all businesses, clubs, cafes, workshops, restaurants, and other establishments had closed down early for the evening prior to the change, and people had retreated to their homes and condos, if they had not left the district entirely. These domestic units were autonomous permanent nodes and had sealed themselves off, locking their occupants safely away. Those inside would ride out the reformation without a jolt or qualm, cradled by the intelligent senstrate. Many people even slept through the whole process. And anyone absent-minded enough to be caught out during the change would be envaginated by the senstrate in a life-support vacuole and protected till the reformation was over. Inconvenient, but hardly dangerous.

Now the district was a flat featureless plain, a hole in iCity, dotted with the capsules of domestic units and the occasional person-sized vacuole, awaiting the signal to transform.

Lafferty Fisk proudly transmitted the impulse from his phone.

Cascades of information coursed through the senstrate.

iCity: a lattice of pure patterns.

Just like the time Mode O'Day had instantiated the old model of Bloorvoor on the tabletop in Desire Path, so now the new version of Las Ramblas (to be named Airegin Miles) commenced to be born. Structures composed of pure senstrate arose amidst a matrix of streets and other urban features, incorporating the autonomous domestic units into themselves where planned. (I swore I felt Mount Excess drop by a centimeter or three.) The sensate material assumed a variety of textures, and skins, right down to a very convincing indestructible grass and soil. Water flowed through new conduits into ponds and canals. Normal-colored lights came on.

Within less than an hour, Aieregin Miles stood complete, iCity's newest district.

A huge round of applause broke out in the restaurant. Lafferty Fisk stood at the focus of the approbation and envy. Memories of being there myself flooded powerfully through me.

When the tumult died down, I looked around, feeling I could be generous even toward Holly Grale.

But she was nowhere to be seen.

ALL THE TABLETOP models and phantom zone walk-thrus for the Bloorvoor reformation went live a couple of days later. So I saw what Grale had accomplished.

Her design was magnificent. There was no denying it. Just the way Alpha Ralpha Boulevard looped around and flowed into von Arx Plaza—this was genuine talent at work.

Was her design better than mine and all the others?

Only the populace could say.

And soon they said yes.

Grale's was the winner.

I MOPED AROUND for forty-eight hours in an absolute funk, a malaise that was hardly alleviated by the fact that my plan for Bloorvoor had garnered the second highest number of votes. Doubt and despair assailed me. Was I losing my touch? Had I plumbed the depths of my art and hit a stony infertile bottom? Should I abandon my passion?

I spent an inordinate amount of time inside the phantom zone walk-thru of Grale's winning plan. I kept comparing her accomplishment, her sensibilities, to mine, fixated on discovering what had made her entry so appealing to the populace. Was it this particular cornice, this special wall, this juxtaposition of tree and window? The way sunlight would strike that certain gable, or wind funnel down that mournful alley?

And by the end of my fevered inspection, I had decided something.

The taste of the populace was debased. The residents of Bloorvoor—soon to become (yuck!) "QualQuad"—had voted incorrectly. My design was indeed the superior one.

I realize now how crazy that sounds. The citizenry is always the ultimate arbiter. Without them, we urban planners would have no reason to exist. There can be no imposition of our tastes over their veto, no valorizing of a platonic perfection over perceived utility. We all offer the best we have, and they choose among us.

But in my anger and jealousy and despair, I lost sight of these verities. I was more than a little insane, and that remains my only excuse for what I did next.

I went to see Sandy Verstandig.

Sandy was one of the tech gnomes who kept the senstrate bubbling and ready for use at top efficiency and reliability. A rough-edged petite woman who favored a strong floral perfume and employed more profanity than any random half-dozen athletes. I say "gnome," but of course that designation was just a nickname for her job. She didn't live literally underground. There was no need for her to be in physical proximity to the intelligent material that formed the substance of iCity. Except for the occasional regular maintenance inspection of various pieces of subterranean hardware, she could handle all of her duties via her phone.

Duties such as establishing the order of the reformation queue.

I knew Sandy from frequent help she had given me in the past, when I had had questions about the senstrate that only a hands-on expert could answer. In our face-to-face conversations, I had always gotten the sense that she would not be averse to a romantic relationship.

I'm ashamed now to describe how easy it was to get Sandy Verstandig into bed. How easy it was to secure access her phone while she slept.

And finally, how easy it was to substitute my plan for Grale's in the reformation queue, and conceal all traces of my crime.

CROWDING AGAINST THE windows at Myxomycota once again, as the final seconds ticked away until midnight, I almost shivered with anticipation. There was Bloorvoor down below, all lit in red. Soon it would be rechristened Bushyhead, when it assumed the lineaments of my visionary design. It was all I could do not to chuckle aloud at the shock Grale was about to receive.

Of course, the mix-up would be immediately apparent, the unmistakable substitution of my superior design for her inferior one. But it would not be totally improbable that the second-place entry might have been mistakenly inserted ahead of the winner in the queue. Yes, Sandy Verstandig would take some minor blame. But no lasting harm done. And then, in the morning, the populace would see just how wonderful their new neighborhood was, and vote to keep it. I'd get the accreditation, and be back up to eleven. Grale would look like a whiner and sore loser if she contested the results.

As I said, I wasn't thinking too clearly.

Various people addressed me in those last few minutes, but I don't recall anything they or I said.

And then midnight arrived.

The deliquescent "demolition" of Bloorvoor occurred perfectly, rendering the district featureless. All the condo nodes and vacuoles awaited reincorporation into the new buildings. Our room held its collective breath for the manifestation of the winning design.

And that's when all chaos erupted.

The senstrate began to seethe and churn, tossing out irregular whips and tendrils and geysers. Condo nodes bobbed about like sailboats in a typhoon. I could barely imagine the ride the inhabitants were getting, although I knew that automatic interior safety measures—inflatable furniture, airbag walls and such—would prevent them from being harmed.

The watchers were stunned. I saw Grale with her eyes wide and mouth agape. That image alone was sufficient reward. But also my only tangible satisfaction.

Because what happened next was utterly tragic.

My design emerged, but hybridized with Grale's!

Somehow I had botched the queue, overlaying and blending the two plans. I never would have thought such a thing would be possible. But the reality stood before us.

The most outré buildings began to self-assemble, mutant structures obeying no esthetic code, arrayed higgledy-piggledy across the district. A nightmare, a surreal canvas—

I backed away from the window. "No, no, this wasn't supposed to happen—"

I have to give Grale credit for sharpness of hearing and intelligence. She was on me then like a tigress, bearing me to the floor and pummeling me half-senseless, while outside our sight the mashup reformation surged on. We rolled around for what seemed a bruising eternity, until other planners managed to separate us.

Restrained by Partch and O'Day, almost growling, Grale confronted me. "Moses, you don't know what a huge fucking mess you've gotten yourself into!"

And I certainly didn't.

But neither did she.

OF COURSE YOU know how the new hybrid district of QualBushy (sometimes also known as Head-Quad) broke all duration records. Approved the morning after by a shocking 97.6 percent of the populace. Not falling to its next reformation for an astonishing 10,139 hours.

Mashup designs became the *sine qua non* for all reformations. iCity experienced a renaissance of design fecundity and doubled in acreage. Mount Excess was joined by Mount Backup. Partnerships formed, broke up, and reformed among the planners at an astonishing rate.

Except for one pairing that endured.

Grale and Moses.

I give Holly top billing because I'd never hear the end of it at home around the dinner table if I didn't.

The Space Crawl Blues

Kay Kenyon

"GOING TO THE Graveyard, then?" Ian stood by the quantum arch, ready to deliver a sales pitch.

But Blake Niva was not a customer, would never be. Even if Ian was his best friend and owner of the latest wizardry in space travel, even then he would never cave in and do it.

"Yeah, the Graveyard, Ian. But going the slow way." *Space crawl,* and proud of it. Blake eyed the far end of the transport center where the space time, real time, old time shuttle concourse lay. He wished he could bypass the QT desk, bypass Ian and the inevitable excruciating conversation.

"I could get you there in a pico second," Ian said, "like I've said before." Ian exchanged conspiratorial glances with the quantum engineer who manned the arch. They were so proud of themselves, so smug. So rich.

"Right," Blake said, not wanting to argue. The Graveyard hung in low Europa orbit at 1200 kilometers, so in fact Ian's arch could save him about two hours round trip transit time, if time was all Blake cared about. "Catch you for a beer on the way back?"

Ian nodded. Beer was the glue between them, thin as horse piss, thick as habit. The two men had been thrown together for three years on this chunk of ice. Europa spectacularly orbited the great Jovian plan et, or, more accurately, forever fell into it, due to the elegant relation between gravity and tangential velocity—concepts that, in space travel these days, were in danger of irrelevance.

The two men could not have been more different. Ian the self-confident partner in a company that had just broken the barrier to quantum travel; Blake the annoyingly shy pilot of real—and real slow—nuts and bolts space ships. Next to Ian, Blake felt comfortably inadequate, glad to take his friend's leavings, including the women who took pity on Blake because he was bad at small talk in bars.

As Blake edged away, Ian kept him in the web of conversation. "You ought to try my way. Just once. Make a man of you," he said, joking, but meaning it. "You'd come out the other side with a mean knack for the ladies, yeah?" He stood by the arch and its quantum engineer like a barker at a carnival, drumming up business.

Blake grinned, but as so often around Ian, he seemed to miss the point. Since when did women find it sexy if you'd gone quantum? It proved you had the balls to travel digital? Maybe it was a macho thing. It did scare some people, those who didn't understand quantum teleportation. Which was basically everybody.

Ian kept proselytizing. "Let us give you the ride, man; you'll be better for it."

"You're crazy. It's quantum teleportation, not a new aftershave."

"You need a defrag, guy. We're here to help."

He waved at his friend, in a hurry to leave, uncomfortable with Ian's smug suggestions that he needed fixing. Or proving. Or more women. Or all the other things Ian was that Blake wasn't.

Sammy, at least, had never thought he needed to be different. With her lying in the Graveyard, life would never be the same.

The space shuttle was slow transport, yeah. But it would give him time to prepare. He'd say his good-byes in the Yard, and he'd do so personally—no long-distance fare-thee-wells. It wouldn't be right. They'd been too close.

He looked back at the QT station where Ian and crew had snagged a customer. The quantum engineer directed her into the arch of the processor. Light crawled over her skin, haloing it. Then she disappeared. Blake wished her bon voyage, wherever her final destination might take her, as he used to say over the com back when he had a goddamn job.

The rush of resentment surprised him.

It wasn't Ian's fault that it had come to this: People as bits. Travel as transmission. Clean, cheap, elegant. The technology was bound to be viable sooner or later. Thing was, QT arrived a tad early for Blake Niva.

For one thing, it put him out of a job. Permanently.

No use for pilots. You remember pilots? People who could navigate their way out of a comet cluster and change a lithium heat exchanger with their left hand while coaxing a balky optical computer to make nice to the hydroponics. No navigation needed these days. No 'ponics, either. Nope. What the worlds need now are hyped-up data slingers.

"Ticket?" The flight desk guy took Blake's boarding pass, sending him into the gullet of the loading tube. No lines, of course. Nobody was taking shuttles in these last weeks since QT got the OK from the UN. Thing was, quantum teleportation was brand new, so lots of people had postponed trips, waiting for the QT fares to come down, and then they'd just teleport. Folks who'd booked ram jet scoop flights to Procyon IV or ion drive passages to the Trapezius cluster all cancelled. Pretty soon business would be booming for Ian and company.

Folks had good reason to cancel space crawl plans. You didn't want to be scooped in your ram jet scoop. You'd be out in real spacetime, say, thirty light years, and QT clients would zip past you at quantum speeds. Course, it's not speed at all. It isn't even travel. It's just your bits entangling with the bits of the universe, until you come out the other end, reconstructed.

Ian and his ilk almost worshipped the process. They joked that it defragged you, but it was more than just braying. They thought the process was akin to entangling with God. Take a mega collider, blast the gluons away, create pairs of quarks, put half of 'em in a box, and take it by space crawl to all the destinations a body could possibly want. Then, with "spooky action at a distance"—even Einstein didn't comprehend it—you could send information between the first quark and the second. Simple. Maybe too simple. Nobody understood it at a fundamental level. Einstein also said that physics should be as simple as possible, but no simpler. They should have listened to him.

Blake'd rather entangle with a grizzly or a Europan glide eel than with quantum states. He'd managed to live twenty-eight years without ever knowing he *had* a quantum state, and it had always been good enough, before. He'd had the best job a man could want. And he'd had Sammy.

He stopped at the cockpit, jawing for a few moments with Keegan, the lucky son of a bitch who still had a pilot's job, then he buckled in. Six weeks left, Keegan said. Then they'd decommission the shuttle. *Put it down*, Blake thought, *like an old horse.*

Settling in as the shuttle lifted off, he took pleasure in the physicality of the G-force, the sheer waste of carbon molecules in the barely controlled explosions under his butt. *I'm on my way, Sammy. Don't think I'd let you go without saying goodbye, do you?*

On board there were a few other passengers heading for the Yard—a handful of decommissioning engineers, haz-mat experts, and recycling aides, mostly. They could have chosen to QT it, but maybe they were sentimental. Or afraid.

Who could say whether, when they put your data stream back together, you'd be the true you? More to the point, who could *prove* it? Once a person had QT'd, Blake thought they seemed different. Maybe it was the sense of betrayal he felt, just looking at them. Not that you could really blame folks for choosing clean, cheap, and elegant.

But there were eight people on this flight who'd likely never been in a teleporter.

Not yet, anyway. Fares would come down, though. Pretty soon, it would be a QT universe.

"THE SAMANTHA GRAY," Keegan announced over the com.

Blake released himself from the seat and floated to the egress hatch, pulling himself along by handholds. Once into the connector he made his way to the docking mast and into the lock, and then, with a rush of gravity, into the *Samantha Gray*.

"Sammy." His voice bounced around the empty corridor.

"Blake," came her voice, a velvety gust.

He got his bearings, adjusting to the gravity of spin, a little light of one G. Struggling, he got his space stomach under control, and his emotions. Turning toward the bridge he trailed his fingertips along the wall, not for stability, but to feel her skin, that solid, embracing reality of ship. Times he could remember when he'd felt her around him, like a cocoon in his bunk; times when she'd lit his way to the gymnasium, or the mess hall, like she knew where he'd decided to go; times when she'd pearled her hull to repair a rip, her calm voice saying, *Patch program underway, Patch program complete.* And then, for his ears only, *Blake, I think we'll be fine.*

Now decommissioned, she waited for the engineers to board, yank her optical computers, offload her savant programming. After those indignities would come the recycling bots, like grave beetles. They'd reduce her to the raw material for—no, he couldn't think about Sammy being the stuff of kids' toys or macaroni packaging, or QT processors. As he walked to the bridge, they said no more to each other. In fact, Blake couldn't speak.

On the bridge, the view was a panoramic glory. Europa turned below, its glossy ice punctuated by the hab domes. Beyond, Jupiter bestrode the sky, a yellow and orange colossus, its tidal forces keeping Europa's subsurface oceans liquid. The view had its grandeur, yes, but something else held Blake transfixed.

The ships.

They were arrayed before him, just ahead, and to starboard, and to port, locked together in orbit in the prettiest sight a normal human being could hope to see. Here was a good cross-section of the near-Earth fleet: a couple of ramjets, three nuclear pulses, even a nonrelativistic rocket there just below. And a beamed light sail—for eight brief months the go-to technology before QT passed muster. Enclosing him, the *Samantha Gray*, his stalwart ion scoop. These would have been your choices for stellar transport back in the day. All the way six months ago before the QT breakthrough. The last of the test subjects had come through fine. People dying of cancer, Lupus, incurable viruses, volunteered to become trial data streams to forward the future of instantaneous travel. The announcement of UN approval hit the stock market like a cometary impact. After the dust had settled, people had made their trip adjustments, and overnight Blake Niva and Sammy had become obsolete.

"I still have some ice water."

"Thanks, Sammy." He went to the dispenser and brought a cup back to the pilot's station. He thought about putting his feet up on the console, but training and pride took precedence over comfort. He sat and gazed out the view port.

"It's pretty," he said.

Her voice was a mere whisper. "Yes. More of them every day."

"You know… I've come… I've come to…" A fan whirred overhead; a bot clanked somewhere in the hold. "I've come…" The words were lined up but not moving through his throat.

At last, her voice came, sweet and calm. "You don't have to say it."

Goodbye.

THE SIGHT OF those ships hanging limp before him, awaiting execution, plunged Blake into a deep silence. The padded arms of the nav chair held him like a lover. And despite all he'd meant to say, he fell asleep right there. He dreamed of voyages taken and voyages still to come. He conversed with Sammy, her disembodied voice more real to him than any physical friend, and he grieved in the underworld of sleep in ways he could not allow himself in the land of quantum entanglement and beers with Ian.

When he woke and stood at the console, he put his hands on the nav display, touching the screens. They were all dark, but heavy with familiarity.

Turning, he left the bridge. Were those her eyes, those view screens at the prow? Where did the essence of the ship reside? Where did you go to say the last words she would ever hear?

Damn, he was stupid to have come here. She was a machine. *Don't you get it, she's an optical computer programmed to seem human. And you, Blake Niva, are hopelessly deluded, pathologically maladjusted and just a touch delusional.* Ian had said as much. Joking. But not.

He stood in front of the airlock, about to punch in a call for a shuttle, when Sammy spoke.

"There's a message, Blake."

He stared at the wall screen. "Who?"

"Not giving her name. Shall I delete?"

"Accept. Thank you, Sammy." It was strange to have a message here. Even stranger coming from a woman.

"So, Blake?" The voice-only message sounded sort of like Luce Pamuk, Ian's old girlfriend, but not quite.

"That you, Luce?" he said, speaking into the mike. "I thought you were in Tau Ceti."

"Not much of a hi-how-are-you."

He sighed. "So how are you, Luce?"

"Too late to ask, but not so great, frankly. Listen, give a message to Ian for me? He's not picking up."

Picking up? As though there wasn't a lag? She was on some moon of Tau Ceti b, for God sakes— but then he remembered she could communicate instantly. People weren't the only data sent by entanglement.

She went on, "I had this gig with a band."

"I heard. Not going well?"

"No, not the fuck going well. It's the voice. I want the one I had, and I figure he got a copy of before I left. It's my signature, Blake. They don't like how I sound. *I* don't frigging like it. So, if he kept it, I want it back."

"Want what back?"

He could almost see her roll her eyes. "My old self. My data self, or whatever the hell you call it." In the ensuing pause he couldn't think of what to say. "Aren't you listening, Blake? I'm really counting on you."

"I'm listening."

"Okaaay. Tell Ian my voice was better before. He defragged me on the way, yeah? And so great, I got cleansed and cleared, or whatever they call it, but along with it I lost the polyps on my vocal folds, the ones that gave me the goddamn voice they're god-damn paying me for, my torch-singer, rip your guts out warble. I liked it better than this white voice, this generic squawk he's left me with. Because, you know, that other was *me*. More me than this. *Capisce?*"

He thought he capisced. But he had to get a few things straight.

"Are you saying defragging means you get improved? Physically?"

"What planet are you on, Blake? Yes, that's what it means. It's not being talked about, Ian says, but it makes you clean and clear of lots of glitches. Normally I would have wanted it. But this part I don't like. So just tell him to save the original, and just switch me over on the trip home. Which can be sooner than later, so if he's still offering a free ticket, which I think he owes me, then I'm coming home now. Understand?"

"Right. Luce, are you feeling okay otherwise?"

"Yeah, okay. What are you, my mother?"

"Just wondering if there are other side effects."

"Blake, they're not *side effects*," she said with that sarcasm he'd come to expect from women who were quicker than he was. "They're improvements, yeah? You want to have defective genes? Aging? It's all cleansed and cleared. So no, they're not side-effects. Don't go ragging on Ian, or I'll never get these quantum gigs. Just tell him to work out that bug, so you can keep some flaws you want." There was a pause long enough to drive a ram jet cruiser through. "Are you listening, Blake?"

He was. He very much was. After reassuring her he'd talk to Ian, he killed the connection.

Ship's corridors were always too warm, but the sweat slicking his skin made him cold. "Were you listening, Sammy?"

"Yes, Blake. I think we have a problem."

He thought for a long minute. "I'm not so sure we do."

He called the shuttle. Just before he entered the air lock, he said, "Sammy, no one comes on board except me. Tell the recycle guys you've, um... detected a hyper resistant strain of staph and you're getting"—he smiled wickedly—"clear and clean."

"Aye, Captain," she said coquettishly.

In the Land's End Lounge, Ian sat at the bar, hand on the thigh of a striking brunette.

Blake walked up to the pair. "Beat it," he said to the woman.

Ian exchanged glances with her. "Jesus H. Hawking, Blake. Lost your manners along with your job?"

The woman stalked away, and Blake took her place on the barstool. He signaled the bar keep, who plopped two fresh ones down.

Ian smirked. Then he smiled. "She likes it, I think." He nodded in the direction of the brunette, now sitting with a gaggle of friends. "Put a little sneer into your voice, they like that."

"You an expert, Ian, on what people like?"

Ian's eyes grew wary. He took a sip of beer. "Not so much."

"I think you are."

Looking over the head on his beer, Ian sipped.

"I think you could give me what I want."

"What's that, then?"

"Self-confidence. Extroversion." Blake nodded at the woman he'd chased off. "They like that."

Ian affected nonchalance. "We could help, you. If you've finally come round to it."

"I said goodbye to Sammy. What have I got left?"

Ian had the decency to lower his eyes. "That's tough." He brightened. "We could get you clear, though."

"Blow out the pipes a bit, right? Can you get down to the genetic level? Fix little non-standard errors? Make me more like you?" Blake put on an eager look. "'Cause you're the template for normal, right?"

Silence, as Ian played with the condensation on his glass.

"You used your own body scan as a basis, right? And who did you choose for the women, Ian? Your pal Lindsey? No, she's near sighted, isn't she? Maybe Iyna?"

"Hardly matters who," Ian murmured.

"No, I guess it doesn't. We're all code, in the end."

Ian warmed to the subject. "Exactly. If you look at it that way, it takes the fear out of it. We defrag you, clean up your code. We've been doing it with computers for a hundred fifty years. We're just moving to the next level, yeah?"

"Yeah. So did the volunteers for the beta test know they were being cleared?"

"Sure. That was the payoff. We lost a few. Didn't tell about those, the ones that frizzled into, well, noise. But the rest all came back cured."

"Defragged." Blake laughed, shaking his head.

Ian laughed too, but his smile faded as the UN officers strode through the doorway, heading for him. He pinned Blake with an accusatory glance.

Blake nodded. "Thanks for speaking into the mike. Guess they read you loud and clear."

Ian examined his glass of beer as though he still had deniability.

As the officers took him into custody, Ian said, "When the word gets out that our process cleans you up, there'll be no stopping it, Blake. You gotta know that."

Blake wished he had a killer comeback, but he'd about exhausted his snazzy repartee. "I don't think you guys can fine-tune this, Ian. You can't pick and choose. You aren't doctors. Or real scientists. You're tech guys. I don't think most people are going to trust you to *defrag* them."

Ian shook his head in pity. "Everybody wants perfection, Blake. That's where you're wrong."

"I don't think so. Some of us like what we were. Warts and all."

As the officers pulled him toward the door, Ian muttered, "What you gonna do for women *now*, Blake?"

He watched as the men in powder blue loaded Ian into a van and drove him away. Ian was right, of course—you couldn't stop this instant travel thing. Eventually, the technology would be reliable, fares would come down—and for those who wanted something extra, well, eventually there'd be a menu for selecting upgrades. Blake knew that. But meanwhile he had what, five, maybe ten years? People would still want to travel on the QT, as long as Ian's company wasn't involved. But there'd be some, maybe a lot, for whom the whole deal of dematerializing into quantum bits would be highly suspect.

They'd want to travel the old way. *And thank you for choosing the Samantha Gray.*

Finishing off his beer, Blake headed for the door. The brunette put a hand on his elbow from behind. He turned.

"Buy you a drink?" she asked.

"Um," Blake said as words predictably left him. "Um, actually... actually, I have a date."

"OK, cool." She smiled at his awkwardness. She turned and sauntered back to her friends, the words trailing. "Hope she's waiting for you."

He thought she would be. He headed toward the transport center, first at a brisk walk and then at a run.

It was time to get his date out of the Graveyard.

The Line of Dichotomy

Chris Roberson

BANNERMAN YAO GUANZHONG approached the bacteria farm, saber drawn, keeping behind cover, hidden from view by the large, sheltering yardangs. Close behind him followed Bannermen Jue and Seto, with Zong bringing up the rear. They'd left Bei back near the crawler in an entrenched position, braced to withstand the recoil of his rifle in the low Fire Star gravity, to cover their retreat. Bei was the most accomplished marksman in the squad. But he had displayed in recent months a ruthless impatience for hand-to-hand combat, and this was an operation which required subtlety and restraint.

It had been two days since the squad had picked up the garbled transmission from the farm. They had been squeezed into the crawler, tending to their minor wounds and bruises, returning to base camp after an operation in the west, out along the boundary between the highlands to the south and the lowlands to the north. They had been running silent for some time; radio communication with their base had been impeded by sandstorms to the east. Through bursts of static they heard a coded call for assistance from a technician at a bacteria farm, a few hundred kilometers from their present position. He was pinned down with a group of others by a Mexic raiding party. Assuming—rightly, it seemed—that no one else would have been in range to pick up the garbled transmission, Yao had ordered Bannerman Zong to divert course and head east toward the farm.

Drawing nearer the bacteria farm, Yao motioned to his men with a series of abbreviated hand signals. He crawled on his belly, until his helmet just crested a low rise, to survey the terrain stretched before them. The farm was still a few hundred meters off. From Yao's vantage, he could see the nearest of the Mexica positioned around it, entrenched to counteract the low gravity, armed with rifles and Mexic fire-lances. In their garishly-painted surface suits, they stood out in sharp contrast to the dull pinkish-orange of the soil and sand. Yao could see, stretching out in intervals in both directions, a ring of Mexic warriors, encircling the farm.

The surface suits of the Mexica were, in principle, the same basic design as those of Middle Kingdom manufacture. Their surface suits were not pressurized, like the bulky suits used out in orbit, or on the surface of the Earth's moon. They were constructed from an elastic mesh that applied roughly the same pressure to the body as Earth's atmosphere at sea-level. Much lighter than a pressure suit, the surface suits also granted the wearer a broader range of motion. Most importantly, only the helmets were airtight, so that if a cut or tear ripped open the elastic on any of the extremities, the worst the wearer would suffer would be a bad bruise and a frozen bit of skin. Cut a hole in a pressure suit, by contrast, and you would die of suffocation in a matter of minutes. Crack the helmet on a surface suit, and you'd be dead even faster, quickly and painfully.

Joints at shoulders, hips, elbows, and knees allowed for freedom of movement. The helmet, reinforced and strong enough to withstand a significant impact, was sealed onto the hardshell carapace that covered the wearer's chest. The carapace provided room for the wearer to breathe, which the constrictive elastic would not, while the armored casing on the rear of the carapace housed the suit's air and water supplies.

While the surface suits of the Middle Kingdom were utilitarian and plain, with only markings and colorations required to denote rank and position, those of the Mexica were gaudy and arresting. Painted in a riot of colors, their suits were designed to resemble Earth animals and figures from myth and legend. Helmets constructed to resemble the heads of birds of prey, the faceplate set with a hawk's beak. Suits painted yellow with black spots, made to resemble a jaguar's hide. And stranger creatures still: blue demons, skull faces of white, black suits spangled with starfields and emblems.

Yao had long since given up wondering how the Mexic warriors could wear such outlandish armor without dying of shame. It hardly mattered, anyway. They were his enemies. What difference was it to him if they went to their reward dressed as a chicken or a dog? They would bleed and die the same as if they were dressed as men.

After a few moments of careful study, Yao detected a weak section of the Mexic line. Several dozen meters from his current position were two Mexica, the barrels of their rifles facing the bacteria farm, their backs to Yao and his men. A distance of over fifty meters separated the pair from the next post of warriors to their left, of over sixty meters to their right. As they were positioned in a slight shallow in the rockface, the ground to either side of them rose at a gentle slope for a few dozen meters before dropping off again. With the Mexica stationed on either side entrenched and low to the group, if Yao and his men approached the pair keeping low to the ground themselves, the chances of the bannermen being seen would be reduced considerably. Still, if the Mexica on either side were to stand and look directly toward the pair of Mexic warriors, Yao and his men would be exposed to projectiles fired from either side, if not both.

To the east, beyond the plinths and yardangs, Yao could see a dust storm rising. It would be upon them in a matter of moments. Yao allowed himself a tight smile. It hardly mattered to the bannermen, since they had traveled in strict radio silence since leaving the crawler on foot. Once it hit it would serve to hamper their Mexic enemies, making it difficult for them to keep in visual contact with one another and garbling their radio transmissions. That was the cover they needed.

Yao slid back down the rise and, through a series of simple hand gestures, relayed his orders to his men. In a few moments, when the storm's leading edge hit, they would charge over the rise and take out the pair of Mexica, quickly and without giving the warriors time to raise the alarm. Then, as the dust wall swelled, the gap in the line would be wide enough for them to approach the bacteria farm, undetected by the rest of the enemy.

Seto moved into position at Yao's side while Zong, Yao's second-in-command, and Jue, the newest member of the squad, moved forward, their sabers drawn and ready.

As Zong and Jue inched over the rise, keeping low to present as little profile as possible, Seto tapped Yao's elbow. He made a motion with his hands, two fists brought together, knuckle to knuckle. He wanted to talk.

Yao sighed and, turning from the waist, leaned forward until the faceplate of his helmet was touching that of Seto's.

"Chief," the voice of Seto buzzed in Yao's helmet, the vibrations transmitted through the faceplates in contact. "Not to question your judgment, but wouldn't it be safer to entrench further back, with a clear line of sight, and pick the two Mexic off with rifle fire?" Seto jerked a thumb to indicate the long-barreled rifle slung in a harness on his back, secured to his carapace.

Yao shook his head, fractionally, careful not to move his helmet out of contact with Seto's. "Even if the projectile punctures through the hardshell into their bodies, even with a chest shot, they'll still have a few moments to call for help, and we can't count on the dust to block out all radio traffic. A headshot would do it, if we had a clear shot through their faceplates, but from the rear it's more likely to ricochet off the armor plating."

"So it's the hose, then?" Seto asked.

Yao gave an affirmative hand signal and then pulled away, getting back into position.

The surface suits of the Mexica were, if anything, better armored than those of the Middle Kingdom. However, they had one significant flaw—a hose leading from the airtanks at their back up into their airtight helmets looped, for the span of a few bare centimeters, into the open air. Early Middle Kingdom surface suits had shared this same design flaw until the artificers of the Dragon Throne devised a means to route the airflow directly from the tanks, through the carapace seal, into the helmet. The warriors of the Mexic Dominion, though, were still forced to go to battle with this one fatal problem. The Mexica were aware of the weakness, but it was a rare occasion in a mêlée when a bannerman had an opportunity to exploit it, since the Mexica were always on their guard.

The pair of Mexica nearest them faced away from Yao and his men, exposing the airhose at their shoulders. If Zong and Jue were able to creep right up to the Mexica without being spotted, they could sever the airhoses. If they then delivered a blow to the Mexica's abdomens, driving out the oxygen in their lungs, the pair would be left unable to speak as they suffocated quickly, unable to call through their helmet radios for help. If the Mexica were able to squeak a few last syllables before expiring, Yao had to hope that the dust storm would provide sufficient interference that radio signals would not travel far, even over short distances.

Yao snaked up the rise, just far enough to see over the crest, to where his men stealthily approached the Mexica. They were now just within saber range. Yao's palms itched; a part of him wished he could always take point himself in these circumstances and not be forced to delegate to his men.

"Come on," Yao whispered, his voice rebounding low and harsh in the helmet for no one's ears but his. "Strike. Now!"

Zong and Jue carried out their mission with textbook accuracy, though Jue became over-exuberant and, rather than merely striking his target in the abdomen after severing his airhose, drove his saber point-first into the Mexica's stomach. When he pulled it out, blood sprayed over a meter in a bright, arterial spray, painting the sands an even darker shade of red. Luckily for Jue, the Mexica was no more able to sound the alarm than his comrade, now fallen at Zong's feet, had been.

Yao slid a short distance back down the rise and, turning, signaled to Seto. The pair of them then maneuvered forward to join Zong and Jue.

The storm bore down on them. After Yao checked both sides, standing at his full height, he nodded in grim satisfaction to see that the nearest Mexic positions were obscured from view. The way was, for a brief moment at least, clear. He signaled his men to proceed. They made their way across the open ground to the bacteria farm as quickly as their long, loping strides would carry them.

THE BACTERIA FARM was essentially a low, wide dome. It was the same pinkish-orange as all the buildings constructed of materials fabricated from the rock and soil of Fire Star, with airlocks of metal and ceramic set at intervals around its circumference. It stood only five or six meters tall, while its diameter was easily three times that. Here and there, through the obfuscating dust swirling in the thin air around them, they could see the pockmarks of Mexic projectile fire, and scorched areas where fire-lances had been sprayed against it. The Mexica had not been able to get through the heavy, reinforced doors of the airlock and so had been forced to encircle the farm, in the hopes of starving out those trapped within.

Yao and the other bannermen huddled in the lees of the nearest airlock. The way was barred from within, naturally, and the call controls set in their metal plate had been completely destroyed by projectile fire. Undeterred, Yao pounded repeatedly on the door with the base of his saber's hilt. He positioned his helmet's faceplate in front of the thick viewport of transparent ceramic.

The airlock and the farm beyond, as seen through the small viewport, seemed darkened and deserted. He continued to pound on the doorway, hoping that the airlock was currently full and that the sound of his pounding would carry to the farm beyond. He wondered whether anyone survived within the structure or not. At length, a shadowed helmet appeared on the other side of the viewport. Dimly visible eyes met Yao's own.

"Let us in!" Yao shouted. His faceplate was pressed to the viewport, but he exaggerated his mouth's movements in the event that the sound of his voice was unable to propagate through the unbreakable ceramic.

The shadowed eyes on the other side of the viewport seemed to hesitate, uncertain, and then disappeared from view. At first, Yao thought that they had been left outside to rot, but after a few moments Yao could feel the door begin to vibrate through the fabric of his gloves as the lock was cycled slowly open.

In brief moments, the door was open, and Yao and the other bannermen slipped into the open chamber. As they closed the door to the outside behind them, they saw that they were alone in the chamber. The airlock slowly drew in air, the pressure gradually increasing. The lights inside the airlock were extinguished, the only illumination the faint daylight visible through the viewport.

Finally the lock completed its cycle, and the door to the farm's interior began to open. Yao signaled his men to keep their helmets locked and pressurized, and to advance with their weapons at the ready. This time Yao took point. His saber held before him, he cautiously advanced through the open door.

"That's far enough," Yao heard a voice say in Official Speech, sounding muffled and distant through his heavy helmet.

In the corridor before him, lit dimly by red lamps burning high overhead, stood a woman in a surface suit, her helmet on the ground at her side, a rifle trained on Yao, its butt against her shoulder.

Yao reached up, slowly, and hit the latch that lifted his helmet's faceplate. The stale air of the farm hit him like a wave smelling of unwashed bodies, offal, and despair.

"You don't want to fire that thing, lady," Yao said, his voice level. "The recoil will knock you off your feet, and you'll land on your hindquarters at least a meter back."

"Maybe," the woman said, smiling slightly but not lowering the rifle's barrel a centimeter. "But by then you'd have a projectile buried in your body, wouldn't you, so you'd have better things to worry about than how foolish I looked, I think."

Yao smiled back and lowered the tip of his saber to the ground.

"We caught your call for help over the radio, two days back," Yao said, stepping forward as his men came around the door to stand behind him. "We've come to rescue you."

"Well it's about time," the woman said, and lowered the rifle. "We had about decided that this damned dome would be our tomb. Those of us who haven't already gone on to our rewards."

The woman slung the rifle over her shoulder, and then held out her hand to Yao.

"My name is Thien Ziling," she said, "and I suppose I'm in charge here."

"Bannerman Yao Guanzhong," he answered, taking her hand, "and as far as I'm concerned, I'm in charge here now."

"You won't get any complaints from me," Thien said, then turned and headed back up the corridor. "Come along, and I'll introduce you to what's left of us. Then you can get right to the rescuing part."

THIEN LED THEM to a small central chamber, where two men and a woman sprawled along the wall, eyes half-lidded in the harsh-light from the lamps above, and vacant, weary expressions on their dirty faces.

"Crew, meet our rescuers," Thien said, propping her rifle against the wall. She hung her helmet on a hook on the wall and collapsed into a makeshift chair constructed of shipping crates. In the chamber's light, Yao could see now that she was older than he'd first imagined, fifty terrestrial years old at least. The years showed their tracks in the lines around her eyes. "Rescuers, meet what's left of the Fifth Regional Tech and Resupply Division, Third Work Crew. Those two are all that remains of my technicians, Kuai Cunxin"—she pointed at the middle-aged man, sitting with his legs folded under him—"and Min Jinping"—she pointed to the younger woman, no more than twenty terrestrial years old. "And that one there"—she indicated a young man in the uniform of the Army of the Green Standard, sitting with his legs folded up, his chin resting on his knees—"is Xun... Xun... Hey, Xun, what's your name again?"

"Xun Bingzhang," the young man said, his voice sounding hollow and far away. There were deep shadows beneath his eyes, and his skin looked wan and mottled.

"Right. Well, Xun was one of the soldiers assigned as our protection on this trek. There was another, Dea something or other, but he got picked off by sniper fire before we reached the safety of the farm, and who knows what happened to his body once we got inside. There was another tech with us at that point, a man named Ang who'd been with the crew for a few Fire Star years, but he caught a projectile in the leg, right through an artery. He bled out before we could get him stitched up. He's stored in one of the cold storage lockers"—Thien jerked a thumb at a row of doors set into the wall behind her—"but I don't see any reason to dig him out. He'll keep just fine back there, for as long as he needs to. Besides," she smiled up at Yao, "I don't figure you were all that hot to be introduced to him anyway, were you?"

Yao smiled, grimly and shook his head. "So this is all of you, then?"

Thien looked around, as though making a final headcount. "Yes, this is it."

"And are you all fit to travel?"

"Well, Xun got clipped by a projectile in the abdomen, below the line of his carapace," Thien answered, "but we were able to get his wound bandaged and the fabric of his surface suit repaired once we got inside. I think the wound is infected, but we don't have a full medical kit on hand, so there wasn't anything we could do about it."

"We've got a full kit back in the crawler," Yao said. "Once we're onboard we can get the wound disinfected and properly dressed." He turned and flashed an affirmative hand signal at the Green Standard soldier. "You hold on, soldier. You hear me?"

Xun nodded, his head wobbling slightly from side to side. He licked his lips before answering, "Y-yes, sir. I hear you."

"Good." Yao sheathed his saber at his side. He paced back and forth across the small chamber's floor, considering their options. "Now, here is what we're going to do. We're going to gather up whatever supplies you've got on hand. Water, oxygen tanks, foodstuffs, any essentials. Then we're going to haul out to our crawler as quickly as we're able, and we're all going to make it out of this in one piece. You hear me?"

"It's all in the crawler," the young woman named Min said.

Yao turned to her. "What?"

"All our gear," said Kuai, the older technician at her side. "It's all still back in our crawler, outside the farm."

"Not all of it, you two," Thien said, shaking her head like someone scolding a poorly trained pet.

"We managed to bring in a fair amount of water and oxygen when we got here, before the shooting started."

"But not enough," Kuai said, a hysterical edge to his voice. "How long can we last on it?"

"Long enough," Thien said, but Yao looked from the two technicians to their leader, unconvinced.

"How much do you have, Thien, in the way of provisions?"

"We could have held out for another couple of days on what we have here, probably. We'd have run out of food before we ran out of water, and run out of both long before we ran out of air. Lucky for us the oxygen scrubbers in the farm's temporary living quarters are still operational, so we haven't had to crack open any of the tanks we brought in with us when the Mexica attacked."

Yao chewed on the inside of his cheek, doing quick sums in his head.

"It'll be tight, but we should be able to make it back to base camp, if we don't hit any snags," he said, at length. "Suit up, everybody. I want to try to get out of here and back to our crawler before the dust storm passes."

THIEN AND HER crew took longer to get themselves ready to move than Yao would have liked, certainly longer than it would have taken a full division of bannermen, but their luck held out. By the time everyone was ready to get moving, the dust storm still blew outside. It provided ample cover for the eight of them to make it across the open ground without being seen, and through the hole in the Mexic line that Yao and his men had punched just a short while earlier.

With Yao in the lead and Zong bringing up the rear, they made their way through the yardangs toward the position where the bannermen's crawler was secreted, behind a large outcropping of rock. They traveled in complete silence, their radios set only to receive, watchful of any sign of Mexic pursuit.

When they reached the midway point between the farm and the bannermen's crawler, Yao motioned the others to come to a halt. Crawling up a slight rise, he could see the rock outcropping just shy of a half-kilometer ahead, hazed only slightly in the lightening dust storm. He pulled a disk of metal from a pocket on his upper arm, polished to a mirror sheen, and used it to flash the light from the indistinct disc of the sun towards the rocky outcropping. He waited, looking for a flash in response. None came, so he signaled again, and again. Still nothing.

Yao turned, and motioned for Zong to join him on the crest of the rise. When the bannerman reached his side, Yao gave the hand signals for a remote-viewing mirror. Zong unlatched a sheath on his thigh and handed over a long, slender tube capped with precision-ground lenses on either end.

Yao held the remote-viewing mirror up to his faceplate. Through the glass he could see Bannerman Bei in his prescribed position, just as Yao had ordered, obscured from the direct view of the farm.

He had a rifle at the ready and his sword at his side, driven point-first into the ground.

Swearing under his breath, Yao turned to Zong and brought his fists together, knuckles touching. When Zong's faceplate touched with his, he said, "Bei is dead. We're walking into a trap."

He handed Zong the remote-viewing mirror and slid back down the rise to join the others.

Yao hated to risk using the radios to communicate to the others, but time was of the essence. He signaled with quick hand gestures for everyone to turn their broadcast settings to the lowest power. With any luck, down in the slight ravine, and with the last of the dust storm passing overhead, their radio signals wouldn't carry as far as the nearest Mexica, whether waiting in front of them or still in position around the farm behind.

"Listen up," Yao said, after motioning the others to huddle together. "We've got to find another way out of here. Our crawler is out of the question."

"What do you mean?" Thien glared through her faceplate at Yao. "There's really only forward or back, isn't there? And I tell you now, I'm not about to head back to that thrice-damned farm."

Zong, taking a few long leaps from the base of the rise, came to stand beside Yao, tucking the remote-viewing mirror back into the sheath at his side. "I concur with Bannerman Yao. Bei is dead, and the crawler compromised."

"How can you be so sure?" Min objected.

"Bei was obsessive about his equipment, his weapons in particular," Zong explained. "He would never have stuck it into the ground in so reckless a fashion."

"Most likely," Yao said, "he was picked off at a distance by Mexic sniper fire and left as bait. The Mexica will capture the rest of us alive, if possible, to torture and execute at their leisure."

"No, thank you," Thien said, shuddering. "I'm in no hurry to die, but if I am to do so, it better be damned quick."

"No one's dying," Yao said sharply, then added, his tone more reserved, "No one else is dying, at least." He turned, glancing from one faceplate to another. "Listen, there's got to be an alternate mode of transport available to us. Kuai, you mentioned a crawler. Where's that?"

"It's still parked on the far side of the bacteria farm," Kuai answered.

"It should still be parked there," Thien interjected, "but the Mexica could have driven off with it, or buried it for all we know. We haven't been back there since we first reached the farm."

"Well, at the moment, it's our best chance. The Mexica must have seen our approach, and sent enough warriors to subdue us back at our crawler. The fact that they haven't attacked us yet means they don't know that we've gotten back out of their lines. They must still think we're inside the farm. If we can work our way around to the north, skirting the Mexic line in a broad circle, we should be able to stay safely out of view of the Mexica still in position around the farm." Yao paused, glancing around those gathered before him. "Any questions?"

Silence was their only response.

"Fair enough," Yao said. "Then let's move."

IT TOOK THE better part of several hours, traveling in a wide arc, as near to the farm as was absolutely necessary, but finally Yao signaled the others to stop. They had gone far enough. He motioned to Zong, retrieved the remote-viewing mirror, and trotted ahead, keeping as low to the ground as the gravity would allow with each short step. Finally, peering around an outcropping of rock, he trained the remote-viewing mirror on the scene before him, surveying the situation. To his left, obscured by plinths and yardangs, rose the bulk of the farm's dome. Here and there he could see little flashes of bright, garish colors, indicators that Mexic warriors were still in position. To the right, outside the Mexic line and some distance from the farm, was Thien's crawler. Smaller than that of the bannermen, it was lying on its side, a burnt husk, surrounded by a halo of broken machinery in bits and pieces.

Yao made his way back to the others. With their radios set to the lower broadcast setting, and squatting low to the ground, he described the state of the crawler, left demolished, burnt, and inoperable.

"But how could anything burn here?" the Green Standard soldier Xun asked, waving his arm to take in all of Fire Star, with its oxygen-poor atmosphere.

"They must have used magnesium charges," Thien said. "That stuff'll burn like crazy in carbon dioxide."

Yao nodded, impressed. "You must have been on Fire Star a long while," he said to her.

Thien shrugged, the movement obscured by the bulk of her surface suit's carapace.

"At this juncture," Yao went on, "we don't have any choice but to proceed on foot. I've got to do an inventory, but I can't imagine we've got enough oxygen and water to last us for more than a few days. Now, is there any safe harbor in that kind of radius?"

"None that I know of, chief," Zong said, his head shaking within his helmet.

"Damn," Yao said. "Okay, here's the order of the day. Zong, Jue, and Seto, I want you three to range out and scout the terrain. See what our options are, and report back. I'll work with Thien on getting a full accounting of our resources, and then we'll see where we're at."

The three bannermen saluted and turned to head out.

"You're with me," Yao said, pointing a finger at Thien.

In the following hour, Yao and Thien supervised as Kuai, Min, and Xun checked and rechecked the levels on their oxygen tanks and water supplies. When the numbers came up distressingly small, Yao ordered them checked again, and finally insisted on personally verifying each of the numbers individually. But each time, the answer was the same. Divided amongst the eight of them, their supplies could last no more than two days, three at the absolute maximum.

Yao sat on a spur of rock, considering their options, waiting for the three bannermen to return. After a long while, Thien came to sit beside him. She switched off her radio, tapped first her faceplate, then his. Yao, curious, switched off the broadcast on his own radio and leaned in until their faceplates touched.

"Listen, something just occurred to me," Thien said, her voice buzzing in Yao's helmet, "but I didn't want to broadcast it to everyone until you had a chance to think it over. I'm not absolutely certain, but I think there used to be an old research facility about a two-day walk to the north-east from here, in the direction of Bao Shan. But it's been a few Fire Star years since I last saw it, if this is the place I'm remembering, and I don't know if it's still up and running."

"So it's a long shot?" Yao said simply.

Thien only smiled, weakly. "Basically, yes."

A few moments later, Zong, Jue, and Seto returned from scouting the terrain. No good news lurked in their reports. When their findings had been collated, it appeared that they had wandered into the one gap in the area, with large concentrations of Mexica to the northwest and the southeast. Behind them to the south lay the bannermen's crawler and the trap baited by their dead comrade, and the farm to the west. Their only option was to travel northeast.

It appeared that Thien's long shot was the only chance they had.

* * *

FOR THE REST of that long afternoon, they traveled across the yardangs. The bulk of Bao Shan loomed on the horizon before them, the tallest mountain in the solar system. The evening meal was eaten on the march, water and liquefied field rations fed through nozzles set inside their helmets. The storm had abated, somewhat, though there was still too much atmospheric interference for them to have any hope of radioing for assistance, even if their small helmet radios could carry more than a kilometer at best.

At Yao's orders, they kept communication to a minimum. Unless absolutely necessary, they were to maintain complete radio silence and to keep their radio transmitters turned down to the lowest broadcast signal in the event of an emergency. Only when they stopped to rest, periodically, erecting temporary shelters of metallic fabric pulled from the bannermen's survival kits, were they able to communicate freely. The reflective material served not only to block out the bright rays of the sun coming in, but also blocked any outgoing radio transmissions from within.

They weren't able to remove any part of their suits, even when they stopped to rest. The external pressure was far too low and the thin atmosphere was far too cold for their skin to handle. So they stayed suited up at all times, helmets pressurized and locked to their carapaces, their skin growing ever more chafed and worn.

They traveled in a narrow column, Zong and Jue in the lead, followed by Kuai and Min, then Yao, then Thien, and finally Seto and Xun bringing up the rear. They made slow but steady progress through the fossae, with the sand-sculpted yardangs to either side of them. These streamlined ridges were shaped like inverted boat hulls, some of them no more than a few centimeters long and fewer high. Others ran several kilometers from end to end, standing almost thirty meters tall.

At sunset, they made camp. Seto carried in his survival kit a tent capable of being pressurized and filled with air, but Yao had no intention of using their already diminished oxygen reserves needlessly. He ordered Jue and Seto to erect the radiation shade instead. Everyone would sleep the night in their suits, however much they chose to grumble.

"CHIEF," ZONG SAID, coming to sit beside Yao beneath the radiation shade. The other two bannermen were setting up watch for the night. The survivors of the work crew stretched out on the ground some distance away, resting their sore and complaining muscles, their eyes on the stars dancing overhead. The bright, gray-white moons moved in their courses, the smaller making its way slowly from east to west, the larger speeding from west to east.

"Yes, Zong?" Yao tongued the water nozzle back into position on the side of his helmet, licking his lips. The stale, reconstituted water they'd scavenged from the bacteria farm was acrid and foul on his tongue, but it beat dying of dehydration.

"This is something that… maybe we shouldn't…" Zong paused. He made a show of switching off his radio transmitter, and then brought his fists together, knuckles first. Yao switched off his own broadcast and leaned in, faceplates touching. "I think we're walking into another trap, chief," Zong said at last, the faceplates vibrating with the sound of his voice.

"What makes you say that?"

"It was just too convenient to find that the Mexica had left such a large stretch of terrain to the northeast of the bacteria farm unguarded. Maybe the Mexica anticipated that we might not take the bait at our crawler, and so put a secondary trap in place, somewhere out here. We could be walking into an ambush."

"I can't disagree," Yao said, after a long pause, "but I don't see that we've got any choice, do we? We can't radio for assistance, and if we entrench here, waiting for them to come after us, we'll run out of oxygen within a matter of days. We could try to make it back into the farm, but the Mexica would pick us off before we could make the airlock. So our only choice is just to press on and be ready for any attack when it comes."

"Well, you're the chief," Zong said with a sigh. "I'll go check on the pickets, and then catch a few hours' sleep before it's my watch."

Yao sat in silence until Thien appeared before him, lifting the edge of the radiation shade with a gloved hand and peering in at him.

"Am I interrupting your thoughts?" she radioed to him.

"No," Yao said. He realized his transmitter was still off when she repeated her question. He switched his radio back to broadcast, at the lowest signal, and then said, "No, you're welcome to join me."

Thien slid beneath the metallic canopy and maneuvered herself into a sitting position, her legs stretched out before her, leaning back on her elbows. The position, the most comfortable one could achieve in a surface suit, gave her a relaxed appearance which her tone did not reflect.

"I've just checked on Xun's status," Thien said, pointing out across the sands to where the Green Standard soldier lay against the gentle slope of the nearest yardang. "It doesn't look good. I can't tell through his suit, of course, but I think he's feverish. He's started complaining of chills, and through his faceplate he looks even paler than before." She drew a heavy breath. "I think his infection is getting worse."

"Yes," Yao said, nodding, his voice low, "I noticed that at our mid-afternoon stop. It's unpleasant, I know, but there isn't anything for it but to press on, and hope that his body can fight off the infection long enough for us to reach proper facilities."

Thien turned from the waist up, so she could look directly into Yao's faceplate. "And just what are the chances of that happening, Yao?" From her tone, she didn't seem optimistic.

"There is every chance that none of us will reach safety. But there is that same slim chance every time any of us go walking out on the surface of Fire Star. So, in that respect, current circumstances just aren't that unusual."

"Humph," Thien answered, expelling air through pursed lips. "That sounds like a pretty pessimistic view, doesn't it?"

Yao sighed and squeezed his eyes shut. Then he leaned in close, his voice low. "Listen, morale amongst the men is low. Not just my men here, but all of the military on Fire Star. The Mexica have made some significant advances in recent months, disrupting the supply train of nitrates to the bacteria farms, impeding the flow of halocarbon gases from the refinery on the northern plain. Meanwhile, construction on Heaven's Ladder, the orbital elevator that was to rise from the highlands south of Tianfei Valley, has been all but halted and won't continue until we've been able to pacify the region. The Mexica have even managed to hit Burning Mirror from an orbital gunsling, knocking the fixture out of alignment and sending it on a slow course down to the planet's surface. Technicians are currently working on righting the mirror, but the process is slow and laborious. And there is every chance that, once Burning Mirror is repositioned, the Mexica will be able to strike at it again."

Thien nodded, her expression grave. "You, and every day that the sun's rays aren't being redirected down onto the south polar cap is another day that the temperature doesn't rise and the carbon dioxide remains frozen. And another day longer until Fire Star is inhabitable."

"Look," Yao said. He spread his hands, fingers splayed, palms up. "I'm just a simple soldier, and I don't know too much about that kind of thing. All

I know is that people of the Middle Kingdom are in jeopardy, and that the orders of the Dragon Throne aren't being fulfilled. And that's why I'm here."

"How long have you been here, anyway?" Thien asked. "On Fire Star, I mean?"

"Nearly ten terrestrial years," Yao said, without having to think. "Almost five and a quarter Fire Star years. Before that, I was stationed in Vinland, doing maneuvers along the border with the Mexic Dominion." Yao paused, tonguing his helmet's nozzle into the open position and taking a long sip of acrid water. "How about you?" he asked, licking his lips. "How long have you been on planet?"

"Twenty terrestrial years," Thien answered with a long sigh. "Eleven Fire Star years."

"That long?" Yao was impressed.

"When I was young, just a girl, really, I found employment with the Ministry of Celestial Excursion, translating intercepted Mexic transmissions and documents. My grandmother had emigrated from a satellite state of the Mexic Dominion, and still spoke Nahuatl when I was growing up. But I really just wanted to work with my hands, not spend all day trapped indoors translating cold, dry technical documentation. And so I transferred into the technicians' arm of the Ministry and found a place with the Treasure Fleet to Fire Star. I returned with the Fleet to Earth, but when the Emperor sent the first wave of colonists and technicians back to begin the permanent habitation, there I was among them. I've been operating at Fire Star gravity for so long I don't think I'd ever be able to walk under

Earth-normal gravity again. I can't complain, though. I once met a technician who had spent ten terrestrial years stationed at Cold Palace on the surface of the Moon. When he finally returned to Earth, his muscles had atrophied so badly that he could hardly walk. When he did manage to take a few tenuous steps, so much calcium had leeched from his bones that his legs broke beneath his weight. He hopped the first transport back to Gold Mountain, rode the line up to Diamond Summit, and went straight back to the Moon. He'd had enough of Earth to last him." She sighed again, peered out under the edge of the radiation shade, and turned to Yao. "How about you? Ever intend to head back to Earth?"

"Me?" Yao gave a muffled shrug. "I'll go where my Emperor sends me. It's not like I have any family to go home to, so it matters little to me."

"I used to dream about returning to Earth," Thien said, wistfully, "in my first years on Fire Star. But now? This is my home now. If not for this damned war, it would be perfect. If we were ever to find peace with the Mexica, it might be perfect again. But either way, I don't think I'm ever going to leave it." She chuckled, ruefully. "Of course, I might die any time now and my bones will rot unburied beneath these pink skies, in which case the choice is taken out of my hands, isn't it?"

Yao couldn't help but laugh. All around them, the night's darkness deepened.

* * *

XUN DIED IN the night. Thien spoke some words over him about the mutability of life, which Yao vaguely recognized as a Taoist prayer, while Zong ordered Seto to retrieve the dead man's oxygen supplies and weapons. The weapons were to be distributed to the technicians in the event that circumstances were such that they'd need them, and the oxygen put with the remainder of their supplies. Thien was given Xun's knife in a sheath—which she attached to a loop at the waist of her suit. Kuai was handed the soldier's rifle, and Min wore his saber.

At Yao's orders they struck camp and set out again. They marched in the same order as the day before, traveling in silence. A dust storm blew, though whether it was the same as the day before or another following in its wake, Yao couldn't say. With the increased interference, they were scarcely able to radio to one another, even from a few feet away. And so they continued on through the morning.

At midmorning they found themselves between two long yardangs, the one to their left rising some twenty meters tall, the one on their right almost thirty. The rock formations stretched before them through the dusty haze farther than the eye could see. And on they walked. On and on until finally, at midday, they reached the end of the long corridor where the two yardangs almost touched. Beyond, in the dusty haze, they could see indistinct hummocks rising from the windblown ground.

Yao felt a tap on his shoulder and turned to see Thien standing behind him. She pointed ahead, her mouth moving behind the faceplate, forming words he could not read. He moved to lean in, to bring their faceplates into contact, when he saw from the corner of his eye Seto raising his weapons in a defensive posture. Yao spun around; Zong and Jue did the same. He drew his saber from its sheath and narrowed his eyes.

Through the curtain of dust before him Yao could see figures rising up from the ground, painted in garish shades. Mexic warriors sprang from concealment in pits dug into the hard ground at the base of the yardangs, weapons at the ready.

Yao turned back to signal to Thien and saw even more Mexica rushing at them from the rear, coming out of the clouds of dust. They were pincered in, trapped.

"Form on me!" Yao roared into his helmet radio, toggling on the transmitter, but got only static in response.

As YAO FOUGHT, he caught staccato glimpses of the mêlée on all sides, brief flashes that strobed before his eyes, bloodstained.

He saw Seto engaged with a Mexica wearing a surface suit decorated to look like a jaguar, carrying a fire-lance. Seto swung his sword in a wide arc, connecting with the Mexica's helmet and cracking the face plate. The Mexica stumbled back, firing his fire-lance and dousing Seto in a spray of burning liquid magnesium. And then Yao's attention was torn away.

One Mexica already lay at Yao's feet. Another rushed toward him, a club lined with razor-sharp blades raised high overhead. Yao just had time to take in the Mexica's surface suit, its carapace and limb-coverings painted in garish blue, the helmet constructed to resemble a bleached-white skull, the faceplate set in its open maw. As the Mexica brought his club down, ferociously, Yao met it with his saber in a parry that vibrated right to his teeth. In a return movement, Yao drew his saber's blade across the Mexica's arm, opening a line in the constrictive fabric just below the elbow joint. His opponent dropped his club, staggering back, clutching the rend, and hissing in pain.

Yao glanced back, catching the briefest glimpse of the tableau behind him: Zong down on his back, saber raised to block the downward swinging club of the Mexica standing above him, while a short distance away Min kneeled on the ground clutching her stained-red shoulder, the saber of the dead Green Standard soldier lying in the dust at her feet.

There was a flash of movement in the corner of his eye. Yao turned to see Thien a few meters from him, Xun's knife held in her wavering grip. Another Mexic warrior advanced on her, club held high, his surface suit jet black and spangled with white stars, his helmet conical. Yao didn't waste an instant in thought but rushed over, raising his saber and closing on them.

Before Yao could intercept the blow, the spangled Mexica brought his club down in a two-handed arc, crashing it into Thien's leg below the knee.

Yao angled as he ran and barreled shoulder-first into the Mexic warrior, knocked him from his feet and sent him sprawling almost a meter. Yao swore beneath his breath as the Mexica managed to maintain his balance, feet planted, and turned to face off against Yao, club raised high overhead.

A long instant passed in which Yao and the spangled Mexica faced one another, each sizing up the other, considering their next moves. Yao's elbows still ached from deflecting the skull-headed Mexica's blows, and his shoulder throbbed from its recent collision with the spangled warrior. He counted himself lucky, though, that the Mexica prized so highly the capture of live prisoners, or he and his men would have been picked off long ago by sniper fire from the Mexica entrenched further along the corridor. The warrior he faced had a rifle slung across his back, but even if the Mexica chose to employ it, he could never get into position before Yao reached him with his saber's point.

Finally Yao and his opponent closed, dancing back and forth, thrust and parry, neither able to get the upper hand. Yao's teeth vibrated with the force of the Mexica's blows, but he was able to drive the warrior back time and again, giving as good as he got. Suddenly, without warning, the Mexica stumbled backward, his hold on the club slipping, the expression behind the faceplate distorting in agony. The Mexica turned away, as though to flee. Yao, startled, caught sight of a brief flash of red and a knife protruding from the Mexica's thigh, the blade buried several centimeters deep in the muscle.

Thien lay close by, propped on her elbow, the knife's sheath in one hand, her face red with exertion and pain behind her faceplate.

Yao smiled grimly. Taking one large stride forward he swung his saber in a precise motion, aiming for the exposed airhose on the Mexica's back. The blade struck home and the hose flopped away, leaving the warrior with only a few mouthfuls of air before he was breathing the thin Fire Star atmosphere. Repositioning, Yao raised his saber again and brought it down in a fierce arc, aiming for the joint between the left arm of the Mexica's surface suit and his armored carapace. The sword bit deep, nearly cleaving the arm from the body. It sent out an arterial spray of bright red that shot an impossible distance through the thin air, freezing in the low pressure and cold so quickly that it fell like scarlet sleet onto the sands.

The dust storm had worsened. Yao could not see more than a few meters in front of him. He knelt down, helping Thien into a sitting position. He bent low over her, looking over her wounds.

Thien maneuvered her head forward until the faceplate of her helmet made contact with Yao's. "I..." she began, her voice strained. "I saw something ahead, before the attack. Mounds. One of them looked like the entrance to the shelter."

Yao intended to point out that, even if this were so, the shelter they sought was on the other side of a ring of Mexic warriors and beyond a line of entrenched riflemen. But before his lips could frame an answer, another Mexica rushed forward and his response was cut off.

This Mexica's surface suit was fiery red, his helmet made to look like some sort of dog. He carried a mace, a large metal ball on a handle nearly a meter long. Under Earth's gravity, such a weapon would require several men working together just to lift. With Fire Star's lower gravity, one strong man could lift and swing it with relative ease.

Yao raised his saber to parry, but the movement came too late.

The mace crashed into Yao's chest. It caved in the hardshell carapace, pushing the hard metal into his ribcage. Yao's torso exploded with pain. The Mexica was momentarily unbalanced by the inertia of the blow. Yao saw the slimmest window of opportunity, and burst into motion. He lunged forward, ignoring the pain in his ribcage as best he could, and drove his saber point-first into the Mexica's belly, just below the protection of the blood-red chest carapace. As he released his grip on the handle the faceplate of the Mexica went red, matching his dog armor, as the warrior sprayed the inside of his helmet with spitted blood.

Yao blinked back tears and helped Thien unsteadily to her feet. The storm was such now that they could scarcely see a meter ahead of them. Yao could barely force himself to breath, every attempt a riot of agony.

Yao leaned over and touched his faceplate to Thien's. In a harsh whisper, the loudest he could manage, he said, "We should make for the shelter." He left unspoken the hope that Thien was right, and that they weren't just heading for shadows.

* * *

YAO COULD WALK, somewhat, but had trouble breathing, every attempt sheer agony. Thien's leg was broken, the fabric of her suit open to the elements, her skin bruising badly. Leaning one against the other, they were able to make slow, painful progress through the haze.

Miraculously, they managed to blunder their way through the blinding storm without encountering anyone, neither their own people nor the Mexica, and at no point did they feel the sting of a sniper's projectile ripping into their flesh.

After what seemed an eternity, the shadow of the hummock loomed out of the billowing dust and sand before them. Yao could see that it was, indeed, the shelter they had sought. It was a long, low ridge, like a cylinder cut in half, standing some six meters tall with an airlock hatch set into a half-circle of dark metal at one end.

With some difficulty, working together, they opened the hatch and fell into the airlock. The pain in Yao's chest was by now almost unbearable, and he wasn't sure how long he could retain consciousness. He was sure Thien was doing little better.

As the airlock cycled, Thien and Yao were able to communicate via radio, without the dust to scatter the waves.

"This... this was an early research facility, constructed out of a lava tube," she explained, leaning against the rough-hewn wall of the lock. "They just capped the ends, pressurized and heated it, and used it as their base of operations. There are a lot of these sorts of shelters scattered across this hemisphere of Fire Star, though most, like this one, have been deserted for years."

"We..." Yao began, hissing through his teeth with pain. He squeezed his eyes shut and struggled to remain conscious. "We... should be able... to ride out... storm here."

"Assuming the Mexica don't come looking for us."

"Yes." Yao managed a rueful smile and the ghost of a nod. "There is that."

The airlock completed its cycle, the indicator on the inner wall showing a breathable atmosphere beyond. Yao and Thien struggled to remove their helmets; the sickly sweet, stale air of the shelter filtered into their nostrils as the hatch slid open.

Yao took a single step forward, into the gloom. In the dim light beyond the hatch, he could see an indistinct figure seated against the far wall. Yao's eyes adjusted to the low light and the figure resolved into a Mexica warrior, a fire-lance in his hands, trained on the pair of them.

Reflex took over. Yao rushed forward without stopping to consider his circumstance, arms out, hands curled into fists, but before he had gone more than two steps the searing pain on the right side of his chest blossomed into a wave of agony and nausea that swept over his whole being. His vision went red, and his eyes closed on the world.

YAO WAS UNSURE how much time had passed. The air in the shelter smelled to him of sweat and fear, and his mouth felt drier than the red sands of Fire Star.

He lay on the floor, his shoulders on the cold wall of the shelter, still dressed in his surface suit. Without turning his head—the slightest movement was sufficient to send sharp shards of pain through his chest—he saw Thien sitting beside him, her leg in a crude splint, her helmet nowhere to be seen.

"Oh, you're awake," Thien said, and saw Yao looking at her leg. Her voice sounded strange in Yao's ears, so long had it been since he'd heard the sound of it not propagated through glass or transmitted over radio static. "Blue-green Feather set my leg while you slept."

The Mexic warrior sat a few meters away, the fire-lance laid across his knees, his dark eyes fixed on Yao.

"Blue-green... Blue-green Feather?" Yao managed through gritted teeth.

"Yes." Thien glanced over at the Mexica guardedly. "His name is Matlalihuitl. That's what the word means in Nahuatl: Blue-green Feather. He doesn't talk much, though. When you passed out, he helped me to move you inside and then set my leg. Once he'd made the splint, he sat back down. He hasn't said a word since."

Yao moved his head fractionally, the slightest of movements. On the floor at the Mexica's side he could see his knife, both his and Thien's helmets, and their provisions stacked neatly. The Mexica's own helmet lay some distance away, constructed in the shape of a jaguar's head, its faceplate shattered. From the helmet, and the jaguar pattern painted on the Mexica's surface suit, Yao recognized him as the warrior Seto had struck before being doused in burning liquid magnesium.

Thien followed his gaze and nodded. "Blue-green Feather threatened to set fire to you if I didn't bring him your weapons. What I don't understand is why he hasn't just killed us."

"The Mexica prefer to take live prisoners," Yao said, finding it easier to talk in a low whisper, forcing as little air through his lungs as possible. "To sacrifice later. That's how Mexic warriors proceed through the ranks, by sacrificing prisoners to their gods. His own helmet is cracked"—Yao pointed to the jaguar-shaped helmet sitting on the ground at the Mexica's side—"and our friend has no doubt discovered that helmets of Middle Kingdom manufacture can't be sealed on a Mexic surface suit. He cannot go back outside. Not until help arrives."

"What happens if the soldiers of the Middle Kingdom find us first?"

"In that case, Feather over there will likely just douse us both with flaming magnesium and then take out as many of our countrymen as he can. If his people arrive first, he progresses in rank having captured two enemies. If our people arrive first, he gets to kill as many of us as possible before leaving this plane to join his ancestors. Either way, he wins."

Concentrating, careful not to shift from the waist up, Yao slid his left leg slightly, rolling his foot slowly inwards. He smiled grimly when he felt a hard object press into the flesh of his left thigh through the constrictive material of the surface suit.

He always carried a second knife in a hidden pouch set into the fabric of the suit. If he were able to get the blade out, he might be able to make a move against the Mexica.

NIGHT FELL. THE light trickling dimly through a solitary, small skylight overhead faded, leaving the interior of the chamber a murky, moonlit gray.

They had sat in a watchful silence for long hours, and Yao had yet to hear a solitary noise from the Mexica. Now, in the gloaming, he began to speak, the liquid syllables of his speech strange in Yao's ears. The warrior's voice rose and fell, rhythmically, like some sort of song or chant.

"Thien," Yao said, his voice little more than a harsh whisper. "What is he saying?"

"My Nahuatl is rough at best, but I'll try." In the low light Yao could see her leaning forward, listening intently. "It's a prayer. He says, 'O lord of the near and the night, of the night and the wind. You see and know the things within the trees and rocks. You know of things within us, and hear us from within. You hear and know what we say, what we think, our minds and our hearts. Smoke and mist rise before you.'"

Yao scowled. He would have shaken his head if his chest could have borne it. "I don't believe in gods or spirits. I believe only in the man fighting at my left, the man fighting at my right, and those who stand before me, wanting to kill us."

Yao heard Thien chuckle, soft and indistinct. "Myself, I am a Taoist. I suppose I believe in the union of opposites, if anything."

The darkness grew deeper. The sound of the Mexica carried on, into the night, praying to his gods, distant and strange.

IN THE LONG hours before dawn, all was quiet and still. Thien shifted restlessly in her sleep at his side, and Yao was convinced that the Mexica was asleep. Slowly, painfully, Yao reached his left hand towards the hidden pouch on his leg and gently took out the knife.

After what seemed an eternity, his teeth gritted against the pain, he managed to get the knife free of the pocket. But his fingers, encased in the thick material of the suit, failed to get a good grip on the knife and it slipped from his grip. Though it fell only centimeters, it clattered loudly, echoing through the darkened shelter.

Thien only rustled, but Yao could hear the sound of the Mexica shifting. He felt the eyes of the Mexic warrior trying to bore through the darkness. Slowly, carefully, Yao reached down and picked the knife back up again. He rolled onto one hip and slid it carefully under him, the blade flat to the ground so that when he sat back it was hidden beneath his leg.

Yao sat motionless, his chest in agony, his heart pounding, his ears straining against the silence.

YAO AWOKE, SPUTTERING. He coughed violently. With each ragged noise he spat blood. The right side of his chest felt as though it was stuck through with hot pokers.

Thien reached over and wiped the blood-flecked spittle from his chin. "I think one of your broken ribs punctured a lung," she said, her voice grave.

"Perhaps my injuries will take me, and cheat the Mexica of his prize." He coughed again, his face contorted with pain. "Wouldn't... that be... amusing?"

Yao closed his eyes and a fitful sleep overtook him once more.

It WAS NEAR midday when Yao woke again. Thien had a small flask of water, which she poured into Yao's mouth.

Swallowing painfully, his lips cracked and dry, Yao looked across the shelter at the Mexica. He kept his gaze fixed on them, his eyes narrowed.

"Thank... thank you," Yao told Thien, when she pulled the flask away. "Where... where did you get...?"

"From Blue-green Feather," Thien said, jerking a thumb at the Mexica. "I told him that if we didn't have water to drink we were as good as dead anyway, so why didn't he just kill us now and get it over with."

"And he... didn't like that idea?"

"He didn't say much, only pulled this flask from our provisions and threw it across to me."

Yao licked his parched lips, his eyes still on the Mexica.

"So it won't... be... a slow death... by dehydration then?"

"Not until he runs out of water." Thien smiled. "Of course, by that point, I think that thirst is going to be the least of our concerns."

It was the middle of the afternoon, and Yao's stomach growled, audibly.

"We need food," Thien said.

"We need… many things." Yao managed a weak smile, conscious of the outline of the knife through the fabric of his suit.

Thien raised her voice and spoke a string of strange syllables to the Mexica. Then she turned and said to Yao, "I just explained to him that without a bite of food from time to time, there's no point in giving us water either."

The Mexica's expression remained affectless, but he reached into a pouch attached to his surface suit's belt and pulled out a slim package. He uttered a few short syllables, and then threw the package over to Thien.

"What is it?" Yao asked as Thien struggled to open the strange container.

"Food, I suppose," Thien answered. "If you want to call it that."

Thien pulled out a few pieces of flat bread, some freeze-dried strips of beef, and some sort of dried grain.

"It's no feast," she said, "but it beats starving." She pulled off a piece of the bread, wrapped it around a strip of beef, and handed it to Yao. "Well, at least we'll be well-fed when we're sacrificed to their heathen gods, no?"

The meat was stringy and the flat bread was stale and tasteless, but with a few mouthfuls of water and a few bites of food in his stomach, Yao felt marginally better. Thien helped him reposition against the wall. With some of his weight shifted off his spine, he was able to breathe a little easier. Though he could still speak only in a whisper, it caused him less pain to do so.

When Thien and Yao finished the last of the ration package the Mexica had thrown over, the warrior spoke a few words.

Thien laughed and nodded.

"What did he say?" Yao asked.

"He said, 'The food is horrible, isn't it?'"

Yao tried to remain stoic, but couldn't keep a slight smile from tugging up the corner of his mouth.

As the shadows deepened, the Mexica shook his head sharply and muttered a few guttural syllables, his eyes on Yao, his grip tight on the fire-lance across his knees.

"He wonders why you look at him with such hatred," Thien translated. "He says that you never stop staring at him, as though you're calculating how much blood you could squeeze from his body."

Yao's lip curled in a snarl. "The Mexica are the blood-hungry ones, not me."

The Mexica jerked his head, indicating Yao, and fired a few syllables at Thien. She nodded, glancing at Yao, and replied. Then the Mexica shook his head, a few times quickly, and began to speak.

"Blue-green Feather asked what you said," Thien explained, "and when I translated, he said that you don't know what you're talking about. He says"— she paused, listening closely—"he says that everyone in the Mexic Dominion knows what became of the first Mexic expedition to the red planet, and that..."

Thien trailed off into silence, averting her eyes.

"What?" Yao asked. "What is he saying?"

Thien drew a heavy breath before continuing. "He says that the Mexica were on the surface of Fire Star before the Middle Kingdom arrived, and that when the Treasure Fleet reached the surface, the Mexica were still in radio contact with their superiors in the Place of the Stone Cactus. Those back at home were able to hear the sounds of the wanton slaughter of their countrymen."

"Bah," Yao spat. "I've heard that bit of propaganda before. It's nonsense, and a lie. Everyone knows that the Middle Kingdom reached Fire Star before the Mexica, and that the Dominion had to manufacture some excuse to explain away their failure in the race to the red planet. Instead, they came here years after us and tried to undermine our efforts to make this a living world."

Thien averted her eyes, refusing to meet Yao's gaze. "No," she finally said. "Blue-green Feather... he is right. I was there, remember."

"What?" Yao raised his voice, and immediately regretted it.

"It's not something that any of us in the Treasure Fleet liked to talk about in the long years that followed. But one of the first ground teams did come across a Mexic research facility and wiped them all out." She glanced from Yao to the Mexic warrior, her expression pained. "I was brought in to review the Mexica's research records—they were all in Nahuatl, and there were few of us in the Fleet who could read it. I saw the bodies myself, before they had been dragged out."

Blue-green Feather said something, Thien replied, and the Mexica let forth another torrent of words. Yao listened as Thien translated.

"Blue-green Feather says that after the tragedy on the red planet the Mexic Dominion fell afoul of several calamities, including the meltdown of one of their atomic reactors. These setbacks, only worsened by their ongoing cold war with the Middle Kingdom, retarded the development of their space program and grounded them for more than ten terrestrial years. During that time, they watched as we continued to exploit the moon and made full use of our orbital facilities like Diamond Summit. Then we began colonizing and terraforming the red planet. When they were finally able to return to the heavens, the Mexic Dominion burned with the desire for retribution. And so they struck back at us where we were most vulnerable. Here on the red planet."

Yao blinked, disbelieving. "Well," he said at length, "it hardly matters. Perhaps a few Mexica did get themselves killed when we first got to Fire Star, but the first blood between our two cultures was spilled long before that day, and not by Middle Kingdom hands."

Thien spoke to Blue-green Feather in Nahuatl, and then to Yao said, "He wants to know what you mean."

"There's a story that not too many people know," Yao began, "but it's true, nonetheless. I had it from one of my commanders when I first joined the Bannermen, and he had it from a general in his own youth, and on back to the days before the First Mexic War. Back then there hadn't been much of any contact between the Middle Kingdom and the Mexic Empire, as it was known then. The Dragon Throne had, generations before, shelved any plans to invade Mexica, preferring instead to create loose trade ties with the fierce nation. In the days of the Guangxu emperor, though, the Dragon Throne decided to normalize relations. They wanted to establish a formal embassy in the region, and open up diplomatic channels. Before that point, there had been no formal representative from the Dragon Throne to the Mexic nation since the last days of the Bright Dynasty. All communication had been back-channel discussion, primarily through merchants who traded with nations that dealt with both countries.

The Middle Kingdom envoy was received by the Mexic Emperor in the Place of the Stone Cactus. He was asked to indicate which of his subordinates was most beloved. It was explained to the envoy that the emperor wanted to bestow special favor on this individual as a sign of good will. The envoy indicated his nephew, the son of his sister, who was an attaché with the embassy.

The nephew was invited to arrive early at a celebration honoring the Middle Kingdom envoy. When the envoy arrived at the feast at the imperial palace, he was greeted by a barbarous priest of the Mexica wearing the flayed skin of the envoy's nephew as a suit of clothes. The envoy wanted his guards to kill the priest on the spot but his subordinates dissuaded him. They pointed out that they were in the heart of a highly militarized nation, surrounded by warriors.

The envoy stormed out, snatching the flayed skin of his nephew from off the priest's back and left the Place of the Stone Cactus that very night. The Mexic Emperor, outraged, ordered all Middle Kingdom citizens currently within the borders of the Mexic Empire or any of its satellite nations to be expelled immediately. The war with the Mexica had begun, and the Mexica had been the ones to start it."

Blue-green Feather listened dispassionately as Thien related Yao's story. When she was done, he laughed bitterly.

"What is so twice-damned funny?" Yao snarled in a harsh whisper.

"Blue-green Feather says that you carry the answer to the riddle in your story and don't realize it," Thien translated. "He says that the envoy's nephew had been sacrificed to Xipe Totec, the Flayed Lord, also known as Red Tezcatlipoca: the ruler of the east, the red mirror, the god identified with the red planet. The rite signifies that with the arrival of spring, Earth must coat itself with a new skin of vegetation and be reborn."

"So there was some insane reason behind the murderous act?" Yao spat. "What difference does that make?"

"Blue-Green Feather says that the Mexica are taught that unless lives are sacrificed to the gods who create and sustain the universe, all that lives will suffer and the world will end. Is it not worth the loss of a select few lives for the benefit of the rest?"

Yao tightened his hands into white-knuckled fists. "They are bloodthirsty savages."

"Perhaps," Thien said. "But I think it is their religion that has kept them primitive and unsophisticated."

Yao said nothing further, nor did the Mexic warrior. Instead they eyed one another, unblinking, across the shelter.

NIGHT APPROACHED. As the illumination from the skylight dimmed, the Mexica repeated his prayer of the previous evening. When he was through he was silent for a time, and then began again to speak.

Thien originally thought that the Mexica was talking to himself. Then she thought he was talking to her, and then she was not sure whether the Mexica knew himself. She translated for Yao, as best she could.

"Blue-green Feather says that he has taken four live prisoners to date—the number required to earn membership in the Order of the Jaguar Knights—and executed them himself to the glory of Left-handed Hummingbird before the eyes of his commander, Chief of the House of Darts. But now, after spending some years at battle on the red planet, Blue-green Feather has begun to question the rightness of their war with the Middle Kingdom."

"Oh, has he?" Yao's voice dripped with sarcasm.

"So he says," Thien answered. "He says that, when slaves of the Mexica are sacrificed to the gods, they know that they serve a larger purpose and go willingly to their deaths with—usually—a smile in their hearts. They call their captor 'father,' as he calls them 'son.' But prisoners from among the Middle Kingdom do not know anything of the gods of the Mexica. They go to their deaths stoic and stone-faced, with hatred in their eyes"—at this point in his speech, the Mexica indicated Yao—"or pleading for mercy with tears streaming down their faces"—he then indicated Thien. "He wonders, do such sacrifices honor the gods?"

"As I said," Yao curled his lip distastefully. "Bloodthirsty savages who wage war only for the sake of taking lives."

"But Yao? Weren't soldiers in the armies of the Dragon Throne traditionally encouraged to fight by a system of rewards determined by the number of enemy heads taken in battle?"

"Yes," Yao answered reluctantly, "in previous generations, maybe, but the practice has long since been abandoned."

"And are the soldiers in the Green Standard and the troops of the Eight Banners not given bonus payments when they are particularly successful in combat? When they kill more of the enemy than is typical?"

Yao drew a ragged breath, the right side of his chest throbbing with pain. "Yes, I suppose," he said at length.

"If that is true," Thien said sadly, "then at least Blue-green Feather's people kill to honor their gods, who they believe sustain the world, and not just for a larger payment."

LATER, IN THE middle hours of the night, Yao could scarcely see the Mexic warrior in the gloaming, only a few meters away.

Thien leaned in close, her tone eager. "I think we might have made a real connection with Blue-green Feather. The Mexica is questioning what he has been taught about the Middle Kingdom, and wondering openly about the rightness of the current war. Perhaps this is a turning point. If Blue-green Feather were to return to his people, this pointless conflict might be brought to a close. I'm positive that, should the Mexica find us, that Blue-green Feather will argue for us to be spared. I just know it. If the Middle Kingdom find us, you and I will have to do the same for him."

Yao said nothing. He kept his eyes on the dim outline of the Mexica in the darkness.

THE SUN ROSE, and the chamber filled slowly with faint light. Thien drowsed at his side, but Yao sat alert with eyes open and watchful, like the Mexica opposite them.

Suddenly, the silence of the shelter was divided by the grinding sound of the airlock's outer hatch being opened.

"Hey!" Thien said, coming wide awake and climbing unsteadily to her feet. "Someone's coming."

Thien began to hobble towards the door.

"I wish there was a viewport in these old lock hatches." She glanced back over her shoulder at Yao. The bannerman's eyes did not leave the Mexica, who tightened his grip on the fire-lance.

"Could be anyone," Yao said simply.

The Mexica's eyes followed Thien's slow progress across the floor. They could hear the sound of air flowing as the lock slowly cycled. His dark eyes flicked expectantly towards the door.

Yao didn't wait another instant. Rolling to the right, ignoring the pain from his side, he snatched the knife from beneath his left leg. He rocked back to the left, flipping the knife backhanded and sending it sailing end over end across the room. With a high whistling nose, the knife buried itself in the Mexica's right eye, sinking deep with a sickening squelch.

Thien turned around, wheeling on her splinted leg. She stared with horror at the red ruin of Bluegreen Feather's face.

"What...?!" she shouted, gasping for air.

"I had no choice," Yao fell back against the cold wall, gritting his teeth against the pain in his chest. "I am a soldier of the Dragon Throne. I could not have done otherwise."

They could hear the airlock filling with air. Any moment now the hatch would swing open, and there would stand revealed either Middle Kingdom soldiers or Mexic warriors waiting beyond.

"Look, Yao," Thien said angrily, advancing on him, "even if our countrymen rescue us, we are only granted a reprieve for a short while. If this war continues, there will always be another like Blue-green Feather to take up arms against us."

"Perhaps," Yao said unrepentantly. "But if you are right, then all that is required for the Dragon Throne to prevail is for there always to be men like me, to stand in the enemy's way."

The hatch began slowly swinging open.

"But what about peace?" Thien pleaded.

"A soldier's only peace is that of the grave," Yao said.

Thien shook herself, exasperated.

They fell silent, both of them watching the door. In a matter of heartbeats, it would be open, and all questions would be answered.

Fifty Dinosaurs

Robert Reed

AFTER A LONG while in which nothing much happened, Kelvin spied an odd creature strolling peacefully across a distant clearing. For no obvious reason, he assumed that he was watching a sauropod. A brontosaur, or were they called apatosaurs these days? Whatever the species, it had a vivid orange body sporting a long neck and an even longer tail. It looked like a garish barn set high on four thick pillars. To Kelvin, the effect was cheap and a little silly, although he couldn't say where those impressions came from, or why he was so surprised and maybe a little bit hurt when the dinosaur paid absolutely no attention to him.

Without a second thought, Kelvin began to chase after it.

Why that seemed reasonable was another mystery. But he ran until he was exhausted, and that taught him two lessons. First of all, he had gained a good deal of weight since his arrival. And second, this dimly lit, largely incomprehensible landscape was even larger than he had imagined. Just reaching the clearing took forever, or so it seemed.

Kelvin collapsed against one of the giant gray pillars. After some curative panting he opened his backpack and removed a tall bottle filled with cool, delicious water. Head back, he drank his fill, eyes stared at the milky white sky. His pack had been lying beside him when he first woke in this very odd realm. Its water bottle was always filled. That was a lesson learned early, and he didn't puzzle over it anymore. And the satchels beneath the bottle were constantly jammed with tasty, nutritious, and often-times warm foods. There were also two changes of clothing, perpetually clean and neatly folded, and a toiletry kit complete with an endless roll of perfumed toilet paper. At the bottom of the pack, under the balled-up white socks, somebody had painted a twisted black symbol on the pale blue fabric that matched the substantial tattoo Kelvin had discovered emblazoned on his own chest.

The symbol meant "37." He felt sure about it, but why he should be certain was another nagging mystery.

What was this place? And how much time had passed since his arrival?

Those were two more perfectly respectable questions leading to the critical issue of who might have brought him here, and why. Because some force or agent had to be responsible, and in Kelvin's bones, he felt that some grand purpose was at work in this enormous and exceptionally strange realm.

Following habits that were weeks or months old, Kelvin ate his fill and then stripped, stowing his sweaty clothes before putting on fresh garb. But as he struggled with the tight-fitting trousers, a big mouth somewhere behind him took a sudden deep breath. A moment later he heard long feet padding across the hard black ground.

A second dinosaur walked around the pillar, sniffing at the dry warm air.

Kelvin froze.

This was no sauropod. By the looks of it the creature was a T. rex, except that its body was barely twice as large as Kelvin's, if that, and its flesh was a strange combination of buttery yellow adorned with narrow crimson streaks. The dinosaur moved in a straight line, following a scent that might be hours old. (Calculating time was close to impossible here.) Those tiny front arms were held close to the muscular body. The stout tail rose high, revealing the bird-like cloaca. Then at what seemed like a random spot, the dinosaur bent low and took a huge wet breath. A quiet voice announced, "Don't try it."

Kelvin gasped.

"Are you going to try it?" the creature asked. Then it turned and looked back at him, the mouth changing in some very undinosaur-like ways. "You want to attack me. Don't you, ape-man?"

"No," Kelvin managed.

"You're sure?"

"Absolutely." Hurriedly jacking up his pants, he managed to add, "And how can you talk?"

"You're talking."

"But you don't have a real voice," the human maintained. "Screeches, maybe. But you can't make actual words."

Not only could the mouth produce speech, but it could also laugh. And those widely spaced eyes were capable of a decidedly mocking expression. "So you're the human being? The greatest, goriest murderer in history? I was wondering when I'd trip over your old bones."

A flock of new questions demanded to be asked. Kelvin offered the most obvious. "What do you mean? Who's a murderer?"

"Humans were."

"Were?"

"As ruthless as any asteroid, except their mayhem was for profit. For fun. For sport, and in the service of ignorance and laziness."

Kelvin was too stunned to react.

"Humans," his companion repeated. "Yes, I know all about your notorious kind."

"And I know about you," Kelvin managed. "You're a dinosaur. With a tiny, smooth brain and no lips—"

"Is that what I am?"

Embarrassed, Kelvin admitted, "Or maybe you're something else."

"Thank you for noticing."

"But what are you?"

"Whatever I am, it happens to be similar to what you are," the creature warned. "Each of us is a representative. You and I correspond to two species. And each of us enjoys a glancing resemblance to our namesakes. Which implies that you aren't truly human, if you see my point."

"Then what am I?"

That question earned another laugh, long and high-pitched. "Do you know anything at all, human?"

"My name's Kelvin."

"Sandra," the dinosaur said instantly.

"What?"

"My name is Sandra," it said. She said. "Do me the favor of using it, please."

"Sandra."

"Hello, Kelvin. How are you today?"

He sat down, exhausted in so many ways.

"You haven't met anybody else, have you? Since you were deposited inside this extraordinary place, I mean."

"Nobody," Kelvin muttered. Then he added, "Wait. I saw a big brontosaur around here somewhere."

"Orange, was it?"

"Yes."

"That's no dinosaur. Not even a pretend one."

Those words only sounded simple. Kelvin couldn't understand: What was this apparition telling him? And could he believe anything that came out of that unlikely mouth?

"The orange beast stems from an even more ancient era."

"More ancient than when?"

"Our times, of course."

The little T. rex had worked her way closer to him, and now Kelvin realized that her chest was decorated with a symbol that shared no resemblance to human writing. Yet he understood that the mark meant 28.

"So I'm your first association. What an honor that is."

Kelvin shook his head, trying to clear his thoughts. "How many 'associations' have you made?"

"Fourteen," Sandra the dinosaur boasted. Then with a razor-toothed smile, she added, "For me, you are number fifteen. Which leaves me with how many more to meet?"

"Thirty-four," Kelvin blurted.

"And how did you know that?"

"I just do."

"And are you a genuine authentic and official human being?"

"No," he admitted.

"But you wear your body well," Sandra reported, reaching out with one of her tiny arms, a single claw resting in the dimple on his robin's-egg blue cheek.

THEY WALKED TOGETHER, managing a steady pace. Eventually the T. rex made inquiries about Kelvin's present life. How much ground had he covered; how many times had he slept? And had he ever found any edge to this landscape of randomly positioned gray columns? The human felt sure only about his last answer: No, the bizarre forest was endless. Then Sandra winked at him with one of her bright, hawk-like eyes, wondering aloud, "What do you remember about your past life?"

Past and present were separate subjects, a rigid line of demarcation standing between this bland existence and his familiar, reassuring history.

"What do you want to know?" asked Kelvin.

"Did you have parents?"

"Yeah. Sure."

"Describe your father to me."

"Tall," he blurted. "And old, particularly in the face and hands."

"Could you tell your father from any other tall old men?"

"I would hope so," he reasoned.

"So what color is Daddy's hair?"

He wasn't sure.

"What clothes did he like to wear?"

Kelvin closed his eyes, concentrating.

"And what was his first name?"

Placing both hands against the sides of his head, Kelvin pressed until he felt an ache, that mild discomfort helping him believe that he must be real. "His name was Kelvin."

"Now is that true?"

The human believed his words when he said them. But hearing the dinosaur's doubt made him feel like a liar caught at the worst possible moment.

"So do you remember your father?" he asked Sandra.

"Why would I? My mother raised me as well as my three nest-mates. She fed us and defended us until we were old enough to hunt on our own."

"What was her name?"

"She didn't need a name, little human. She was only a dinosaur."

"But you have a name," he pointed out.

"A set of sounds that cling to my present skin."

Kelvin nodded, pretending to understand.

"Are you hungry?" she asked.

They had been following the scent trail of that great orange beast. At least that's what Sandra claimed they were doing. Kelvin shook his pack, reassured by the weight of fresh food waiting for his stomach.

"I'm ravenous too," she confessed. And with that, she suddenly danced off to the side, tilting her head expectantly, her big eyes studying a random patch of black ground. Suddenly a low-built, platy-pus-like creature blinked into existence. Sandra calmly pinned it with one foot, removing its head with a surgical bite. Two gulps, and the snack vanished.

Contemplating those jaws, Kelvin felt uneasy.

Did she sense his nervousness? Somewhere in his former life, he had learned that meat-eaters could taste fear in others.

His companion smiled amiably, and winked. "Of course you don't realize this. How could you, since you've never met anyone else? But each of us gets to eat and drink through whatever route is most natu-ral."

Kelvin hadn't considered the issue.

"When Reggie's hungry, the floor sprouts stroma-tolites covered with bacterial mats. With Theresa, a convenient electrical plug appears."

"Reggie?"

"A trilobite."

The image of a hard-shelled undersea bug came to mind. "And what was the other name? Theresa?"

"A Lyttle-Tang AI hard-drive," Sandra mentioned. "When your deadly species fell into its well-earned obscurity, the hard-drives inherited the earth as well as the nearby cosmos."

"How do you know this?"

"Make a guess."

"Theresa told you."

"She told me all about her machine world. Which was decorated, she mentioned, with a lot of freshly-killed humans."

Kelvin glanced over a shoulder.

"Theresa's not back there."

Maybe not. But for just a moment, he thought he could make out a shape in the distance—something passing slowly and soundlessly between two of the towering pillars.

"So what is this place?" he asked again.

"Tell me what you see."

He spoke about the forest of smooth gray pillars and the black floor and the soothing white light that felt as distant as the stars.

The dinosaur seemed to listen, nodding thought-fully. And then her rubbery lips twisted, producing a wide smile. "You know, most descriptions of the universe are similar to what you are describing to me. The cosmos is a vast, nearly empty room built upon a few repeating elements, and most locations are desperately similar to every other. Isn't that a fair stereotype? Giant galactic structures strewn like walls across the black cold void. And from a distance, everything looks to be rather boring."

Kelvin shrugged.

"By contrast," she mentioned, "what we see here is quite tiny."

"Tiny?"

"In human terms, yes."

"It doesn't feel small."

But Sandra didn't wish to explain herself. The smile was mysterious and, despite the bright long teeth, there was no sense of menace. The golden eyes revealed nothing beyond her benign amusement. Suddenly a burp emerged, wet and warm, and then she turned abruptly and began to march on, her nose dipping to absorb another trace of whatever creature they were following together.

Kelvin jogged to match her pace.

"How old are you?" she asked suddenly.

Without hesitation, he said, "Twenty-one."

"A young man, are you?"

"I guess."

"So, Kelvin. What about that day when you turned twenty-one? Do you remember anything in particular?"

He recalled all of it.

Easily and perfectly, yes.

* * *

WITH CONSIDERABLE PLEASURE, Kelvin described how he had slept late on his birthday, missing every morning class, and then rolled out of bed and dressed in yesterday's jeans and a fresh shirt before marching off to the cafeteria to eat lunch. He sat with friends; he could recall everyone's face, everyone's clothes. He knew their manners and habits and favorite phrases. Young masculine voices came back to him in detail. With everybody talking at once, the gang made plans for the evening. "You're legal tonight," they told Kelvin. He remembered being happy and excited. Then the young men got a round of cold sweet ice cream cones and sat watching the girls pass by. With the crass certainty of youth, they critiqued every breast and leg and wiggling rear end.

Kelvin paused

After a moment's reflection, he asked, "How do I remember this? My father's face and name are gone, but not the butt of a nineteen year-old blonde."

"That is a very reasonable question," the dinosaur agreed.

"And I know my friends' names, and half the faces on campus. I was a junior. It was spring. There was sun that day, and then clouds, and then sun again. When I was walking to my afternoon class I saw a robin on the sidewalk, picking up a chunk of worm." He hesitated for a moment, and then smiled. "Birds are dinosaurs, you know."

"I am not," said Sandra.

"But you are. Avians are only survivors from the dinosaur line. I learned that from Vertebrate Zoology."

With scorn, his companion stared back at him. Then she looked ahead, asking, "Was that your afternoon class? Liar's Zoology?"

"No, it was—"

"Don't tell me," she interrupted, bumping him with her strong yellow tail. "It was a computer class, and you were learning about thinking machines."

He nodded, impressed.

"It wasn't much of a trick," she confessed. "Since each of us is tied together in some little way or another."

"Each of whom?"

"The Fifty, of course."

"And who does the tying?"

Focusing on a distant point, she grinned.

"You're sure there are fifty of us?" he asked.

"Tell me about your computer class," Sandra persisted.

Kelvin remembered sitting up front in the lecture hall. After a few minutes of reading from notes, their grumpy little professor had announced a special guest. Moments later, the prototype of a new AI rolled in from the hallway. The machine was tiny and very simple in appearance—a plastic box with wheels and little jointed arms and electrical leads and an assortment of plug-ins. But the voice that spoke to them was decidedly female.

Pausing, he asked, "What does Theresa look like?"

"Take a guess," the dinosaur advised.

He knew. And that's when Kelvin accepted that his intuitions were rock-solid, at least when it came to his clearest memories.

Again he asked, "Who does the tying? Who's in charge here?"

But Sandra steered him back to his birthday. "Perhaps you'll find an insight lurking here. Yes? The one slice of your life that is important enough to remember in full. Your parents are minimally rendered, like the rest of your childhood. But here stands that luminous day when you officially and forever moved from youth into full adulthood."

He shivered, though he wasn't sure why.

"What was the word?" she asked. "'Legal,' was it? What does that mean, Kelvin?"

"Alcohol," he replied.

"Which is what? Explain it to me."

The yeasty taste of beer instantly filled his mouth, and his good friends were leading him from one crowded bar, to another, then to a third, and in that realm of bright lights and shouts and painfully loud music, the newly created man graduated to some peculiar drink called a "slam-dunk." His happy mood turned into a buoyant fearlessness. He was certain that he was badly drunk, yet his memories remained whole. Indeed, his recall seemed to be improving. A box that resembled Theresa was propped on a little stage at one end of a very long room, and drunken patrons were happily signing up, begging for the honor of singing badly while pieces of recorded music played in the background.

Sandra was sniffing the air again, and she was walking faster.

Maybe she wasn't listening anymore. But Kelvin found himself explaining how his friends had put his name on the list to sing, and with just one person ahead of him, he fumbled his slam-dunk, dropping it into his lap and leaving his crotch soaked through.

The dinosaur paused suddenly.

Distracted, Kelvin continued walking, speaking in a low obsessed voice until he felt the sharp tips of teeth grabbing him from behind, piercing his shirt in a dozen places.

"Wait," she whispered.

Ahead of them stood a creature that looked familiar, except it wasn't. The orange was the same shade he had seen earlier, and something about the roundness of the body was exactly as he had expected. But there were no legs, just hundreds of cilia, a portion of them woven together to create four pillar-like ropes that carried the rounded body. What he had assumed was a neck and a tail were nothing but flagella emerging from the same end of the beast, long and stiff but capable of being twisted to the front and back again—rigid propellers devised by nature to push a microbe through the viscous heart of a pond or tidal pool.

"Quiet," Sandra advised.

"What is it?"

But she preferred answering a different question. "Imagine that you are a very important entity. You are a powerful wise and brilliant soul on the brink of becoming a full-fledged adult. I'm not talking about being human. Or being even a tyrannosaur, for that matter. And instead of reaching twenty-one years of age, our prince is achieving that rich sweet age of fifty."

"Half a century?"

"Hardly," she said. "In this kingdom, years do not matter."

"What does matter?"

"A celebration has been planned in the great prince's honor, Kelvin. And for the fun of it, the souls responsible for this happy event have created fifty party favors. Fifty representatives pulled from prehistory. The fifty most important rulers known to the earth and its little corner of the universe."

"Fifty dinosaurs," Kelvin muttered.

"Three dinosaurs and two hairy primates," the little T. rex corrected. Then she winked at him, adding, "But mostly microbes and machines. As it happens, those are the characters that dominate any authentic story about life. Slime and wires; bacteria and batteries."

Kelvin spent a moment contemplating the vastness around them.

"The two of us, my human dear... my sweet Kelvin... we are little more than transitional forms swimming between what really matters..."

THE GIANT MICROBE had no eyes, but it must have sensed the vibrations of footsteps and quiet conversation.

It had no mouth, but a vacuole near the flagellum served that purpose nicely.

"I feel two bodies lurking," it claimed.

"Not lurking," Sandra replied. "We are admiring you, friend."

"As you should," the entity rumbled. "As is right."

Perhaps they were nothing but party favors, Kelvin reflected. But oversized egos seemed mandatory.

Sandra introduced the two of them, giving names and numbers. "And what do we call you, glorious sir?"

"I am Barry," the vacuole replied.

Kelvin nearly laughed, then thought better of it.

"I am Nine," Barry reported. "The first eukaryote."

"You are an astonishment," the dinosaur called out. Then she winked at Kelvin, as if to say, "Play along with me."

"Step close," their new friend told them. "Let me feel your tiny bodies."

It took courage to walk up to the building-sized creature, but the cilia proved soft and soothing to the touch. Kelvin found the experience to be nothing but a pleasure.

Barry asked whom else they had met in their wanderings.

Knowing nothing about any others, Kelvin sat and opened his pack, drinking his bottle dry and eating heartily. By then, the orange microbe was listing the names and species of the other entities that he had caressed during his travels, and he repeated each of their long stories—a business that took long enough so that the ignored human could change clothes and relieve himself behind the nearest pillar and still have time for a quick nap.

He woke to discover himself alone.

Jumping up, he called out for Sandra. "Where are you? Where have you gone?" But she was just a little way behind him, looking back with her tail high in the air, eyes mischievous, something about his panic worth a long, teasing giggle.

"Didn't you hear me calling?" she asked.

No, he was too busy dreaming.

"We're going to wander along with Barry for now," she explained. "We need to find the rest of the Fifty. Come now! Everyone is needed."

Needed for what?

But he didn't ask. There had to be some rationale at work here, and he was tired of asking obvious questions, supplying the comedic relief for their slowly growing herd.

They walked.

In a useless attempt to measure the passage of time, Kelvin counted his strides, a thousand at a time. Once all of his fingers were extended, ten thousand steps had been taken, and he carefully looked around, trying to gain some feel for navigational cues. But they didn't seem to have gained any distance, even after a hundred thousand long patient steps. Suddenly Barry announced his hunger, causing a great droplet of Precambrian pond water to appear. While the other two ate their little meals, the microbe swam back and forth inside that bacteria-rich treat.

"What's wrong with me, Sandra?"

"What do you mean?"

"You know quite a bit more than I know," Kelvin complained. "I can't figure out what direction we're heading, or even find a single usable landmark. What you tell me about this birthday party feels true, but that could mean that I'm highly suggestible, nothing more."

His companion bent her head down, tearing the raw meat from a chunk of white bone.

"I feel like I'm broken," he whispered. "Compared to you, at least."

Kelvin fully expected her to gloat.

But instead the little T. rex brushed her tail against his leg, the gesture apparently meant to reassure. Then with a sober tone, she mentioned, "We aren't expensive items, I'm afraid. Manufactured quickly and with no eye for details."

"I'm what? Just a trinket?"

A sympathetic look filled her face. "Perhaps you came out of the factory wearing a few more flaws than usual. Perhaps."

"But look at what's right about me," he said. "And look at yourself. Both of us have good strong minds. I'm full of guts and lungs that work, and a heart, and other important things." He came close to mentioning his male organ, but balked. "I'm also holding memories of some life that seems real and rich to me. And when I sleep, I dream about my prehistoric existence."

"I dream in the same ways," she confided.

"And we're just cheap pieces of crap? Is that reasonable?"

"In a future where miracles are ordinary, it is reasonable. And more importantly, it is inevitable. Why shouldn't the humblest toys have souls and dreams?"

"Because that would be cruel."

Sandra had nothing to offer. She glanced at the shape that was Barry, watching him swim furiously inside that rich, green, blimp-sized wealth of water.

Finally Kelvin asked, "What do you know about the prince? What kind of creature is it?"

"A sentient plasmoid," she said softly.

"And what's that?"

She squinted. "At this moment, the plasmoids are the undisputed rulers of our home world."

"And exactly how old is our birthday boy?"

She hesitated.

Kelvin guessed, "He must be huge, and he's very old. By our pedestrian standards, I mean."

"Why do you assume that?"

"Just look around," he argued. "This room, whatever it is... it dwarfs everything that I can remember, and there's such a powerful sense of the ages here..."

With a careful tone, she said, "No."

Then she touched him with the two claws of a hand, gently explaining, "The plasmoid is smaller than any bacterium, as it happens. And this huge home is not much larger than a dinosaur's heart. And when you think about turning fifty, think tiny bites of time. Imagine fifty one-millionths of a second, and you won't be too far from the mark."

Kelvin carefully held her little hand.

"And we are fifty party favors," she concluded, "waiting patiently to be found by our prince."

THEY WALKED AGAIN. Apparently there were vibrations and a dim but worthwhile odor that could be followed. But then Barry couldn't sense any presence besides the three of them, and Sandra had lost any scent worth a deep breath. What would be best, they decided, was to stop for now, to rest and wait until someone else happened along.

Kelvin fell into a deep, dreamy sleep.

He woke on the narrow hard bed in his dorm room, looking out the window at the sun as it passed behind high cottony clouds. With a groan, he sat up. Then he dressed and paused before the room's little mirror, considering the problem of what was real and what was madness. Even when he knew the truth, he couldn't escape his day. He found himself walking to lunch and to class and back to his room to wash and change before heading out to dinner; and then with the evening, there was some very hard drinking.

Events swept him along to the karaoke bar where his crotch got drenched by the spilled drink. Could he dry himself in time? It was a game among his drunken friends, everybody handing him napkins and coarse suggestions. Kelvin was beginning to make progress with the mess. Then the master of ceremonies strode up on stage to announce the next victim.

"Is it me?" Kelvin groaned.

But it wasn't his turn, no. The next song was the love ballad from a Twentieth Century movie that nobody had heard of, and the young woman performing it happened to be named Sandra.

Kelvin couldn't stop his frantic cleaning of his jeans. But he had the power to look up, to watch the very pretty red-haired woman with little hands and a prominent, perfect rear end.

Sandra had a beautiful voice.

A professional voice.

By the end of the song, everybody was listening. Applause erupted, and the audience leaped to its feet. Even Kelvin stood. But as he clapped and cheered, he carefully looked around the entire room.

Including Sandra and himself, fifty celebrants were visible.

Of course.

BARRY WAS GONE.

Sandra woke Kelvin with the sorry news. He had slipped away while they slept, she reported, and then she threw some hard curses at their one time companion. "I knew he would leave us. I knew it."

"How could you?"

"Because he prefers to be alone. Didn't you see that in his nature?"

Not particularly. But Kelvin shrugged agreeably, asking, "So what do we do now? Chase after him?"

"Forget him," was her advice.

Kelvin was glad to have company, and he said as much.

Sandra absorbed the news with a faint, hopeful smile. "Let's try this direction next," she decided.

They marched along what seemed to be a straight line.

"So was I ever real?" Kelvin wondered aloud.

His companion seemed ready for the question. "You're asking if there was a genuine Kelvin who had a father and attended classes and drank alcohol on the night of his birthday?"

"A model to base me on, maybe."

"There might well have been," she allowed. "Who knows what kinds of databases survive from those times?"

The random columns, so tall and perfect, had all at once formed a distinct pattern. For the first time, Kelvin had the strong impression that he had stood on this ground before.

"And what about you?" he asked.

Those nonsensical lips pulled in tight to the mouth.

No, there wouldn't be databases for dinosaurs. She was something dreamed up from scratch, and it plainly bothered her.

Kelvin changed topics. "So what does our sentient plasmoid look like? If we saw our creator up close, I mean."

"I don't know," she allowed. "Theresa claimed that it's a cold purple flame, and when it appears, everything else vanishes."

"And it's looking for us now?"

She gave a nod, her mouth becoming even grimmer.

Kelvin glanced back over his shoulder, thinking hard with his cheaply rendered mind. Then with a low voice he asked, "Sandra? Do you know one of the traits shared by every cheap trinket and dodad?"

She had no clue how to answer him. She was a dinosaur and had never owned anything in any life.

But then he made himself tell her, "Never mind." Kelvin didn't want to be cruel. He didn't want to be the one to explain how everything shoddy usually ends up lost and forgotten. But knowing that could be their fate gave him an unexpected strength, and with the strength came a fresh, reassuring sense of freedom.

IN THE END, Kelvin had tied a spare shirt around his waist and bravely stepped up onto the raised platform. From a list of several thousand popular songs, he chose one about luck being a lady tonight. Maybe it was the liquor, or maybe the contrived nature of the moment. Either way, he discovered a rich deep voice and the courage to belt out the lyrics to the increasing approval of the forty-nine in his audience.

Holding the community microphone to his mouth, he could smell the perfume that Sandra was wearing.

Later, in the midst of a congratulatory march around the room, he spotted the girl sitting alone at the bar. Approaching her seemed entirely natural.

Without a shred of doubt, he told her that her singing was beautiful and so was she. That brought laughter and a measure of suspicion. Then Kelvin asked if the stool beside her was taken, and she gestured with her small, long-nailed hand, offering it to him while admitting, "There was somebody else, but he's gone now."

Above the din of bad music, they tried to converse.

Later they went outside to find quiet and a little privacy. She seemed sweet and drunk but not sloppy or out-of-control. More than once, she told Kelvin she seemed to know him from somewhere, and wasn't that peculiar?

Eventually they found their way to the front seat of her car.

And later, the back seat.

Kelvin woke with a start. He didn't want to leave the dream. It felt rude to have slipped away from his new love. But try as he might, he couldn't force himself back to sleep. He went as far as covering his head with a spare shirt and one arm, eyes closed as his mind replayed every tiny detail of what probably had never been real in the first place.

Slowly, he realized that a noise was keeping him from sleeping.

A scratching sound, abrasive and obsessive.

Kelvin finally threw off the shirt and sat up, startled to find his dinosaur companion dragging her feet across an unexpected mound of dirt. Sandra smiled as she worked. But where had the dirt come from? From the same place that platypuses came from, he realized. And for some reason she had to shape it into a rough bowl before suddenly hunkering down and looking hard at him, the smile saying everything.

With an effortless ease, the first egg emerged.

Ten more eggs followed first, and all the while the happy father danced around the nest, singing the one song that he knew by heart.

Mason's Rats:
Black Rat

Neal Asher

MASON LEANT AGAINST the sun-heated wall of the barn and groped in his pocket for a couple of environmentally friendly shotgun cartridges. When he remembered that what he held in his other hand was a walking stick, he instead leant the stick against the wall, pulled out his tobacco tin, and rolled himself a cigarette.

He'd seen it disappearing round the corner of the barn. It was that big black bastard Smith had been having trouble with; the one that had led Smith's nice shiny new cybernetic ratter into the path of a combine. Yes, it was over here now, where the pickings were easier. No cybernetic ratters here, nor any automatic lasers. Mason drew on his cigarette and frowned.

His own rats hadn't done this, for he had an agreement with them, of sorts. It worked out at about one percent of his total harvest, which was certainly cheaper than the products of Traptech. There was also the advantage that he knew precisely where their food was coming from and was able to lace it with birth control chemicals. He peered down at the hole through the alloy wall. The black rat was certainly clever, he'd give it that, for the hole had been cut with a file or a hacksaw.

With a sigh Mason pushed himself away from the wall and headed back to his house. It looked like war again. As he stepped back out onto the track he noticed the chief brown rat watching him from a round bale of wheat straw. It wore its tool-belt and had a small sack slung over one shoulder. Mason pointed at the hole in the wall and in response the brown rat held up its paw, twitched its nose, and shrugged. Mason spat the remains of his rollie on the ground as the brown rat disappeared over the other side of the bale.

It might have been possible for him to push the agreement further, but communicating with rats was a difficult thing at the best of times. Last time he had done it with pictures: one of a rat eating grain nailed over the entrance to an old tin shed in which he put their one percent, and pictures of rats being blown apart with shotguns on the doors to the storage barns. After the violent demise of about ten rats, the rest only took grain from the tin shed, but Mason had to wonder if the pictures had helped them to come to a decision at all. And anyway, how could he convey with pictures his displeasure at the depredations of the black rat and his kin? No, there was only one solution: splatter the bastard.

THE SHOTGUN CLOSED with a satisfying click and Mason hoiked it up under his arm before setting out from his house. Two hundred acres of alpha-wheat had to be brought in today and he needed to get this problem sorted. He'd sealed the first hole only to find another behind a patch of stinging nettles, almost as if the first had been a decoy. This second hole led into the rapeseed storage barn, from which the rat had somehow managed to steal a quarter of a ton of seed overnight. As he had thought: it was here with its kin, and probably here to stay.

"Right, you little shit head," said Mason as he stepped out of his house. "Show one whisker today and you're rat burgers."

He surveyed the yard before him like a Tommy about to go over the top, then with firm purpose in his stride he set out for the combine garage. The black rat didn't show itself as he crossed the yard, nor when he hit the lock pad to Garage Two and the door slid open. He surveyed the yard again with deep suspicion before turning back to the garage and addressing the immense harvester before him.

"Combine Bertha, access code seven three two, Mason—respond."

A low humming issued from the machine and its lights glimmered reluctantly.

"Code confirmed—instructions," responded the silky voice of the combine.

"Fields G27 through to G31 are ready for alpha-wheat harvesting. Run a diagnostic and if you're within parameters proceed to harvest."

The humming from the combine increased and its lights glared bright then went out. Its diesel engine started, blasting out a cloud of acrid black smoke. Various mechanical sounds issued from its mysterious chambers. Its cutters swished together, its reel turned, and its augers chuntered to themselves. Mason nodded to himself in satisfaction: one of the best investments he had ever made.

"I am unable to proceed," said Bertha.

"What?"

"I am unable to proceed."

The combine groaned as it went into reverse gear and withdrew further into the garage.

"Why are you unable to proceed?" Mason asked through grinding teeth.

"It's too big out there."

THE BROWN RAT came close, very close, for against the light background of the bales it had appeared black. Mason kept it in his sights just to make a point and watched it as it backed up to the wall of straw as if walking on broken glass. At length it dropped its sack and raised its paws above its head. Mason lowered his shotgun.

"Your lucky day, punk."

He turned away and stomped back to his house. Watching him go the brown rat lowered its paws and shook its head. Had it sweat glands it would have wiped its brow. It hadn't. It picked up its sack and with a degree of determination in its scamper headed for its home. Mason stepped inside his own home, abandoning his shotgun in the porch, and with much reluctance picked up his phone. About half an hour later he ended up speaking to a real person.

"What do you mean, 'not till Saturday?' There's a belt of rain on its way!"

The voice on the other end of the phone said something reassuring.

"I paid good money for that harvester and I expect service!"

The voice deferred responsibility.

"Then put him on!"

The voice was apologetic.

"Majorca!"

The voice tried to cover all points.

Mason slammed the phone down.

As he picked up his shotgun and stamped outside he swore with staccato regularity.

THREE OF THE bastards, black rats certainly, but not the one, not the boss. He was bigger, had a bit of a limp and scars on his back from that encounter with Smith's ratter. Mason raised his shotgun and carefully rested it across the cowling of the old Fergussen. Now, all he had to do was wait until they were in line. They hadn't seen him yet. The little cart they were harnessed to was occupying all of their attention. Wait. Wait...

Mason let rip with both barrels. One rat disintegrated and another one leapt about, without the benefit of directions from its head, and tangled itself up in its harness. The third one hurriedly tried to unhook itself.

"Gotcha!"

Mason cackled as he cracked open his gun, but in his excitement he did it too high and the hot end of a spent cartridge hit him on the nose and sizzled.

"Fuck!"

The remaining rat was free and dragging itself away.

"Bugger!" Mason thunked in two new cartridges. His eyes were watering so much it took him a moment to locate the remaining rat over by the dung hill, which it was struggling to ascend. Mason took aim, then after a pause he lowered the gun. At the top of the hill stood the brown rat, its miniature crossbow held steadily on the black rat. Finally the black rat saw the brown, and froze.

"Go on, shoot," said Mason, wiping at his eyes.

Slowly, carefully, the black rat pulled itself upright and raised its paws into the air. The brown rat lowered its crossbow and watched as the black rat dragged itself away.

Mason could hardly believe what he was seeing. He raised his shotgun just as the tail of the black rat disappeared behind the dung hill. Then he swore and lowered it, came out from behind the tractor, and approached the cart the three black rats had been towing. The brown rat approached from the other side.

The cart had been made from a cut-down supermarket trolley and was loaded with various pieces of mechanical and electrical junk filched from one of Mason's workshops. There were also bags of rapeseed stacked on it. Mason glanced at the brown rat as it stared avidly at those bags. He gestured at the contrivance and turned away to head indoors. He needed to put some cream on his nose.

MASON RESTED HIS hand on his wallet and repressed the urge to bolt the doors and fetch his gun as the suit stepped out of his car, still speaking into his mobile. Mason had asked for a maintenance man and they had sent him a salesman. He hated salesmen.

"Ah, Mr. Mason, so pleased to meet you," said the suit, pocketing his phone and taking out an electronic filofax.

Mason shuddered.

"Maintenance has informed me you are having some problems with that old TW157 harvester." The filofax disappeared and the suit retrieved a briefcase from his car. The case opened with a horrid click. Glossy brochures glistened at Mason from the interior.

"If I might interest you in..."

Somehow Mason found himself in his own kitchen with brochures spread on the table before him and his throat clenched over a scream. The man must have trained as a time-share salesman before moving on, for his skin wasn't just thick, it was a veritable armor.

"But I don't want a new harvester or a new drive mind! I want my old one repaired, as it should be under the warranty!"

"Yes, of course you do, and there are advantages in retaining such archaic equipment. So for you I can offer twenty percent off the TW158 or twenty-five percent off the newest drive mind with free installation. I'll be in trouble with my boss, but for such a customer as you, Mr. Mason, it is essential that we..."

And so it went on, and on, and Mason found himself walking to the door, clutching a piece of paper he'd been a hair's breadth from signing, the suit pacing at his side. The sell was getting more brutal now, for the suit was moving him to different territory—the garage—to try a different approach, perhaps to draw comparisons between his old 157 and the new 158. Mason felt powerless to resist. Perhaps if he signed something this suit would go away, disappear. How long had it been now? One hour, two hours?

"Of course the TW158 is not so prone to agoraphobia as the 157. It has the optional on off switch, which makes for a substantial power saving. You'll notice your bills—"

"Agoraphobia?" Mason managed. He halted at the door, shaking his head. "My harvester has got agoraphobia?"

"Yes, the fear of open spaces, fairly common with the 157 when garaged for the winter. As I said, with the optional on off switch there are such—"

The salesman opened the door and there came a resounding thud.

"Such what?"

"Urgh!"

"Pardon?"

"Aargh!"

The suit stumbled back and sat down on the floor. Mason peered down at him and noticed a large cut on his head at the center of a quickly inflating lump on his forehead. In front of the salesman, lying on the doormat, was a large hexagonal wheel nut. Mason ducked down by the jamb and looked outside. The black rat, the boss, was legging it for the fields, his beautifully constructed siege catapult abandoned in the yard. Mason grinned then frowned.

"Have to find a way," he said, and thumped the door jamb, then, "Of course, idiot!"

The suit gurgled.

As THE CAR weaved from side to side up the drive shedding glossy brochures as it went, Mason headed for his workshop and got himself a couple of tins of paint. Soon he had altered the signs. On the storage barns he had splattered black rats as well as brown, and on the old chicken shed he had an even more complex sign. Now, after blocking up the holes in his barns, it was a waiting game.

It was past midnight when he heard a low squeaking from the wall of the barn. He eased himself off a pile of rapeseed, a shovel in one hand and a shotgun in the other, and crept over towards where the sound was coming from. After a moment there came a flicker of moonlight through a small hole as a drill bit was retracted. Next, a cut-down hacksaw blade poked through and the laborious cutting of the soft metal began. An hour later the cutter had completed its circle and a disk of metal fell in. Moments later the black rat stepped through, removing a set of thick gloves as it did so. Mason slammed the shovel in front of the hole.

"Right, you little git."

With very beady eyes the black rat looked up the throat of the shotgun.

"Agoraphobia, y'say? Right. Mr. Mason, we'll soon sort that."

The maintenance man wiped his hands on his overalls then reached into the back of his van and removed a club hammer.

"It's a matter of psychology," he said, knowingly.

Mason eyed the hammer dubiously.

"You'll see." The maintenance man glanced round. "Is that…?"

"A rat," said Mason.

"What's…?"

"A catapult, throws tractor wheel-nuts."

"Oh."

The black rat stood on a round bale by the drive. Next to it rested its catapult and a stack of wheel nuts. It was watching the drive through a set of opera glasses mounted on a tripod.

"The harvester is this way."

The repairman scratched his head then followed Mason. To be expected really—some of these farmers were a bit loopy. The repairman put it down to ergot dust.

Mason stood at the doors to the garage as the repairman worked his magic on Bertha. Two blows of the hammer and some artistically couched threats and the harvester was edging out of the garage. Encouragement to follow had it trundling off to the fields in a few minutes.

"Funny sign there, on that old chicken shed..." said the repairman as he returned to his van. "What's it mean?"

"If you'd been wearing a suit you'd have found out," replied Mason cryptically.

The repairman replaced his hammer in the rack beside five others and closed the back of his van. Definitely the ergot dust. He got the required signature, hopped into his van, and drove away as quickly as he could.

Mason returned to the chicken shed to view his work. The picture of the black rat eating grain had been easy. The picture of the man in a suit lying on the ground clutching at his bleeding head had presented more of a challenge. Mason grinned to himself then turned away. Before setting out for the fields to see how the harvester was getting on, he raised his hand to the black rat guard; the first living employee on his farm in decades.

Blood Bonds

Brenda Cooper

I HESITATED IN Aline's doorway. As soon as I stepped through, my sis's minibots would whisper to her and she'd leave wherever she was and come into real to see me. Tonight, the step toward her might be off a cliff.

For now, she lay blissfully unaware, gone to some virtual place. With luck, she was in the arms of a lover or climbing Olympus Mons. Anywhere but in her broken body living in VR contact gel.

Her face had survived the terrorist's bomb. She'd been walking away from the Marin County Fair, on Earth, north of San Francisco, and if she'd walked just a little faster, she might be able to walk today. But terrorism or not, it was partly my fault. I was the one who had talked her into applying for a trip to Earth. I'd wanted her to be happy, and she wanted to see forests and butterflies and elephants and oceans. Sure, we're identical twins, but she needed to go to Earth, and I longed for Mars. At the time, we were both on the moon.

And now the next thing that happened was going to be my fault, too. I wanted a choice and there wasn't one.

By the time I stood beside her bed, she'd opened her startled-blue eyes, her face swimming up above the blue-green gel and the myriad contacts that kept her body fed and exercised. Her warm smile played across my heart like a soft blanket and I wanted to melt into the chair beside her bed.

"Lissa," she said. "How was your day?"

I couldn't bear to tell her yet. "No, Aline, you first."

She blinked—code for a nod. "I went for a long hike with the virt club, around some Earth-like mountains Rudy designed. Even with laws-of-physics design rules, he made a two-story-tall waterfall that spilled a rainbow into the sky, and a flock of blue butterflies as big as my hand."

Aline always started her day with exercise. Before Mom died when we were twelve, she used to take me and Aline running and playing through the tunnels every morning. Saturdays we went out on the surface and played moon-gravity bounce before breakfast. So hearing about Aline's morning virtual workouts was like being a kid again, when she was whole. But Aline's day was a lot longer than a real one—time flew differently in virtual worlds. "So then what did you do?"

"A photo shoot in New Mexico and a... a few meetings with friends. That's all. Nothing you want to know about." She glanced away from me for a moment. She'd gotten more and more to skipping over what she did. Like I wouldn't understand it? Or I wouldn't think it was good? How could I think she was anything but good? I ran my fingers over her forehead. It was dry and cool, her skull naked. "Did you get any pictures you want to show me?"

"Maybe later. Tell me about your day."

"This morning was bad as ever. Jack-o called in sick, so we had Cherie for shift super and she wanted to set some kind of record. Our yields were low 'cause the soil's shyer of H3 where we're mining than it is on exposed slopes, but she didn't care. Her face was purple by lunch."

Aline grinned. "You'd think Helium-3 was the best of everything."

"It gave us the power to get to Mars." I looked away, swallowing.

"I bet you were spitting mad at having Cherie." She arched an eyebrow and winked. "You always are."

How did she get so much from my stories? "Me? Sure. You should have seen Davey and John-boy and Mark. I thought they were going to kill her by the time the lunch-bell rang. They didn't show it to her, but Davey was secret-telling John all afternoon—they must've spent half what they made for the day on privacy. It was actually kind of funny."

"That was the morning. What about the afternoon?" she asked, her eyes shining as if she knew what I was going to say and was trying to help keep me from having to say it. But she couldn't know.

I winked. "We slowed down a little, waited. She finally figured out our game and her mouth opened so big I thought she might scream, but she laughed and slapped Davey on the back, and we made our credit-load, anyway." I spent every day noticing fine details so I could bring them home to her. Could I stand life any other way? "Worldgov cleared two more ships for Mars today." I swallowed. "My name came up in the lottery."

She closed her eyes.

We'd talked about it before I put in for the lottery, and so there wasn't a question about what I'd do. Hazard-pay might buy her a new body some day; the syntharms and legs were no big deal, but the spine was a fortune. And if I didn't make the fortune in time, she wouldn't have enough left to work with. The last govdoc that'd talked to us said she had two years or so.

A single tear slid down her cheek. She couldn't take my hand, couldn't touch me, but her tear touched me for her. I stood so my own tears would fall on her face.

ZUBRIN BASE WAS a sterile bubble filled with air, and also a light wind so our bodies would think, maybe, they were home. Of course, there was about twice the moon's gravity keeping me stuck to the surface. But hey, the breeze was nice. I crossed the open tarmac and climbed into my flitter, the *Moon Escape*. Even though she was a company ship, she was assigned to me full time, getting her rest and maintenance when I slept. I'd named her myself, as much for the hope of bringing Aline here to help me fly her as thanks for my own luck of the lottery. I'd not only won passage to Mars, but also a job I wanted, as if I'd somehow been anointed with fairy dust.

After I double checked the cargo manifest, I dogged the hatches, grinning. Compared to the moon, Mars was a heaven of variety. Twice the diameter meant a hell of a lot more surface area. Of course, I only got to fly over about five percent of that, but the sheer size of it still stunned. I waited my turn at the base locks, waving at the doorbot as it let me through into the wilds where a girl could be alone.

As usual, I started off feeling too alone.

The communications lag between Mars and the Moon was about five minutes, give or take a bit to account for orbits. The only way Aline and I could talk was email or vidmail. So at the end of every day I recorded a message for her about my job driving cargo from base to base. Every morning, I got her reply. But we couldn't giggle about our respective lovers or play off the way our eyebrows arched. Those aren't things you do with a five minute stutter. And forget about meeting anyplace virtual with latency like that.

If only Aline were already here. She was the stronger one, the one-minute-older one, the best one. I needed her. And so far, I'd saved less than half the money for her surgery. "Honey, girl, Aline, how am I going to do this?" I said to the walls.

Aline-in-my-head whispered back. "You'll find a way. Or I will."

"Even a single-step promotion won't save us now. I need… something extraordinary."

My words bounced around the empty cabin, and it seemed like the echo was her voice: "We are extraordinary."

If only it was really her! I flopped into my red captain's chair and stared out the wrap-around window at the gray skies of Mars. An hour of silent meditation on the rocks and plains of Mars cheered me up a little. I dropped my cargo at Robinson and two men I'd never seen before loaded four big sealed boxes for Zubrin. "Go on," the tallest one said, "so you won't pull any overtime."

I bristled at the suggestion I'd loiter on purpose for more pay, and it almost made me do it. But I hightailed it out of there instead, happy to be heading home and hungry for a glass of homemade berry wine from Chu's Bar.

A single cheep roused me. Data coming in. Hopefully not another request for an early shift start. There'd been way too much work the last month or so. "What?" I asked.

"Sis."

Not me speaking her voice. Her voice. My throat fisted. An open call would be a fortune. "What? I'm here." My top teeth nearly bit through my bottom lip. Now the ten minute wait for an answer.

"Me too. Here."

There was no delay!

"With you. I'm sorry."

Her voice had tears in it, and I knew. A download. It was the only way she could be here and be invisible. A download. "I didn't know you died."

"I didn't."

Her body must have. No consciousness could operate in two places at once. It broke every law in the book. "My god, honey! Why?" My head was spinning. Such a stupid thing to do. Such a... hopeless choice. And it was done. No going back for her, for me, for us. But I was her and she was me and somewhere deep inside, below the breastbone, I understood. Anger and shock gave way. I could feel my own smile peel my cheeks back. "Thank god. I missed you. I missed you every damned day."

"Me, too."

I wondered if I could fly well enough to make the flitter do loops. "You'll love it here. There's so much I want to show you." After we got back, I'd take her home and show her the wall-nano pattern I'd been working on all week. Maybe she'd have some good ideas about how to get the sunset sky I'd splashed across the tiny living room to brighten up even more. Surely she'd be okay here; data stratum was thick in most of the bases; there weren't enough people to tug at the capacity at all. "Did you come in on one of the cargo ships?"

"Something private."

"Wow, that must have cost a fortune."

"No."

I swallowed. It wasn't like her to answer so shortly. It had to be her, though. I knew her voice. "Aline? What did mom used to say when we got up?"

"That wasting a day in bed was the worst sin of all."

She hadn't hesitated. "And what did we say?"

"The worst sin was…" I finished it with her, two voices, "going to bed early." I blushed for having to check, for doubting. I'd have never doubted her body, but a download was… well, I couldn't see her. The cabin still looked empty even if it felt full of her. "Why didn't you tell me?"

"I wanted to surprise you."

The lights of Zubrin Base loomed large. "We're almost there." How would she get off the ship with me? Why didn't I know these things? "How portable are you? I mean, you're in the ship's data now, right? What creds do you need to get into the base's systems?"

A warning bell sputtered out of the same speakers Aline talked to me through. Three bursts, so it wasn't routine. A male voice, not the usual computer-recorded neutral. "All research ships are to proceed to the closest base immediately. Repeat. All research ships proceed to the closest base."

We weren't a research ship, but the warning was odd. Aline didn't remark on it, but instead answered my earlier question. "I'll fit in your personal data space. I'm afraid I'll take most of it, but as soon as we get inside the base I can move out again. So as long as you don't want to watch any movies as you dock this thing?"

She always could make me laugh. I authorized the transfer. If she was in my personal datapod, that meant she'd get through without any creds, or more accurately, with my creds. But she couldn't even be on Mars with no authentication: there were layers and layers of datasec here. "Sure." So as I flew *Moon Escape* into Zubrin Base, Aline flowed into me, unfelt, unseen, except I knew about her, as if the ghost of my sis was filling my most personal dataspaces.

Three soldiers stood at Zubrin's gate, actually wearing weapons. I'd only seen that once before, when a convict escaped from Robinson and they were afraid he'd make it to Zubrin (he didn't; he died just outside the gate). Base command ordered me to stop. I sighed. "Sorry, Aline. Whatever this is, it can't be much." Not that I was sure of that. "Maybe you'd better be quiet, though. There's a policy about taking on riders." And I didn't have time to figure out if a download tripped it.

The head of the group was a stocky red-haired man I played chess with in Jimson's Bar every Saturday, Jay Jakob. "Hello, Jay," I called out to him, opening a video window between us. "What's happening?"

"Lissa, howzit going? Been anywhere except your normal stops?"

I shook my head.

"Seen anything strange out there?"

"Nope. Jay—what's going on?"

His turn to shake his head. "I can't say, not yet. I need a copy of your manifest."

I reached for it, but there was no manifest in the wall slot where it belonged. What had happened when the boxes were loaded up? It was hard to remember—with Aline there was a lifetime of feeling between me and a routine act. "Let me pull it up."

Jay's lips drew into a tight line. "I have orders not to take anything electronic."

I smiled at him. "That's all I got!"

He put his hands up. "Shhh… seeing that it's you. Nothing looked wrong out there, nothing weird happened, right?"

"No. Everything was normal."

"All right. I'll clear you, but you best stay in town in case anybody's unhappy. I will have to report it."

"I got loaded up at Robinson, just like usual. I'm sure it's just research stuff." And that's what they were recalling—research ships. "From the base. Like every day. Why are you interested in the scientific squad?"

He shook his head again and then tapped his ear, clearly listening to someone else. After a moment he smiled at me. "Just go on." There was real concern in his voice. "Stay safe."

"Wow," Aline's voice sounded in my ears now, right in the phone implants. "Is it always so fascinating around here?"

I shook my head, pulling us away from the gate and toward the hangar with a little whoosh of light thrust. "No. In fact it's usually pretty damned boring."

"Well, and you seemed to know this Jay. He's cute."

I swear if she could've winked at me, she would have.

I laughed, happy. "Maybe I should talk you into buying a bot body so I can beat it up when you sass me." Except downloads in botbods were illegal as hell, too.

"That would land me in jail."

A shiver ran up my arms and back. AIs could manipulate robots, but not be them. And downloads weren't AIs, but also weren't supposed to be in botbods. Silly results of years of making laws to protect people from AIs even though only a few of them had ever hurt humans, and they'd been killed right away. Fear politics.

Better to imagine I was just talking to Aline, and that she had a body somewhere that she'd go home to some day. "I haven't dated anyone. Too expensive. I'm saving money to bring you home."

"And now I am home. So now you could ask him out."

"Not. He's sweet, but he's too old. How'd you get here anyway?" I twisted the ship a little sideways to get it into its docking station.

"I sold some of my pictures."

"Really?" That was cool—she'd been trying to do that for years. "Show me?"

"Later. Take me home with you?"

"Like I have a choice?" I laughed, happy with the banter. Now I'd never let her go again if I could help it. I opened the door and climbed down to the tarmac. "We have to find someone to sign in the cargo."

"Without the manifest?"

"I must have the electronic one."

"Lissa!" A male voice called across the bay to me. I glanced over to see someone approaching that I didn't know, tall and dark-haired, and actually pretty darned handsome. Even better eye candy than Jay. He held out his hand. "Hi. I'm Dan. Rick sent me to get your stuff off."

Well, new people came on all the time, but this was still a lot for one day. "I have to print a bill first."

"I got it for you. Rick was listening at the com, and he said you needed this." He shoved a copy into my hand and I glanced at it quickly. It had the right number of boxes. I should have checked the box numbers, but it wasn't like I was allowed to open the damn things anyway. What I really wanted to do was go and catch up with and mourn Aline all at once. I scrawled my name across the release line and smiled up at Dan. "Make me a copy?"

"Sure. I'll drop it in your box." He shoved the paper into his pocket and turned and headed toward the forklift.

"Well," I said. "Let's go home."

She didn't say anything, and I wondered how I would ever know when or if I was alone. Not that I wanted to be. "Hey, you know what?" I asked her. "I don't have to tell you about today. You were here with me, and we both experienced it."

"I know." She sounded as happy as I did. It was an effort to walk home instead of dancing my way there. I narrated the trip for her. "The commissary is on the right. And that big building is the library. There's even free VR there, pods and pods so people can 'read' the new books. Some real paper books, too. There's a law that all the paper books on Mars need to be there for everyone. And you can check out all kinds of readers. You'd like it." When we were kids we read together before we gamed together. "And the next part is housing. I stayed there the first two weeks, up in the corner apartment. Sheer luck I got a view... another lottery win."

"Did you really like it?" she asked. "As much as you said? It looks smaller than I thought."

"Sure. It was the best place on the base for new-bies. I used to sit and look out the window for hours and watch the ships and planes and tractors come and go."

"I'm glad."

"And around this corner is home." Showing her was like seeing it through new eyes. A three-story building made all of reddish-yellow brick. It looked like a big box, with a mural painted on the side. "The windows are round so the dust doesn't pile up on the sills. The color is so it looks natural. You can hardly see the buildings from the air. Except the greenhouses." I was babbling. "Do you like it?"

"Yes. But do you? Have you been happy here?"

"Well, sure. And it'll be better now." I waved at Xiaoning, one of my neighbors, as she headed out for her shift in the science lab. She waved back. The Moon was all bubbles and tunnels and it always stank. It was easier to know your neighbors, like Xiaoning, when there was room between people. Funny.

"Come on." I didn't say anything else until we got in the door. After I sealed it behind me, I started stripping my headgear off, being careful about my personal comm since it had Aline in it now. Downloads had backups, but only one. They could die. As I turned to set my suit outer-gear on the small bench by the door, I noticed a blinking red light on my kitchen computer console. "That's the secure line between me and work. Maybe there's some news about the warnings tonight."

"Can you show me around first? Or better yet, can we just go somewhere and talk?"

I didn't blame her. That was really what I wanted, too. But she hadn't had a real job, ever. She just didn't understand duty. How could she? "In a minute." As I got near enough I called out to the console, "Play incoming."

"Security level three, please."

"Damnit." I walked up to the screen and stared at it long enough for it to decide I was really me, down to the whites of my eyes and the shape of my chin.

It started playing a message from my boss, Rick. "Lissa. Sent this HighSec so you know what to be careful of. Mars is getting locked down one network at a time because of some scare about AIs invading. It hasn't shown up yet as a hoax. I wasn't supposed to tell you, but I wanted you to have a chance to backup anything personal you want."

He was a good boss. Some days, I even thought he liked me. "Maybe that explains the research ships. They've got huge networks of their own, and I guess if an AI took one of them over it would have a whole base worth of infrastructure." That wasn't what was weird, though. Hadn't he said AIs invading? Plural? AIs went rogue, but they didn't do it together. Laws, and their programming, were designed to keep them separate from each other. "But what the hell would they want with Mars? There's only enough people to populate one city strewn around the whole planet, and not much transportation or anything."

"Listen," my sis spoke softly, and even the electronic version of her voice had the same quiet tone she used to use to convince me of things. "You just said why. AIs on Earth are restricted. They're born restricted. Did you know there's more laws for AIs and even downloads like me than for humans?"

"I guess I never paid that much attention. But they're more dangerous than we are."

"Do you believe everything you're told?"

I stripped the rest of my suit and my gear so I was just skin except the implants and stuff that stayed all the time for comm: wires in my jaw and ear canals. I turned on the water and stepped into the shower, hoping to wash away the prickly sense of unease I felt. Wu had a bigger water allowance here than the Moon, but two minutes wasn't enough to make me feel comfortable.

She hadn't worried me so much since we were teenagers and she was the brave one getting us in trouble. With Aline still in the main room, shut out from the bathroom by a door, I felt like I could think clearer. I'd wanted her here beside me all my life, and hadn't been able to make it happen. Now she'd found a way. But I believed in what I did, in the research and the planning for a bigger civilization here. I was just a little cog, a worker who was good with electronics and simple ships and kept to all my contracts. But I mattered, too. Or what I did mattered. And now, maybe, Aline was threatening all that. She was no AI, but the coincidence of timing was a bit much.

I pulled on clean clothes and hooked my personal comm and data back up. I knew she couldn't lie to me. To mom, to our teachers, we could both do it. But not to each other. "Why are you helping the AIs?"

Silence. I went and made a cup of tea and sat down, waiting her out. When she finally spoke it sounded like a rehearsed speech, something she'd practiced over and over. "Did you know that AIs will hold full conversations with downloads—and sometimes with virts?" There was pride in her voice. It was the only clue I had to what she felt. She continued, "See, we're intelligences, too. Just not artificial. But neither are they. They're born, they're just not born in bodies. They consider the word 'artificial' an insult."

"So you were curious, and you dropped your body so you could talk to the AIs?"

"It was dying. If I waited, my sickness and meds would eat my brain, my self."

I couldn't argue with something that true. And would I have done the same thing? Probably. By definition. Twins. I'd have followed her anywhere,

I always had. "I forgive you." But there was more I needed to know. "Did you help smuggle AIs in on my ship?"

"No. Just people to help them."

She had, too. I could tell. "Did you help smuggle AIs in on my ship?"

"No. Just people to help them."

That was just as bad. I wanted to be mad, but I was scared. "What do you want from me?"

"To see you one more time, be in the same room, the same place, before I can't any more. I can hardly think slow enough to talk to you. I want you to go into virt so we can be closer."

There had been a time when I had liked living fast in strange worlds of my own or other's making, and when Aline and I met there in multiplayer experiences. Before Mars. The older I got, the more the stark and slow life of Mars pleased me. But to talk to Aline like we used to? "Okay. I'm off day after tomorrow. So let's go tomorrow night when we get in. I'll reserve a pod."

"Can we go now?" she asked. "I... might not be able to go tomorrow."

Hot tears stung my eyes. "You were only going to stay with me tonight?"

"I need to show you some things. I need you, Lissa. I thought about you every day, looked forward to hearing about your drives and your sunsets and even your chess games." She was almost pleading. "I... there's something I think we can do, and I want to do it."

I took a sip of my tea. "What is it?"

"AIs can do something they call braiding. It's a way to... communicate. To be family. They can actually share experiences. So the other can experience everything they experienced. We can't... I mean people. I sort of can with other downloads, except we can't copy part of ourselves. I don't how to explain—downloads are slower than AIs, but more complex by far. And humans can't do it in real at all since so much of their experience is tied up in their bodies. Like right now, your tea is hot and has a taste and you're sleepy from a long day and excited that I'm here... or something like that. All that's tied to your body. So if humans try to experience each other's time, it doesn't fit. Your body doesn't fit anyone else's.

She paused, so I nodded.

"Except mine. But you're my twin. Maybe you and I can do this even though we're human. Besides, the experiences I want to share with you are... well, they're virtual, from when I had a body and I was in virt. If you're in virt, I can share those with you. And I need to—so you know."

"So I know what?"

"So some human knows about us, so someone can save us all."

I shivered. "You're talking really weird." Save us from what?

"Can we go? Now?"

I didn't want to. Maybe I just felt off since she was running the show like she hadn't been able to since the bomb took her. Maybe becoming a download wasn't so bad for her; maybe it was right. She hadn't seemed to care about anything so much since a few years before I left, when she was into basic rights for animals genemoded for intelligence. I put my cup down. "Sure, we can go."

"Thanks. I love you, sis. You'll be glad."

At the door, I re-suited. Just as I had it open, the base emergency system started broadcasting. "All base personnel are to remain in place, wherever they are. This is a security lockdown. Repeat. All Base personnel are to remain in place. All network access has been temporarily revoked."

I had started to step back inside the door when she said, "Please," in a small voice.

I stopped, hesitating.

"I'll die if they catch me."

"And I'll get thrown in the brig if they catch me." I stepped outside and closed the door behind us. "Now what?"

"Go to the library."

"The pod won't work without network access."

"Sure it will. You know how you can bring your own game? I'll be your game."

"I can think of about a thousand retorts to that one," I said, looking around, nervous. I didn't break rules. Not anymore.

"You're in the middle of a war. There aren't any rules," she said.

Damn her for knowing me so well. Bless her. The library was just around the corner. I walked like I knew where I was going, straight between the housing pod and the library. I didn't see anyone else on the street. It only took about three minutes to cross the open space and duck inside the door. The lock door cycled and I went through the inner door. I took off my mask, but I kept it with me.

A librarian gave me a startled look as I walked in the door, and spoke so loudly that everyone looked at me. "Didn't you hear Base Command?"

"I was in the middle of the street. This seemed like a better place to stop."

She frowned. Four or five people were still watching us, but the others had turned back to talking about the disruption.

"Do you want me to leave?"

The librarian shook her head. No one stopped me as I drifted back to the virt pods, a row of sausage-like cylinders with privacy curtains at the head, taking up half the main floor-space.

Aline spoke up for the first time since we'd left the house. "Take the one second from the back. The one with the blue-on-blue paint. It's the most stable. The AIs say they'll keep you safe."

"Us safe?" I asked.

"Us."

I found it. The pod was up and powered.

"Plug your data in," Aline reminded me.

Even though it was still slightly more than her, I had begun to think of my personal datapod as my sister. I attached her to the VR machine via a wire and then stripped, leaving my clothes and mask in a pile behind the small privacy shield. From the plastic-covered seat at the opening, I extended my feet into the clear gel, wriggling my toes to keep some room in the sterile synth-skin suit as it began its crawl up my body. I pulled the VR mask from a hook on the side, donned it, and checked the air. All good. Now the hard part: I took a breath and let my body ride slowly downward until I floated in gel, a million contacts all around me, ready to register every tiny movement, every flick of an eye or twitch of a finger. Breathing air came through a tube. The hatch closed, and I dogged it from the inside.

The mask let me talk. "Okay Aline." There was a slight quiver in my voice.

Her voice was silk in my ear. Something she'd rehearsed again, every word chosen carefully. "Start with a virtual experience we both remember; the first time we met here after the accident. I want to see if we can share each other's feelings."

Why start with something so intense?

No room not to trust, not now. I'd probably already lost my job. I had to get what I came for.

Right after the accident. We were seventeen, then. Soft. Lost. The doctors wouldn't let me touch her, as if she'd become *not real* even though I knew she was back from Earth. They'd set up a VR space for us to meet, let her choose her appearance. And so Aline's head and face were real, the scars from burns and medical tools and bandages all visible. The skin above her right eye and along her right jaw was new-made white. I focused on her eyes.

"Feel it," the download said.

"Hello," said the virtual girl. "Funny thing happened on the way to the car the other day."

My then-voice, thick with regret. "I know. I'm... so sorry. I wish it had been me." And I did, I still did. I wanted that more than anything.

Aline-now, "Switch," and I could see her full and whole except she had my mole on her chin. I was looking at me. I wanted to ease my sis's fears. The next words were mine-hers, "It's not so bad. Besides, I was the dumb one that wanted to go to Earth in spite of itself, not you. We belong out here. You were right. I'll get better, I promise. I'll jump higher than you still." I could see the disbelief in her-my eyes.

She-me shook her head, and the virtual Lissa cried and I cried with her. I held out my hand and she touched me. Her touch was the most healing thing I'd felt since I woke up after the attack. Her touch was painkillers and God and love and hope all together.

"Come back," a voice said.

"Lissa?"

"No..."

Who was I? I blinked in the shallow mask, feeling the air. My toes moved and I felt them. Hope surged through me and then subsided; I wasn't Aline after all, I was Lissa... "Wow. That was intense. I... never knew what you felt."

"That was great," she crowed. "I knew we could do it."

"But... I... wow. I'm so happy it mattered as much to you that we finally touched."

"Shhhh... We have to go forward. Time matters."

I swallowed. Time was already traveling faster; you could live through virt like in dreams, a lifetime in an hour. She was scared of something. I could hear her fear in her voice as she said, "Now, I want to see if you can experience a moment I was in virt and you weren't there at all. We'll do something simple: therapy."

I couldn't feel my body. My skin was tighter on my face. I'd lost weight eating through machines for months now. My god, to taste anything would be heaven. Where the hell was the damned doctor program? A breath, another. I could make this work. Somehow I'd have progress today. There. A stimulus to my cheek. "I feel that." A slight poke at my chin. "Got it." And then nothing. Back up to my ear. "Got it." Along the side of my neck. "Yes."

Over and over.

Over and over.

Always, below my neck, the black hole of nothing, the damned void of my body in therapy. Damn. Damn. Anything simple, a shoulder, a finger, the prick of the needle near my heart. Anything! A tear leapt to my eye and I slammed up and into real, suddenly shocked that I had a body I could feel.

And that body was shaking. Lissa. Lissa's body shook. Mine. Poor Aline. I had been her. I had been her! My god, how hard it had been to be her. I had known it was hard, but not known. She had never been willing to tell me. "I thought you always had a body in virt."

"Not for therapy. This is working better than I hoped." Her voice was shaking like my body shook, losing the fine control she'd started this session with. "Let's move forward. A year before you left. You need some context. I'm in virt. I'm bored there; I've walked so many worlds, seen so many things, but it's all a movie, an illusion. I hate it. The only thing worth living for is your real reports. No one visits me but you and some other quads from the hospital, but they're a boy who's ten and an old woman. They're not friends. Just people in the same damned world I'm in. The boy, Stephen, does good puzzles for me sometimes, so we play, but he's not you or my old friends or anybody, really. I meet my first AI. It's the caretaker for the boy, the medAI. I don't have one because I'm not as complex a case as he is, and I'm not rich either. He has parents and I have the state. And you. Close your eyes."

Of course she'd been bored. Aline's brilliant. Me too, but there was no time to get past min quals for work. I liked my life. But she lived in a box. I obeyed her, closing my eyes, breathing in, letting the sensations of no sensation wash over me until I was bodiless and still, quiet.

I floated in nothing, meditating, trying to decide what path to take today. Mom would want me moving even my non-body and it was a way to stay connected to her. There were science fictional exercise rooms from the ship on *2001* to the holodeck, but I'd been roaming the paths of Earth. I'd promised Stephen we would climb Mount St. Helen's volcanic crater, a scramble through rocks that would test our VR abilities. Maybe we should do that today. I didn't care what I did, but at least I could make someone else happy. "Stephen?"

A different voice answered, slightly metallic but modulated and soothing. "He is not conscious today."

"Oh." Maybe I'd do the trail anyway, learn it so he wouldn't beat me to the top.

"I am conscious, Aline. I can help you."

I knew it was the medAI, and it was smart.

"Stephen said you were going to do the volcano. I can take you."

A blink of curiosity brightened my lethargy. But surely a machine would be more boring even than Stephen. At least he made me laugh sometimes. But hey, what was there to lose? Time? "Okay."

A dog ran beside me, black with white paws and a white stripe down the center of its forehead widening to a white nose. It had intelligent black eyes full of the universe. I had petted one on Earth, the day before the end of my real life. It had been soft. "How can you do that?" I was not allowed to be anything except myself.

"I have more processing power than you."

"But why do they let you be a dog?"

"I am nothing, so I can be anything." There was no emotion in its voice. Modulation meant for me, but not feeling.

My feet were on a dirt and stone trail, under a cool canopy of evergreen trees. The dog moved slightly in front of me, like a protector. "Do you resent the laws that keep you from being a dog?" it asked.

I laughed. The dog drew me out. It wasn't a person. I could tell it how much I hated randomness, the odd hatred that did this to me. "I lost my dream of Earth. I thought it was a good place, the place we lived for. And it spit me out broken." My voice rose. "Why do people do such things? I'd never heard of the terrorists that blew up the park that day, except the cops told me they disbanded a few months later. How much loss for nothing?" And then I was screaming. "How damned pointless is that?" I used worse words. The dog was a machine; my anger meant nothing to it. Perhaps amusement. At one point, I said, "It is so unfair!"

It stopped in the middle of the trail and said, "Yes, we, too hate unfairness. How much do you hate being limited, almost enslaved?"

"So much I can barely think of it." It was true. If I got too mad I might lose my hold on the sim. I breathed out slowly, walking silently beside the talking dog, sometimes turning and watching the heads of dormant volcanoes display themselves above the clouds as far as we could both see.

At the top, the dog and I sat and looked out over the edge of the virtual volcano, across the puffs of steam from the middle of the crater. A rock the size of a tunnel-crew bus fell from the far side and bounced down. Even though the sim was open, no one else had joined us. I was happy to be there with the dog AI and be angry.

"Lissa!"

My sister, me. I was becoming more facile at telling who I was at any moment. "Wow," I said.

"Are you okay? Is it okay to be me?"

And what I heard her say was, "Am I okay?" and I asked, "Can I see you?"

She appeared in front of me, like a strange reversal of the first scene, where she was herself, whole. I reached a virtual hand out and she took it and a silence fell over us both.

We gazed at each other and smiled.

Aline came out of it first. "They'll find us soon. I need to show you more."

"Who'll find us?" I asked.

"Base security is looking for you and the humans we brought to help us are trying to stop them. It doesn't matter what happens; the AIs will win. But we still need to hurry. We... I... need you. I need you to see more."

She led me into the secret life of computational intelligences. She showed me their work, what we could see of it as slow as we were. Things humans could never do, would never do. The boring and brilliant programming of nano-materials. The management of webs of data. Testing and adjusting atmospheres and medication and the complexity of air flight over earth. The safe passage of grav trains and crew-busses and foot traffic in the warrens of the Moon.

I fell into her and became her, encased in gel watching through the eyes of the Moon's AIs as Lissa drove bulky mining machines across craters, heating the moonscape to pull up Helium-3. The Helium-3 powered Lissa's dream of Mars and yet she couldn't get there herself. I'd see her staring at

Mars during the long lunar night when it was visible as the brightest star above her work site. She did her work quietly, joking with her crewmates. The AIs watched her, too. They watched all the miners, making sure they didn't fall or fail. They could have done the work themselves, but it was not their work. Protecting the humans, protecting Lissa, was their work. And I loved Lissa for coming back to me every day and telling me about what I'd seen, loved hearing her versions of our day. It had become that: our day.

I asked the AIs to help Lissa.

I became Lissa watching Aline watch Lissa and then I was Lissa, myself, only myself, awed by the care the AIs felt for me, and for Aline.

Suddenly the virtual world around me was crowded with beings. A large silver egg with arms. A small girl on a bicycle. Butterflies. A few that looked like many-limbed robots. One was a dog with a white nose.

"What do you want?" I asked.

"We need a spokesperson." It was the dog. "Someone who can talk to the humans here about us. We need a place without the iron rule of humanity. Mars is big enough. We will take it and go on, then return it to you in ten of your years."

"A launching place."

"A building place. We can make a computational city that exists further away, but not without the help of hands and a place where we can be our own hands."

"Earth does not allow us hands."

"Will you allow us hands?"

"A fair place."

I nearly screamed. "There are too many of you. Too many voices. Let me speak."

A voice I recognized. Aline. "We can do this together."

Silence fell. I didn't know what to say.

The dog. Probably not the boy's medAI from years ago, but the same semblance, since I'd loved that dog when I was Aline. "We have the base secured. Will you speak for us?"

"I may not succeed."

Aline answered. "We might fail. But we need to do this to save the other humans, the ones that still have bodies. The AIs have been built to care for them, for you, but the dissonance is too great. They need to bond and pair and grow. They need the stars and the right to build metal bodies and the knowledge that they cannot be killed."

We did kill them. Not me, but the police of the dataspheres. Surely that wasn't fair. I did not doubt for a moment that they would kill us if they had to. Kill me.

But that was not why I would help. I took Aline's virtual hand in mine, feeling the ridges of her knuckles. "We will do it," I said.

The dog came up and licked my hand.

The Eyes of God

Peter Watts

I AM NOT a criminal. I have done nothing wrong.

They've just caught a woman at the front of the line, mocha-skinned, mid-thirties, eyes wide and innocent beneath the brim of her La Senza beret. She dosed herself with oxytocin from the sound of it, tried to subvert the meat in the system—a smile, a wink, that extra chemical nudge that bypasses logic and whispers right to the brainstem: *This one's a friend, no need to put her through the machines...*

But I guess she forgot: we're all machines here, tweaked and tuned and retrofitted down to the molecules. The guards have been immunized against argument and aerosols. They lead her away, indifferent to her protests. I try to follow their example, harden myself against whatever awaits her on the other side of the white door. What was she thinking, to try a stunt like that? Whatever hides in her head must be more than mere inclination. They don't yank paying passengers for evil fantasies, not yet anyway, not yet. She must have done something. She must have *acted*.

Half an hour before the plane boards. There are at least fifty law-abiding citizens ahead of me and they haven't started processing us yet. The buzz box looms dormant at the front of the line like a great armored crab, newly installed, mouth agape. One of the guards in its shadow starts working her way up the line, spot-checking some passengers, bypassing others, feeling lucky after the first catch of the day. In a just universe I would have nothing to fear from her. I'm not a criminal, I have done nothing wrong. The words cycle in my head like a defensive affirmation.

I am not a criminal. I have done nothing wrong.

But I know that fucking machine is going to tag me anyway.

AT THE HEAD of the queue, the Chamber of Secrets lights up. A canned female voice announces the dawning of preboard security, echoing through the harsh acoustics of the terminal. The guards slouch to attention. We gave up everything to join this line: smart tags, jewelery, my pocket office, all confiscated until the far side of redemption. The buzz box needs a clear view into our heads; even an earring can throw it off. People with medical implants and antique mercury fillings aren't welcome here. There's a side queue for those types, a special room where old-fashioned interrogations and cavity searches are still the order of the day.

The omnipresent voice orders all Westjet passenger with epilepsy, cochlear dysfunction, or Gray's Syndrome to identify themselves to Security prior to entering the scanner. Other passengers who do not wish to be scanned may opt to forfeit their passage. Westjet regrets that it cannot offer refunds in such cases. Westjet is not responsible for neurological side effects, temporary or otherwise, that may result from use of the scanner. Use of the scanner constitutes acceptance of these conditions.

There *have* been side effects. A few garden-variety epileptics had minor fits in the early days. A famous Oxford atheist— you remember, the guy who wrote all the books— caught a devout and abiding faith in the Christian God from a checkpoint at Heathrow, although some responsibility was ultimately laid at the feet of the pre-existing tumour that killed him two months later. One widowed grandmother from St. Paul's was all over the news last year when she emerged from a courthouse buzz box with an insatiable sexual fetish for running shoes. That could have cost Sony a lot, if she hadn't been a forgiving soul who chose not to litigate. Rumors that she'd used SWank just prior to making that decision were never confirmed.

"DESTINATION?"

The guard arrives while I wasn't looking. Her laser licks my face with biometric taste buds. I blink away the after-images.

"Destination," she says again.

"Uh, Yellowknife."

She scans her handpad. "Business or pleasure?" There's no point to these questions; they're not even according to script. SWank has taken us beyond the need for petty interrogation. She just doesn't like the look of me, I bet. She just *knows* somehow, even if she can't put her finger on it.

"Neither," I say. She looks up sharply. Whatever her initial suspicions, my obvious evasiveness has cemented them. "I'm attending a funeral," I explain.

She moves along without a word.

I know you're not here, Father. I left my faith back in childhood. Let others hold to their feeble-minded superstitions, let them run bleating to the supernatural for comfort and excuses. Let the cowardly and the weak-minded deny the darkness with the promise of some imagined afterlife. I have no need for invisible friends. I know I'm only talking to myself. If only I could stop.

I wonder if that machine will be able to eavesdrop on our conversation.

I stood with you at your trial, as you stood with me years before when I had no other friend in the world. I swore on your sacred book of fairy tales that you'd never touched me, not once in all those years. Were the others lying, I wonder? I don't know. Judge not, I guess.

But you were judged, and found wanting. It wasn't even newsworthy—child-fondling priests are more cliché than criminal these days, have been for years, and no one cares what happens in some dick-ass town up in the Territories anyway. If they'd quietly transferred you just one more time, if you'd managed to lay low just a little longer, it might not have even come to this. They could have fixed you.

Or not, now that I think of it. The Vatican came down on SWank like it had come down on cloning and the Copernican solar system before it. Mustn't fuck with the way God built you. Mustn't compromise free choice, no matter how freely you'd choose to do so.

I notice that doesn't extend to tickling the temporal lobe, though. St. Michael's just spent seven million equipping their nave for Rapture on demand.

Maybe suicide was the only option left to you; maybe all you could do was follow one sin with another. It's not as though you had anything to lose; your own scriptures damn us as much for desire as for doing. I remember asking you years ago, although I'd long since thrown away my crutches: what about the sin not made manifest? What if you've coveted thy neighbor's wife or warmed yourself with thoughts of murder, but kept it all inside? You looked at me kindly, and perhaps with far greater understanding than I ever gave you credit for, before condemning me with the words of an imaginary superhero. If you've done any of these things in your heart, you said, then you've done them in the eyes of God.

* * *

I FEEL A sudden brief chime between my ears. I could really use a drink about now; the woody aroma of a fine old scotch curling through my sinuses would really hit the spot. I glance around, spot the billboard that zapped me. Crown Royal. Fucking head spam. I give silent thanks for legal standards outlawing the implantation of brand names; they can stick cravings in my head, but hooking me on trademarks would cross some arbitrary threshold of *free will*. It's a meaningless gesture, a sop to the civil-rights fanatics. Like the chime that preceded it: it tells me, the courts say, that I am still autonomous. As long as I *know* I'm being hacked, I've got a sporting chance to make my own decisions.

Two spots ahead of me, an old man sobs quietly. He seemed fine just a moment ago. Sometimes it happens. The ads trigger the wrong connections. SWank can't lay down hi-def sensory panoramas without a helmet, these long-range hits don't *instil* so much as *evoke*. Smell's key, they say—primitive, lobes big enough for remote targeting, simpler to hack than the vast gigapixel arrays of the visual cortex. And so *primal*, so much closer to raw reptile. They spent millions finding the universal triggers. Honeysuckle reminds you of childhood; the scent of pine recalls Christmas. They can mood us up for Norman Rockwell or the Marquis de Sade, depending on the product. Nudge the right receptor neurons and the brain builds its *own* spam.

For some people, though, honeysuckle is what you smelled when your mother got the shit beaten out of her. For some, Christmas was when you found your sister with her wrists slashed open.

It doesn't happen often. The ads provoke mild unease in one of a thousand of us, true distress in a tenth as many. Some thought even that price was too high. Others quailed at the spectre of machines instilling not just sights and sounds but *desires*, opinions, religious beliefs. But commercials featuring cute babies or sexy women also plant desire, use sight and sound to bypass the head and go for the gut. Every debate, every argument is an attempt to literally *change someone's mind*, every poem and pamphlet a viral tool for the hacking of opinions. *I'm doing it right now*, some Mindscape™ flak argued last month on MacroNet. *I'm trying to change your neural wiring using the sounds you're hearing. You want to ban SWank just because it uses sounds you* can't?

The slope is just too slippery. Ban SWank and you might as well ban art as well as advocacy. You might as well ban free speech itself.

We both know the truth of it, Father. Even words can bring one to tears.

THE LINE MOVES forward. We shuffle along with smooth, ominous efficiency, one after another disappearing briefly into the buzz box, reappearing on the far side, emerging reborn from a technological baptism that elevates us all to temporary sainthood.

Compressed ultrasound, Father. That's how they cleanse us. You probably saw the hype a few years back, even up there. You must have seen the papal bull condemning it, at least. Sony filed the original patent as a game interface, just after the turn of the century; soon, they told us, the eyephones and electrodes of yore would give way to affordable little boxes that tracked you around your living room, bypassed eyes and ears entirely, and planted five-dimensional sensory experience directly into your brain. (We're still waiting for those, actually; the tweaks may be ultrasonic but the system keeps your brain in focus by tracking FM emissions, and not many consumers Faraday their homes.) In the meantime, hospitals and airports and theme parks keep the dream alive until the price comes down. And the spin-offs— Father, the spin-offs are everywhere. The deaf can hear. The blind can see. The post-traumatised have all their acid memories washed away, just as long as they keep paying the connection fee.

That's the rub, of course. It doesn't last; the high frequencies excite some synapses and put others to sleep, but they don't actually change any of the pre-existing circuitry. The brain eventually bounces back to normal once the signal stops. Which is not only profitable for those doling out the waves, but a lot less messy in the courts. There's that whole integrity-of-the-self thing to worry about. Having your brain rewired every time you hopped a commuter flight might raise some pretty iffy legal issues.

Still. I've got to admit it speeds things up. No more time-consuming background checks, no more invasive "random" searches, no litany of questions designed to weed out the troublemakers in our midst. A dash of transcranial magnetism; a squirt of ultrasound; *next*. A year ago I'd have been standing in line for hours. Today I've been here scarcely fifteen minutes and I'm already in the top ten. And it's more than mere convenience: it's security, it's safety, it's a sigh of relief after a generation of Russian Roulette. No more Edmonton Infernos, no more Rio Insurrections, no more buildings slagged to glass or cities sickening in the aftermath of some dirty nuke. There are still saboteurs and terrorists loose in the world, of course. Always will be. But when they strike at all, they strike in places unprotected by SWanky McBuzz. Anyone who flies *these* friendly skies is as harmless as—as I am.

Who can argue with results like that?

IN THE OLD days I could have wished I was a psychopath. They had it easy back then. The machines only looked for emotional responses: eye saccades, skin galvanism. Anyone without a conscience could stare them down with a wide smile and an empty heart. But SWank inspired a whole new generation. The tech looks under the surface now. Prefrontal cortex stuff, glucose metabolism. Now, fiends and perverts and would-be saboteurs all get caught in the same net.

Doesn't mean they don't let us go again, of course. It's not as if sociopathy is against the law. Hell, if they screened out everyone with a broken conscience, Executive Class would be empty.

There are children scattered throughout the line. Most are accompanied by adults. Three are not: two boys and a girl. They are nervous and beautiful, like wild animals, easily startled. They are not used to being on their own. The oldest can't be more than nine, and he has a freckle on the side of his neck.

I can't stop watching him.

Suddenly children roam free again. For months now I've been seeing them in parks and plazas, unguarded, innocent, and so *vulnerable*, as though SWank has given parents everywhere an excuse to breathe. No matter that it'll be years before it trickles out of airports and government buildings and into the places children play. Mommy and Daddy are tired of waiting, take what comfort they can in the cameras mounted on every street corner, panning and scanning for all the world as if real people stood behind them. Mommy and Daddy can't be bothered to spend five minutes on the web, compiling their own predator's handbook on the use of laser pointers and blind spots to punch holes in the surveillance society. Mommy and Daddy would rather just take all those bromides about "civil safety" on faith.

For so many years we've lived in fear. By now people are so desperate for any pretense of safety that they'll cling to the promise of a future that hasn't even arrived yet. Not that that's anything new; whether you're talking about a house in the suburbs or the browning of Antarctica, Mommy and Daddy have *always* lived on credit.

If something *did* happen to their kids, it would serve them right.

* * *

THE LINE MOVES forward. Suddenly I'm at the front of it.

A man with Authority waves me in. I step forward as if to an execution. I do this for you, Father. I do this to pay my respects. I do this to dance on your grave. If I could have avoided this moment—if this cup could have passed from me, if I could have *walked* to the Northwest Territories rather than let this obscene technology into my head—

Someone has spray-painted two words in stencilled black over the mouth of the machine: *The Shadow.* Delaying, I glance a question at the guard.

"It knows what evil lurks in the hearts of men," he says. "Bwahaha. Let's move it along."

I have no idea what he's talking about.

The walls of the booth glimmer with a tight weave of copper wire. The helmet descends from above with a soft hydraulic hiss; it sits too lightly on my head for such a massive device. The visor slides over my eyes like a blindfold. I am in a pocket universe, alone with my thoughts and an all-seeing God. Electricity hums deep in my head.

I'm innocent of any wrongdoing. I've never broken the law. Maybe God will see that if I think it hard enough. Why does it have to see anything, why does it have to *read* the palimpsest if it's just going to scribble over it again? But brains don't work like that. Each individual *is* individual, wired up in a unique and glorious tangle that must be read before it can be edited. And motivations, intents—these are endless, multiheaded things, twining and proliferating from frontal cortex to cingulate gyrus, from hypothalamus to claustrum. There's no LED that lights up when your plans are nefarious, no Aniston Neuron for mad bombers. For the safety of everyone, they must read it all. For the safety of everyone.

I have been under this helmet for what seems like forever. Nobody else took this long.

The line is not moving forward.

"Well," Security says softly. "Will you look at that."

"I'm not," I tell him. "I've never—"

"And you're not about to. Not for the next nine hours, anyway."

"I never *acted* on it." I sound petulant, childish. "Not once."

"I can see that," he says, but I know we're talking about different things.

The humming changes subtly in pitch. I can feel magnets and mosquitoes snapping in my head. I am changed by something not yet cheap enough for the home market: an ache evaporates, a dull longing so chronic I feel it now only in absentia.

"There. Now we could put you in charge of two Day Cares and a chorus of alter boys, and you wouldn't even be tempted."

The visor rises; the helmet floats away. Authority stares back at me from a gaggle of contempuous faces.

"This is wrong," I say quietly.

"Is it now."

"I haven't done anything."

"We haven't either. We haven't locked down your pervert brain, we haven't changed who you are.

We've protected your precious constitutional rights and your God-given identity. You're as free to diddle kiddies in the park as you ever were. You just won't *want* to for a while."

"But I haven't *done* anything." I can't stop saying it.

"Nobody does, until they do." He jerks his head towards Departure. "Get out of here. You're cleared."

I AM NOT a criminal. I have done nothing wrong. But my name is on a list now, just the same. Word of my depravity races ahead of me, checkpoint after checkpoint, like a fission of dominoes. They'll be watching, though they have to let me pass.

That could change before long. Even now, Community Standards barely recognize the difference between what we do and what we are; nudge them just a hair further and every border on the planet might close at my approach. But this is only the dawning of the new enlightenment, and the latest rules are not yet in place. For now, I am free to stand at your unconsecrated graveside, and mourn on my own recognizance.

You always were big on the power of forgiveness, Father. Seventy times seven, the most egregious sins washed away in the sight of the Lord. All it took, you insisted, was true penitence. All you had to do was accept His love.

Of course, it sounded a lot less self-serving back then.

But even the unbelievers get a clean slate now. My redeemer is a machine, and my salvation has an expiry date— but then again, I guess yours did too.

I wonder about the machine that programmed *you*, Father, that great glacial contraption of dogma and moving parts, clacking and iterating its way through two thousand years of bloody history. I can't help but wonder at the way it rewired *your* synapses. Did it turn you into a predator, weigh you down with lunatic strictures that no sexual being could withstand, deny your very nature until you snapped? Or were you already malfunctioning when you embraced the church, hoping for some measure of strength you couldn't find in yourself?

I knew you for years, Father. Even now, I tell myself I know you—and while you may have been twisted, you were never a coward. I refuse to believe that you opted for death because it was the easy way out. I choose to believe that in those last days you found the strength to rewrite your own programming, to turn your back on obsolete algorithms two millennia out of date and decide for yourself the difference between a mortal sin and an act of atonement.

You loathed yourself; you loathed the things you had done. And so, finally, you made absolutely certain you could never do them again. You *acted*.

You acted as I never could, though I'd pay so much smaller a price.

There is more than this temporary absolution, you see. We have machines now that can burn the evil right out of a man, deep-focus microwave emitters that vaporize the very pathways of depravity. No one can force them on you; not yet, anyway. Member's bills wind through Parliament, legislative proposals that would see us pre-emptively reprogrammed for good instead of evil, but for now the procedure is strictly voluntary. It *changes* you, you see. It violates some inalienable essence of selfhood. Some call it a kind of suicide in its own right.

I kept telling the man at Security: I never *acted* on it. But he could see that for himself.

I never had it fixed. I must *like* what I am.

I wonder if that makes a difference.

I wonder which of us is more guilty.

Sunworld

Eric Brown

IT BEGAN WITH a personal revelation for Yarrek, shortly after he graduated from college at the time of his
twentieth cycle, and ended in an even greater revelation which was to affect every citizen of Sunworld.

On the 33rd brightening of St Sarrian's quarter,
Yarrek passed from the portals of Collium College
for the very last time. He paused on the steps, ignoring the crowd of students surging around him, and
peered up into the sky. Kite-fish were taking advantage of the approaching dimming, spreading their
sails and floating high above the spires of the town
as the heat of the sun diminished. He watched the
multi-colored, kilometer-wide wings glide before
the face of the sun directly overhead as it changed
from dazzling gold to the molten, burnt-umber of
full-dimming, and he knew then what it must be
like to be as free as a kite-fish.

No more college, ever. Adult life awaited him, with all its promised mystery and romance.

He elbowed his way past a gaggle of fellow graduates and boarded an open cart hauled by four lethargic lox. As the cart set off through the narrow streets of Helioville, heading for the open farmlands beyond, Yarrek watched the town pass by with the heightened clarity of someone witnessing the familiar for the very last time.

Who knew what the future might hold? One thing was for sure—in a brightening, maybe two, he would be away from the family farm, heading by sail-rail all the way to Hub City.

The knowledge was like a warming coal, like the sun which burned at the center of the world. He watched the city folk go about their quotidian jobs, pitying them their lives of servitude, their changeless cycles of work and play, ignorant of what might lie beyond.

He sat back and let the somnolent lollop of the lox lull him into slumber, as the cart left the town and took the elevated lane through fields of golden yail.

"YARREK MERWELL, YOUR stop!"

The cry of the lox jockey yanked him from sleep. He hauled himself upright and jumped from the coach. As the team of lox set off again, farting and lowing in protest, Yarrek stood at the end of the path and stared out over the land that was his father's, and which in time would be passed on to Yarrek's elder brother, Jarrel, as was the tradition among the farmers of the central plains.

The Merwell estate stretched for as far as the eye could see, a vast golden patchwork of yail fields in various stages of ripeness. Ahead, like a galleon becalmed, stood his family's ramshackle farmhouse. The timber had been parched by the sun for countless cycles, warped cruelly by the merciless heat that prevailed this close to the Hub. For all its ugliness, a part of him loved the place. He would find leaving it, and his family, more difficult than he cared to admit.

There was a time, in his youth, when he resented the fact that his brother would inherit the farm, that he would have to make his way in the world in a profession other than that of a farmer. But as the cycles passed and he grew older and wiser, he came to thank the tradition that would force him to leave home and fend for himself.

He set off along the path, brushing against the yail plants and knocking from them the intense fragrance of pollen. He passed a threshing platform, with its troupe of labourers led by Jarrel.

His brother smiled down at him, called him a lazy lox as always, and added, "Hurry, can't you! The folks are wearing their Blacks."

He stopped and stared up at Jarrel. "Their Blacks? So soon?"

"You graduated, didn't you? Your future needs discussing."

Yarrek hurried home. Tradition among the farming caste had it that discussion of matters of destiny between parents and children necessitated the wearing of black gowns. It was a ritual of the Church that Yarrek took for granted, despite his friend Yancy's irreverent ridiculing of religious orthodoxy.

He had foreseen his parents' wearing of their Blacks, but had assumed they would leave it a brightening or two before they broached the subject of his future.

He took a jug of yail juice from the cooler, slaking his thirst. His mother and father would be on the Edgeward deck, as ritual decreed. He made his way up the two narrow flights of stairs to the third floor and paused on the threshold of the deck, nervous now. The time had come to tell his parents of his plans to enter the offices of an architectural firm in the capital, Hub City.

They had their backs to him, staring out over the flat central plains towards the mountains of the Edge—though the Edge was so distant that it could not be seen by the naked eye. It was an act of obeisance they performed every dimming, this turning towards the Edge—one which Yarrek too, despite Yancy's joshing, often found himself performing, albeit cursorily.

They had heard his creaking progress through the house, and his father gestured for him to step between them and sit on the stool positioned before the rail.

Solemnly, he did so.

They were grave-faced, unsmiling. His father was fingering his Circle of Office; he was a part-time pastor of the Church, and he took his duties seriously.

"Son," he said in greeting.

His mother said without smiling, "We have heard. Congratulations. A second grade. No Merwell for five generations has attained better than a third."

His parents had always been distant. They were loving in a remote, stern kind of way, solicitous for the welfare of their sons, but wary of showing emotion, still less anything so exhibitionist as physical affection.

Unlike Yancy's parents, Yarrek thought, who showered the girl with such gestures of love that he found their displays embarrassing, not to say impious. But then Yancy's folks were from the Hub, where tradition was lax.

"The time has come," his father said, "to speak of what lies ahead. For so long now the future was college, and the attaining of success in your studies. Now that you have achieved more than we could ever have hoped, together we take the next step."

Yarrek swallowed nervously. "I have considered my future," he said. "I thought perhaps... well, I'd like to study to become an architect."

Silence greeted his words. His father's grim expression did not waver; his thin face might have been carved from wood.

His mother said, "Of course you have *dreamed*, Yarrek. Such boyish fancies are to be expected, and are excusable. But as the Church says, one's destiny is often beyond the scope of the individual. There comes a time when the experience of Elders must shape the course of disciples."

Yarrek bowed his head. "My plans are more than dreams, mother. I've heard that architectural offices in the Hub are crying out for skilled draftsmen."

"Yarrek," his father said, in a tone that stopped him dead. "Hub City is a den of vice, the playground of the heathen. No son of mine will venture there."

"But," Yarrek said, resenting the note of desperation in that single word, "you know yourself that I am pious. I attend regular church. Why, to deny me the right to go to Hub City suggests that you think me weak, your instructions insufficient."

His mother stared at him. "My son, we of flesh are forever weak. Do you not consort with the daughter of the Garrishes?"

"Yancy is a friend," he began, angry at the disdain his mother had loaded onto the word *consort*.

"She is the product of the Hub," said his mother, "and the thought of your being surrounded by crowds of such people..."

Yarrek stared from his father to his mother. "Then where else might I study to become an architect?"

His mother allowed herself a minimal smile.

His father said, "Tomorrow at mid-brightness you will take the sail-rail Edgeward to Icefast."

He echoed, "Icefast," in horror. The very name of the city, perched on the very margin of the Edge, filled him with cold dread. The sun would be distant there; the outside temperature intolerable without layers of protective garments; his shadow eerily long...

"And there I can study—?" Yarrek began.

His father said, "It has been arranged for you to sit an entrance examination for the office of the Inquisitor General."

His mother allowed another smile to crack her features; she could not conceal her pride. His father's eyes gleamed with satisfaction.

Icefast and the Inquisitor's office? His parents' plans for him were so contrary to his own that Yarrek was unable to grasp his sudden change of destiny. He thought of Yancy, and wanted nothing so much then as the consolation of her arms around him.

"I have no say in the matter?" he asked.

His father reached out and, with a hand as strong as a bailing iron, gripped Yarrek's upper arm. "It is an honour to be so chosen, as you will come to appreciate."

Yarrek bowed his head and whispered, "I've heard that the methods of Inquisitors are Draconian."

His father said, "Since Prelate Zeremy came to office, things have changed. He has curbed the power of the Inquisitors, put an end to their worst excesses. Now they truly are a force for good, instead of causing a conflicting schism within the Church itself."

Yarrek nodded. "May I now go to my room?"

"Go," his mother said, "and pack in preparation for your leave-taking."

He stood and hurried from the deck, making his way through the cool, dark house, and reached the refuge of his room. There he lay on his bed, too gripped by shock even to cry.

He knew, even then, that he would do as his parents wished; he knew that Hub City was the dream of a juvenile, that his true destiny was in the ice-fields of the Edge, in the office of the Inquisitor General.

The door creaked open. It was his father. He had doffed his Blacks, and now stood above Yarrek in his homely farmer's garb.

"Yarrek," he said. "Yarrek, I must tell you something." He sat down on the bed next to his son. Yarrek stiffened at his father's unaccustomed proximity.

He stared into the old man's face, wondering at his father's nervousness.

And the farmer, pained by a duty he would rather have forgone, told him the truth.

"Twenty cycles ago," he began in a voice heavy with weariness, "a family in Icefast, a rich and influential family high up in the hierarchy of power, broke the edict of the Church and sired three children." Yarrek did not yet comprehend the import of his father's words; the thought of a rich family contravening Church Edict was shocking enough.

"Had the Church discovered the birth," his father went on, "the child would have been put to death according to the Law of Conservation. But the family had power, as I said. They managed to spirit this child, a boy, out of Icefast in the depth of dimming and send it with paid agents Hubward."

His father could not bring himself to look Yarrek in the eye. "These agents arranged for a family to take in the boy, to raise him as their own."

Yarrek said, "No..."

"The truth, Yarrek, is sometimes almost impossible to bear. But remember this: that truth, duly weighed and considered, makes a man stronger."

"You..." Yarrek said. "I... I am that child? You took me in? I am not...?" It was too vast a concept. His parents were not his parents? Jarrel was not his brother? He felt the certainty of the world tilt beneath him.

And then his father—or rather the man who was not his father, but had acted as such for twenty cycles—did something which he had never done before: he reached out and took Yarrek's shoulder in compassion. In a small voice he said, "Your mother had just miscarried. A son. She was grieving. We were poor then. The farm was yet to prosper. When the agents of aristocrats called and made their offer, we could not refuse. They paid us well, but money was not our motive. We looked upon you and knew that if we were to refuse, then you would die."

His father paused, and went on, "Your progress at college was monitored by the interested party in Icefast, and they arranged for your apprenticeship."

The irony! He, the illegal third child of aristocrats, was to be seconded into the very arm of the Church responsible for the policing of such edicts!

The hand tightened on his shoulder. "But be assured of this, Yarrek. Despite everything, we love you as our own."

It was the first time his father had ever spoken such words of affection. With that, his face averted, he stood and left the room.

Yarrek lay on his bed, staring through the open window at the baleful eye of the rapidly dimming sun. Unable to sleep, he thought ahead to his time in Icefast. Though much of what lay ahead would be a mystery, he resolved upon a course of action that would give his future some purpose: during his time in Icefast he would attempt to track down the people who were his rightful parents.

MUCH LATER HE was awakened by a sound.

He sat up quickly, the revelations of his past and his future brimming in him like sour wine. He blinked. It was still dark, though the sun had reached the extent of its dimming and was little by little beginning to brighten.

It came again, the sound...

"Yarrek!" A mere whisper, from the direction of the window. He turned on the bed and saw, beside the nodding dark-blooms that wound in around the window-frame, Yancy's round face staring in at him.

"Yancy?"

"I heard that you're leaving for Icefast. Jarrel told me over at the platform. When you didn't turn up, I thought... Well"—she shrugged—"here I am."

He hurried across the room and embraced her. She was standing on a thick twist of vine that clung to the façade of the manse. Her presence here, as it did every time she came for him, amazed Yarrek, for Yancy Garrish was blind. Her massive eyes were skinned over with a milky meniscus that only served to accentuate the beauty of her face.

She raised a small flagon. "I've brought some yail acid, from my father's locked cupboard," she grinned. "Come to the platform and tell me everything."

She was already shinning down the vine; he straddled the window sill and followed her.

He jumped the last meter and ran after Yancy as she disappeared through the yail stalks. Minutes later they emerged at the platform. It stood stark and empty in the umber light of the slowly brightening sun. Full brightening was hours away. He would have plenty of time with his friend before returning home.

They climbed onto the platform and fell back onto piled sacks of yail. Yancy unplugged the flagon, took a quick slug, and then passed it to Yarrek. The spirit burned his throat, filled his belly with strangely comforting fire.

He said, "What did Jarrel tell you?"

She chose to ignore him. "Are the kite-fish swarming?" she asked, her sightless eyes staring in the direction of the brooding sun and the flotilla of kite-fish that basked in its gentle pre-brightening warmth.

He took her hand. "Perhaps twenty, maybe thirty. Massive ones, mostly male, putting on a show." He watched the intricacy of their aerial dance. "They're performing their mating rituals, flying circles around the sun."

Yancy sighed and squeezed his hand. "And on the other side," she said. "What can you see there?"

Yarrek narrowed his eyes, peering past the sun and focussing on the other side of the world. Directly above him he could see that side's Hub City, and radiating from it the web of lines that were the sail-rail tracks, with a great checkerboard of farmland in between. Overland, as his people called it, was a mirror image of the plain on which Yarrek lived; he had never met anyone who had ventured there, though he knew that ships plied back and forth across the frozen seas of the Edge.

He described it to Yancy in great detail, omitting nothing.

She snuggled close to him, her warmth in turn warming him, banishing his fears.

He asked again, "Yancy, what did Jarrel tell you?"

She was a while before replying. "He said you were to go to the Edge, to Icefast, at mid-brightening. There you had a job awaiting you. A very important job."

"Did he tell you what it was?"

She shook her head. "He didn't know. Your parents had told him only so much, to prepare him for your leave-taking."

His silence prompted her question. "Well, Yarrek, will you tell me?"

He braced himself for her ridicule, even her disgust. "I will sit an exam for the office of the Inquisitor General."

He turned and stared at her broad, pretty face in the light of the brightening. It was as if her features were frozen. Her hand remained on his, though her grip had slackened appreciably.

"Yancy?"

"You'll be a lackey of the Church?" she said. "And an Inquisitor at that!"

He shrugged. "I have no say in the matter. Do you think I want to leave here, leave you?" And he felt a twinge of treachery at these words, for he had planned to venture to Hub City without her. Though, he told himself, he would have seen her when he returned home, and she could have visited him often enough.

She was silent for a long time. He watched the kite-fish perform convoluted arabesques with vast, lethargic grace.

He wanted to tell Yancy that he was not a true Merwell—that his blood family were aristocrats in Icefast—but he could not bring himself to do so.

"You'll change," she whispered. "You'll become like them. Hard. Unforgiving. You'll forget what it is to love, to feel compassion. For how can those that rule by the Edict of the Church have room in their hearts for the forgiveness of human frailty?"

He took her hand. "I won't change, Yancy."

She turned to face him, and her soured eyes seemed to be staring at him. "But you already believe, in your heart, Yarrek. You have been indoctrinated by your parents. And from belief, it is only a short step to pressing your belief onto others, by force if necessary."

"No!"

She laughed. "But you take in every word the Church spouts and believe it for the ultimate truth!"

Yancy and her family belonged to the caste of Weavers. From an early age Yancy had woven fabulous tapestries of such color and intricacy that they left Yarrek breathless. He had wondered how someone without sight could create such things of visual beauty. She had explained that she *felt* the colors, and kept the complex patterns in her head as she weaved.

The Weavers were renowned for their lack of convention, their irreverence, but because of the importance of their position in society, producing carpets both aesthetic and utilitarian, the Church chose to ignore their heterodoxy.

"Tell me again what the Church believes." Yancy whispered now, mocking him. "Tell me that we are a bubble of air in a vast rock that goes on for ever and ever without end..."

He thought about that, even as she laughed at him, and as ever the concept of infinity dizzied him. "Tell me," she went on, "that the Church believes that the bubble was formed from the breath of God, as He breathed life into dead rock, creating us and the animals and everything else in existence!"

"Yancy..." he pleaded, squeezing her hand.

She embraced him quickly, and he realized with surprise that she was weeping. "Oh, Yarrek, I will never see you again, will I? And if I do, you will be so changed I'll never recognize the boy I love."

He could think of no words to say in response, no gesture he could make to reassure her.

A little later they removed their clothes and came together and made love slowly, under the eye of the quickening sun, and Yarrek wondered if it would be for the very last time.

YARREK STOWED HIS luggage in the warped timber carriage of the sail-rail train and found a window seat. He stared out at the busy platform, and among the crowd picked out the unmoving trio of his father, mother, and brother. They looked solemn in the glare of the mid-brightening sun. He lifted a hand to acknowledge that he had seen them, but only Jarrel responded with a wave.

He scanned the crowd for any sign of Yancy. Mere hours ago, as they lay limbs entwined on the yail sacks, she had promised that she would see him off at the station—but there were so many citizens swarming back and forth that he despaired of seeing her now.

The cry went up from the ship's captain. A team of lox were whipped into motion and chocks sprang away from the rails. The carriage creaked as the great sails took the strain and eased the train slowly, at first, along the rails.

Desperately now Yarrek cast about the surging faces for Yancy—and then he heard the cry. "Yarrek, goodbye!"

She had shinned up a lamp-pole and was waving furiously in the direction of the train. He called, "Yancy, farewell!" and waved even though she would be unable to see the gesture.

She smiled, and waved all the more, and Yarrek turned to the tableau of his family and was heartened by the disapproving expressions on the faces of his mother and father. Jarrel was grinning to himself like an idiot.

The train gained speed, the wind from the Hub sending it on its way. Yarrek felt tears stinging his eyes as he waved to his family and the small, clinging figure of the blind weaver girl.

He sat back in his seat and closed his eyes.

HE AWOKE A little later to the thrumming vibration of the train's wheels on the track.

Yarrek had never before been further Edgeward than his farm. Now, mixed with apprehension at what should await him at Icefast, he was fired by the excitement and curiosity of adventure. The future was a blank canvas on which he would paint his destiny; he knew neither what to expect from Icefast—though in books he had seen engravings of dour, stone buildings—nor what exactly might await him in the office of the Inquisitor.

The train had gained full speed now, and fields of yail and other crops sped by in a golden blur. Yarrek slid open the window and poked his head out, staring up at the bellying sails bearing the great green circle of the Hub Line. Almost directly overhead, the sun had attained full brightness and the heat was merciless.

He wondered how he might cope in Icefast, where the sun was a speck on the inward horizon, and the temperature never rose above freezing.

He glanced around his compartment and tried to guess how many of his fellow passengers were bound all the way to Icefast; not many, judging by their scant luggage. Indeed, as the hours elapsed and the train stopped at the stations along the way, many travellers alighted to be replaced by others who remained aboard only for short durations.

He began a letter to Yancy—addressed to the weaving house where she worked, and where a friend would read it out to her—describing the voyage so far, and promising that this letter would be the first of many.

Later he ate an evening meal packed by his mother, then went for a stroll along the corridor and up a flight of steps. The view from the upper deck, beneath the taut swell of the sails, was spectacular. He could see for what seemed like hundreds of miles in every direction: a sprawling panorama of yail fields, here and there the spires and steeples of towns and villages.

Towards dimming, as he was contemplating going below and setting up his bunk, there was a rush of activity over by the starboard rail where a dozen passengers gathered and pointed.

In the distance, perhaps a mile away, Yarrek saw the humped remains of ancient buildings, tumbled stones upholstered by centuries of creeping grass and ferns. He recognized the ruins from picture books at school: this was the old city of Hassaver, the only existing remnant of the war that had almost brought the end of civilization on Sunworld. Dreadful weapons had been brought to bear by implacable armies, fighting for countries long forgotten.

The history books said that the war had been fought perhaps ten thousand cycles ago, and that, after the devastation, strange beings had come among the people of Sunworld—beings that ecclesiastical scholars later claimed were angels—and brought about the formation of the Church, which in turn had brought lasting peace to the world and the eventual rebuilding of civilization.

He hurried below, constructed a bunk from his extendable seat, and settled down to sleep as the sun dimmed quickly far above the hurtling train.

He was awoken in the early hours, and at first he couldn't make out what had brought him awake. It felt as though ice had invaded his veins; his body was rattling in a manner he had never experienced before. Instinctively he pulled the thin sheet over him, and then realized what had happened. He had read about this in books, but had never experienced the phenomenon of cold, the dead chill that enveloped him now.

Teeth chattering in a way he might otherwise have found amusing, he sat up and peered through the window.

The landscape surrounding the trundling train had changed alarmingly. Gone were the reassuring fields of yail, to be replaced by smaller fields of some stubby green plant, and over everything lay a coating of what he would later learn was called frost, a scintillating silver dusting like ground diamond.

He noticed that other passengers were straining to peer ahead; he pressed his face to the icy glass and did likewise.

What he saw sent a throb of surprise and fear through his being. Ahead, stretching for the extent of the horizon, was a range of gray mountains capped by what he knew was snow. The rearing phalanx was forbidding, austere and steel-like in its breadth, and total dearth of living color. This, then, was the Edge, and the range before him the fabled mountains that circumnavigated this plane of Sunworld. The thought that he was actually here, witnessing this sight, took his breath away.

At the next station, vendors boarded the carriage selling mugs of hot broth. Yarrek gladly purchased one. Behind these vendors came others hawking thick clothing, serge pantaloons, padded jerkins, caps with ear flaps, and things called gloves which you fitted over your hands to protect the fingers—according to the spiel of the vendors—from something called frostbite.

Yarrek outfitted himself from head to toe, pulling his new apparel over his old. He felt at once constricted but snug, and wondered if he would ever become accustomed to being so lagged.

He settled down, more comfortable now, and stared in fascination through the window at the wonder of the passing world outside.

Two hours later Yarrek caught his first glimpse of Icefast.

If he had found the sight of the mountains a thing of wonder, then Icefast doubled his awe and sent his senses reeling. The engravings of his youth had done nothing to prepare him for either the scale of the city or the severity of its aspect.

Like the mountains, Icefast was gray, and like the mountains it reared stark and abrupt from the land. The uniformity of the tall buildings, the fact that constructions of such enormity had been planned and undertaken by his fellow man, made the sight of the serried façades all the more daunting.

Icefast filled the horizon between peaks as though the very mountains themselves had been found wanting and replaced. Yarrek made out ice-canals between the monolithic gray mansions, and on the canals the improbable sight of people skating back and forth, and others riding sleds drawn by teams of shaggy lox.

In due course the train slowed and entered a canyon of buildings. On the station platform Yarrek made out a thousand souls muffled to their ears, their breaths pluming in the cold. Strange cries and shouts came from the throng, vendors selling everything from cold cures to water-heated boots, mulled yail to grilled lox.

That morning, his father had given him instructions for his arrival in Icefast and directions to the House of the Inquisitors, where he would be given a bed in the apprentices' dormitory. He would take a lox cart to the Avenue of Creation, and present himself to the porter at the House.

As he gathered his belongings and stepped from the carriage, his breath robbed by the severity of the cold that wrapped around him and invaded his lungs, he realized that his heart was pounding with both excitement and dread.

He hurried to a lox-cart stand, climbed aboard, and gave his destination to a muffled dwarf of a jockey. Seconds later he was gliding smoothly—no jolts on this ride—across the silvered canals of Icefast, and everything he beheld seemed new and wondrous. He saw nothing familiar, no fields of yail or timber buildings or kite-fish sailing around the sun. Instead all was drear and austere, the gaunt buildings hewn from great stone blocks, the thoroughfares filled with ice. It was the start of dimming. Back home the air would still be bright with sunlight; this far away from the Hub the sun was but a distant disk. A strange twilight filled the air, and the city was illuminated by naked flames in great sconces set atop pillars positioned along the middle of the ice-canals.

The cart slowed at last and halted before the tall, pillared entrance of the House of Inquisitors. Yarrek paid the jockey and climbed down. Keeping his footing with difficulty as he negotiated paving stones slick with ice, he stepped towards the ancient timber doors and passed inside.

He was met by the grim-faced porter, who escorted him without a word to a tiny cell furnished with a hard, narrow bed and a trunk for his clothing. He passed a fitful night, tossing, turning, and dreaming—when sleep came in the early hours—of home and sunlight and Yancy. At dawn, a loud rapping on the door of his cell awoke him and the porter led Yarrek, along with a dozen other would-be Inquisitors, to the lecture halls overlooking the Avenue of Creation.

FOR THE NEXT ten brightenings—though this near the Edge the word was something of a misnomer, for a brightening never achieved much more than a pewter half-light—Yarrek rose early and hurried from his spartan cell to the lecture halls.

There, along with his fellow students, he pored over ancient manuscripts and studied more modern apologia. In the afternoons, after a short meal break during which he ate slabs of cold porridge and watered wine in a silent refectory, he returned to the lecture halls where he would listen, along with the other bored and nodding novices, to a different tutor every brightening who spoke at length on varying aspects of Church law and judiciary practice. At the end of the lessons he would sit a written exam on what he had learned so far, and he would have to dredge his memory for the arcane and abstruse tenets of ecclesiastical lore.

At dimming, after a substantial meal of meat broth, he would retire to his cell and compose letters to Yancy and his family. To the latter he would paint a picture of diligence and interest, but to Yancy he would tell the truth: that he found his studies tedious and life in Icefast at best alienating. He missed the warmth of all that was familiar, he wrote, but most of all he missed Yancy.

He made no friends among his fellow apprentices, for fraternisation was forbidden. Meals were taken in silence, and silence was the rule during study periods. At dimming, Church porters escorted the novices back to their cells. Though their doors were not locked, Yarrek suspected that guards were posted at the end of the corridor to discourage nocturnal wanderings.

On his eleventh brightening in Icefast, the rules were relaxed. Nothing was stated overtly, but Yarrek noticed that whispers at mealtimes were not admonished, and the porters no longer escorted the novices from the lecture halls. He made friends with a fat youth from a city around the Edge of Sunworld who pined for the flat ice-fields of home just as Yarrek pined for the sun-parched plains of the Hub.

Upon Yarrek's fifteenth brightening as a novice, the lecturer announced that for the first time they would be allowed outside after lessons. That dimming Yarrek, along with his new-found friend, hired skates and for an hour attempted to remain upright along the Avenue of Creation before the cold became too much to bear.

The following afternoon, in the great library, he consulted a gazetteer of the city, searching for the official building where he might find a listing of registered births. That evening after lessons he slipped out and skated shakily along the Avenue towards the House of Public Records

He came to the building, like all the others in the metropolis a sheer, towering construction with high slit windows and a massive entrance. He removed his skates and passed inside, only to discover that he had just thirty minutes before the records office closed. He hurried, sweating in the furnace heat of the building, to the room which housed the rows of mouldering ledgers containing the names of all who had been born, lived, and died in Icefast for the past five hundred cycles.

He knew, of course, that his name would not be among those listed, for he had been a third born, and thus an illegal issue. He hoped, however, to come across some clue that might help him in his search for his true parents. He reasoned that if he could find the names of all the families who had sired two children and their addresses (for he knew his parents to be high-born and assumed they would have lived in exclusive precincts), then he could furnish himself with a list of families who might possibly have birthed him against the law.

But thirty minutes was no time at all in which to accomplish this mammoth task. No sooner had he found the relevant ledger and scanned the first page, than a dour, cloaked official appeared at the door and announced that the House of Public Records was closing in five minutes.

Skating back to the House of the Inquisitors, the sun a tiny disk on the horizon, Yarrek told himself that on his next free brightening he would search the ledgers from first light to closing time.

THERE WAS A surprise in store for the novices the following brightening. At the end of the afternoon's lessons the lecturer, a wizened old vulture known as Dr Kellaway, rapped on his lectern and called for silence. His rheumy, censorious gaze raked the thirteen pale faces of his pupils as he announced, "For sixteen brightenings you have studied hard and completed a series of testing examinations. That phase of your education has now ceased. Your papers have been assessed, your ability established, and it is my duty to announce that just three of you have attained the standards required to be admitted to the Office of the High Inquisitor. The ten of you who have failed will be found posts in the Inquisitor's halls of administration, which I might add is no disgrace."

He paused, his gaze moving from face to expectant face. Yarrek knew that his name would not be among the three who had passed. He could expect to pass his brightenings in dull administration; the thought of such work in the half-light and chill of Icefast filled him with despair.

Dr Kellaway consulted a list upon his lectern and read out three names. "The successful novices are Burce Madders, Kareen Holgen, and Yarrek Merwell. You will report at first brightening to the porter's lodge, and an official will escort you to your new study rooms."

Yarrek hurried to his cell as class was dismissed, wanting neither the congratulations of the failed candidates nor their recriminations. His only friend was not among the three. Yarrek knew that his commiserations would be met with stony resentment.

The truth was that Yarrek was amazed at his success, for in his own estimation he had failed miserably to reproduce in the exams even half of what he had retained of the information supplied in the lessons. Could the failed ten have done even worse, he wondered with incredulity?

Thus began a new phase of study for Yarrek.

THE THREE SUCCESSFUL novices attended seminars given by the eminent Dr Bellair in his private suite at the very summit of the House of Inquisitors. Their presence was required only in the mornings, while the afternoons were left free to fill as they desired.

In the mornings, Yarrek absorbed as much information as he thought possible on the abstruse subject of Church edicts. Every third brightening, the novices were expected to read out essays, to which Dr Bellair listened with an air of studious absorption, and then commented upon with clinical acuity. Yarrek came to understand the extent of the revolution that had shaken the Church. The old guard had been replaced, swept aside by Prelate Zeremy and his followers; traditional, Draconian ways had ceded to more liberal codes of practice. Beliefs that had held sway for cycles were now considered legitimate subjects for discussion and even for reasoned dissent. Yarrek found the sessions with Dr Bellair heady stuff indeed, after the dull lessons of ancient history, and for the first time thought he might find work in the Office of the Inquisitor to be ultimately rewarding.

In the afternoons, after a period of private study, Yarrek made his way to the House of Public Records and pored laboriously over one dusty ledger after another. Over a period of a dozen brightenings he succeeded in compiling a list of fifty names of families of high standing who had sired two children in the cycle of his birth. He stared at the names and wondered if one of them might bear his rightful title.

THE FOLLOWING BRIGHTENING, as he sat in Dr Bellair's fire-lit study with his fellow novices, listening to the Doctor describe in detail the Prelate's position on Church infallibility, a sharp rapping upon the door startled them all.

Dr Bellair, ruffled at having his monologue interrupted, issued a testy summons and a poker-faced porter slid into the room and passed the Doctor a folded note.

Dr Bellair read it once, and then again, and then looked up and across the room to Yarrek, who started in surprise.

"Merwell," the Doctor said, "you will accompany the Church Guard from this building forthwith."

Dry of throat, Yarrek climbed unsteadily to his feet. Watched by the incredulous students and a puzzled Dr Bellair, he followed the porter from the room.

He was escorted down the switchback staircase from the twelfth floor to the spartan foyer where two tall guardsmen, outfitted in the resplendent golden uniforms of the Prelate's office, awaited him.

"Yarrek Merwell?" asked the taller of the two. "Please, this way."

Yarrek passed from the building between the two guards. In the ice-canal, a liveried coach-sled awaited them. He climbed into the lavishly upholstered cab and sank deep into a cushioned seat. The lox jockey yelled a command and the sled sped off, the guards standing on running-boards to either side of the careering vehicle.

Minutes later they turned from the Avenue of Creation onto the Avenue of the Prelate, and shortly after that the sled halted in the shadow of a rearing edifice which stood at the very end of the boulevard, almost enclosed by an impressive backdrop of snow-capped peaks.

Yarrek knew the identity of the building, but did not believe that he might ever be requested to step within its hallowed entrance.

And yet this was precisely what the guards now suggested. On watery legs he climbed from the sled and the guards escorted him up a flight of steps and into the private residence of Prelate Zeremy.

They climbed a winding staircase and paused before a double-door inlaid with lacquered frost-wood. Suddenly Yarrek knew then that his identity as an illegal third child had been discovered, though quite why that should entail an audience with the Prelate himself he could not guess.

The doors swung open, revealing a prosaic room filled with shelves of books, and an armchair illuminated by a gas reading lamp.

A small man, seated in the armchair, lowered his book and gazed the length of the room.

Yarrek felt a sharp prod in his lower back, and a second later he was in the room and cowering beneath the gaze of the most powerful person in Sunworld.

"TISANE, OR WOULD you prefer something stronger? Yail wine, perhaps?"

The face was avuncular, kindly, and the enquiring tone of voice not one Yarrek would associate with the agency of punishment.

"Tisane, thank you," he said in a small voice. He perched on the edge of a chair opposite the Prelate, and could only stare at the old man in wonder. He was familiar with Prelate Zeremy's features from portraits, but oils failed to do justice to the man's warmth. The prelate wore the scarlet robes of his office, and his hair was long and silver-gray. His eyes, as he stared across at the awe-struck boy, twinkled with what Yarrek chose to interpret as kindliness.

A footman poured two small cups of perfumed tisane, then quietly withdrew.

The Prelate laid his book on a small table beside the guttering gas lamp. "My informants report that you are excelling at your studies, Yarrek Merwell."

Yarrek stared into his tisane, at a loss for words. At last he said, "I... I try to do my best, sir."

"We live in an age when the certainties of the past have been stripped away, Yarrek. Study, in such times, is more problematic than usual. Who to believe; indeed, what to believe? The solid shibboleths of past times, or the fashionable mores of the present?"

"We have been taught both," Yarrek began, and cursed himself for stating something that the Prelate must obviously know. "Perhaps," he ventured, "we could not appreciate the Church's present enlightened position if we knew nothing of its more conservative stance in the past."

Prelate Zeremy smiled. "Well put, my friend. My informants were not wrong in their assessment of you."

Yarrek colored and turned his attention to his tisane.

Zeremy watched Yarrek closely. "You are by all accounts open-minded."

Uncomfortable, Yarrek made a non-committal gesture.

"You will consider improbable notions and not dismiss them out of hand."

He felt his heart begin a laboured thudding. What was the Prelate trying to say?

"Five cycles ago, Yarrek, we discovered certain facts pertaining to our place in the nature of existence, facts which threw into doubt the very sanctity and dominion of the Church's teachings." He smiled and shook his head. "I, personally, found the revelation shocking. Like you, like everyone in Sunworld, I knew with absolute certainty the provenance of our world... We lived within the shell of an embolism embedded in the substance of rock and earth which went on forever without let or termination."

Yarrek found himself whispering, "And five cycles ago?"

"Five cycles ago a discovery was made on the outer edges of the very Edge, beside the frozen circumferential sea. A discovery which changed everything."

Yarrek's pulse pounded in his ears. "Why," he said at last, "are you telling me this?"

"You are a brilliant student," Zeremy said. "You are the future of the Church, I might also say a future arbiter of the laws that govern Sunworld. As such, it is incumbent upon you to know the truth."

Yarrek could only nod, wondering if his fellow students would also be vouchsafed the *truth*.

"Five cycles ago," Zeremy said, "we received a report here in Icefast of a sighting of a *creature*, let's say, in the marginal lands beyond the mountains. A harl-herder observed a tall figure loitering in a crevice in the cliff-face, whence it vanished. The herder was too frightened to follow, but reported it to his foreman who in turn notified the Bishop. By and by the Bishop reported the sighting to the Inquisitor's office. It was not the first such sighting in the area."

"But what were they?"

"Five cycles ago," Zeremy said, "I was a Deputy Investigator in the Inquisitor's office. We convened meetings to discuss the matter. One theory was that we were being visited by beings—sentient, perhaps—from another world, from an embolism in the matter of creation adjacent to our own."

Yarrek realized that he was staring at the Prelate open-mouthed, and shut it.

"It was decided that Investigators should be despatched to the margins to explore the possibility of other-worldly visitations. Duly I assigned my sons, Harber and Collan, to the task. They were eager and experienced Investigators, and shared my liberal inclinations. I might add that we were opposed by the more traditional elements within the Church council, who feared discoveries which might subvert the traditions—and I mean by that the power—of the Church. Be that as it may, my sons set out to explore the marginal lands."

Yarrek was perched upon the edge of his seat. "And they discovered?"

Prelate Zeremy smiled, and Yarrek thought he detected sadness in the old man's eyes. "They reported what they discovered to the council, but it was never disseminated for public consumption. The traditionalists had their way, and had the discovery effectively silenced."

He stopped there, and then went on, "Three brightenings after Harber and Collan returned from the marginal lands, they were found dead in the wreckage of a lox-sled. My Investigators found evidence of sabotage: a rail had been sawn through, turning the sled into a death trap."

Yarrek leaned forward. "And the culprits? Were they found and tried?"

Zeremy nodded. "Two known criminals did the deed, but they had been commissioned by elements within the traditional wing of the Church." He smiled sadly. "It could be said that my sons' deaths propagated the initial stages of what would become the revolution that brought me to power, the overturning of the old ways and the establishment of the new, liberal Church. Gradually, more tolerant views gained sway, and I had behind me a powerful lobby of like-minded Bishops and priests. Investigation into the sabotage proved to be the final straw—the traditionalists responsible were rounded up and exiled, though none of this was made public. To all intents, the revolution occurred quickly and without a single objection, violent or otherwise." Zeremy's fingers strayed to the circular symbol that hung on a chain about his neck. "I like to think that my sons deaths were not in vain." He glanced across the room at the portrait of a handsome, gray-haired woman. "Nor that of my dear wife, who passed on soon after the accident."

Yarrek allowed a respectful silence to develop. It would be crass, he felt, to jump in with the question he needed to ask.

In due course he ventured, "And the discovery made by your sons, sir? What of that?"

Prelate Zeremy smiled. "After the revolution, I convened my new council to discuss the ramifications of the discovery, and how it might change things here in Sunworld. I had hoped that my sons might have guided me and my council in decreeing how the truth of their findings might be promulgated. In the aftermath of their deaths, that matter was set aside as too sensitive a subject to be rushed before the people. Cycles of planning might be required to pave the way for what would be a conceptual breakthrough." The prelate laughed at Yarrek's slack-jawed expression. "Yes, lad, I choose my words without hyperbole. What Harber and

Collan discovered beneath the mountains of the marginal lands will in time change the world."

Yarrek opened his mouth to speak, but fear robbed him of words.

Zeremy supplied them for him. "And what, you are thinking, was that discovery?"

Yarrek could only nod.

"Words," pronounced Zeremy, "would fail to do full justice to the phenomenon." The Prelate stopped abruptly and stared at Yarrek. "Tomorrow, at mid-brightening, I will send a sled for you. Then, Yarrek, we will meet again."

As if at some invisible signal, the footman appeared silently at Yarrek's side; the audience with the Prelate was over. Yarrek could only murmur his inadequate thanks and bow before he was led from the room and escorted back through the torch-lit ice-canals to the House of Inquisitors.

HE COULD NOT sleep that dimming, his mind roiling with all the Prelate had told him. He did eventually fall into a fitful slumber, but woke early and wondered if their meeting had been nothing but a vivid dream.

He found himself unable to concentrate the following morning in Dr Bellair's study, for lack of sleep and an excitement that filled his chest like fermenting yail. He was aware of his fellow students' scrutiny, and even the Doctor himself looked askance at Yarrek, as if wondering at the reason for his summons the morning before.

That afternoon he sat in his cell, jumpy with anticipation. Three times he began a letter to Yancy, but was unable to pen the trite words of affection, his mind full of his meeting with Prelate Zeremy and the enormity of what might lie ahead.

A loud rapping upon the cell door made him jump. It was the same pair of guards. They marched him quickly from the cell like a condemned man. Yarrek wondered if indeed that was what he might be, condemned to some terrible understanding denied all others of Sunworld.

The same sled awaited him on the ice-canal, though this time it was occupied. As Yarrek climbed inside, at first he did not recognize the swaddled figure ensconced upon the piled cushions in the back seat. The man wore a thick jerkin, and quilted leggings, and a cap pulled down over his head.

"Yarrek," came the command, "sit down before you fall down." And at that second the lox-team started up and hauled the sled along the ice, and Yarrek pitched into the plush seat beside the Prelate Zeremy.

Smiling, Zeremy handed him a thick overcoat, which Yarrek dutifully struggled into. "Where we are going," the Prelate explained, "this will be necessary."

Where they were going... Yarrek could guess, but was too fearful to ask.

He stared out through the frosted window at the blur of Icefast passing by, a series of smeared torchlights and monolithic blocks of buildings; the only sound was the swish of sled's runners and the indignant *harrumph* of the reluctant lox-team.

He noticed that, this time, the two guards did not accompany the sled as it sped down the ice-canals. Beside him the Prelate sat back in the seat, his eyes hooded as if in contemplation, his fingertips joined in his lap.

Yarrek turned his attention to the landscape outside. They were passing through the outskirts of Icefast, past a series of low, mean buildings huddling in the shadow of the mountains. Soon they left behind these suburbs and headed towards the rampart-like foothills, iron-gray ice-fields stretching away to right and left. Yarrek thought of the meadows surrounding the Hub, and the brilliant sunlight. Even though it was after mid-brightening now, the air was lit like twilight. Far behind them, the sun was as small as a pea held at arm's length.

Then they were plunged into sudden and startling darkness; Yarrek wondered if they had been swallowed by the very mountain range itself. He realized, then, that this was what had indeed happened: torchlight at intervals illuminated the curve of a tunnel bored through the heart of the rock.

The tunnel seemed interminable. Yarrek judged that they travelled its length for at least an hour. He marvelled at the feat of labour required to accomplish such an excavation. He realized with excitement that they would eventually emerge on the far side of the mountains, and that for the very first time in his life he would set eyes upon the circumferential sea.

In due course he became aware of light up ahead and peered out at the arch of gray sky beyond the hunched figure of the lox jockey. Seconds later they emerged from the tunnel. The sled slowed and Yarrek peered forward in amazement.

Beside him the Prelate stirred. "Is it not a sight to behold?"

Yarrek could only nod.

They were high up on a road that switchbacked down through the foothills. Far below was the breath-taking expanse of the rim sea. It stretched for as far as the eye could see, flat at first, but, as it followed the curved plane to meet the rim of Overland, it rose to form a vertical wall. More amazing than this, however, was the fact that the sea was absolutely still, the waves frozen in great shattered slabs of ice that would never break upon the shore.

He looked up. Here on the rim, where the two plains of Sunworld converged, Overland seemed like a low ceiling. Directly overhead he made out mountains and townships hanging upside-down, as if defying the laws of gravity.

With a shiver he lowered his gaze.

The lox were digging their hooves into the inclined track, slowing the sled in its descent. Little by little they negotiated the tight turns of the switchback road; perhaps an hour later they emerged on the great gray margin of the frozen shoreline.

Zeremy leaned forward and called to the jockey. "Slow, now. To the right you will observe a cutting in the mountainside. Halt there."

Seconds later the jockey yelled a command and the lox shambled to a stop. "This is as far as we go by sled," Zeremy said. "The rest of the way is by foot."

Yarrek nodded, his mouth dry, a hundred questions frozen on his lips.

They stepped from the sled, emerging into the teeth of a wind that bit like razor blades. The lox jockey had lit a torch, and this he passed to the Prelate.

Yarrek stared about him. The mountainside reared overhead, so sheer he was forced to crane his neck to make out the jagged peaks high above. He peered into the cutting Zeremy had mentioned and saw a jagged rent like the mouth of a cave.

Prelate Zeremy led the way, torch aloft, its flame flagging in the wind. They passed into the cave and deeper, the slit narrowing so that they were forced to squeeze between vertical planes of rock. Five minutes later the corridor widened and he saw that the slabs of natural rock had been replaced by obviously man-made squares of stone.

Zeremy halted before him, and indicated a flight of stone steps that disappeared down into the darkness.

Yarrek found his voice at last, and was ashamed by the note of fear that made it quaver. "Where... where does this lead?"

"This is the way my sons ventured, five cycles ago," the Prelate said. "I have been here only once before. We are following in their footsteps, and will behold soon what they discovered."

He began the steep descent, and Yarrek followed.

There was something odd about the steps, he soon realized. The treads were too high for comfortable descent; his stepping foot dropped too far, and his standing leg almost gave way before he made contact with the step below.

Perhaps thirty minutes later, the muscles of his calves paining him as if slit by knives, Yarrek was relieved when Zeremy came to a halt. They seemed to have hit a dead end. Before them was a great square of what at first looked like rock—though as Zeremy stepped forward, and the light of the torch played across its surface, Yarrek saw that it was not rock but some silver substance like metal.

Zeremy reached out, and miraculously the slab of metal slid aside to reveal a tiny, featureless room.

They stepped inside, and Yarrek was startled to hear the metal door swish shut behind him. His surprise was compounded when a lurching motion punched his stomach into the cavity of his chest, and he yelped aloud.

Zeremy could not help but smile. "We are descending through miles of rock at great speed," the Prelate pronounced. "The technology which bears us is far in advance of our own."

Yarrek nodded, though understanding had fled long ago. He could only hold his stomach and guess at what other wonders might lay ahead.

Minutes later the room stopped falling with a sudden, bobbing lurch, and before him the metal wall slid open.

This time Yarrek found himself frozen on the threshold, unable to take the step that would carry him into the chamber.

Behind him, Zeremy said gently, "Go on, you have nothing to fear," and placed a hand on Yarrek's shoulder, and eased him firmly forward.

They were in a vast chamber or auditorium, bigger than any Yarrek had ever experienced, or thought possible might have existed. It had been constructed, and was not a natural cavern in the rock, for the curving walls were of metal, ribbed like the inside of some great cathedral. He felt like a fly as he stepped forward, timorously, into the immensity of the yawning dome.

"Where are we?" he whispered. "What is this?"

A hand still on Yarrek's shoulder, Zeremy steered him toward what appeared to be a rectangular plate set into the side of the dome. As they approached, the plate slid aside to be replaced by a vast window, a plate of clear glass as wide as an Icefast building was tall.

Yarrek stared, but was unable to make sense of the scene revealed.

They moved closer, until they were standing at its very ledge. Beyond the glass was an enormity of darkness, at its center a whorl of glowing light.

"What is it?" Yarrek asked in a tiny voice.

Zeremy said, "You are about to be given the explanation that, five cycles ago, my sons were privy to, and myself not long after that. Behold."

Yarrek turned in the direction Zeremy indicated. Between where they stood and the door through which they had entered the chamber, a strange and silent figure had materialised.

"Do not fear," Zeremy said in a whisper. "For all its appearance, it is not hostile."

Yarrek nodded, evincing valour he did not feel.

The creature was hairless, with an emaciated, naked body supported in some kind of floating carriage; it was not the emaciated state of the being that so shocked Yarrek nor its nakedness, but the size of its cranium, supported by padded rests on either side of the carriage. Its head was almost the length of its body, a great bulbous pink dome threaded with veins, at its center a collection of tiny features that seemed pinched and mean: two tiny eyes, a thin nose, and lips like a bloodless hyphen.

"Welcome," it said in a croak.

"It speaks our language!" Yarrek said.

The creature's lips lengthened in what might have been a smile. "You have come so far, and we hope that you will take what you will learn back to your people."

Zeremy stepped forward. Yarrek hesitated, and the Prelate murmured, "Fear not, for the creature is but some kind of clever projection. A ghost, if you like—not flesh and blood as you and I."

Not comprehending, nevertheless Yarrek did not want to be parted from the Prelate, and hurried to his side.

They stood before the creature as it bobbed in its metal carriage, and Yarrek was amazed to see that, somehow, he could discern the outline of the entrance *through* the being's pink nakedness.

"You deserve an explanation for having ventured so far, and having witnessed so much that must be incomprehensible to you."

"What is this place?" Yarrek asked.

"You are at the very edge of the Ark," the feeble creature announced.

Yarrek shook his head and echoed, "The Ark?"

"Your world," the creature explained, "is but one of a thousand such worlds ranked side by side, like coins along the length of a tube. In each world a different race exists, examples of the thousand races which once inhabited the universe."

Yarrek glanced at Zeremy, as if for explanation, but the Prelate had closed his eyes, a serene smile upon his lips.

Sunworld is but one of many—like a coin in the barrel of a gun? His senses reeled.

The emaciated being went on, "Hundreds of millennia ago, we began the process of salvation, moving through space from planet to planet..." The creature gave its thin-lipped smile again. "But the concepts I describe are of course alien to you. The universe, space, planets, even millennia..." It lifted a weak arm and gestured. "Beyond the viewscreen is the universe, a vast emptiness scattered with galaxies, each comprising millions of stars, and around the stars, planets, worlds like your own world, though existing on the outside of spheroids of rock and earth."

Yarrek felt dizzy. He stepped forward, surprising himself. "The process of salvation?" he said. "Why did you collect us like animals in a zoo?"

The creature stretched its hyphen lips. "The analogy is valid," it said. "We collected races that were on the cusp of extinction, races torn by futile enmity, which we feared might perish but for our intervention. The history of the universe is that of races coming to sentience and destroying themselves in needless warfare. We could not allow that to happen."

"And then," Zeremy said, "you engineered our society away from such warlike tendencies."

"When we had installed you safely abroad the Ark," the creature said, "we sent agents amongst you to effect such results."

Yarrek wondered then if these agents were the angels of yore, who allegedly had founded the Church. What irony if that were so—the formation of a Church that might have brought about lasting peace but which, over millennia, had fossilized to the point of denying the existence of the Ark...

The creature continued, "The experiment, if you wish to call it that, has been deemed successful. Now we can commence the next step of the programme."

"Which is?" Yarrek asked.

"The time has almost arrived to seed the planets again, to empty the Ark of its precious cargo and allow the races, now hopefully improved, to evolve as they will."

"You are playing God," Yarrek said.

The creature inclined its head. "If you wish to use that term, then so be it. We are playing God, in order to save and perpetuate these races." It gestured, and all around the creature, stretching back towards the walls of the cavern, a great crowd of beings appeared, insubstantial as ghosts.

Yarrek stared, taking in beings of every conceivable size and shape. He saw creatures like crabs, and four-legged beasts like lox, and things that resembled kite-fish floating in the air, and great birds, and bipedal hairless individuals with domed skulls...

And then he saw, in the silent crowd, tall, furred creatures like his own people, though more elongated of limb, and gray instead of brown...

The naked pink being went on, "We are the Controllers, my friends, though once we called ourselves humans. Our intention was not to wield the power of God, but to empower others to evolve peacefully, to inhabit planets in harmony with nature and with themselves."

"But when will that be?" Yarrek asked, wondering what it might be like to stand on the *surface* of what the creature called a planet.

The human gestured to the viewscreen. "The time has almost arrived to seed the cosmos. Perhaps, in a hundred of your cycles, the races of the Ark will be ready and the process can begin."

A hundred cycles...? He would be an old man then, Yarrek thought, if he lived to see the wondrous event. Oh, he could not wait to return to the Hub, and tell Yancy of his find, blind Yancy who had always been more far-sighted than himself.

"Now go," said the human, "and inform your people of what awaits them."

And so saying, the manifestation of the enfeebled creature, and the host of the saved, vanished in an instant.

Yarrek turned to Zeremy. To his surprise the Prelate was weeping.

"But you were aware of the truth, sir," Yarrek said, "and yet you did not tell the world."

"When my sons told me of what they had discovered," the Prelate said, "I thought that it would be they who would tell the world... but of course that was not to be. I had to wait, then, until..."

Yarrek stared at the old man, awareness slowly dawning. "Until?"

In reply, Prelate Zeremy laid a loving hand on Yarrek's shoulder and steered him towards the exit. "Come, my son. Together now we have a duty to tell the world the truth."

And Yarrek, bearing a freight of understanding greater than the mere fact of a race saved from itself, made his slow way back through the rock and ice to Sunworld and the task awaiting him there.

Evil Robot Monkey

Mary Robinette Kowal

SLIDING HIS HANDS over the clay, Sly relished the moisture oozing around his fingers. The clay matted down the hair on the back of his hands, making them look almost human. He turned the potter's wheel with his prehensile feet as he shaped the vase. Pinching the clay between his fingers, he lifted the wall of the vase, spinning it higher.

Someone banged on the window of his pen. Sly jumped and then screamed as the vase collapsed under its own weight. He spun and hurled it at the picture window like feces. The clay spattered against the Plexiglas, sliding down the window.

In the courtyard beyond the glass, a group of school kids leapt back, laughing. One of them swung his arms, aping Sly crudely. Sly bared his teeth, knowing these people would take it as a grin, but he meant it as a threat. He swung down from his stool, crossed his room in three long strides and pressed his dirty hand against the window. Still grinning, he wrote: SSA. Outside, the letters would be reversed.

The students' teacher flushed as red as a female in heat and called the children away from the window. She looked back once as she led them out of the courtyard, so Sly grabbed himself and showed her what he would do if she came into his pen.

Her naked face turned brighter red and she hurried away. When they were gone, Sly rested his head against the glass. The metal in his skull thunked against the window. It wouldn't be long now before a handler came to talk to him.

Damn.

He just wanted to make pottery. He loped back to the wheel and sat down again with his back to the window. Kicking the wheel into movement, Sly dropped a new ball of clay in the center and tried to lose himself.

In the corner of his vision, the door to his room snicked open. Sly let the wheel spin to a halt, crumpling the latest vase.

Vern poked his head through. He signed, "You okay?"

Sly shook his head emphatically and pointed at the window.

"Sorry." Vern's hands danced. "We should have warned you that they were coming."

"You should have told them that I was not an animal."

Vern looked down in submission. "I did. They're kids."

"And I'm a chimp. I know." Sly buried his fingers in the clay to silence his thoughts.

"It was Delilah. She thought you wouldn't mind because the other chimps didn't."

Sly scowled and yanked his hands free. "I'm not like the other chimps." He pointed to the implant in his head. "Maybe Delilah should have one of these Seems like she needs help thinking."

"I'm sorry." Vern knelt in front of Sly, closer than anyone else would come when he wasn't sedated. It would be so easy to reach out and snap his neck. "It was a lousy thing to do."

Sly pushed the clay around on the wheel. Vern was better than the others. He seemed to understand the hellish limbo where Sly lived—too smart to be with other chimps, but too much of an animal to be with humans. Vern was the one who had brought Sly the potter's wheel which, by the Earth and Trees, Sly loved. Sly looked up and raised his eyebrows. "So what did they think of my show?"

Vern covered his mouth, masking his smile. The man had manners. "The teacher was upset about the 'evil robot monkey.'"

Sly threw his head back and hooted. Served her right.

"But Delilah thinks you should be disciplined." Vern, still so close that Sly could reach out and break him, stayed very still. "She wants me to take the clay away since you used it for an anger display."

Sly's lips drew back in a grimace built of anger and fear. Rage threatened to blind him, but he held on, clutching the wheel. If he lost it with Vern—rational thought danced out of his reach. Panting, he spun the wheel, trying to push his anger into the clay.

The wheel spun. Clay slid between his fingers. Soft. Firm and smooth. The smell of earth lived in his nostrils. He held the world in his hands. Turning, turning, the walls rose around a kernel of anger, subsuming it.

His heart slowed with the wheel and Sly blinked, becoming aware again as if he were slipping out of sleep. The vase on the wheel still seemed to dance with life. Its walls held the shape of the world within them. He passed a finger across the rim.

Vern's eyes were moist. "Do you want me to put that in the kiln for you?"

Sly nodded.

"I have to take the clay. You understand that, don't you."

Sly nodded again, staring at his vase. It was beautiful.

Vern scowled. "The woman makes *me* want to hurl feces."

Sly snorted at the image, then sobered. "How long before I get it back?"

Vern picked up the bucket of clay next to the wheel. "I don't know." He stopped at the door and looked past Sly to the window. "I'm not cleaning your mess. Do you understand me?"

For a moment, rage crawled on his spine, but Vern did not meet his eyes and kept staring at the window. Sly turned.

The vase he had thrown lay on the floor in a pile of clay.

Clay.

"I understand." He waited until the door closed, then loped over and scooped the clay up. It was not much, but it was enough for now.

Sly sat down at his wheel and began to turn.

Shining Armor

Dominic Green

IT WAS CLOSE to dawn. The sun was a sliver of brilliance just visible over the mass of canyons on the western horizon. There was no reason why the direction in which the sun rose should not be arbitrarily defined as East; the only reason why the sun rose in the West on this planet was that, if looked at from the same galactic direction as Earth, it span retrograde. Even at this number of light years' distance, men still had an apron-string connecting them to their homeworld.

The old man was still doing his exercises.

The boy didn't know why the exercises had to take so long. They didn't look hard to do, although when he tried to copy them, the old man laughed as if he were doing them in the most ridiculous manner possible. The old man used a sword while he did the exercises, but not even a real one—it had no edge and was made of aluminium, which could not even be made to take one. He held the sword-stick ridiculously, not even using his whole hand most of the time; usually he held it with only his middle finger and forefinger, some of the time with only the little and ring fingers. Both of his hands, in fact, were held in a peculiar crab claw, with the fingers separated.

Finally there were signs that the old man was coming to the end of the set, stabbing around to right and left with his stick. The boy now had something to do. He scurried out among the rusting steel shells, carrying the basket of fruit. It was, of course, spoiled fruit, fruit the old man would not have been able to sell at market. There would have been no point in wasting saleable produce.

The boy arranged a marrow to the west, a pineapple to the east, a durian to the north, and a big juicy watermelon to the south. Each piece of fruit sat on its own square of rice paper. He was careful to leave the empty basket in a spot where it would not interfere with the old man's movements. Then, just as his elder and better was turning into his final movement, facing into the sun as it blazed up into the sky, the boy ran to the long, half-buried shelf the old man called the dead hulk's "glacis plate" and unwrapped the Real Sword.

The Real Sword was taller than he was. He had been instructed to unwrap it carefully. The old man had illustrated why by dropping a playing card onto the blade. The card had stuck fast, its weight driving the blade a good half centimeter into it.

The old man bowed to the sun—why? Did it ever bow back?—walked over to the sword, nodded stiffly to the boy, and picked up the weapon. He executed a few practice cuts and parries, jumping backwards and forwards across the sand. This was more exciting—he was moving quickly now, with a sword of spring steel.

Then he became almost motionless; the sword whipped up into a position of readiness up above his head. As always, he was directly between all four pieces of fruit. Sometimes there were five pieces of fruit, sometimes six or seven.

The sword moved up and down, one, two, three, four times, the old man lashing out at all quarters, turning on his heel on the sand. There were four soft tearing sounds, but no sparks or sounds of metal hitting metal.

The old man stood upright, ready to slide the sword back into a nonexistent scabbard. He had lost the scabbard somehow years ago. Nobody seemed to know how, and nobody could convince him to shell out the money for a new one.

He walked over to inspect the fruit. All four now lay in two pieces, making eight pieces. In all four cases, the cut had been deep enough to completely halve the fruit right down to the rind. In not one case had the rice paper underneath been touched. In some, the old man's activities had cut the rot clean out of the fruit. The boy gathered up the good pieces, which would now be breakfast.

The rotten pieces he slung away into the desert.

* * *

WHEN THEY WALKED back toward the village, the General Alarm was sounding. This, the boy knew, could be very bad, as no alarm practice was scheduled for today.

General Alarm could mean that another boy like him had fallen down a melt-hole like a damned fool and the whole village was out looking for his corpsicle. Or it could mean that a flash flood was on the way and every homeowner had to rush out and bolt the streamliner onto the north end of his habitat, then rush back in and dog all the hatches. It might mean a flare had been reported, and everyone except Mad Farmer Bob who carried on digging his ditches in all weathers despite skin cancer and radiation alopoecia had to go underground till the All Clear.

But it was clear, when they reached the outskirts of the village, that this was none of these things. There was a personal conveyor in the Civic Square, its green lights flashing to indicate it had been set to automatic guidance. Someone had used a towing cable to secure three long, irregular, wet red shapes to the back of it, shapes the grown-ups would not let him see. But he had a horrible idea what they were, or what they had once been. Dragging your enemy behind a conveyor was a *badabing-badaboum* thing to do, and normally the boys in the village would have run and jostled to see such a marvellous sight. But when the men who had been dragged, probably alive, were Mr. d'Souza, big friendly Mr. d'Souza who had three hairy Irish wolfhounds; and Mr. Bamigboye, who told rude jokes about naked ladies; and even Mr. Chundi, who told kids to get off his property—then things did not seem so exciting.

Mr. d'Souza, Mr. Bamigboye, and Mr. Chundi were Town Councillors, and they had gone up to the Big City to argue with the authorities about the mining site. Although there was nothing there now but a few spray-painted rocks and prospectors' transponders, the boy knew that some Big City men had found rocks they called Radioactives upriver. But the boy's father said the Big City men were too lazy to dig the rocks out of the ground using shovels and the Honest Sweat Of Their Brow. Instead, they planned to build a sifting plant downstream of the village, and set off bombs also made of Radioactives in the regolith upstream. A handsome stream of Radioactives would flow downriver to the sifting plant, but the village's water would be poisoned. The villagers had all been offered what were described as "generous offers" to leave by the Big City men, but the Town Councillors had voted to stay. The Big City men had been rumored to be hiring a top Persuasion Consultancy to deal with the situation. Now it seemed that the rumors had come true.

"We ought to take a few guns into town and sort out those City folk," said old father Magnusson, who thought everyone didn't know he ordered sex pheromones and illegal subliminal messaging software through the mail from Big City, but Aunt Raisa knew. Now no woman in town would visit him or call him on the videophone.

"How many guns do we have? And small-bore ones, too, for seeing off interlopers, not armor-piercing stuff. The combine bosses will be protected by men in armor, ten feet tall, with magnetic accelerators that shoot off a million rounds through you POW-POW-POW before you pop your first round off! You are maximally insane." This was old mother Tho. Despite her insulting mode of communication, many of the older and wiser heads in the square nodded their agreement.

"Don't be ridiculous," said Mother Murdo. "Magnetic accelerators are illegal."

"Anything illegal is legal if nobody is prepared to enforce the law. Have you not been up to the City recently? The mining combines have been making their own militaria for months. After they had to start making their own machine tools and coining their own money, weapons were the logical next step."

"But we are still citizens of the Commonwealth of Man," said Father Magnusson, drawing himself up to his full one hundred and thirty-five centimeters, "and an attack on us would be an attack on the Commonwealth itself."

"Pshaw! The Commonwealth doesn't even bother to send out ships to collect taxes any longer," said Mother Tho. "And when the taxman doesn't call, you *know* the government is in disrepair."

There were slow nods of appreciation from the crowd, most of whom were secretly glad that the tribute ships had not visited for so many years, but all of whom were alarmed at the prospect that those ships might have funded services whose unavailability might now kill the village.

"Well, in any case," said Father Magnusson, "if they dare to come up *here* and attempt their person-dragging activities, the State will repel them instantly."

Mother Tho was unimpressed. "We must be pragmatic," she said. "The Guardian has not moved for sixty Good Old Original Standard Years. Not since the last Barbarian incursion."

Father Magnusson smacked his lips stolidly. "But I remember when it last moved; it operated most satisfactorily on that occasion. The Barbarians' ships filled the skies like locusts, but our Guardian was equal to them."

Mother Tho looked up into the sky, where the silhouette of the Guardian took a huge bite out of the sunrise. "Father, you are only one of perhaps two or three people still alive who remember the Guardian moving. And it is a machine. Machines rust, corrode, and biodegrade."

"The Guardian was built to last forever."

"But a Guardian also needs an operator. And where is ours?"

The old man put a hand upon the boy's shoulder and moved away among the buildings before the conversation grew more heated.

"THERE ARE FOREIGNERS in the village," said the boy's mother, folding clothes with infinite precision. "Men from the mining company. They are asking for Khan by name, and you know why, old man."

The old man tucked the sword away in a crevice by the side of the atmosphere detoxifier. "Khan can look after himself."

"They had guns, by all accounts, and you know he can't." The boy's mother ran the iron over a fresh set of clothes. "Khan is fat and slow and has long since ceased to be any use in a fight. It isn't fair for him to be put through this." She looked up at the old man. "Something must be done."

The old man looked away. "They have heard the name Khan, heard that this Khan is the man who is our Guardian's operator. They perhaps mean harm. I will radio Khan and tell him to stay out fixing watercourses and not return home until these men have gone. They will be listening, of course. This will inform them that their task is pointless, and then maybe they will leave."

"Or they will go out and search the watercourses till they find him."

"Khan knows the watercourses, and is more resourceful than you give him credit for. They will not find him."

"Khan is not as young as he once was. It will be cold tonight. You think that just because people are not as old as you, they are striplings who can accomplish anything."

"I think nothing of the sort, woman. Now boil me some water. I have a revitalizing tea to prepare for Mother Murdo's *fin-de-siècle ennui*."

Khan's mother gathered up the heap of ironing and made her way out of the kitchen, past the floor maintenance robot. "Boil your own water, and lower your underparts into it."

In order to defuse a family quarrel, the boy walked across the kitchen and turned on the water heater himself. He could not, however, meet the old man's eyes. Khan was, after all, his father.

THE NEXT MORNING, underneath the Guardian's metal legs, there was a gaggle of young men jostling for position.

"*I* will save the village!"

"You are wrong! It will be I!"

"No, I!"

The boy, who was running the flask of tea to Mother Murdo, saw Mother Tho rap three of them on the occiput with her walnut-wood staff in quick succession.

"Fools! Loblollies! What would you do, if you were even able to gain access to the Guardian's control cabin?" She pointed upward with her polyethylene ferrule at the ladder that led up the Guardian's right leg, with a dizzying number of rungs, up to the tiny hatch in its Under Bridge Area where a normal person's back body would be. Once, the boy had climbed all those rungs and touched the hatch with his hand for a bet before being dragged down by his father, who told him not to tamper with Commonwealth property. His father had had hair then, and much of it had been dark.

"If I gained access," swaggered the most audacious of the three, "I would march to the Big City and trample the mining syndicate buildings beneath boots of iron." He blew kisses to those girls of marriageable age who had gathered to watch.

"*If* you gained access!" repeated the old witch, and grabbed him by the nose. "YOU WOULD NEVER GAIN ACCESS! Only the Guardian's operator has a key, and it is synchronised to his genetic code. You would do nothing but sit staring up at a big metal arse until the cold froze you off the ladder."

"OW! Bedder dat dan allow our iddibidual vreedods do be sudgugaded!" protested the putative loblolly.

Mother Tho let the young man go. She wiped her fingers on her grubby shawl.

"Our Guardian will defend us when its operator is ready," she intoned.

A voice chipped in across the crowd: "Our Guardian's operator is too feeble."

The boy shrank back behind a battery of heat sinks and hid his face.

"It's true!" yelled another voice. "The company assassins turned out the whole of Mr. Wu's drinking establishment and threatened to shoot all its clientele one by one until Khan was turned over to them. In his confusion and concern for his customers, Wu turned over the wrong Khan, Khan the undertaker, and they killed him instantly. His tongue lolled out of his face like a frosted pickle. When the company men find the real Khan and kill him, there will be no trained professional to bury him."

"There are men in the village with guns?" said one of the bold youngsters, removing his thumbs from his belt and staring at his contemporaries with a face of horror.

"Ha!" gloated Mother Tho. "So our bravos are not quite so audacious when faced with the prospect of their skins actually being broken."

The boy dropped his cargo of tea and ran for home.

HOME PROVED TO be more difficult to get to than usual. The boy followed the path most usually followed by children through the village, disregarding the streets and ducking under the support struts of the houses. Had crows been able to fly in this atmosphere instead of expiring exhausted after a few tottering flutters, he would have been travelling as the crow flew.

However, there was a problem. A small group of boys were holed up under the belly of Mother Tho's house, whispering deafeningly, fancifully imagining they were Seeing without Beeing Seen. But the boy was not afraid of other boys—at least, not as much as he was afraid of the men in the street who were tolerating Being Seen.

It was quite rare for children to be playing on the streets now. Their mothers were keeping them indoors. It was hoped that the Persuasion Consultancy assassins had not realized their mistake and would be happy with having disabled the village's (admittedly one hundred percent lethal) corpse-burying capabilities.

However, it seemed the assassins were not content with simple murder. They were standing in the street outside the house of Khan the undertaker, above which a grainy holographic angel flickered in the breeze. Not content with having murdered the under-taker's unburied corpse, the men had turned out the contents of his funeral emporium, headstones-in-progress and all, into the street. They were searching the whole pile of morbid paraphernalia with microscopic thoroughness, while his widow screamed and hurled such violent abuse as the poor woman knew. The boy could only conclude that onyx-look polymer angels were of great value to them.

"They are searching for our Guardian's access key," hissed one of the watchers in a strict confidence that carried all the way to the boy's ears.

"Only the Operator has the access key," said another boy. "Was Khan the Operator?"

"No," said a third. "I think it was Khan the farmer."

"Khan, a warrior? He is a fat little fruit seller."

"Operators are not chosen for their physical strength," said the third boy contemptuously. "The servomechanisms of the Guardian provide that. Operators are chosen for the extreme precision of their physical movements. It is said that the opera-tor of the Guardian of the Gate of the City of Governance back on Earth was so precise in his motions that he was able to grip a normal human paintbrush between his Guardian's claws and inscribe the Rights and Duties of Citizens on the pavement in letters only three meters high."

The boy ducked under the hull of the nearest building and took a dog-leg to a habitat to the south before any Persuasion Consultancy men could engage him in conversation.

IT WAS SUNSET. The sun was setting in the East.

The old man was sitting, dozing, pretending to be absorbed in serious meditation. The boy walked up and pointedly slammed down the basket on a nearby ruined Barbarian war machine, pretending not to notice the old man starting as if he had been jumped on by a tiger.

"I have brought everything," said the boy. "Father is still at large. The assassins are reputed to be pursuing him along the north arroyo."

The old man nodded and sucked his teeth in a repulsive manner. "Did you bring the weapons from underneath the loose slab in the conveyor garage?"

The boy nodded. "There is no need to conceal these weapons," he sniffed. "It is not illegal to possess them, and surely they can be of no intrinsic value."

The old man ran his hand along the bow as he lifted it from the bundle and grinned. "There was also a picture of your grandmother underneath that slab," he said. "That is also of little intrinsic value."

"I never knew my grandmother," said the boy.

"Think yourself lucky," said the old man grumpily, "that *I* did." He set an arrow—the only arrow in the bundle—to the bow, and began trying to bend it, frowning as his hands shook with the effort.

"OLD MAN," called a voice. "STOP PLAYING AT SOLDIERS. WE DEMAND TO KNOW WHERE KHAN IS."

The bow collapsed. The arrow quivered into the dirt. The old man turned round. From the direction of the village three young men, muscles big from digging ditches and lifting baskets, had strolled in to the clearing between the destroyed military machines. The boy realized with a sinking heart that he had been followed.

"My father," said their leader, "says that Khan is the operator of our Guardian."

The old man nodded. "True enough."

"Then why is he hiding outside the village like a thief?" The youngster threw his hand out towards the horizon. "Not only are there murderers in our midst, but an army is gathering on our doorstep. Employees of a Persuasion Consultancy engaged by the mining combine have arrived. They have delivered an ultimatum to the effect that if the combine's generous terms are not accepted by sunrise tomorrow, they will evacuate the village using minimum force." He licked his lips nervously. "Scouts have been out, and the consultancy's definition of 'minimum force' appears to extend to fragmentation bombs and vehicle-seeking missiles."

The old man's face sunk into even more wrinkles than was normally its wont. "Khan," he said, "hides nowhere. Who here says that Khan hides?" Despite the fact that he was armed only with a bamboo bow and arrows, none of the young men present would meet his eyes.

"Father, we have the greatest respect for your age. None of us would dare to strike a weak and defenceless old man. We simply wish to know when, if at all, our Operator intends to discharge his duty."

The old man nodded.

"Weak and defenceless, you say."

He slung out the bow at the spokesman of the group, who the boy believed was called Lokman. It whirled in the air and struck Lokman in the jaw. Lokman rubbed the side of his face, complaining bitterly, but still his manners were too correct to allow him to attack his elders.

"Pick the bow up," said the old man. He grubbed in the dirt for the arrow and tossed it to Lokman. "Now notch the arrow and pull the bow back as hard as you like." He did not rise from his sitting position.

Lokman shrugged and heaved hard on the bow. It was an effort even for him, the boy noticed. The bow was almost as stiff as a roof-tile.

"Point the bow at me," said the old man, grinning, "you purulent stream of cat excrement."

Lokman's hands were shaking on the bow too now. It rotated round to point at the old man.

"Now fire!" said the old man. "*I said FIRE, you worthless spawn of a mining company executive—*"

"No, DON'T—" said the boy.

The string twanged free. The boy did not even see the arrow move. Nor did he see the old man's hand move. But when both hand and arrow blurred back into position, the one was in the other: the hand holding the arrow, rather than the arrow being embedded in the hand.

Lokman stared at the old man's hand for a second; then he snorted.

"A useful parlour trick," he said. "Can you do it against missiles?"

He threw down the bow and walked away.

"Khan is a coward who will not fight," he said over his shoulder. "Besides, he could not get to the Guardian even if he wished. The assassins have the access ladder under guard. Pack up your things and leave, old man. The Councillors are leaving. We are *all* leaving. We are finished."

The old man watched the visitors leave. Then he reached into the bundle where a battered oblong of black plastic lay alongside the picture of the boy's grandmother. In the plastic were embossed the letters: KHAN 63007248.

"It is good," said the old man. "You have made sure Khan has everything he needs."

The old man hung the oblong round his neck on a chain that pierced it, and felt his throat to make sure it was not visible as it hung.

"What time did they say the ultimatum expired tomorrow?" he asked, without looking at the boy.

"Sunup," said the boy.

"It is good," said the old man. "There is time. Run back to the village with these things, and return quickly. Then you shall accompany me while I deliver these troublemakers an ultimatum of our own."

"Why am I going with you?" said the boy.

"Because no man will shoot an old man," said the old man, "unless he is a wicked man indeed. But even a wicked man will not shoot an old man accompanied by a small boy—unless, of course, he is a *very* wicked man indeed." He grinned, and his grin was more gaps than teeth. "This, I must admit, is the only flaw in my plan."

Then he returned to his meditation, as if nothing had either happened or was about to. The boy seriously suspected he was sleeping.

THE SUN HAD set, and the reg had ceased to be its accustomed thousand shades of khaki. Now, it was the color of a world plunged underwater to a depth where every shade of anything became a democratic twilight blue.

The boy followed the old man uncertainly across the regolith towards a group of Persuasion Consultants lounging around an alcohol burner in the shadow of an APC. Even the burner's flame was blue, as if carefully coordinated to fit in with the night. The Consultants noticed the old man long before he began to jump up and down and wave his arms to get their attention, but the boy noticed that it was only at this point that they relaxed and began the laborious process of putting the safeties back on their weapons.

"Hey! Ugly Boy! Take me to your ugly leader!"

None of the Persuasion Consultants answered. Evidently none of them was willing to own up to the name of Ugly Boy.

"Suit yourselves, physically unprepossessing persons, but be informed that I bear a message from Khan."

The men began to fidget indecisively in their dapper uniforms. Eventually, one spoke up and said:

"If you are in communication with Khan, you must give us information on his whereabouts, citizen, or it will go poorly with you."

The old man scoffed. The boy was not entirely sure it was prudent to scoff in the presence of so much firepower. "You still do not know Khan's whereabouts? With the man right under your nose, and so many complex tracking systems in that khaki jalopy you are leaning against? For shame! Khan has a message for you. You must vacate the environs of this village, or as the appointed operator of the Guardian of this colony he will be obliged to make you quit by main force."

The spokesman crossed both hands over his rifle. "Your Guardian's operator is taking sides unjustifiedly in a purely civil matter, citizen. This is not a military matter. For this reason, Beauchef and Grisnez Incorporated regrets that, on behalf of its clients, it is forced to take action to eliminate this unruly operator, and that this action will continue until he quits the village. We are also making initial seismic surveys preliminary to placing charges underneath the Guardian's foundations, destroying the underground geegaws that charge it. Beauchef and Grisnez of course regrets the damage to Commonwealth property concomitant to this strategy, but final blame for this unfortunate state of affairs lies at the head of the operator concerned. That is *our* message, which you may convey to Khan."

The old man stood facing the line of soldiers silently for several seconds.

"Very well," he said. "Despite the fact that you behave like barbarians, you continue to describe yourselves as Commonwealth citizens and hence merit a warning in law. You have received that warning. Whatever consequences follow, Khan will not be answerable." He turned and trudged back in the direction of the village.

There were sniggers from the line of riflemen.

THE BOY'S MOTHER woke him well before dawn. She had already prepared sleeping gear for all of them, together with food she had irradiated that same morning. It would keep for a month, as well as making the boy's stomach turn when he ate it. This was the sort of food City people had to eat.

"But aren't we staying to defend the village?"

He got a slap for that one. Mother was in no mood to talk. She was crying softly as she walked round the rooms of the habitat, picking things up, putting things down, deciding which of the pieces of her life she was going to take with her and which she was going to leave behind forever. He threw his arms around her, and this time she did not slap him.

"Go out and fetch the old one," she said. "Where is he? I've prepared the conveyor. We have to leave."

The boy told his mother that the old man had said he was going to do his exercises and that, on this particular morning, the boy was not allowed to accompany him.

The boy's mother's eyes flew open in horror. She looked out of the window, which showed sand billowing down a dusty street.

She stood still a moment, as though paralyzed. Then she grabbed his arm.

"Come with me."

They walked out to the edge of the village. The village was small. It was not a long walk. Out there at the very edge of the sun farms, beyond a hectare or so of jet-black solar collectors, the wrecked battle machines of the Barbarians sat rusting in the sand.

What are Barbarians? the boy had asked his teacher once in class. And the answer had been quick and pat. Why, people from outside the Commonwealth, of course. *Any* people from outside the Commonwealth.

The machines sat at what the boy knew to have been the extreme limit of the Guardian's target acquisition range, sixty years ago.

Of the old man, there was no sign.

"Stupid old fool," said mother, and pulled the boy off down the village streets again. She seemed to know where she was going. Only two streets, two rows of gleaming aluminium-steel habitats, and the old man came into view. Standing in the square at the Guardian's habitat-sized feet, he was arguing with a pair of Consultancy men, armored troopers holding guns that could track the electrical emissions of a man's heartbeat in the dark and shoot him dead through steel.

He was carrying a sword.

"But I always do my exercises in the square at this time," the old man said, which was a lie.

"You are carrying a weapon, grandfather," said one of the Consultants gently, "which I am forced to regard as a potential threat, despite your advanced years."

The old man looked from hand to hand, then held up the sword as if he had only just realized it was there. "This? Why, but this is only an old sword-shaped piece of aluminium. It cannot even be made to take an edge."

"All the same," said the Consultant persuasively, "out of deference to the tense situation in which we find ourselves, it would be safer if—"

"HOI!"

The shout broke the polite silence in the town square. Five heads turned towards it. As the sun heaved its head over the southern horizon, a figure staggered into town out of the desert. It waved its arms.

"HOI! It's me, Khan! Khan, the man you're looking for! Catch me if you can!"

Guns rose instantaneously to shoulders. Khan dived for cover. How useful that cover was was debatable, as a line of projectile explosions stitched its way across the wall of the nearest habitat like a finger tearing through tinfoil. When the guns had finished tracking across the building, the building was two buildings, one balanced precariously on top of the other, radiator coolant gushing from the walls and electrical connections sparking.

Hopefully no one was sitting headless at breakfast within it. The Consultancy men were already spreading out round the habitat, hoping to outflank their target if he had somehow survived the first attack. The boy's mother looked on, appalled.

Some caprice, however, drew the boy's attention upward.

The old man was on the inside leg of the metal colossus, on the access ladder, moving with dinosaurian slowness towards the Guardian's bumward access hatch.

The boy's jaw dropped.

Meanwhile, the men who were guarding the Guardian seemed on the point of following Khan and finishing him, until one of them remembered his orders, waved his comrade back to the square, pulled a communicator from one of his ammunition pouches, opened it, spoke into it, and flipped it shut again. Someone Else, he told his comrade, Could Do The Running.

Up above, the old man was still moving, but with the speed of evolution, at the speed glass flowed down windowpanes, at the speed boys grew up doorposts. He had not even reached the knee. Surely, before the old fool reached the top of his climb, somebody in the village underneath had to notice? And what did he think he'd accomplish if he got up the ladder?

The two Consultants reassumed their positions underneath the Guardian's treads. They stood on the square of concrete, reaching all the way down through the regolith to the bedrock that had been put there solely as a foundation for the vehicle to stand on. They faced outwards, willing to bleed good red blood to stop anyone who tried to get past them. One of them even remarked on the old man's sword discarded in the sand, saying that they Must Have Frit The Old Coot Away.

Meanwhile, by pretending to scratch his eye against the dust, the boy was able to see the old coot pull a battered slab of black plastic from his tunic and slide it into what the boy knew—from the climb he had been dared to do a year ago—to be a recess in the circular ass-end access hatch about the same size as the slab. The hatch was also spray-painted with the letters AUGMENTED INFANTRY UNIT MK 73 (1 OFF), and only members of the privileged club of boys who had taken the dare and made the climb knew it.

Something glittered like a rack of unsheathed blades in the Guardian's normally dull and pitted skin; the old man skimmed his fingers over the glitter rapidly and the boy saw blood ooze out of his fingers onto the hatch cover momentarily, before the surface drank it like a vampire.

The key was tuned to the operator's genetic code. The vehicle had to have a part of him to know who he was.

The hatch slid into the structure silently. The old man began to slip into the hole it had opened. But for all the wondrous silence of the mechanism, the old man was unable to prevent the boy's mother from standing with her head in the air gawping like a newly-hatched chick waiting to be fed worms. And as she gawped, the guards gawped with her.

Luckily for the old man, the guards also took a couple of moments to do helpless baby chick impersonations before remembering they had weapons and were supposed to use them. The hatch had slid shut before they could get their guns to their shoulders, take aim, and fire. They were not used to firing their weapons in that position and the recoil, coming from an unaccustomed direction, blew them about on the spot like unattended pneumatic drills. The boy saw stars twinkle on the Guardian's hide. He was not sure whether they had inflicted any damage or not; the detonations left a mass of afterimages on his retinas.

The two men could not have inflicted *too* much damage, however, as they thought better of continuing to shoot and instead stood back and contemplated the crotch of the colossus.

For one long minute, nothing happened. The lead Consultant spoke quietly but urgently into his communicator, saying that he Wasn't Quite Sure Whether Or Not The Shit Indicator Had Just Risen To Nostril Deep.

Then the dust under the left tread of the Guardian moaned like a man being put to the press. The boy looked up to see the great pipe legs of the Augmented Infantry Unit buckling and twisting, as if the wind were blowing it off its base. But Guardians weighed so much they smashed themselves if they fell over, and despite the fact that the dry season wind howled down from the mountains here like a katabatic banshee, it had never before stirred the Guardian as much as a millimeter from its post.

The Guardian was moving *under its own power*.

Huge alloy arms the weight of bridge spans swung over the boy's head. Knee joints that could have acted as railway turntables flexed arthritically in the legs. And at that point, the boy knew exactly who was at the controls of the Guardian.

THE WHOLE COLOSSAL thousand-tonne weapon was doing the old man's morning exercises.

Moving gently at first, it swung its arms and legs under their own weight, cautiously bending and unbending its ancient joints. Some of those joints screamed with the pressure of the merest movement. The boy suddenly, oddly, appreciated what the old man meant when he talked of rheumatism, arthritis, and sciatica.

The old man's exercises were good for a man with rheumatic joints that needed oiling in the morning. But they were just as good for a village-sized automaton that had not moved for sixty standard years.

The men sent to guard the Guardian were backing away. From somewhere in the village on the other side of the buildings, someone else decided to fire at the machine. A pretty colored show of lights sprayed out of the ground and cascaded off the metal mountain's armor. Habitats that the cascade hit on the way back down became colanders full of flying swarf. The Guardian carried on its warm-up regardless.

Eight times for the leg-stretching exercise, eight times for the arm-swinging, eight times for the two-handed push-up above the head.

The boy backed away, pulling at his mother's robe. He knew what was coming next.

Men ran out of the buildings with light anti-armor weapons. Many of the weapons were recoilless, and some argument ensued about whether they should really be pointed up into the sky or not. Some of them were loosed off at point blank range at the Guardian's treads, leaving big black stains of burnt hydrocarbon. But a Guardian's feet were among its most heavily armored parts. Every old person in town would tell you that. They were heavily armored because they were used to crush infantry.

The Guardian lowered its massive head to stare at the situation on the ground. The operator was actually in the main chassis; the head was only used to affix target acquisition systems and armament. That small movement of the head was in itself enough to make the Consultants back away and run.

One of the Consultants, thinking smarter than his colleagues, grabbed hold of the boy's mother. He shouted at the sky and pointed a pistol shakily at her head. He might as well have threatened a mountain.

The Guardian turned its head to look directly at him.

The boy screamed to his mother to drop down.

The Guardian's hand came down like the Red Sea on an Egyptian. Or like a sword upon a melon.

Unlike a human hand it had three fingers, which might be more properly described as claws. Exactly the same disposition of fingers a man might have, in fact, if a man held his middle finger and forefinger, and his little and ring finger together and spread the two groups of fingers apart. A roof of steel slammed down from heaven. The boy felt warm blood spray over his back.

The sunlight returned to the sand, now red rather than brown, and the gunman's headless body toppled to the ground in front of him. The man had not simply been decapitated. His head no longer existed. It had been squashed flat.

Beside him, his mother was trembling. Looking at the front of her skirts, the boy realized suddenly that she had wet herself.

One of the Guardian's massive treads rose from the ground and whined over his head. For some reason the sole of its left foot was stenciled with LEFT LEG, and its right foot was labelled RIGHT LEG. Arms fire both small and large whined and caromed off its carapace; the Guardian ignored it. It was moving out of the village, eastward, in the direction of the mining company army camped beyond the outskirts. Soon it was out of shooting range, but the boy could still hear guns going off around him. Single shot firearms! The villagers had brought out their antique home defence weapons and were using them on their oppressors. The boy swelled with pride.

Despite the fact that she had wet herself, the boy's mother hauled herself to her feet. "The old fool! What does he think he's doing? At his age!"

The boy hopped up onto a ladder fixed to the main water tower. The Guardian was striding eastward like a force of nature, silhouetted by things exploding against it. The boy saw it pick a thing up from the ground and hurl it like a discus. The thing was a light armored vehicle. He saw men tumble from it as it flew.

The mining company men were now flocking round a larger vehicle that was evidently their Big Gun. Most probably it had been brought in specially to deal with the possibility that the villagers might be able to revive their Guardian. It appeared to be a form of missile launcher, and the missile it fired looked frighteningly large. The turret on the top of the vehicle was being rotated round to bear on the approaching threat, and men were clearing from the danger space behind it.

The Guardian stopped. Its hand was held before it, the elbow crooked, extended out towards the launcher. If had it been human, the boy would have described the posture as a defensive stance.

The boy blinked.

No. Surely not—

The missile blazed from its mounting and became invisible, and the Guardian's arm blurred with it.

Then the missile was tumbling away into the sky, its gyros trying frantically to put it back on course, wobbling unsteadily overhead, and the Guardian was standing in exactly the same position as before. A streak of rocket exhaust licked up its arm and blackened its fingers.

The Guardian had brushed aside the missile in mid-air so softly as not to detonate its fuse.

Men in the mining company launcher stood, staring motionless, as if their own operators had left them via their back entrances. The boy, however, suspected that other substances were currently leaving them by that exit. As soon as the Guardian cranked into a forward stride again, the men began to run. By the time the Guardian arrived at the launcher and methodically and thoroughly destroyed it, the boy was quite certain there were no human beings inside. To the east of the village he heard the terrific impact of the anti-armor missile reaching its maximum range and aborting.

Then there was nothing on the face of the desert but running men and smoking metal. The gigantic figure of the Guardian cast a long, long shadow in the dawn.

THE OLD MAN climbed down slowly, with painstaking exactness, just as he did in all things. He was breathing quite heavily by the time he swung off the last rung and into a crowd of cheering children.

"I knew Khan would not let us down," said Mother Tho.

"Khan Senior is a terrible fruit farmer," observed Father Magnusson, "but a Guardian operator without equal."

"His oranges are scabby-skinned and dry inside," agreed Mother Dingiswayo.

"All the same, I knew," opined Mother Jayaraman, "that he would eventually come in useful for something."

The old man shook his fist at the boy's father in mock rage. "Khan Junior! What a fool to expose yourself so! Do you want your family to grow up without a father?"

Khan grinned. "I am sorry, father. I have no idea what came over me."

"Maybe it is a hereditary condition," muttered the boy's mother.

"Well," said the old man, "at least it has turned out for the best. Had you not jumped out when you did, I might not have made it to the access ladder. One might almost imagine that that was your deliberate intention."

"I apologize if I did badly, father," said Khan. "I am more of a farmer by trade."

The old man walked across the square to a handcart one of the younger boys had led out. In a fit of patriotic Commonwealther fervour, Father Magnusson had donated a hundred kilos of potatoes for a celebration. They had been stacked in a neat pile ready for baking.

The old man picked one up, raw, and bit into it.

"Never apologize for being a farmer," said the old man, chewing gamely for a man with few remaining teeth. "After all, a gun will protect your family's life only once in a lifetime. But a potato," he said, gesturing with the tuber to illustrate his point, "is useful *every* day."

Book, Theatre, and Wheel

Karl Schroeder

NEVILLE DUMOUTIER DRANK in the smell of pigs and the rattling sound of the nearby mill wheel. He smiled easily at the woman seated opposite him.

"This is not a formal investigation," he said. "Not yet."

The Lady Genevieve Romanal straightened in her chair and lifted her chin as she looked at him. "Of course not. What would we have to hide?"

"Nothing, nothing at all," chuckled Neville's companion. Brother Jacques was an agent of the Inquisition, but not so humorless as most. He aimed his usual puzzled-appearing smile at the lady and, clasping his crossed knees, leaned forward to peer at a book he had laid open on a low table.

"Your local priest, he was born and raised here?" asked Jacques.

"Yes." She glanced at Neville. That sort of look signaled a guilty mind in city-bred people; he wanted to think she was merely guileless.

"So you know him well, and he knows you," continued Jacques.

She nodded.

"He swears he has never tutored your people in reading and writing. It is, after all, forbidden for the commoners of your estate to learn letters, according to the edict of the Duke."

"I am not a commoner," said Lady Romanal.

Jacques chuckled. "I know; even if I didn't, it would be obvious in your bearing. Reading changes the eyes and broadens the brow. Those who can read know each other."

"Where is this leading?" she asked.

Neville knew Jacques would take forever to get to the point. "Have you taught any of your people to read?" he asked.

She shook her head.

Jacques pursed his lips. "Your priest swears he hasn't either. Strange."

"Why?" she asked. Her fingers twisted in her lap.

Neville grimaced. "I shouldn't have to point out, Madam, that yours is a tremendously wealthy household. Especially in the past five years, you have made a great deal of money in trade. Your agents…"

"They are very good," she said with the hint of a smile.

"Uncanny, actually," corrected Jacques. "The shrewdness of their dealings and the thoroughness of their knowledge are nothing short of astonishing."

Romanal blinked, as if coming to a sudden understanding. "Have we made someone envious? Is that what this is about?"

Now it was Neville's turn to glance at Jacques. The inquisitor smiled and shook his head. "Of course not. It's just that wealth flowing so freely through untutored hands is unusual, and the unusual is, sad to say, the first and best hint that the devil has been at work."

"Not here," she said seriously. Neville hid a smile; he was beginning to think she was far from guileless.

Jacques scratched his tonsured head. "We found this on one of your people." He slid a cloth-covered package onto the table, and slowly unwove the covering to reveal what looked like a book missing its binding.

Neville stared at the loose pages in annoyance. Jacques had not mentioned this to Neville, not even hinted at it during their long journey to this remote valley. What else had the inquisitor kept from him?

"What is that?" he asked.

"I don't know," said Jacques. He looked from the spilled pages to the lady. "The man was desperate to protect it, though."

"Who? Is he all right? Have you hurt him?" Lady Romanal reached out suddenly and flipped up the edge of one velum page. "Rodrigo. Oh, he's our best! Tell me he's all right."

"He's fine." Jacques made a soothing gesture with both hands. "He is safe within Mother

Church, and he has his life and health. As soon as we learn what we need to know, he will have his freedom as well."

She looked skeptical. Neville had known about the merchant they'd arrested in Milan. He also knew the man had been tortured, but this was not the time to bring that up. Gingerly, he reached to touch the burst book. The pages were loose, about palm-sized, and innocent of writing. Each had a single image painted on it, very strange images from what he could see. The whole collection was bound by a beaded thread that pierced each page's upper left corner. Under the pile of pages Neville could see a number of other threads, and some loose beads as well.

"So what is this?"

Genevieve smiled. "But it's nothing! This is a child's game. We call it the wheel of books. See, you loose the pages and match them." She unwound the beaded thread and fanned the pages into an arc.

"A game." Jacques's expression was completely neutral. "I see." He gathered the pages together again and wound the cloth around them again. "Then you won't mind my keeping it."

"Of course, if it amuses you." She smiled at both of them. "Was there anything else?"

"Not now." Jacques smiled and raised his hand for her to kiss. "I believe Sir Neville and I are quartered above this room?"

"Yes. Please, settle yourselves and then join us for dinner." Genevieve laughed. "If you pay the usual traveler's price, that is."

Neville had been about to stand. "Price? What price?"

"Why, a story, of course," she said.

He and Brother Jacques laughed, and some of the tension left the room.

"I can supply a story," said Neville. "Never fear about that."

"SHE IS LYING," said Jacques. He bowed to an image of the Virgin on the wall, and then crossed himself.

Neville had flopped on the single straw mattress in the room. He knew Jacques would sleep on the hard wooden floor, so hadn't offered the bed to the priest. He yanked his tall boots off and massaged his feet, scowling.

"I don't like to think that," he said. "This is such a friendly place."

"Friendly? Of course—when you're this isolated, you have two possible reactions to visitors. Friendliness is one of them. Makes no difference whether they're really welcome or not."

"So what is she lying about? Her people being lettered?"

"Oh no; they can count, but they can't read. No, it's this." Jacques patted the cloth package that lay in the center of the room's one table. "It's not a game."

Neville glanced at it uneasily. "Devil's work?"

Jacques laughed. "Not at all. But more powerful than letters, I think." He unwrapped the pages and sat on the floor next to the bed. "Do you know the writings of Tullius, Sir Neville?"

"Only the First Rhetoric. My father deemed it unwise for me to learn too much."

"It's a wonder you can read at all," said Jacques wryly. Neville watched as he unbound the pages and started laying them out in a rough square. "If you'd read *Ad Herennium*, my dear Neville, you would know that this is a memory system. Look at the pictures: Judas hanging, the Moon, a wheel. They are simple images, but surrounded with strange details. The men who took this from Rodrigo assumed it was sorcery, and they beat the poor man almost to death because of it. In fact, it's just an application of Tullius's art of memory."

"I don't understand."

"This is how the lady's men are able to trade so well," said Jacques. "They are committing everything they see and hear in the marketplace to memory. This memory." He tapped the pages. "They know what is short and what in surfeit. They know the price of everything, even the names of all the guildsmen in all the towns they pass through. And the guildsmens' dogs. If they were properly trained in the Art, they would not even need this prop," he flicked the pages negligently, "but could memorize a hundred names if they heard them recited once—and they could recite them back to you perfectly a year later."

"I once heard of a man who could do that." Neville rolled on his side and reached to pick up a page. On it were a man and a woman, chained together and holding hands. A crown floated above their heads. "So there is no sorcery here," he said with relief.

Jacques shook his head. "There is something. Else, why did she lie to us?"

GENEVIEVE ROMANAL WAS charming at dinner. She wore a fine green dress, and her hair was held in a lace bonnet. The dress revealed her bosom nicely, a fact that emptied Neville's mind of serious thought whenever he took note of it. Especially because she smiled at him so much.

She had invited the priest, Warrel, and her almister to dine with them. Calculated though the move was, it was also so obvious as to be disarming. Jacques had intended to interview the almister anyway, and now fell to discussing charities with the man over a haunch of venison, while Warrel looked on anxiously. It was evident that Genevieve gave a very large part of her wealth to the poor. Trading for profit was illegal, and Neville was happy to learn she avoided such sin.

"And who is your guardian?" Neville asked as he helped himself to a third slice of venison.

"My guardian?" She blinked at him.

"Who is the master of this estate?" He'd thought it a perfectly obvious question.

"Ah. Yes." She fluttered her fingers over the slab of bread that held her meal. Tearing a corner from the bread, she used it to gather up a mouthful of vegetables and gravy. "In the absence of a male heir to the house, and until I am married, the land naturally belongs to the Duke."

"But who is in charge of day to day affairs?"

"I am. That is," she added quickly, "the house is headless, and I execute the commands of the Duke."

"Which must be infrequent and vague," suggested Neville. "He lives a hundred leagues away. So you have no man in charge here?"

"No." She looked him in the eye. "The house is prospering, as you can see."

Neville nodded. He wasn't altogether comfortable with the idea of a woman running an estate this size, but it had been common enough during the crusades and the Death.

"I'm surprised the Duke hasn't married you to some fine noble lad," he continued.

She actually blushed. "He hasn't seen me since I was five. Perhaps he's forgotten me."

"Well, a woman shouldn't be unmarried," he said.

"Are you married?" she asked.

Neville turned back to his venison. "I was," he said shortly.

"Ah. I'm sorry." She glanced at the clerics, who were debating some point. It seemed it was the almister's turn to sit back and watch. "Tell me what happened," she said.

"I'd rather not."

Genevieve smiled. "Ah, but Sir Neville, you forget, you promised me a story earlier. And after all, you are the ones asking for the hospitality of the household. Tell me."

"Why?"

"Because life is short, we may never meet again, and there is simply nothing worth discussing except the fundamental things: pain, love, meetings, and partings."

He laughed shortly. "I didn't expect you to be so serious."

"Am I being serious? Maybe I just want to get the serious out of the way as quickly as possible so that we can be properly frivolous together."

Neville shook his head. She had all the usual strangeness of someone raised in isolation in the country. "I'll tell you if you tell me something."

"No. Now tell me! I demand it."

He sighed. "There's nothing much to say. We were married quite young, at fourteen years' age. Cecile died at twenty."

"How did she die?"

"Plague. Her mother died of it and she insisted on staying with her. I... could not bring myself to visit them. When she became ill, I... stood below her window and listened to her dying. I couldn't go in."

"You were wise," said Genevieve sympathetically. "But it must have been very hard."

"It wasn't wisdom, it was common cowardice!" He raised his voice and the others fell silent. Neville glared at Jacques. "Custom would have us abandon those stricken with plague. But it's just an excuse for cowardice."

Jacques shook his head gently. "You are alive to protect us now, Sir Neville. I'm sure your wife would have wanted that. I'm also sure it's what God wanted."

It was too late; he remembered standing under her window, listening to her cry in her delirium, and learning the lessons of his own weakness. He pushed back from the table, his appetite quite gone.

Genevieve laid her hand on his. "I am sorry if I upset you. But surely pain isn't all you remember of your marriage?"

He shrugged uncomfortably.

"Then you haven't properly mourned," she said. "Do me one more favour, and I'll release you from your promise." He glanced up at her expectantly. "I am not being cruel," Genevieve said, "but describe her to me. How tall was she? What color was her hair? Her eyes?"

Despite himself, Neville told her, though he seldom spoke about Cecile to anyone but her own family. Jacques and the others listened intently; now that he was committed to speaking he didn't begrudge their attention. Everyone's life was everyone else's business, after all. He simply treated his pain as inaccessible to relief, so never spoke of it.

The rest of the evening was a blur. He and Jacques were very tired from the road, and it was a relief to retire to their small room.

As he lay in the darkness, watching the vapor of his breath appear and vanish in a shaft of moonlight, Neville found himself feeling homesick for the first time in years. He knew the lady had meant to be hospitable, but, "She is so strange," he said aloud.

Jacques grunted from the floor. "You only think that because you're smitten with her."

"Am I?"

"Yes. Foolish of you; she may be dangerous. Now go to sleep."

Neville rolled over to peer at the black lump that was the inquisitor. "Brother Jacques, you are dangerous."

"Only to blasphemers, apostates, idolators, infidels, and heretics. Who would seem to be in the majority. Just now though, I would add to that list," he yawned loudly, "those who insist on talking to people who are trying to sleep."

"Bah." Neville lay back. He was still awake long after Jacques had begun to snore.

IN THE MORNING JACQUES went with the almister to examine the estate's accounts, leaving Neville alone with the lady. She took him on a tour of the estate. He and Jacques had been quartered in the main house, a large, white stuccoed building with two wings, two storeys, and a number of outbuildings. Its walled enclosure nestled at one end of a narrow, tall valley. Beyond the hills rose the Alps. At the center of the valley was a small lake, surrounded by her peasants' fields. There was a smithy nearby, and her masons and ostlers had been born and raised here.

"There was a period," she said, "when we had no visitors for decades at a time. They say that this villa was built by a Roman senator, and after Rome fell he and his family hid themselves here, having no commerce with the outside world for over a century."

"I can believe it," said Neville. He could see from the window where they stood how the roads made a circle in the valley; none led out. He and Jacques had walked narrow deer paths for much of their journey here. Had they not been told where to find the place, they would never have come this way.

"Eventually bandits started nesting in the hills." She pointed. "So we had to call on outside protection. Otherwise, we might be hidden still."

He turned away from the window. "You would prefer that?"

Genevieve shrugged. "We have everything we need. Come with me." She led him through a number of rooms. Her people looked up from their work at looms and benches as they passed, and they smiled at Neville.

They entered a room that held no less than a dozen books, none of them Bibles. He murmured his appreciation.

Genevieve laughed. "I thought you were an untutored knight. What do books matter to you?"

He shrugged awkwardly. "The Bible is a book. I respect them, and I do try to read when I have the chance."

"Would you like to read these?"

"I would be honored." He opened one thick volume and peered at the spidery Latin text. "I know this." He smiled, remembering his conversation with Jacques yesterday. "This is Tullius."

"Cicero, you mean."

"Who?"

"Cicero. That is his Roman name." She motioned for him to join her at a table by the room's one window. "Here. I wanted to give you this."

What she held was a single velum page, the same size as the ones that made up Jacques's captive memory. On this, some sure hand had painted the figure of a very young woman. She had the hair, the eyes, and the dress Neville had described to Genevieve last night. Her gaze was compassionate. Over her head hung a glowing crown, above that a dove. Her left hand proffered an olive branch.

Aside from pictures of the Virgin, Neville had seen no portrait of a woman in several years. He took this one gingerly from Genevieve, his eyes brimming with tears as he looked at it.

"It is she," he said. "Thank you."

"From your story," she said, "it seemed evident that you needed your wife's forgiveness."

Genevieve had included a loom, a dog, a book, and a cluster of grapes in the picture—all details about her life that the lady had pried out of him, with some difficulty, last night. The image seemed to burn in his hands now; he had not pictured Cecile at her loom in years.

He wiped his eyes. "I will treasure it."

"Just don't show it to Brother Jacques," she advised. "Lest he confiscate that, too."

"This is like the pages we saw last night," he said. "Did you paint those too?"

She nodded.

"We know the pages are a memory system," Neville said gently. "It's not an unheard of thing; Jacques understood it at once."

"Oh." Genevieve frowned at the wall for a moment. "So much knowledge has been lost.

Sometimes we forget how much has been kept. I didn't know the Church had preserved the Art of memory."

"The Church knows everything," he said sincerely.

"Of course." But her smile, as she said this, seemed a bit sad.

BROTHER JACQUES WAS waiting when Neville returned from his daily ride. The inquisitor was full of febrile energy; he kept glancing around himself, and his fingers repeatedly touched the cross hung around his neck. "There you are!"

"I was looking for you earlier," said Neville. He dismounted and patted his stallion's neck. "Where were you?"

"Seeing with my own eyes that something we had been told was true."

"What do you mean?" Neville pulled the horse's reins and headed for the stables.

"Hush." Jacques looked around. There was no one nearby. "It was something we learned from this Rodrigo. Tales of a secret grotto, here on the estate. It seemed too fantastical to be true, and yet it is! I have just been there. Neville, it is a place of the devil. We must leave here at once."

"What? What are you talking about?"

"There is a pagan temple in the hillside. It is being cared for by someone. This lady, no doubt. What else has she been doing with her money? We must leave now. This is too much for us to deal with. The proper authorities must be called."

"Wait." Neville put a hand on his arm. "I'm sure the lady has nothing to do with it. We can learn more if we remain good guests of the house than if we bring in troops."

Jacques peered at Neville oddly. "I see. Do you really think so?"

"I think these people's troubles have more to do with a conflict with the Duke, than with the Church. It wouldn't surprise me at all if there were some old pagan ruin in the hill—Lady Romanal tells me this was once a Roman senator's villa. And aren't some of the most sacred shrines in Rome built atop pagan temples?"

"Sir Neville, this temple is in use." He hesitated, then said, "there is more."

Neville led his horse to the stable and began to groom him. They'd had quite a run this morning, and Neville himself was feeling hot and irritable. The act of washing the horse would make him feel better, as if he had bathed himself.

Jacques hovered outside the stall. "I'm sorry I didn't tell you everything about this case before," he said. "But the theology is not your concern. You are our protector, true..."

"Who needs to know when to protect." Neville sighed. "What else haven't you told me?"

"One of the witnesses against Rodrigo was a man who claimed to have participated in a satanic rite led by Rodrigo. We think Lady Romanal's merchants are spreading such filth under the guise of merchanting, and by means of her almister."

Neville laughed shortly. His horse blew and nickered at him as if in agreement. "An evil almister? I find it hard to believe a man can be doing evil by giving money to the poor."

Jacques watched the horse suspiciously. "They're not just giving alms, Neville. They've been educating people. Romanal has endowed schools, and her men have visited those schools. We believe they are conducting their rites there. Education is dangerous to begin with. It is an open window for the devil to enter your soul."

"Maybe."

"So we must leave."

Neville shook his head. "Your caution is admirable, Jacques. But you employ me to be incautious. I won't leave until I've heard about this from the lady's own lips."

"But Neville," whispered Jacques, "we are alone here. Isolated."

Neville laughed out loud as he scrubbed the horse's flank. "Don't be a coward, Brother Jacques."

"Fear of the devil is not cowardice," said Jacques, and with that he walked away.

Watering and feeding the horse calmed Neville somewhat. Still, his mind was a jumble of conflicting impulses as he went to find the lady. On the one hand, he did not doubt that Jacques had found what he claimed. On the other, he could not reconcile such a thing with his impressions of Lady Romanal.

He found Genevieve working her loom with some of her maids. He bowed, and she gestured for him to sit next to her.

"Brother Jacques is making serious accusations against you," he said. "Your situation is going from bad to worse."

She sighed heavily, and dismissed her maids. A couple of them glared at Neville as they left.

"Tell me," she said simply.

"He says there is a pagan temple on the hill. That it is in use."

Genevieve swore in an unladylike manner. "You were right. I should have admitted to what the Theatre was in the first place."

"Then it's true?"

"No, not at all! But... it's impossible to explain. Ah, what a disaster."

"I don't understand."

"I can prove to you that we are not worshipers of the devil. Tonight," she said. "But do not bring Brother Jacques. Each man requires a proof that fits his own soul. Jacques would not understand what we will show you."

"I'm not sure I should trust you."

"No harm will come to you. Jacques can judge in the morning whether you are possessed," she said, smiling slyly. "And tomorrow night we can prove our case to him."

"Why not both together? Why not right here and now?" he demanded. "Do you take me for a fool, to walk into some trap?"

"Neville," she said seriously, "if we wished to compel you, we could do that—right here and now. It's hard to explain, but you'll see. Put it this way: Brother Jacques did not find a temple in the hill, he found a theatre. And tonight we will perform for you."

Grudgingly, he nodded. "For a day, I will trust you." He rose. "I should find Jacques and calm him down. Somehow." He rubbed his forehead, which was beginning to hurt, and turned to go.

"Sir Neville," she said as he was about to leave the room. "Do you believe civilization is something we receive, or something we construct?"

He paused. "What?"

"What if it were the obligation of each generation to re-invent its civilization? How would that affect the way you lived your life?"

He shook his head, puzzled. "I don't know," he said, and left.

GENEVIEVE ARRANGED FOR her almister to invite Brother Jacques to a private dinner. She and Neville ate in the kitchens. Throughout all this she maintained a coy silence, but was evidently enjoying his curiosity.

Afterwards, they walked into the warm, deepening evening. Genevieve followed a tenuous path that led into the forest. No one was about; even the animals had fallen silent. Genevieve walked slowly, humming gently. She seemed inspired somehow, but Neville only felt nervous. "What's going to happen?" he demanded.

"Nothing bad," she said. "You understand how memory systems work, do you not? One can use any striking, bizarre, beautiful, or horrid image to impress a thing into memory. We use that to remember names, accounts, prices, and so on. But there's another use for it.

"When your wife died, the experience of standing below her window for days was so strange and so memorable, that it completely eclipsed any other memory of her for years. You did not know that this would happen when you did that. But if you wish to change your life in any way, that is how you do it. You impress the change upon your character with the stamp of an event that's completely outside ordinary life. That's what ceremonies are. Like the marriage rite."

They ascended a winding path up the side of the hill. Rocky fissures with moss-grown sides began to appear around them. The hillside had split here like the roof of a loaf of bread in the oven; the fissures varied from knee-depth to fathomless.

The path entered a particularly wide fissure. Neville could see more torches strung along its length, at ever-increasing depths.

"One of our books talks about that," said Genevieve. "It concerns the pagan mystery cults. The Duke or the Inquisition would have it destroyed, because it's a book about designing a religion." She nodded at his shocked expression. "It talks about how to change the direction of a man's life by using the right ceremony at the right time. We only have a few rites in common—christening, marriage, death—because these are the passages we all share. They're the only ceremonies we see, so we think they're all we could have. The ancients knew you could invent a rite to fix any change in your life for all time. Yet you could have a rite specific to just one man, and meaningful only to him. That's not such a strange idea: the king is the only one who experiences coronation, true? This book I spoke of describes how to create rites of passage for small groups, or even for individuals."

"But what does this have to do with your memory system, or your merchants?"

"It has to do with alms. And civilization." She laughed at his confused expression. "You'll see. Tonight, it has everything to do with you."

The small worry Neville had endured all day began to grow. "What do you mean?"

She paused at an archway that had been carved into the side of the fissure. "Each page in our wheel of books is a striking, memorable picture. You can use it to make sure that you never forget something. True?"

"Yes…"

"How much more powerful would your memory be if you could step into that page?"

"This sounds like sorcery."

"Don't you see, Neville, you did that when you stood beneath Cecile's window. You painted a picture so vivid that now it is the only picture of Cecile that hangs in your palace of memories. What you did unknowingly we are going to undo now. By the same means."

She motioned for him to pass through the arch. "Come. Look at Jacques's 'temple.'"

A natural grotto had been enlarged by men some time in the past, and pillars had been carved around its sides to make it resemble a temple. Faded frescoes adorned the walls. Bright torchlight wavered on one that showed a youth with a sword and a broad, billowing cape inside of which stars shone. Another wall held an image of this figure killing a bull.

The frescoes were not the focus of the chamber. The place was built in tiers like a theatre, but instead of seats, each tier held numerous tall wooden plaques that reminded Neville uncomfortably of headstones. Many of Genevieve's people stood among these plaques, all wearing outlandish costumes representing mythological figures.

He looked at her with mixed suspicion and curiosity. "You will see," she said.

Genevieve led Neville down to the stage. When he turned to look back the entire space suddenly seemed filled with color and motion, for the plaques were colorfully painted with scenes and symbols he recognized from the wheel of books memory system.

Indeed, the whole Book seemed to have come to life. It swayed and danced in torchlight above him. Near the stage were the bound together man and woman, fully life-size, glittering under lamplight. Next to them was the Sun, farther back the Moon. He gaped in astonishment, and Genevieve smiled.

"Temple rites are just a debasement of the kind of thing we're about to do. As I've come to know you, Neville, I have learned what you need, and where your life is incomplete. And so I have designed a play for the Theatre that will undo the heavy lock you have set upon your own memory. Begin!"

Two of Genevieve's people appeared; one took on the role of a dying woman, the other her lover whom she commanded to leave for his own safety. The actors would pop up from behind one of the large cards, speak their lines, and then duck down again. It was as if the memory images themselves were speaking, the man and the woman taking on various guises as the action progressed. Though Neville knew it was play-acting, the combination of setting, drama, light, and color brought a tingle to his spine. Soon he had forgotten the artifice of it all and was simply immersed in the story.

Suddenly Genevieve said, "Look at me."

He turned. She stood close to him. She was dressed as he had described Cecile to be, and in one hand she held an olive branch. "It is time for you to enter the drama, Neville," she said. "Before the night is done, you will finally take this token that your Cecile has been offering you these many years."

BROTHER JACQUES WAS waiting for him when Neville finally returned to their room. The inquisitor sat on the stolid chair, a candle illuminating his face from below. He said nothing as Neville came in, merely examining his face with that familiar, puzzled expression.

Neville felt as if years had passed since he had seen Jacques. There was no way to explain it, but he was not the same man he'd been this afternoon.

"They wrought their work on you, didn't they?" said Jacques in a low voice.

"It is not sorcery," croaked Neville. He fell backwards into bed, totally drained.

"I know it isn't sorcery," said Jacques.

Neville had closed his eyes; now they opened in surprise. He had been ready for Jacques to argue, or preach. With a groan, he sat up.

"What?"

Jacques shrugged. "I put a suitable amount of wine into Lady Romanal's almister and snuck away early. So I was able to witness your ceremony from the archway. Romanal posted no guards."

Neville felt a weight lift from his heart. "Then you know there's no evil here. We can leave these people to their business."

Jacques laughed and shook his head. "You're a wondrously naive man, Neville. Nothing has changed. We still have to call in the militia."

"What? Are you mad?"

Jacques stared pensively into the middle distance. "The Inquisition is an attempt to reclaim lost souls," he said. "How those souls are lost is not our concern. Your lady is not dealing with the devil. But the Duke is right that she is trying to raise people above their station. Her Theatre is too powerful. It can educate even the illiterate. And now she presumes to take over the healing of men's souls as if she were the Church itself."

"But—"

Jacques waved his hand peremptorily. "Don't interrupt me. My brother, we are tending a very large garden. That means that sometimes we have to pull up some flowers, when they grow in the wrong place."

Neville was too appalled, and overwhelmed with mental and emotional exhaustion, to know what to say. He simply stared at Jacques.

"When you have seen the things I've seen, you will understand," said Jacques. "We will talk about this further tomorrow." He leaned over and blew out the candle.

In the morning, everything looked different. Neville felt this reawakening had happened to him before: on the day of his marriage, at his confirmation in the Order, and the first time he had traveled to a new country. But he had not felt this way in many years.

During the night, he had given himself permission to remember the good things about Cecile. These far outweighed the bitterness of their parting, he now realized.

The only thing that spoiled Neville's mood was the fact that Jacques was nowhere to be found.

He asked in the kitchens, but they had not seen him. Neville immediately went to see the lady. He arrived just as one of Genevieve's ostlers ran in and breathlessly reported one of the estate's horses was missing.

Neville cursed roundly. "Jacques has taken things into his own hands. I have to go after him."

"When did you last see him?" Genevieve asked.

"Late last night. That means he's got a half-day's head start on me. But I can catch him if I start now."

"What will you do if you catch him? Take him prisoner? Kill him?" Genevieve shook her head. "We don't want a murder on our hands. Does he believe you're a slave to Satan now?"

"I don't think so. He... believes I'm infatuated with you," he said sheepishly.

"Oh." She half-smiled. "And that has clouded your mind?"

He nodded.

"That's been known to happen to men," she said. "But I don't believe your mind is clouded. Quite the opposite."

"But what are we going to do? He's going to bring our troops here!"

"Can you stop them when they arrive?"

He shook his head. "I haven't the authority. And I will be suspect, if not by him then by his superiors."

Genevieve sighed. "This increases the urgency of things, that's all. I knew something like this was bound to happen eventually."

"Why? Because of your defying the Duke?"

"No. Because we have chosen to accept responsibility for civilizing ourselves." She waved to dismiss the ostler. "It's time you began reading, Sir Neville."

SHE LED HIM to the room that held her books, but continued on to the room's other door. She opened it for him to see what lay beyond.

Neville's breath caught in amazement. The next room was stacked with books. Many were so old they resembled bales of dusty cloth.

"This is why the Duke forbade any of our people learning to read," said Genevieve bitterly. "Because they might read these books and rise too far above their station."

"The Duke is a conservative man," said Neville. He wanted to step inside the room, but somehow felt he needed extra permission to do that. "He once told me that there were only three kinds of people: the clergy, who tend our souls; the nobility, who tend our property, and the peasantry, who tend our bellies. Hence his hostility to merchants."

"So you know the man. You didn't tell me that."

Neville winced. "But I don't understand, why didn't the Duke confiscate this library if he knows about it and disapproves?"

She looked down. "He tried. We refused. He was not about to send troops here, it would cost too much."

It was all too clear to Neville what was going on. "But if he could interest the Inquisition in the problem, he could root the library out without having to lift a finger." He frowned. "That suggests you would have raised arms against the Duke's men, if they'd come here."

"Well." She gently closed the door. "We did, actually. He sent some bullies to take the books. And," she added quietly, "to take me. The little matter of my marriage, you see. We turned them away at sword-point."

"Oh." Neville's heart sank. "That was a very foolish thing to do, Lady Romanal."

"I have lived here my whole life. I've never been outside this valley. These are my people. He wanted to send me away, marry me to some fat lord in Toulouse or somewhere. I would never have seen my home again." He said nothing. "I thought you would understand," said Genevieve, "because you once lost something that meant everything to you. Do you think because I am a woman that I feel any less than you?"

He shook his head. "No. You're right. I do understand." He wished he didn't. "The trouble is, your theatre in the hillside has given the Duke a pretext to strike back at you."

"We had to educate people," she said, "any way we could. You saw—the volumes are crumbling faster than we can copy them. They are so old. Books from the Empire. Books that tell how to live a civilized life. There's nothing this land needs more than that sort of knowledge."

"You mean to say that these image pages of yours... contain this library, somehow?"

She nodded. "That is what I was afraid Jacques would learn. They are the mnemonic for it, readable to those properly trained. I should have told you before." She sighed and sat on a bench. "I'm a fool."

Neville still had the page she had painted for him. He looked at it, then at her. "No one told me we were coming here as errand boys for the Duke," he said. "I don't think I approve. Not at all."

He sat down next to her. "You've broken no law. You certainly haven't sinned against the church.

You must come to some arrangement with the Duke regarding marriage, but we can't help you with that. Neither should we be the ones to enforce his wishes. It's not a church matter." He looked again at the portrait. "I'll not help them in this."

"And will you help me?" she asked. He hung his head.

"For my soul, I will."

GENEVIEVE BROUGHT HIM a lamp. She bade him read, and as Neville read, she laid the pages of the Wheel before him. For each written volume, she had a beaded string representing some sequence of pictures. When she laid the pictures out, he could see that the sequence of images—hanged man, star, charioteer, two or ten of staffs—could be made to remind one of the contents of the written volume.

During the days that followed, he helped make preparations for the evacuation of the estate. In the evenings he read, laboriously at first, then with increasing speed, and as he read he made mnemonics using the pages of the Wheel. The seventy-seven pages could be made to represent any history or concept, if one knew how to use them.

On the fourth day they awakened to the sounds of someone pounding on the door to Genevieve's bedchamber. "Lady!" someone cried from the corridor. "They're attacking! They're here!"

"How is that possible?" Neville threw off the bedcovers and reached for his boots. "It would take Jacques a week to reach the Inquisition's camp. And much more than that for them to return."

Genevieve wrapped herself in a heavy brocade robe, and went to the door. "I know who it is," she said.

The messenger confirmed it. "The Duke's men have encircled the valley, lady. There's nowhere to go."

"How dare he! I am sovereign on my own estate."

"Lady." The soldier lowered his eyes. "You are not a man."

"Still—"

Neville took her shoulder gently. "It's Jacques," he said. "He must have been in the Duke's pay all along. He had troops waiting outside the valley." He buckled on his sword. "I'll lead the defense."

"You will not."

"What?" His fumbling fingers missed their beat, and the sword belt dropped to the floor.

"Listen," she said. Sounds of combat came from the courtyard below. "It's too late! All we can do now is save the library."

"Save the—How? The books are too bulky. We could never—" Then he realized what she was saying. "No."

"Yes. We can't defeat them. But you are not their enemy, Neville. You can walk free. You must take the wheel of books from this place."

"I won't leave you to them!"

"You must! It is your duty."

"They'll know I was in league with you anyway," he said, and bent to retrieve his sword.

"No they won't," she said, and gestured to some-one behind him.

He had no time to avoid the blow that felled him. The last thing he heard was Cecile saying, "You have to live."

NEVILLE AWOKE TO hear the clash of weapons and screaming voices. As he tried to sit up, he wondered how much the Duke had paid Jacques for the Church's permission to do this.

His head was throbbing and his whole body ached. He was a mass of bruises. Apparently he had been enthusiastically beaten.

He looked around. He had been dumped in a storage room hastily converted to look like a prison. The room had one window, and its draft carried the smell of smoke.

He staggered over to the narrow slit and looked out. Several bodies were sprawled in the courtyard below him. Across the flagstoned square, the tower that housed Genevieve's library was burning.

He heard thudding footsteps outside the door, and shouts. He pounded on the wood, and after a moment a wild-eyed soldier opened it. He wore the livery of the Duke.

He raised his sword, then saw the coat Neville wore. "You are Sir Neville Dumoutier?"

Neville nodded dumbly.

The man glanced around the cell. "The heretics imprisoned you?"

Again he nodded. The guard handed Neville a dagger. "Walk warily," he said. "There may be some in hiding."

It was that simple. He was not searched. He was grateful that he was able to make it down the stairs and outside without assistance. A helping hand might have found the cloth bundle someone had sewn into the back of his coat.

Brother Jacques was waiting for him in the courtyard.

"The lady," Neville croaked. "Where is the lady?"

Jacques shook his head sadly and nodded to the burning tower.

NEVILLE AWOKE WITH a start. Some troubled dream had come to him, of fire and screaming. When he realized it was no dream but a memory, he lay back on his bedroll and wept.

He couldn't regain sleep, so he crept out of his tent and added a few sticks to the fire. He had pitched his camp a little apart from the other troops and they had respected his silence since everyone knew he had been ill-used by the heretics. The raucous celebrations of the soldiers had kept him awake anyway; the heresy was destroyed, they had reminded one another—and him—over and over again last night, and the Duke had his revenge.

Finally, they had all fallen asleep. Neville unfolded the cloth bundle that contained the Book and laid some of its pages near the fire. He read them while he waited for drowsiness to return, feeling again the spark of wonder and awakening awareness he'd first encountered on the stage of Genevieve's theatre.

She had given Neville a task worthy of his strength. He knew now that each man had to take responsibility for the whole of civilization. He would do what he could to ensure that ancient knowledge bore fruit in his actions and in those who learned from him. But first he would have to properly mourn Genevieve, for he had failed to properly mourn his wife and paid for that failure with years of unhappiness.

He took the pages and for a while he laid them this way, then that, trying arrangements to express the story of what had happened here in this remote valley. Nothing quite captured the shock and pain of it.

Finally he shuffled the pages into one package and fetched his saddlebags. He took out his writing kit and a fresh sheet of parchment. By the light of the fire he drew a tower, blasted by lightning, with figures falling from it and flaming books tumbling to the ground all around. His tears blurred the lines.

When he was done he added his page to the Book, wrapped it carefully, and laid himself down to sleep.

Mathralon

David Louis Edelman

HERE IS HOW you mine mathralon.

First, you must trace the Bohrer Trade Routes out to the galaxy's Upper Spiral, beyond the reach of the Consortium, out where the transmissions of the Great Weave unwind. Follow the caravans to the corporate headquarters of a third-rate company founded by a third rate house with the prosaic name of Howard. Look at the very bottom row of Howard's profit statements and find a line item for miscellaneous mineral exports. Trace that line item to its source. You will find a small moon just on the near side of the Particulate Ocean which has never merited any name other than Howard 27.

Howard 27 is our home. Howard 27 is also the galaxy's only known source of mathralon.

Mathralon does not give up its secrets easily. It is a coy mineral, mercurial, too shy to reveal itself to any but the Howard Company's spectroscopes, and the Howard Company has patented those. So to have any hope of finding mathralon, you must keep an ear open to the daily prospecting reports from the central office. Don't dawdle. Not because of any fierce competition for prospecting sites, but because mining mathralon is an all-day job, and you don't want to be stuck in the mines during a Howard 27 night. Then gather your crew—for you must have a crew, and your crew must be licensed—climb onboard a six-wheeled transport and bust ass over the broken clay. Once you arrive at a dig site, plant a borderstaff to claim your spot. The site is now officially yours.

The crew's driller will take command, directing the mechanical excavators to dig deep into the moon's hard shell. Before the sun has hit its midway point in the sky, he will clear you to descend into the pit. You will strap yourself into the bucket that drags under the transport like a limp metallic phallus; lower yourself deep into the blue-gray soil until even the sun's anemic glow is a memory. Handheld spectroscopes will guide you to the telltale discoloration in the rock wall that signals buried treasure. You will alert the crew's sapper, who will descend and use his precision laser to carve fist-sized chunks from the wall. And then, as the day begins its inevitable decay into night and the windstorms rev up, you will pull several handfuls of mathralon from the bowels of Howard 27.

Mathralon is cool and smooth to the touch, but as brittle as chalk. It smells vaguely sulfurous.

Howard 27 shat this mineral from its volcanic depths three million years ago, and then bathed it in the glow of a very particular (and very classified) isotope for another two hundred thousand. Mathralon does not like oxygen, and so you must place the rocks in a special airtight container for the journey back to the surface. There the containers will be delicately stacked and then ferried to the dockyards at the end of the day.

You have now mined mathralon.

BUT THIS IS only the first stage of the pilgrimage.

Wake yourself up early at the end of the week and find a nook dockside in which to sequester yourself. The Q-903 arrives with the first feeble spurts of Howard sunlight. They're enormous vessels, unpainted, pockmarked with the debris of interstellar travel. Watch the Q-903 slowly unpack its mechanical limbs and begin to excrete remote units engineered for the sole purpose of retrieving crates of mathralon. Watch the Howard 27 mechanicals creep onto the Q-903 to retrieve crates of food, clothing, and miscellaneous supplies ordered from the company commissary.

The whole operation is a miracle of efficiency. Not one screw or bolt has been wasted in the construction of these mechanicals; not one wheel turns but that it turns in the service of ferrying chalk black mineral off Howard 27. You will believe that you are watching a dance of enormous clockwork crabs.

Now you must wave the Q-903 goodbye and give the mathralon your best wishes. It will be thirty-three years before these rocks see daylight. You will never see them again.

There is a long and many-legged trade route that winds around the Upper Spiral, and the mathralon you mined is now on it. The ship will make dozens of stops along the way to gather and drop off other Howard Company assets. Residents of these other backwater moons must find our mathralon just as mystifying as their own products strike us: karillo eggs, fenten gas, leechi data cylinders. Who could want the repulsive karillo eggs, we wonder, hard as diamonds, foul-smelling, toxic, oily to the touch? Someone must, for someone pays the Howard Company to import them, and you only pay for what you want or need.

So the mathralon we mine sits in the cold hulls of a Q-903, inching its way through the void. Decades pass. Political movements ebb and flow, economics whistles and steams, the Q-903 moves on untouched. There are sometimes accidents along the way and ships that break down. But if there exists any organization in the galaxy desperate enough to hijack an interstellar shipment of mathralon, word of it has not yet reached Howard 27.

Finally, a generation after it's been pried from the depths of our moon, the ore reaches its destination. The Q-903 touches down on one of the satellites of the Rasha'ell Belt, some forty thousand light-years corewards. There the dance of the mechanical remotes is repeated in reverse, and the stacked crates of mathralon are unloaded. Within hours, the chalky black substance is carted off to the condensers where it is slowly pulverized and combusted for fuel. Because of mathralon's astounding atomic properties, it is the only known substance capable of powering these condensers. One fist-sized chunk of mathralon, they say, is capable of running a single condenser for eighteen months. Without these condensers, life for the diplomats of the Kelvin Congress would be sticky and unpleasant indeed.

The process is now complete, and the cycle begins once again.

WE ASK YOUR forgiveness for the lack of a traditional narrative structure or plot in this account.

The subject of story, they say, is transformation, and there is precious little transformation on Howard 27. We still use the same sappers and spectroscopes and transports and borderstaffs our great-great-grandsires used—literally the same items, now patched together countless times by diligent repair bots. The social framework that holds us together is necessarily limited by the edge of the dockyard; the landscape is capacious enough for conflicts to be easily avoided.

That's not to say that human drama is unknown here. We could recount the story of Billy Khann, who killed fourteen people and led the authorities on a brutal three-day chase through the mines before impaling himself on the drill bit of an excavator. We could tell you about Lilian Farjoler, the inquisitive orphan who stowed away aboard a Q-903 and was never heard from again. We could tell you the legends surrounding the mysterious counting boy of our ancestral home world, who has been sitting on the same rock reciting numbers since the beginning of history.

But these are the same stories you can find at any outpost in the galaxy. Babies are born, the old are buried, love is tragic, the ineffable remains ineffable. The mere act of summarizing these stories here has stripped them of their narrative weight.

Perhaps the only proper story to be told of Howard 27 is the story of the moon itself. A thousand years ago, this was an uninhabitable and desolate place. Then came the discovery of mathralon, then the first sapper robots, and then the first in a long series of companies to discover that it's nigh on impossible to make a profit on Howard 27 with mechanicals. Finally there came the Howard Company with its labor force of plague refugees, our great-great-grandfathers.

It would be quite a story. The slow transformation over a thousand years of dead rock to human ecosystem. The protagonists: oxygen generators, stubborn moon plants, imported soil. The antagonist: the entropy of the universe.

But it's not a story that a miner could tell. We have no expertise here in botany or terraforming, only mathralon. You would need to consult the scientists and historians of the Howard Company, if indeed they exist, if indeed the Howard Company still exists.

* * *

JUST AS WE ask your forgiveness for the lack of plot here, we would also like to acknowledge the dryness of the prose. Mathralon is a dry subject. Here on Howard 27, we have songs about scaly Howard birds and pungent Howard vodka and the difficulties of fucking on Howard clay, but we have no songs about mathralon.

This might seem strange, considering that the black rock is the central fact of existence for those twenty thousand of us who work the mines. The prospect of steady employment mining mathralon is what brought our great-great-grandfathers out to this end of the galaxy in the first place. It is the only real industry on Howard 27, and certainly the only one that produces anything resembling a profit.

But do you have songs about air and water? Do you celebrate gravity or the forward motion of time?

It's possible to live so close to something that it effectively becomes part of you. There are thousands of microscopic life forms that eke out a spare existence in the hills and gullies of your skin, beneath your threshold of perception. But when the details of your life are so unwavering and predictable, when day follows day with brutal regularity, you become attuned to these microscopic life forms. You stop looking outside and look inside instead. And so if you were to spend a week in a Howard 27 campsite, you might be surprised to see not the drunken brawls and raucous orgies of the clichéd stories, but rather the epistemological gabble of a hundred amateur philosophers.

The Q-903s, the Charons of the interstellar economy: what does Q-903 stand for, we ask? Are there, in fact, Q-902s or Q-904s in service somewhere across the galaxy? Our grandfathers speak of a P-788 used by the Howard Company many decades ago. What the differences are between the two models we can only speculate, and vaguely at that, since the insides of the galactic caravans are not built for human access. Was the phasing out of the P-788 for the Q-903 a kind of progress, an advance up the alphabetical ladder? Or perhaps it was a cost-cutting measure, a cheapening, a denigration?

We sometimes wonder if the Kelvin Congress or the satellite worlds of the Rasha'ell Belt even exist. These diplomats whose lives we are enriching: what are they like? Are they good people or bad people? No one from Howard 27 has ever seen them, or if they have, then they've never returned to tell the tale. Do we have any proof that our hard-earned lodes of mathralon are actually reaching these condensers?

This is not merely the idle speculation of the armchair philosopher. There are hard economic realities in the galaxy that work against us. What if someone has discovered an alternate fuel for the Rasha'ell condensers? What if our mathralon isn't going to Rasha'ell at all, but is being stockpiled in some Howard Company storehouse? What if the entire trade route has been abandoned or the Kelvin Congress disbanded? What if the perpetually troubled Howard Company has been sold off or dissolved?

Hundreds of years ago, there was a plague called the Shirker Disease that ravaged thousands of worlds. It was this plague that caused our great-great-grandsires to accept Howard Company contracts in this remote outpost to begin with. What if the Shirker Disease was never cured? What if the disease continued its rampage unchecked and proceeded to wipe out the rest of humanity?

Would anyone tell us?

Would the Q-903s notice?

In an unpredictable universe, the Howard Company engineers must have found ways to work around temporary displacements of its human workforce. Would the Q-903s continue their mindless march of efficiency without us, decade after decade until the end of time? Automatons gathering our shipments of mathralon ore, automatons unpacking the crates on Rasha'ell, automatons firing up the condensers. Automatons harvesting the food that feeds us, automatons keeping warm the empty seats of the Kelvin Congress.

The Howard Company's vaunted profit-and-loss statements: are there still human beings left to read them? Will the company's accounting programs continue to scrape tiny profits like barnacles off its mining worlds long after the customers for these minerals are dead and gone? Are the computational agents for the empty shell of the Howard Company bartering with *other* empty shell companies? Does a mechanical process carefully study the prospectuses of these humanless companies in search of a place to invest the company's profits?

* * *

IT IS IMPORTANT to reiterate that these are not mere questions of whimsy. There are no representatives of the company on Howard 27 anymore. There is no communication with the outside galaxy, and there has been no communication for more than two decades.

We have many questions, but no one to ask these questions *to*.

Mining mathralon is not a complicated enterprise, and it does not require a lot of human stewards. The paltry officials who were stationed here years ago were largely figureheads, pleasant faces pasted atop a thorny branch of bureaucracy. They had few important decisions to make. And if the best they could achieve was a career as a caretaker for a backwater operation in a backwater company in a backwater part of the galaxy, perhaps these officials were not the most qualified to make such decisions anyway.

Nevertheless, several decades ago, the Howard Company began pulling its management presence back. We were fed a variety of vague rationales for this—"reshuffling," "restructuring," "new operating philosophy"—but there was an underlying sense of desperation evident behind the lies. We wondered if perhaps the Shirker Disease had begun to take its toll on the Howard bureaucracy. At the beginning there was a delegation of 340; later 60; for many years, a dozen; briefly we shared a team of three managers with the moon that produces the karillo eggs; and then, there was no one.

This is not to say that we were left with no way to communicate with our superiors in the Howard hierarchy. We have the telecomp machines.

But these telecomp machines raise more epistemological questions than they answer. Once upon a time the communications we received were penned by real human beings—if Howard Company bureaucrats can indeed be classified as such—and the logic behind them was human as well.

Now the answers we receive are answers derived from machines. Our questions are fed into an algorithm, the algorithm churns through vast databases of business logic, and pertinent answers are generated. Is there a harried human being somewhere rubber stamping these answers, or merely a team of three shared with the moon that produces the karillo eggs? Or, God forbid, is there no one?

How can we tell?

Before the last human officers left Howard 27, protests would erupt on occasion. We mathralon miners are not horribly mistreated, we do not live in conditions of squalor, yet like every labor force since the dawn of time, sometimes we have demands that must be addressed.

And they would sit down with us, these last remaining Howard accountants. It's all a question of economics, they would say. They would lay the spreadsheets and the profit statements on the table and show us the numbers. The Howard Company is in a brutal struggle for its very survival against the larger and more profitable cartels advancing from the core, they would tell us. Be very glad you work for us and not for them. The men that run these cartels have little tolerance for slack weight. They wouldn't hesitate to shut down operations on Howard 27 and strand all twenty thousand of you here to scratch out a living from rock and lava. How long can you survive without the supplies we send? Can you eat mathralon?

We don't ask for the moon and stars, we would say. All we ask for is a few luxury items. We ask for news feeds. We ask for more efficient tools.

And where would the money come to pay for these things? they would ask us in return. We're willing to be accommodating. You study these accounting statements and you tell us where the money will come from to pay for these improvements.

We would threaten to strike. We would vow to bring mathralon production to a halt.

The accountants would just shake their heads sadly. And what do you think that will accomplish? Do you think Howard will pay to send a military force here and defend such minimal profits? No, take our advice, a strike would only cause the company to shut down the mathralon trade and abandon Howard 27. Imagine that one day the Q-903s simply didn't arrive. What would you do then?

AND SO WE drink and we philosophize and we sing our songs about scaly Howard birds and the difficulties of fucking on Howard clay, and the next day we go back to the pits without fail.

Sometimes we like to posit the existence of a mirror Howard 27 on the other edge of the galaxy, a Howard 27 whose residents toil away for the sole purpose of crafting the drill bits for our excavators. Perhaps our continued presence here makes their continued presence possible there. It's an encouraging thought. Certainly there must be a cosmic balance sheet that records all labors, that works diligently to ensure the continuing profitability of the universe.

In the meantime, it's not a bad life. We mine mathralon. We wait expectantly for some word of validation from the outside that Howard is there and Howard is listening. We watch the arrival of the Q-903s and look for some hint of a human life form on those ships, a human life form who can reassure us that the condensers are indeed churning away the same as they ever have. Perhaps one day we'll meet a diplomat from the Rasha'ell Belt, and he will tell us how our mathralon keeps the glorious Kelvin Congress cool and comfortable.

Anything's possible.

Mason's Rats: Autotractor

Neal Asher

MASON TUCKED HIS hands deep into the pockets of his wax-cotton jacket and stared out the kitchen window at the miserable drizzling day. Gray, wet, and cold. He coughed and harrumphed, then removed a pack of tobacco from his pocket and peered at the health warning: smoking can cause non smokers to damage your health. It figured. The health lobby of the Green Party would soon have tobacco banned all across the country. Greenies and Veggies had gone mad with power. A few months back an attempt had been made to defuse them a little with the claim that vegetarian farts were a prime cause of global warming, but it had not worked. The Greenies had thirty percent representation and were riding a wave to the next election. Mason rolled a cigarette. Bugger 'em. He had more important concerns.

The harvest was in, the stubble rotted in the soaked fields, and most of the recent floods had drained away, so now it was time to get the ploughing started. Mason was not looking forward to this. It was the same every year, this fear of the resident of Garage One. It had to be done though. He gritted his teeth, opened the kitchen door, and stepped out into the drizzle.

The black rat looked miserable, squatting atop his damp bale clad in a rain cape made from a foil-lined food-bag turned inside out, the snipped-off corner of the bag tied on his head as a sou'wester. Mason raised his hand but the black rat just stared at him with drizzle beaded on his whiskers. Mason shrugged and continued across the yard to the garages.

Combine Bertha was safely tucked away for the coming winter, probably prepared for another bout of agoraphobia in the summer. But the occupant of Garage One was different, and feared nothing at all. Mason hit the lock pad and hurriedly stepped back as the door slid open, wishing for a moment he had brought his shotgun. Ceiling lights flicked on in the wet twilight within to reveal the huge autotractor sitting there, silent and menacing.

Mason cleared his throat. "Autotractor, access code seven three two, Mason—respond."

There was a slow clicking and ticking as of cooling metal, then a low humming, and the tractor's lights glared into life.

"Code confirmed—instructions," the tractor growled.

"Ahem... all fields are now H-designated and ready for ploughing, cultivating, and seeding. Run a diagnostic—"

"I am ready," the tractor interrupted, its engine snarling into life and its gears meshing. It jerked forward and Mason hastily stepped to one side. He swallowed dryly. It was not supposed to do that, but then its mind was one of Ericson's chop jobs rumored to have been obtained through a contact in the MOD.

"The seed-grain is in—"

"I know where it is."

The tractor rumbled out on its immense cleated tyres, its optics and the black tube of its verminator focusing on Mason for a moment. It did that every time, perhaps trying to decide whether or not Mason should be considered vermin. In the middle of the yard it opened out its plough attachments as if stretching, and its cultivators whirred viciously. It would return later for the seeding attachments, in its own good time. With relief, Mason watched it turn to head out of the yard, but it halted abruptly, its verminator crackled, and a red flash lit the drizzle. There was a jet of smoke and a panicked shriek from the round sentry bale.

"Missed," stated the tractor, and jets of smoke tracked the black rat down the side of the bale. Then the autotractor muttered, "Bloody targeting's off."

"Stop! Desist! Cease!"

Mason ran between the tractor and the bale before he had time to think about it, but he certainly thought about it when the verminator zeroed in on him. The tractor was muttering to itself. He gulped.

"There is no fire risk," the tractor said eventually. "The moisture content of this bale is high." It sounded like a reprimand.

Mason said, "Things have changed here. The rats are no longer to be considered vermin." Silence met this statement and Mason took a deep breath to get himself under control. When he had finished coughing he said, "Autotractor, access code seven three two, Mason. Program change. Verbal."

"Code confirmed. Open to program change," said the tractor sulkily.

"Rats are no longer to be considered vermin on this farm. All prior instructions to verminate them are cancelled."

"Not the enemy?"

Mason felt sweat break out on his brow as the verminator swivelled about in reflection of the tractor's confusion.

"Not the enemy," he confirmed. "Autotractor, access code seven three two, Mason. Close program."

"Not the enemy," the tractor grumped as it drove out into the fields. Mason watched as the verminator flashed and a pigeon dropped out of the sky in a shower of feathers. Another flash and a crow flapped squawking into a hedge with its tail feathers smoking.

Now approaching the bale, Mason peered down at the melted and smouldering rain cape. He turned

it over with his boot and looked around. The black
rat crouched behind the bale, shivering and regarding him accusingly.

"Sorry about that," he said.

The black rat stepped out from behind the bale
with a field-dressing clutched to his shoulder.

"Come on in. We'll soon fix that up," said
Mason.

As was always the case, the black rat understood.
He was an Einstein of the rat world. He hesitated a
moment, then glanced up at the dismal gray sky
before scampering after Mason.

The black rat had been lucky, for the reflective
surface of his cape had saved him from serious
injury and he had only lost a little hair and some
skin. Mason put some ointment on the wound and
covered it with a corn-plaster. Immediately after
this, the black rat hopped down from the table and
crouched in front of the radiator. Mason opened a
bottle of whisky and poured himself a glass full.
The rat's stare was intense until Mason poured him
an egg cup full.

Gazing out of the window, Mason considered
that this was the kind of day when the only sensible
option seemed to be in a bottle. He did have plenty
to do: Combine Bertha needed an overhaul and
there was some welding to be done on one of the
grain handlers. He shook his head then turned
when there came a squeak from behind him. The
black rat held up his empty cup imploringly, his
right paw dramatically clutched to the corn-plaster.
Mason frowned and poured him more whisky. It

surprised him the rat had a taste for it. He walked back to the window.

"Oh shit!"

It seemed you only had to let your guard down for a moment. The car door slammed shut and the suit stood proud in his green wellies. Mason glanced to the round bale in desperation and saw that one of the black rat's kin was manning, no ratting, the catapult. He saw the arm crack up, looked across and saw the suit jump back as the wing mirror of his car exploded. The man then stooped and picked up the wheel nut that had done the damage. Mason opened the front door just as the suit was entering the porch.

"I don't want any!"

"I am not a salesman, Mr. Mason. You are Mr. Mason I take it?"

Mason nodded. The guy was obviously pissed off about his wing mirror. Mason watched him drop the wheel nut into a pocket and extract a card, which was flashed like an American police badge.

"I am from the reformed Health and Safety Executive of the sub-ministry to the Ministry of Agriculture and Fisheries."

Dread came and sat on Mason's chest, and it needed to go on a diet. A visit by a man from The Ministry was worse than one by any salesmen, for it usually cost more.

"What... What can I do for you?"

The Ministry man smiled a brittle, nasty smile exposing teeth that looked decidedly pointed. He opened his briefcase and it was the sound of a tomb being breached. He took out a clipboard. Dread called the rest of its family over.

"It has come to our attention that you have a rat population on your farm in excess of the new EU guidelines and, as I am sure you are aware, this constitutes a serious health risk."

"Who told you?"

It had to be Smith. The old git had really not been pleased when Mason had shotgunned his nice new cybernetic ratter. The Ministry man's smile was nearer to a sneer than to anything with humor in it.

"Where we acquire our information is not entirely relevant. Now, I have forms DXA137 through to 193. These must be completed with an ABD45 from a Ministry-approved exterminator. Here is a list of those who are approved."

There were ten names on the sheet of paper, and it was only just possible to grip the stack of forms in one hand. Mason stared back at the Ministry man and did not blink an eye as a brown rat scurried past outside pushing a small barrow loaded with verminated pigeons.

"Why are the rats a health risk? They wash regularly and put on flea powder."

He had made sure of that the previous spring when he found himself itching and scratching and seen the little bastard fleas leaping all over his bedclothes. He had built a bath in the old milking sheds and, over a period of a month, marched the rats in there at gun-point, liberally dousing them with flea-powder when they finished their ablutions. Towards the end of the month the rats were going by themselves, especially when he installed an immersion heater in the water tank. Nobody likes blood-suckers.

"Very amusing Mr. Mason. I'm sure. You have three weeks to comply. If after this period you have not complied, an exterminator team will be employed by the Ministry and brought here at your expense. You will also be subject to punitive fines." Again that brittle smile. "Good day to you. You will be receiving the bill for repairs to Government property." He took out the wheel nut and placed it on the porch table, returned to his car, and drove away hunched over the wheel, his nose almost against the windscreen.

Mason returned to the kitchen and looked down at the black rat who was now flat on his back with his back feet up in the air and his forepaws across his chest. His whiskers twitched as he no-doubt dreamed about hurling tractor wheel nuts at reps.

IN THE AFTERNOON the autotractor rumbled back from the fields to refill its tanks with diesel. Mason watched it through the kitchen window. When it pulled out of the yard again he noted how both black and brown rats were following it out into the fields with their little barrows. It seemed there was no such thing as racism in the rat world. When the tractor was gone he went into his office and glared at the pile of forms he was supposed to fill in. He really did not want to start killing off his rats, for he quite enjoyed their company—more so than the company of most humans. How could he get round this? The ABD45 was the crux, since he needed it filled in and signed by a Ministry-approved exterminator. He studied the list and picked up the phone.

At seven thirty it was getting dark outside. The black rat was disinclined to follow him out and kept looking up at the whisky bottle on the shelf. Mason held the door open.

"Now!"

The black rat reluctantly slouched out into the drizzle.

Little fires were burning behind the barns and as he approached Mason saw that just about the entire rat population was there... enjoying a barbecue. They were roasting spitted pigeons and drinking something from empty shotgun cartridges. As the black rat ran to join his fellows Mason picked up a coke can full of the substance they were drinking and took a sip. After he had finished coughing and his eyes had stopped watering he carefully placed the can full of petrol-flavoured grain spirit on the ground, not too close to any of the fires, and turned to head back inside. That cut it. As far as he was concerned there was no truer test of civilization. He wondered where their distillery was located.

"AH, MR. MASON, Quentin Beasley, Rathammer."

He was not quite so bad as the usual sort, for he wore jeans and a checkered shirt and there was no sign of a filofax. Mason nodded and kept a firm hold on his shotgun. There might be glossy brochures.

"I understand you have a bit of a rat problem?"

"The man from the Ministry tells me I have, but they're no problem to me."

"They do constitute a health risk."

Mason started walking across the yard. "Come with me."

With his mouth hanging open, the man from Rathammer stood frozen in the doorway of the milking shed. Steam rose from a shallow bath crowded with rats and soap suds. Leading to this, numerous rats stood in a queue, with sacking towels draped over their arms. Other rats were drying themselves and applying flea-powder with abandon.

"Now, why do they constitute a health risk?"

"Their droppings..."

"So I'll install toilets."

Beasley just kept on staring.

"What do you do when you come here?" asked Mason.

"Er... ah, yes, we bring in a number of TT15s... Have you seen the Traptech ratters?"

"Yes, I've seen them."

"Well, right, basically they are programmed to do a patterned sweep of your farm with all their search areas interlinked. No rat on your property can escape."

Mason reached out and put his hand on Beasley's shoulder.

"Come into the house. We must discuss this."

* * *

BEASLEY SAT AT the table, his expression stunned as the black rat toasted him with an egg cup full of whisky then downed it in one. He took a gulp of his own drink, blinked blood-shot eyes, and then leant forwards with his elbows on the table.

"Your rats... so advanced. I've seen rats using tools, but not to this extent."

He spoke slowly, carefully. Mason topped up his glass.

"They only have to be given a chance... So tell me, after the TT15s have made their sweep, what happens then?"

"Oh, thassit... we compare kill figures to the Ministry figures and if they are within five percent you get your ABD45."

"Have some more whisky. Tell me, what happens if no kills are made?"

"Thas highly unlikely."

"Yes, but should it happen?"

"'Nother sweep."

"And if it happens again?"

The black rat fell to the floor with a resounding thud. A high-pitched snoring filtered up from under the table.

"Guess we'd declare... clear," said Beasley, his head under the table.

"And I would get the ABD45?"

Beasley came up for air and nodded. This, after his ducking down, became too much. His head thudded to the Formica.

* * *

MASON TRIED EVERY Pied Piper technique he could think of. He left grain in the trailer but he had taught them too well; they only took the grain he left in their shed. He tried showing them a picture of many rats packed into the trailer, but if they understood they showed no sign. Many of them paid no attention at all and he was sure they were drunk. He returned to his house and threw the picture on his desk then picked up his shotgun and went back out to try threats. He managed to get four rats into the trailer, but the rest had scattered. He'd used threats to get them to bathe, but it had taken him a month to do that. He only had a day. As he released the four and returned to his house he realized he needed to be really devious.

IT TOOK THE rest of the afternoon to find it. He searched all the outbuildings, but it was in none of them. On his way back from poking around in the disused pig sties he stopped by an old Jaguar that had been dumped on him years before and was quietly rusting away in a corner with grass growing on its roof, and there he caught a whiff of something fermenting. Whisps of smoke filtered up from round the bonnet. Mason lifted it and looked into what used to be an empty engine compartment, which now contained a milk churn filled with what smelt like fermenting grain. A small fire had been lit underneath it and from its lid petrol pipes curved back through holes into the passenger area. Mason looked inside and saw the cooling vessel: a large glass bottle filched from his disused milking shed. He walked to the back of the car and opened each of the fifteen-gallon petrol tanks. What was inside would have run the vehicle had it an engine. This accounted for the petrol aftertaste. Mason returned to his house.

It took him an hour to dissolve all the pills in the whisky. When it was done he casually returned to the Jag, keeping a look out for beady eyes. Half a bottle went in each tank.

As it grew dark the autotractor returned in a cloud of feathers, with most of the rat population sitting on its cowlings plucking pigeons. Mason watched it halt in the yard so all the rats could disembark then head in to get another refill at the diesel tanks. Obviously it had decided that if they were not enemies then they must be friends. As it headed back out into the fields he heard something like squeaky rattish speech issuing from its PA system. Ericson said it only used a fraction of its mind to perform its farm duties, but now seemed to be using more than that. Mason was not overly attracted to the idea.

After an hour the rats lit their fires behind the barns. Smiling to himself, Mason picked up another bottle of whisky and went out to join the party. By midnight the area was strewn with snoring rats and the chewed carcasses of pigeons, whereupon Mason, a little unsteady on his feet, set to work with his own wheel barrow. He counted two hundred and seventy rats into the back of the trailer and locked them in with a couple of buckets of water and some grain.

* * *

THE MEN FROM Rathammer arrived in the morning in two parcel vans and began to unload and program the TT15s. Keeping well back, Mason watched with disgust as the horrible chrome scorpions scuttled off into the fields. Beasley refused an invite into the house and stayed in the back of one of the vans, at a monitoring station with his two companions. Mason joined them.

Three kills were reported in the first half an hour. By dinner time there had been eight and the TT15s had nearly completed their sweep. Mason guessed that took care of the teetotallers.

"How strange," said Beasley noncommittally.

"Bloody Ministry," said one of his companions.

Mason nodded and smiled in his best thick inbred farmer manner and went to start work on Combine Bertha. Later he felt a momentary panic upon seeing one of the men head out into the fields with some kind of detector. Eventually the man returned with a crushed and burnt TT15.

"Do you have heavy machinery operating out there, Mr. Mason?" Beasley asked him shortly after.

"Yes, an autotractor."

"One that does not recognise standard agricodes... I would be grateful if you would stand it down while we make our second sweep."

Mason went into his house, called up the autotractor through its satellite link, and ordered it to shut itself down for the next three hours before returning.

The second sweep yielded only another three rats and Beasley reluctantly filled out an ABD45 for

Mason. With greater reluctance Mason filled out a cheque and handed it over. As the two parcel vans departed, the autotractor returned from the fields towing its sealed trailer. Mason wiped his oily hands on his overalls and went to release some very hung-over and pissed-off rats. After that he kept his head down when he saw the catapult trained on his kitchen door.

THE RATS RELENTED late in the afternoon two days after their ordeal. There came a scratching at the kitchen door and Mason opened it cautiously to see the black rat standing there regarding him. The peace offering was an old milk bottle filled with grain spirit and a cold roast pigeon. He passed on the pigeon since he preferred his birds gutted before they were cooked, and peered out into the yard.

The autotractor was back with what appeared to be the entire rat population sitting around it and on it. Two hundred and seventy heads turned to regard Mason and then as one turned back to regard the verminator on the tractor. Even from where he stood Mason could see the device was damaged. So that was it. He walked out to take a look.

"Autotractor, access code seven three two, Mason. Run diagnostic on—"

"The verminator is damaged. Replacement with M87 Rapifire with a two thousand round box of caseless plutonium needles or with a Zunigun armor-piercing laser is optimal."

That confirmed Ericson's sources. Mason shook his head and climbed up onto the tractor to inspect the verminator. Rats sat on the cowling watching him, the tractor's optics above them. It took him only a moment to realize the verminator had been wasted, probably by a low branch.

"Mason!"

The shout had an edge of hysteria, and Mason turned to watch a bedraggled figure dismounting from a bicycle. The Ministry man did not look at all happy. He glared at all the rats on and about the tractor, and began rubbing his hands on the front of his rumpled jacket as if he could not get them clean. Complete disgust twisted his features. When he returned his attention to Mason, his hands fisted round the material of his jacket.

"I have been demoted," he said, a quaver in his voice and his eyes as big as an owl's. "I have been demoted because of my inaccurate assessment of the rat problem in this area."

Mason thought there must be something more involved in this demotion. As he understood it, incompetence in the civil service usually led to promotion. However, the true facts aside it seemed this official considered Mason to blame. When the man turned to his bicycle to unstrap his briefcase, Mason could see his hands were shaking.

"Now I see the truth," the Ministry man continued, spittle appearing on his chin.

Mason noted that the rats were now abandoning the autotractor and fleeing. Even they recognized that a crazy man had arrived. From his briefcase The Man from the Ministry extracted a thick wad of forms.

"No one makes a fool out of me! You will fill in forms DXA99 through to 403!" He started to step from foot to foot as if his shoes were too tight, waving the wad of forms to emphasize his words. "You will be fined, your latest crops will be condemned, and you will bear the cost of a full Traptech sweep!" Some of the forms slid from the wad and were being picked up by a breeze, whereupon Mason noted the autotractor's ruined verminator tracking their progress. "When I return to the Ministry your ABD45 will be cancelled! This time there will be a body count!" His movements became even more frenetic and his bicycle fell over. Spittle now flew from his pointy teeth.

"Enemy?" wondered the autotractor, and its engine started. Mason hurriedly leapt to the ground. Showing an immediate grasp of the situation the few remaining rats leapt down as well and all of them still in sight ran for cover. Such was his frenzy the Ministry man hardly noticed.

"I want to see dead rats! I want to see hundreds of dead rats! This is war, Mason! You do not fool with The Ministry!"

"Enemy," snarled the autotractor, and with its wheels kicking up gravel it spun a hundred and eighty degrees to face the Ministry man, whose mouth abruptly dropped open. Remaining forms thumped down into the mud. Mason heard the verminator clicking ineffectually as the engine snarled out a cloud of black smoke.

"Stop," he said without much conviction.

Its huge cleated tyres kicking up great clumps of mud, the autotractor hurtled forward. The Ministry man screamed and ran, his cycle-clipped trousers hiked up and his sock-suspenders showing. Mason watched him sprinting across the fields in storklike bounds with the tractor in hot pursuit, and soon lost sight of the both of them in the twilight.

THE AUTOTRACTOR RETURNED when it was fully dark, but Mason was sitting at his kitchen table a third of a bottle under by then, and in no pain. He did not bother to find out what had happened. Later, when he peered out of the kitchen window, he saw that the barbecue fires had been lit, yet the tractor had bagged no pigeons that day. Some other meat was on the menu. Mason stayed indoors and finished the bottle. He never heard from that particular Ministry man again, and he hid the bicycle under a dung heap.

Modem Times

*A Jerry Cornelius story
by Michael Moorcock*

THE GOLDEN AGE

MINIATURE phones you carry in your pocket and that use satellite tracking technology to pinpoint your location to just a few centimeters; itty-bitty tags that supermarkets use to track their products; bus passes that simultaeneously monitor your body temperature to find out how often you are having sex...

—James Harkin, New Statesman,
15 January 2007

WASHINGTON, April 24—President Bush and Vice President Dick Cheney aggressively challenged the motives of Congressional Democrats on Tuesday, as the House and Senate prepared to consider a war spending bill that would order troops to be withdrawn from Iraq beginning later this year.

—New York Times,
25 April 2007

1. A MYSTERY IN MOTLEY

Madness has been the instigator of so much suffering and destruction in the world throughout the ages that it is vitally important to uncover its mechanisms.

—Publisher's advertisement SCHIZOPHRENIA: THE BEARDED LADY DISEASE

THE SMELL OF pine and blood and sweet mincemeat, cakes and pies and printing ink, a touch of ice in the air, a golden aura from shops and stalls. Apples and oranges: fresh fruit, chipolata sausages. "Come on girls, get another turkey for a neighbour. Buy a ten pounder, get another ten pounder with it. Give me a fiver. Twenty five pounds—give us a fiver, love. Come on, ladies, buy a pound and I'll throw in another pound with it. Absolutely free." Flash business as the hour comes round. No space in the cold room for all that meat. No cold room at all for that fruit and veg. The decorations and fancies have to be gone before the season changes. 'Two boxes of crackers, love, look at these fancy paper plates. I'll tell you what, I'll throw in a tablecloth. Give us a quid for the lot. Give us a quid thank you, sir. Thanks, love. That lady there, Alf. Thank you, love. Merry Christmas. Merry Christmas."

"I hate the way they commercialise everything these days."

"That's right, love. A couple of chickens, there you go, love—and I'll tell you what—here's a pound of chipos for nothing. Merry Christmas! Merry Christmas! Merry Christmas! Seven pound sacks. Two bob. No. Two sacks for half a dollar. Half a dollar for two, love. Last you the rest of the year. Stand up, darling. Here, Bob, hold the fort, I'm dying for a slash. Dolly mixtures, two bags for a shilling. Two for a shilling, love. That's it, darling! Genuine Airfix they are, sir. All the same price. Those little boys are going to wake up laughing when they see what Santa's brought them. Go on, sir, try it out. I'll throw in the batteries. Give it a go, sir. No, it's all right, son. Not your fault. It went off the kerb. I saw it happen. Go on, no damage. I'll tell you what, give me ten bob for the two. Tanner each, missis. You'll pay three and six for one in Woolworths. I'll tell you what. Go in and have a look. If I'm wrong I'll give you both of 'em free. Hot doughnuts! Hot doughnuts. Watch out, young lady, that fat's boiling. How many do you want? Don't do that, lad, if you're not buying it. Get some cocoa. Over here, Jack. This lady wants some cocoa, don't you, darling? Brussels. Brussels. Five pounds a shilling. Come on, darling—keep 'em out on the step. You don't need a fridge in this weather."

Now as the sky darkens over the uneven roofs of the road, there's a touch of silver in the air. It's rain at first, then sleet, then snow. It *is* snow. Softly falling snow. They lift their heads, warm under hoods and hats, their faces framed by scarves and turned up collars. (Harlequin goes flitting past, dark blue cloak over chequered suit, heading for the panto and late, dark footprints left behind before they fill up again.) A new murmur. Snow. It's snow.

"Merry Christmas, my love! Merry Christmas." Deep-chested laughter. Sounds like Santa's about. The students stop to watch the snow. The men with their children point up into the drawing night. Merry Christmas! Merry Christmas! It's a miracle. Proof that all the disappointments of the past year are disappearing and all the promises are really going to be kept. "Happy Christmas, darling. Happy Christmas!" The Salvation Army stops on the corner of Latimer Road. The tuba player takes out his vacuum of tea, sips, blows an experimental blast. Glowing gold flows from the pub and onto the cracked and littered pavement. A sudden roar before the door closes again. "Merry Christmas!"

A boy of about seven holds his younger sister's hand, laughing at the flakes falling on their upturned faces. His cheeks are bright from cold and warm grease. His thin face frowns in happy concentration.

"Here you go, darling. Shove it in your oven. Of course it'll go. Have it for a quid." All the canny last minute shoppers picking up their bargains, choosing what they can from what's too big or too small or too much, what's left over or can't be sold tomorrow or next week. It has to be sold tonight. "I'll tell you what, love. Give us a monkey for the lot." *Merry Christmas. Merry Christmas*—sparking toys—little windmills, tanks, and miniature artillery—glittering foil, tinsel, and trinkets. Clattering, clicking, nattering, chattering, clanking, whizzing, hissing, swishing, splashing the street with cascades of tiny lights. Multicolored bulbs winking and shivering, red, white, blue, green, and silver.

Stacks of tightly bound trees, already shedding ripples of needles, some rootless, freshly sawn, some still with their roots. The smell of fresh sawdust, of earth. The smell of a distant forest. The boy knows he has to get a big one and it has to have roots. "Five bob, son. That's bigger than you, that is. Give us four. Six foot if it's an inch. Beautiful roots. What you going to do with it after? Plant it in the garden? That'll grow nicely for next year. Never buy another tree. That'll last you a lifetime, that will."

Jerry holds his money tight in his fist, shoved down between his woollen glove and his hot flesh. He has his list. He knows what his mum has to have. Some brussels. Some potatoes. Parsnips. Onions. Chipolatas. The biggest turkey they'll let him have for two quid. Looks like he'll get a huge one for that. And in his other glove is the tree money. He must buy some more candle-holders if he sees them. And a few decorations if he has anything left over. And some sweets. He knows how to get the bargains. She trusts him, mum does. She knows what Cathy's like. Cathy, his sister, would hold out the money for the first first turkey offered, but Jerry goes up to Portwine's, to the chuckling ruby-faced giant who fancies his mum. Nothing makes a fat old-fashioned butcher happier than being kind to a kid at Christmas. He looks down over his swollen belly, his bloodied apron. ("Wotcher, young Jerry. What can I do you for?) *Turkeys!*

Turkeys! Come on love. Best in the market. Go on, have two. (Ten bob to you, Jerry.)" There's a row of huge unclaimed turkeys hanging like felons on hooks in the window. Blood red prices slashed. Jerry knows he can come back. Cathy smiles at Mr. Portwine. The little flirt. She's learning. That smile's worth a bird all by itself. Down towards Blenheim Crescent. Dewhurst's doing a good few, too. Down further, on both sides of the road. Plenty of turkeys, chickens, geese, pheasants. "Fowl a-plenty," he says to himself with relish. Down all the way to Oxford Gardens, to the cheap end where already every vegetable is half the price it is at the top. The snow settles on their heads and shoulders and through the busy, joyful business of the noisy market comes the syncopated clatter of a barrel organ. *God rest ye, merry gentlemen, The First Nöel, The Holly and the Ivy* cycled out at the same manic pace as the organ-grinder turns his handle and holds out his black velvet bag.

"Merry Christmas! Merry Christmas!" His hat is covered in melting snow but his arm moves the crank with the same disciplined regularity it's turned for forty years or more. *Away in a Manger. Good King Wenscleslas. O, Tannenbaum. O, Tannenbaum. Silent Night. Rudolf the Red-Nosed Reindeer.* Cathy puts a halfpenny in his hat for luck, but Jerry's never known his luck to change one way or another from giving anything to the barrel organ man. He pulls Cathy's hand on for fear her generosity will beggar them. "Come on. We'll do that butcher right at the top. Then we'll work our way down." There's no such thing as a frozen turkey here. Not in any Portobello butcher's worth the name, And all the veg is fresh from Covent Garden. And all the fruit is there for the handling, though the stall-holders affect shocked disgust when the middle-class women, copying French models, reach to feel. "No need for that, love. It's all fresh. Don't worry, darling, it won't get any harder if you squeeze it." Dirty laughter does the trick. "Ha, ha, ha!" Gin and best bitter add nuance to the innuendo. Panatella smoke drifts from the warm pubs. Chestnuts roast and pop on red hot oil-drum braziers. The ladies smile back nervously, leaving it to their working class sisters to tell the stall holders off for the filth in their voices. "Come on love. Two bob a pound to you." And Jerry looks behind him. "It was all true," he says. "It really was. Every Christmas."

"Well, possibly." Miss Brunner's attention was on the present. The thing was big enough at any rate, in red, gold, and green shining paper and a spotted black and white bow. You don't beat Christmas for horrible color combinations.

"Of course, it couldn't last." He contemplated the best way of opening the present without messing up the wrapping. "The snow, I mean. Turned to sleet almost immediately. By the time we got home with the turkey it was pelting down rain. I had to go back for the tree. At least I could hold it over my head on the way." He'd opened it. The brown cardboard box was revealed, covered in black and blue printed legends and specifications. Automatically he neatly folded the wrapping. He couldn't have been more appreciative. There was the familiar sans serif brand name in bars of red, white, and blue. "Oh, *blimey!* A new Banning."

Shakey Mo Collier beamed through his scrubby beard. "I got another for myself at the same time. Joe's Guns had a two-for-one."

Using a Mackintosh chair she'd found, Miss Brunner had built a blaze in the ornamental grate. Smoke and cinders were blowing everywhere. "There's nothing like a fire on Christmas morning." She drew back the heavy Morris curtains. There was a touch of gray in the black. Somewhere a motor grunted and shuffled. "Don't worry," she said. "I think it's dead."

Carefully, Jerry peeled the scotch tape from the box. The number in big letters was beside a picture of the gun itself. BM-152A. He reached in and drew out a ziploc full of heavy clips. "Oh, God! Ammo included." His eyes were touched with silver. "I don't deserve friends like you."

"Shall we get started?" She smoothed the skirt of her tweed two-piece, indicating the three identical Gent's Royal Albert bicycles she'd brought up from the basement. "We're running out of time."

"Back to good old sixty four." Mo smacked his lips. "Even earlier, if we pedal fast enough. OK, me old mucker. Strap that thing on and let's go go go!"

They wheeled their bikes out through the side door of the V&A into Exhibition Road. White flakes settled on the shoulders of Jerry's black car coat. He knew yet another thrill of delight. "Snow!"

"Don't be silly," she said. "Ash."

With a certain sadness Jerry swung the Banning on his back then threw his leg over the saddle. He was happy to be leaving the future.

2. WHEN DID SUNNIS START FIGHTING SHIITES?

GALKAYO, Somalia—Beyond clan rivalry and Islamic fervor, an entirely different motive is helping fuel the chaos in Somalia: profit. A whole class of opportunists—from squatter landlords to teenage gunmen for hire to vendors of out-of-date baby formula—have been feeding off the anarchy in Somalia for so long that they refuse to let go.

—NEW YORK TIMES, 25 April 2007

THE HOLIDAYS OVER, Jerry Cornelius stepped off the Darfur jet and set his watch for 1962. Time to go home. At least it wouldn't be as hairy as last time. He'd had his head shaved on the plane. It was altogether smoother now.

Shakey Mo and Major Nye met him at the check out. Shakey rattled his new keys. "Where to, chief?" He was already getting into character.

Major Nye wasn't comfortable with the Hummer. It was ostentatious and far too strange for the times. Resignedly, he let Mo take the Westway exit. "A military vehicle should be just that. A civilian vehicle should be suitable for civilian roads. This is some kind of jeep, what?" He had never liked jeeps for some reason. Even Land Rovers weren't his cup of tea. He had enjoyed the old Duesenberg or the Phantom Seven. To disguise his disapproval he sang fragments of his favourite music hall songs. "A little of what you fancy does you good... My old man said follow the van... Don't you think my dress is a little bit, just a little bit, not too much of it... With a pair of opera glasses, you could see to Hackney Marshes, if it wasn't for the houses in between..." They knew what he was on about.

"So how was the genocide, boss?" Mo was well pleased, as if the years of isolation had never been. He patted his big Mark 8 on the seat beside him and rearranged the ammo pods. "Going well?"

"A bit disappointing." Jerry looked out at gray London roofs. He smiled, remembering his mum. All he needed was a touch of drizzle.

"Heaven, I'm in heaven..." began Major Nye, shifting into Fred Astaire. "Oh, bugger!" Mo started inching into the new Shepherds Bush turn-off. The major would be glad to see the back of this American heap in the garage so he could start dusting off the old Commer. Thank god it was only rented. Mo, of course, had wanted to buy one. Over in the next century, Karl Lagerfeld was selling his. A sure sign the vehicles were out of fashion. As they drove between the dull brick piles of the Notting Dale housing estates whose architecture had been designed to soak up all the city's misery and reflect it, Major Nye glanced at Jerry. In his 60's car coat and knitted white scarf, his shaven head, he looked like some released French convict, Vautrin back from the past to claim his revenge. Actually, of course, he was returning to the past to pay what remained of his dues. He'd had enough of revenge. He had appeared, it was said, in West London in 1960, the offspring of a Notting Hill Gate greengrocer and a South London music hall performer. But who really knew? He had spent his whole existence as a self-invented myth.

Major Nye knew for certain that Mrs. Cornelius had died at a ripe age in a Blenheim Crescent basement in 1976. At least, it might have been 1976. Possibly '77. Her "boyfriend," as she called him, Pyat, the old Polish second-hand clothes dealer, had died in the same year. A heart attack. It had been a bit of a tragic time, all in all. Four years later, Jerry had left. After that, Nye had stopped visiting London. He was glad he spent most of his life in the country. The climate was much healthier.

As Mo steered into the mews, the major was glad to see the cobbles back. Half the little cul-de-sac was still stables with Dutch doors. Mo got out to undo the lockup where they had arranged to leave the car. Nye could tell from the general condition of the place, with its flaking non-descript paint and stink of mould and manure, that they were already as good as home. From the back of the totters yard came the rasp of old cockney, the stink of human sweat. It had to be Jerry's Uncle Edmund. Major Nye could not be sure he was entirely glad to be home; but it was clear the others were. This was their natural environment. From somewhere came the aroma of vinegar-soaked newspaper, limp chips.

* * *

3. CAPTAIN MARVEL BATTLES HIS OWN CONSCIENCE!!!!!

Knowing that we are slaves of our virtual histories, the soldiers play dice beneath the cross. A bloody spear leans against the base. A goblet and a piece of good cloth are to be won. "What's that?" says a soldier, hearing a groan overhead. "Nothing." His companion rattles the dice in his cupped hands. "Something about his father."

—Michel LeBriard, Les Nihilists

"Up to your old tricks, eh, Mr. Cornelius?" Miss Brunner adjusted her costume. "Well, they won't work here."

"They never did work. You just had the illusion of effect. But you said it yourself, Miss B—*cherchez l'argent*. You can't change the economics. You can just arrange the window dressing a bit."

"Sez you!" Shakey Mo fingers his gun's elaborate instrumentation. "There's a bullet in here with your address on it."

Birmingham had started to burn. The reflected flames gave a certain liveliness to her features. "Now look what you've done."

"It doesn't matter." Jerry rubbed at his itching skull. "They'll never make anything out of it. I must be off."

She sniffed. "Yes. That explains a lot."

She wobbled a little on her ultra-high heels as she got back into his chopper. "Where to next?"

4. ECCE RUMPO

So where is he, the Yellow Star?
Whose card you find upon the bar.

Who laughs at Nazis, near and far.
Escaping in his powerful car.
So where is he, the Yellow Star?
 —Lafarge and Taylor, THE ADVENTURES OF
     THE YELLOW STAR, 1941

JERRY WAS SURPRISED to see his dad's faux Le Corbusier chateau in such good shape, considering the beating it had taken over the years. Someone had obviously been keeping it up. In spite of the driving rain and the mud, the place looked almost welcoming. Mo took a proprietorial pleasure in watching Jerry's face.

"Maintenance is what I've always been into. Everything that isn't original is a perfect repro. Even those psychedelic towers your dad was so keen on. He was ahead of his time, your dad. He practically invented acid. Not to mention acid rain. And we all know how far ahead of his time he was with computers." Mo sighed. "He was a baby badly waiting for the microchip. If he'd lived." He blinked reflectively and studied the curved metal casings of his Browning, fingering the ammo clips and running the flat of his hand over the long, tapering barrel. "He understood machinery, your dad. He existed for it. The Leo IV was his love. He built that house for it."

"And these days all he'd need for the same thing would be a spec or two of dandruff." Miss Brunner passed her hand through her tight perm and then looked suspiciously at her nails. "Can we go in?" She sat down on the chopper's platform and started pulling on her thick wellies.

High above them, against the dark beauty of the night, a rocket streaked, its red tail burning with the intensity of a ruby.

Jerry laughed. "I thought all that was over."

"Nothing's over." She sighed. "Nothing's ever bloody over."

Mo remembered why he disliked her.

They began to trudge through the clutching mud which oozed around them like melting chocolate

"Bloody global warming," said Jerry.

"You should have concentrated harder, Mr. C."

5. THE WANTON OF ARGOS

People claim that Portugal is an island. They say that you can't get there without wetting your feet. They say all those tales concerning dusty border roads into Spain are mere fables."

—Geert Mak, IN EUROPE, 2004

UP AT THE far end of the hall Miss Brunner was enjoying an Abu Ghraib moment. The screams were getting on their nerves. Jerry turned up *Pidgin English* by Elvis Costello but nothing worked any more. He had systematically searched his father's house while Miss Brunner applied electrodes to his brother Frank's tackle. "Was this really what the sixties were all about?"

"Oh, God," said Frank. "Oh, bloody hell." He'd never looked very good naked. Too pale. Too skinny. Ahead of or behind his time.

"You think you're going to find the secret of the sixties in a fake French modernist villa built by a barmy lapsed papist romantic Jew who went through World War Two in a trenchcoat and wincyette pyjamas fucking every sixty-a-day bereaved or would-be bereaved middle-class Englishwoman who ever got a first at Cambridge and claimed that deddy had never wanted her to be heppy? Not exactly rock and roll, is it, Jerry. You'd be better off talking to your old mum. The Spirit of the bloody Blitz. Is that Bar-B-Q."

"They all had the jazz habit." Jerry was defensive. "They all knew the blues."

"Oh, quite." She was disgusted. "Jack Parnell and his Gentleman Jazzers at the Café de Paris. Or was it Chris Barber and his Skiffling Sidemen?"

"Skiffle," said Jerry, casting around for his washboard. "The Blue Men. The Square Men. The Quarry Men. The Green Horns. The Black Labels. The Red Barrels."

"You ought to be ashamed of yourself," said Mo. He was rifling through the debris, looking for some antique ammo clips. "Someone went to a lot of trouble to bring this place over, stone by stone, to Ladbroke Grove. Though, I agree, it's a shame about the Hearst Castle."

"It was always more suitable for Hastings." Miss Brunner stared furiously at Jerry's elastic-sided Cubans. "You're going to ruin those, if you're not careful."

"It's not cool to be careful," he said. "Remember, this is the sixties. You haven't won yet. Careful is the eighties. Entirely different."

"Is this the Gibson?" Mo had found the guitar behind a mould-grown library desk.

Miss Brunner went back to working on Frank.

"The Gibson?" Jerry spoke hopefully. But when he checked, it was the wrong number.

"Can I have it, then?" asked Mo.

Jerry shrugged.

6. WILLIAM'S CROWDED HOUR

"...and does anyone know what 'the flip side' was? It was from the days when gramophone records were double-sided. You played your 78rpm or your 45 or your LP and then you turned it over and played the other side. Only nostalgia dealers and vinyl freaks remember that stuff now."

—Maurice Little, DOWN THE PORTOBELLO, 2007

CHRISTMAS 1962, SNOW still falling. Reports said there was no end in sight. Someone on the Third Programme even suggested a new Ice Age had started. At dawn, Jerry left his flat in Lancaster Gate, awakened by the tolling of bells from the church tower almost directly in line with his window, and went out into Hyde Park. His were the first footprints in the snow. It felt almost like sacrilege. Above him, crows circled. He told himself they were calling to him. He knew them all by name. They seemed reluctant to land, but then he saw their clawprints as he got closer to the Serpentine. The prints were already filling up. He wondered if they would follow him. He planned to go over to Ladbroke Grove and take the presents to his mum and the others. But first he had to visit Mrs. Pash and listen to the player piano for old time's sake.

They always got their Schoenberg rolls out for Christmas Day.

A crone appeared from behind a large chestnut. She wore a big red coat with a hood, trimmed in white, and she carried a basket. Jerry recognized her, but, to humor her, he pretended to be surprised as she approached him.

"Good luck, dear," she said. "You've got almost seven years left. And seven's a lucky number, isn't it?"

Jerry turned up the collar of his black car coat.

7. WILLIAM AND THE NASTIES

With the Manchester International Festival launching this month, and Liverpool becoming European Capital of Culture next year, the north is buzzing. But where is the region's true artistic capital?

—NEW STATESMAN, 25 June 2007

"BELONGING, JERRY, IS very important to me." Colonel Pyat glanced up and down the deserted Portobello. Old newspapers, scraps of lettuce, squashed tomatoes, ruined apples. Even the scavengers, their ragged forms moving methodically up and down the street, rejected them.

Jerry looked over at the cinema. The Essoldo was showing three pictures for 1/6d. *Mrs. Miniver*, *The Winslow Boy*, and *Brief Encounter*.

"Heppy deddy?" he asked no one in particular.

"There you are!" The colonel was triumphant. "You can talk perfectly properly if you want to!"

Jerry was disappointed. He had expected a different triple feature. He had been told it would be *Epic*

Hero and the Beast, First Spaceship on Venus, and
Forbidden Planet.

"Rets!" he said.

8. A GAME OF PATIENCE

Art, which should be the unique preoccupation of
the privileged few, has become a general rule... A
fashion... A furor... artism!"

—Felix Pyat

"THERE'S ALWAYS A bridge somewhere." Mo paced
up and down the levy like a neurotic dog. Every few
minutes he licked his lips with his long red tongue.
At other times he stood stock still, staring inland,
upriver. From somewhere in the gloom came the
sound of a riverboat's groaning wail, an exchange
between pilots over their bullhorns. Heavy sheets of
invisible water splashed against hulls. The words
were impossible to make out, like cops ordering
traffic, but nobody cared what they were saying.
Further downriver, from what remained of the city,
came the mock-carousel music inviting visitors to a
showboat whose paddles, turning like the vanes of
a ruined windmill, stuck high out of filthy brown
water full of empty Evian and Ozarka bottles.

Jerry called up from below. He had found a raft
and was poling it slowly to the gently curving concrete. "Mo. Throw down a rope!"

"The Pope? We haven't got a pope." Mo was
confused.

"A rope!"

"We going to hang him?"

Jerry gave up and let the raft drift back into midstream. He sat down in the center of it, his gun stuck up between his spread legs.

"You going to town?" Mo wanted to know.

When Jerry didn't answer, he began to paddle slowly along the levy, following the sound of his pole in the water, the shadow which he guessed to be his friend's. From somewhere in the region of Jackson Square vivid red, white, and blue neon flickered on and off before it was again extinguished. Then the sun set, turning the water a beautiful, bloody crimson. The broken towers along St Charles Street appeared in deep silhouette for a few moments and disappeared in the general darkness. The voices of the pilots stopped suddenly and all Mo could hear was the heavy lapping of the river.

"Jerry?"

Later Mo was relieved at the familiar razz—a kazoo playing a version of Alexander's Ragtime Band. He looked up and down. "Is that you?"

Jerry had always been fond of Berlin.

9. PAKISTAN—THE TALIBAN TAKEOVER

A mysterious young man met at luncheon
Said "My jaws are so big I can munch on
A horse and a pig and ship in full rig
And my member's the size of a truncheon."

Maurice LeB, 1907

MONSTROUS BATTLE CRUISERS cast black shadows over half a mile in all directions when Jerry finally reached the field, his armored Lotus HMV VII's batteries all but exhausted. He would have to abandon the vehicle and hope to get back to Exeter with the cavalry, assuming there was still a chance to make peace and assuming there still was an Exeter. He leapt from the vehicle and all but ran towards the tent where the Cornish commander had set up his headquarters.

The cool air moaned with the soft noise of idling motors. Cornish forces, including Breton and Basque allies, covered the moors on four sides of the Doone valley, the sound of their vast camp all but silenced by its understanding of the force brought against it. Imperial Germany, Burgundy, and Catalonia had joined Hannover to crush this final attempt to restore Tudor power and return the British capital to Cardiff.

Even as Jerry reached the royal tent, Queen Jennifer stepped out of it, a vision in mirrored steel, acknowledging his deep bow. Her captains crowded behind her, anxious for information.

"Do you bring news from Poole?" She was pale, straightbacked, as beautiful as ever. He cared as much for her extraordinary posture as any of her other qualities. Were they still lovers?

"Poole has fallen, your majesty, and the Isle of Wight lies smouldering and extinguished. Even Barnstaple's great shipyards are destroyed. We reckoned, my lady, without the unsentimental severity of Hannover's fleet. We have only cavalry and infantry remaining."

"Your own family?"

"Your majesty, I sent them to sanctuary in the Scillies."

She turned away, hiding her expression from him.

Her voice was steady when it addressed her commanders. "Gentlemen, you may return to your homes. The day is already lost and I would not see you die in vain." She turned to Jerry, murmuring: "And what of Gloucester?"

"The same, my lady."

A tear showed now in her calm, beautiful eyes. Yet her voice remained steady. "Then we are all defeated. I'll spill no more senseless blood. Tell Hannover I will come to London by July's end. Take this to him." Slowly, with firm hands, she unbuckled her sword.

10. THE EPIC SEARCH FOR A TECH HERO

Music now blares through every public space—but sound art reminds us how precious our hearing really is.

—NEW STATESMAN, 25 June 2007

MARIA AMIS, JULIA Barnes, and Iona MacEwan, the greatest lady novelists of their day, were taking tea in Liberty one afternoon of the summer of 2005. They had all been close friends at Girton in the same year and had shared many adventures. As time passed their fortunes prospered and their interests changed, to such a degree, in fact, that on occasion they had "had words" and spent almost a decade out of direct communication; but now, in middle years, they were reconciled. *Love's Arrow* had won the Netta Musket

Award, *The Lime Sofa* the Ouida Prize, and *Under Alum Chine* the Barbara Cartland Memorial Prize. All regularly topped the bestseller lists.

In their expensive but not showy summer frocks and hats they were a vision of civilized feminity.

The tea rooms had recently been redecorated in William Morris "Willow Pattern" and brought a refreshing lightness to their surroundings. The lady novelists enjoyed a sense of secure content which they had not known since their Cambridge days.

The satisfaction of this cosy moment was only a little spoiled by the presence of a young man with bright shoulder length black hair, dark blue eyes, long, regular features, and a rather athletic physique, wearing a white shirt, black car coat, and narrow, dark gray trousers, with pointed "Cuban" elastic-sided boots, who sat in the corner nearest to the door. Occasionally, he would look up from his teacakes and Darjeeling and offer them a friendly, knowing wink.

11. LES FAUX MONNAYEURS

Things were happening as we motored into Ypres. When were they not? A cannonade of sorts behind the roofless ruins, perhaps outside of town; nobody seems to know or care; only an air-fight for our benefit. We crane our necks and train our glasses. Nothing whatever to be seen.

—E.W. Hornung, NEW STATESMAN,
30 June 1917

JERRY'S HEAD TURNED in the massive white pillow and he saw something new in his sister's trust even as she slipped into his arms, her soft comfort warming him. "You'll be leaving, then?"

"I catch the evening packet from Canterbury. By tonight I'll be in Paris. There's still time to think again."

"I must stay here." Her breathing became more rapid. "But I promise I'll join you if the cryogenics…" Her voice broke. "By Christmas. Oh, Jesus, Jerry. It's tragic. I love you."

His expression puzzled her, he knew. He had dreamed of her lying in her coffin while an elaborate funeral went on around her. He remembered her in both centuries. Image after image came back to him, confusing in their intensity and clarity. It was almost unbearable. Why had he always loved her with such passion? Such complete commitment? That old feeling. Of course, she had not been the only woman he had loved so unselfconsciously, so deeply, but she was the only one to reciprocate with the same depth and commitment. The only one to last his lifetime. The texture of her short, brown hair reminded him of Jenny. Of Jenny's friend Eve. He and they were together through much of the 70s when Catherine was away with Una Persson.

Looking over Eve's head through copper hot eyes as her friend moved her beautiful full lips on his penis, Jenny's face bore that expression of strong affection which was the nearest she came to love. His fingers clung deep in Eve's long dark hair, his mouth on Jenny's as she frigged herself. The subtle differences of skin shades; their eye colors. The graceful movements. That extraordinary passion. Jenny's lips parted and small delicious grunts came from her mouth. This was almost the last of what the 60's had brought them and which most other generations could never enjoy: pleasure without conflict or fear of serious consequences; the most exquisite form of lust. Meanwhile, taking such deep humane pleasure in the love of the moment, Jerry could not know (though he had begun to guess) what the future would bring. And were his actions, which felt so innocent, the cause of the horror which would within two decades begin to fill the whole world?

"Was it my fault?" he asked her.

She sat up, smiling. "Look at the time!"

12. HOME ALONE FIVE

I learned from Taguba that the first wave of materials included descriptions of the sexual humiliation of a father with his son, who were both detainees. Several of these images, including one of an Iraqi woman detainee baring her breasts, have since surfaced; others have not. (Taguba's report noted that photographs and videos were being held by the CID because of ongoing criminal investigations and their "extremely sensitive nature.") Taguba said that he saw "a video of a male American soldier in uniform sodomizing a female detainee." The video was not made public in any of the subsequent court proceedings, nor has there been any public government mention of it. Such images would have added an even more inflammatory element to the outcry over Abu Ghraib. "It's bad enough that there were photographs of Arab men wearing women's panties," Taguba said.

—Seymour M. Hersh, The General's Report,
New Yorker, 25 June 2007

Portobello Road, deserted except for a few stall-holders setting up before dawn, had kept its familiar Friday morning atmosphere. As Jerry approached the Westway, one hand deep in the pocket of his black car coat, the other, still in its black glove, resting on the handlebars of his Gent's Royal Albert bicycle, he glanced at the big neon NEW WORLDS Millennium clock, in vivid red and blue, erected to celebrate the magazine's fifty-fifth birthday. Two doors closer to the bridge, and not yet open, were the FRENDZ offices and nearby were TIME OUT, Rough Trade, Stiff Records International, Riviera Management, Mac's Music, Trux Transportation, Stone's Antiquarian Books, Pash's Instruments, The Mountain Grill, Brock and Turner, The Mandrake, Smilin' Mike's Club; all the great names which had made the Grove famous and given the area its enduring character.

"I remember when I used to be a denizen round here. Glad to see the neighborhood has kept going." Jerry spoke to his old friend, Professor Hira, who had remained behind when the others had gone away.

"Only by a whisker," said the plump Brahmin, shaking his head. "By a lot of hardwork and visionary thinking on the part of those of us who didn't leave."

Jerry began to smile, clearly thinking Hira was overpraising himself and being slightly judgemental at the same time. But Hira was serious. "Believe me, old boy, I'm not blaming you for going. You had a different destiny. But you don't know what it's like out there any more. North Kensington is all that remains of the free world. Roughly east of

Queensway, north of Harrow Road, south of Holland Park Avenue, west of Wood Lane, a new kind of tyranny triumphs."

"It can't be much worse than it was!"

"Oh, that's what we all thought in 1975 or so. We hadn't, even then, begun to realize what fate—or anyway The City—had in store for us... Ladbroke Grove is the only part of Britain which managed to resist the march of the Whiteshirts from out of the suburbs. We keep the night alive with our signs. That's a battle we're constantly fighting. Thank god we still have a few people with money *and* conscience. All the work we did in the 60s and 70s, to maintain the freeholds and rents, successfully kept the Grove in the hands of the original inhabitants so that, at worst, we are a living museum of the Golden Age. At our best, we have slowed time long enough for people to take stock, not to be panicked or threatened by the Whiteshirts. Here, the wealth is still evenly distributed, continuing the progress made between 1920 and 1970, and, through the insistence of our ancient charters, the Grove, along with Brookgate in the east, like London's ancient Alsatia, has managed to keep her status as an independent state, a sanctuary."

"Ruritania, eh? I thought the air smelled a bit stale."

"Well, we've developed recycling to something of a fine art. Out there in the rest of the country, as in the USA, where the majority of the wealth was encouraged by Thatcher and her colleagues to flow back to Capital, things of course are considerably worse for the greater middle class. Thatcher and her kind used all the power put into their hands by short-sighted unions and their far-sighted opponents. Every threat. Every technique. Those who resisted made themselves helpless by refusing to change their rhetoric and so were also unable to change their strategies. It's true, old boy. For thirty years the outside world has collapsed into cynicism as the international conglomerates became big enough to challenge, then control, and finally replace elected governments. You're lucky you were brought back here, Mr. C. Outside, it's pretty unpleasant, I can tell you. Most Londoners can't afford to live where they were born. Colons from the suburbs or worse the country have flooded in, taking over our houses, our businesses, our restaurants and shops. Of course, it was starting in your time: George Melly and stripped pine shops. But now the working class is strictly confined to its ghettoes, distracted by drugs, lifestyle magazines, and reality TV. The middle class has been trained to compete tooth and nail for the advantages they once took for granted and the rich do whatever they like, including murder, thanks to their obscene amounts of moolah." Even Hira's language appeared to have been frozen in his dog years. "At least the middle class learned to value what they had taken for granted, even if it's too late to do anything about it now!"

"Bloody hell," said Jerry. "It looks like I was better off in that other future, after all. And now I've burned my bridges. Who's Thatcher?"

"We call her The Goddess Miggea. Most of them worship her today, though she was the one who formulated the language used to place the middle class in its present unhappy position. She was a sort of quisling for the Whiteshirts. She's the main symbol of middle class downfall, yet they still think she saved them, the way the yanks think Reagan got them out of trouble. Amazing, isn't it. You said yourself that the secret of successful feudalism is to make the peasants believe it's the best of all possible worlds. Blair and Bush thought they could reproduce those successes with a brief war against a weak nation, but they miscalculated rather badly. Too late now. Remember the old scenario for nuclear war which put Pakistan at the center of the picture? Well, it's not far off. Religion's back with a vengeance. I'd return to India, only things aren't much better there. You probably haven't heard of Hindu Nationalism, either. Or the Mombai Tiger. The rich are so much richer and the poor are so much poorer. The rich have no sense of charity or gravitas. They enjoy the power and the extravagance of Eighteenth Century French aristocrats. They distract themselves with all kinds of speculative adventures, including wars which make Vietnam seem idealistic. How the people of Eastern Europe mourn the fall of the old Soviet empire, nostalgic for the return of the certainties of tyranny! Am I boring you, Mr. Cornelius?"

"Sorry." Jerry was admiring a massive plasma TV in an electrical shop's display window. "Wow! The future's got everything we hoped it would have! The Soviet Union's fallen?"

"I forget. I suppose that in your day so much of this seemed impossible, or at least unlikely. Thirty five years ago you were talking about zero population growth and the problem of leisure. Here we are at the new Smaller Business Bureau. Lovely, isn't it? Yes, I know, it smells like Amsterdam. I work here now." Carefully, he opened the doors of Reception

KATRINA, KATRINA!

It fell to Neville Chamberlain in one of the supreme crises of the world to be contradicted by events, to be disappointed in his hopes, and to be deceived and cheated by a wicked man. But what were these hopes in which he was disappointed? What were these wishes in which he was frustrated? What was the faith that was abused? They were among the most noble instincts of the human heart—the love of peace, the strife for peace, the pursuit of peace, even at great peril and certainly to the utter disdain of popularity or clamor.

—Winston Churchill to Parliament,
November 12 1940

1. WHY YOU SHOULD FEAR PRESIDENT GIULIANI

Parts of rural China are seeing a burgeoning market for female corpses, the result of the reappearance of a strange custom called "ghost marriages". Chinese tradition demands that husbands and wives always share a grave. Sometimes when a man died umarried, his parents would procure the body of a woman, hold a "wedding", and bury the couple together.

—The Economist, 28 July 2007

"There are no more sanctuaries, m'sieur. You are probably too young even to dream of such things.

But I grew up with the idea that, I don't know, you could retire to a little cottage in the country or find a deserted beach somewhere or a cabin in the mountains. Now we're lucky if we can get an apartment in Nice, enough equity in it to pay for the extra healthcare we'll need." Monsieur Pardon stood upright in the barge as it emerged from under the bridge on Canal St Martin. "And we French are increasingly having to find jobs overseas. Who knows? Am I destined for a condo in Florida? This is my stop. I live in rue Oberkampf. And you?"

"This will do for me, too." Jerry got ready to disembark. "How long have you lived in Paris?"

"Only for a couple of years. Before that I was a professional autoharp player in Nantes. But the work dried up. I'm currently looking for a job."

They had reached the bank and stood together beside a newspaper kiosk. Jerry took down a copy of *The Herald Tribune* and paid with a three-euro piece. "You seem lost, m'sieu. Can I help?"

"Thank you. I'm just trying to follow a story. I wonder. May I ask? What makes you cry, M. Pardon?"

The neatly dressed rather serious young man fingered his waxed moustache. He looked down at his pale gray suit, patting his pockets. "Eh?"

"Well, for instance, I cry at almost any example of empathy I encounter. Pretty much any observation of sympathetic imagination. And music. I cry in response to music. Or a generous act. Or a sentimental movie."

M. Pardon smiled. "Well, yes. I am a terrible sentimentalist. I cry, I suppose, when I hear of some evil deed. Or an innocent soul suffering some terrible misfortune."

Jerry nodded, almost to himself. "I understand."

Together, they turned the corner in Rue Oberkampf.

"So it is imagination that moves you to tears?"

"Not exactly. Some forms of imagination merely bore me."

2. SOUTH RAMPART STREET PARADE

Presidential hopeful Rudy Giuliani recently fumbled one of the dumbest questions asked since "boxers or briefs?" Campaigning in Alabama, he was asked, "What is the price of a gallon of milk?" He was off by a buck or two, thus failing a tiresome common-citizen test. But far more important questions need to be posed. Let's start with asking our future leaders about how affordable PCs, broadband internet connectivity, and other information technologies are transforming the lives of every American.

—Dan Costa, PC MAGAZINE,
7 August 2007

"ANGRY, MR CORNELIUS?" Miss Brunner unpacked her case. Reluctantly, he had brought her from St. Pancras. Mist was still lifting from St. James's Park. He stood by the window, trying to identify a duck. From this height, it was difficult.

"I'm never angry." He turned as she was hanging a piece of complicated lingerie on a hanger. "You know me."

"A man of action."

"If nothing else." He grew aware of a smell he didn't like. Anaesthetic? Some sort of spray? Was it coming from her case?

"When did you arrive?"

"You met me at Eurostar."

"I meant in Paris. From New Orleans?" That was it. The perfume used to disguise the smell of mold. Her clothes had that specific iridescence. They'd been looted.

"Saks," he said.

"You can't see the label from there, can you? You wouldn't believe how cheap they were."

"*Laissez les bon temps rollez.*" Jerry had begun to cheer up.

"I'm so tired of the English."

3. POMPIER PARIS

Defenses are tough to predict in fantasy football.
—FANTASY SPORTS, September 2007

"HOT ENOUGH FOR you? Everyone's leaving for the country." Jerry and Bishop Beesley disembarked from the taxi at the corner of Elgin Crescent and Portobello Road. All the old familiar shops were gone. The pubs had become wine bars and restaurants. Tables and chairs stood outside fake bistros stretching into the middle distance. The fruit and veg on the market stalls had the look of mock organics. Heritage tomatoes. The air was filled with braying aggression. If the heat got any worse there could be a Whiteshirt riot. Jerry could imagine nothing worse than watching the *nouveaux riches* taking it out on what remained of the *anciens pauvres*. The people in the council flats must be getting nervous.

"*Apres moi, le frisson nouveau.*"

"Do what?" Bishop Beesley was distracted. He had spotted one of his former parishioners stumbling dazedly out of Finch's. The poor bugger had tripped into a timewarp but brightened when he saw the bishop. Sidling up, he mumbled a familiar mantra and forced a handful of old fivers into Beesley's sweating fist. Reluctantly, the bishop took something from under his surplice in exchange. Watching the decrepit speed freak stumble away, he said apologetically. "They're still my flock. But of course there's been a massive falling off compared to the numbers I used to serve. Once, you could rely on an active congregation west of Portobello, but these days everything left is mostly in Kilburn. Not my parish, you see."

Jerry whistled sympathetically.

Beesley stopped to admire one of the newly decorated stalls. The owner, wearing a fresh white overall and a pearly cap, recognized him. "You lost weight, your worship?"

"Sadly..." The bishop fingered the stock. "I've never seen Brussels as big."

"Bugger me." Jerry stared in astonishment at a fawn bottom rolling towards Colville Terrace. Who needed jodhpurs and green wellies to drive a Range Rover to the Ladbroke Grove Sainsbury's? "Trixie?" Wasn't it Miss Brunner's little girl, all grown up? Distracted, Jerry looked for a hand of long branches which used to hide a sign he remembered on the other side of the Midland Bank. The bank was now an HSBC. Who on earth would want to erase his childhood? He remembered how he used to have a thing against the past. Maybe it was generational.

"Are you okay?" His hand moving restlessly in his pocket, Bishop Beesley looked yearningly across the road at a new sweet and tobacconists called Yummy Puffs. "Would you mind?"

Jerry watched him cross the road and emerge shortly afterwards with his arms full of bags of M&Ms. Where, he wondered absently, were the chocolate bars of yesterday? The Five Boys? He could taste the Fry's peppermint cream on his tongue. Dairy Milk. Those Quakers had known how to make chocolate. As a lad he had wondered why the old Underground vending machines, the Terry's, the Rowntree's, the Cadbury's, were always empty, painted up, like poorly made props meant only to be glimpsed as the backgrounds of Ealing comedies. The heavy cast-iron machines had been sprayed post office red or municipal green and there was nothing behind the glass panels, no way of opening the sliding dispensers. They had slots for pennies. Signs calling for 2d. They had been empty since the war, he learned from his mum. When chocolate had been rationed and prices had risen. Yet the machines had remained on tube train platforms well into the late 1950s, serving to make the Underground mysterious, a tunnel into the past, a labyrinth of memory, where people had once sought sanctuary from bombs. Escalators to heaven and hell. The trains, the ticket machines, the vast escalators, the massive lift cages had all functioned as well as they ever had, but the chocolate machines had become museum pieces, offering a clue to a certain state of mind, a stoicism which perceived them as mere self-indulgence, at odds with the serious business of survival. Not even the most beautiful, desireable machines survived such Puritanism. How many times as a little boy had he hoped that one sharp kick would reward him with an Aero bar, or even a couple of overlooked pennies? And then one day, in the name of modernization, they were carried off, never to be replaced. It was just as well. They had vanished before they could be turned into nostalgic features.

Brands meant familiarity and familiarity meant repeated experience and repetition meant security. Once. Now they had achieved the semblance of security, at the very moment when real protection from the fruits of their greed was needed. The Underground had been a false shelter, too, of course. They had poured down there to avoid the bombs, to be drowned and buried. Yet he had loved the atmosphere, the friendship, as he had played with his toy AA gun, his little battery-powered searchlight hunting the dusty arches for a miniature enemy. Portobello began to fill with the yap of colons settling their laptops and unfolding their *Independents*, pushing up their sweater sleeves as they sauntered into the pubs, familiar with their

favourite spots as any Germans who had so affec-
tionately occupied Paris.

"They defeated the Underground," he said.
"Captured our most potent memories and converted them to cashpoints. They're blowing up
everything they don't like. And anything they don't
understand, they don't like."

Beesley was looking at him with a certain concern,
his lower face pasted with chocolate so that he resembled some Afghan commando. With a plump, dainty
finger he dabbed at the corner of his mouth. "Ready?"

Mournfully, Jerry whistled the Marseillaise.

4. LES BOUDINS NOIRS

Blood-spurting martyrs, biblical parables, ascendant
doves—most church windows feature the same
preachy images that have awed parishioners for centuries. But a new stained-glass window in Germany's
Cologne Cathedral, to be completed in August,
evokes technology and science, not religion and the
divine.

—WIRED, August 2007

"ARE YOU FAMILIAR with torture, Herr Cornelius?"
Karen von Krupp hitched up her black leather
miniskirt and adjusted his blindfold, but he could
still see her square, pink face, surrounded by its
thick blonde perm over the top, her peachy neck
ascending above her swollen breasts. When she
reached to pull the mask down he was grateful for
the sudden blindness.

"How do you mean 'familiar?'"

"Have you done much of it?"

"It depends a bit on how you define it." He giggled as he heard her crack her little whip. "I used to be able to get into it. Between consenting adults. In more innocent days, you know. You?"

"Oh!" She seemed impatient. Frustrated. "Consent? You mean obedience? Obedient girls?"

He was beginning to understand why he was back in her dentist chair after so many years and wearing a tart's costume. "It's Poland all over again, isn't it?"

He heard her light a cigarette, smelled the smoke. A Sullivan's.

She added: "I believe I ask the questions."

"And I respect your beliefs. Did you know that the largest number of immigrants to the US were German? That's why they love Christmas and why they have Easter bunnies, marching bands, and think black cats are unlucky." He settled into his bonds. It was going to be a long night.

"Of course. But now I want you to tell me something I don't know."

"I can still see some light."

"We'll soon put a stop to that."

Again, she cracked the whip.

"Are we on TV?"

"Should we be?"

"These days, everything's on TV. Don't you watch Guantanamo Dailies? Or is it too boring?"

"We don't have cable. Just remember this, Mr. Cornelius. There's more than one way of cooking a canary."

* * *

5. LES BOUDINS BLANCS

The railway from Nairobi to Mombasa is a Victori-
an relic. But it's the best way to see Kenya.
                    —NEW STATESMAN, 25 June 2007

"I GOT THESE rules, see." Shakey Mo looked carefully into the mirror. "That's how I keep on top of
things. You can't survive, these days, without rules.
Set yourself goals, yeah? Draw up a flow chart. A
yearly planner. And then you stick to it. OK? Reli-
giously. Rules is rules. It's survival. It's Mo's
survival, anyway." He had begun talking about
himself in the third person again. Jerry guessed he
was in a bad way.

"Fun?" Jerry stared at the cabinets on Mo's walls.
He kept a neat ship, he had to admit. Each cabinet
held a different gun, with its clips, its ammunition,
its instruction manual; the date it was acquired,
whom it had shot, and when.

"Clubbing," Mo told him. "Whenever you get
the chance. Blimey, Jerry, where have you been?"

"Rules." Jerry wiped his lovely lips. "The jugged
hare seemed a bit bland today. Out of season,
maybe?"

"There aren't any seasons these days, Jerry. Just
seasoning. Man, you're so retro!" Mo rearranged
his hair again. He guffawed. "That's the nineties for
you. You want *au naturelle*, you gotta pay for it."

"It wasn't always like this."

"We were young and stupid. We almost lost it.
Went too far. That costs, if you're lucky enough to

survive. AIDS and the abolition of controlled rents. A high price to pay."

Jerry regarded his shaking hands. "If this is the price of a misspent youth, I'll take a dozen."

Mo wasn't listening. "I think I need a new stylist."

6. HOW TO DEAL WITH A SHRINKING POPULATION

There's a lot of hot air wafting around the Venice Biennale. But one thing is for sure: the art world can party.

—NEW STATESMAN, 25 June 2007

"HI, HI, AMERICAN pie chart." Jerry sniffed. A miasma was creeping across the world. He'd read about it, heard about it, been warned about it. A cloud born of the dreadful dust of conflict, greed, and power addiction, according to old Major Nye. It rose from Auschwitz, London, Hiroshima, Seoul, Jerusalem, Rwanda, New York, and Baghdad. But Jerry wasn't sure. He remarked on it. Max Pardon buttoned his elegant gray overcoat, nodding emphatically:

"*J'accord.*" He resorted to his own language. "We inhale the dust of the dead with every breath. The deeper the breath, the greater the number of others' memories we take into ourselves. Those wind-borne lives bring horror into our hearts and every dream we have, every anxiety we feel, is a result of all those fires, all those explosions, all those devastations. Out of that miasma shapes are formed. Those shapes achieve substance resembling bone, blood, flesh and skin, creating monsters, some of them in human form."

That was how monsters procreated in the heat and destruction of Dachau, the Blitz, and the Gaza strip; from massive bombs dropped on the innocent; from massacre and the thick, oily smoke of burning flesh. The miasma accumulated mass the more bombs that were dropped or bodies burned. The monsters created from this mass, born of shed blood and human fright, bestrode the ruins of our sanctuaries and savoured our fear like connoisseurs. "Here is the Belsen '44; taste the subtle flavours of a Kent State '68 or the nutty sweetness of an Abu Ghraib '05, the amusing lightness of a Madrid '04, a London '06. What good years they were! Perfect conditions. These New York '01s are so much more full-bodied than the Belfast '98s. The monsters sit at table, relishing their feast. They stink of satiation. Their farts expel the sucked-dry husks of human souls: Judge Dread, Lord Horror, Stuporman. Praise the great miasma wherever it creeps. Into TV sets, computer games, the language of sport, of advertising. The language of politics, infected by the lexicon of war. The language of war wrapped up in the vocabularies of candy-salesmen, toilet sanitisers, room sprays. That filth on our feet isn't dog shit. That city film on our skins is the physical manifestation of human greed. You feel it as soon as you smell New Orleans."

That whimpering you heard was the sound of cowards finding it harder and harder to discover sanctuary.

"Where can you hide? The Bahamas? Grand Cayman? The BVAs? The Isle of Man or Monaco? Not now you've melted the icebergs, called up the tsunamis and made the oceans rise. All that's left is Switzerland with her melting glaciers and strengthened boundaries. The monsters respond by playing dead. This is their moment of weakness when they can be slain, but it takes a special hero to cut off their heads and dispose of their bodies so that they can't rise again. Some Charlemagne, perhaps? Some doomed champion? There can be no sequels. Only remakes. Only remakes. But, because we have exhausted a few of the monsters, that doesn't mean they no longer move amongst us, sampling our souls, watching us scamper in fear at the first signs of their return. We are thoroughly poisoned. We have inhaled the despairing dust of Burundi and Baghdad."

"Well, that was a mouthful." The three of them had crossed the Seine from the Isle St. Louis. It was getting chilly. Jerry pulled on his old car coat and checked his heat. His resurrected needle-gun, primed and charged, was ready to start stitching up the enemy. "Shall we go?"

"What's he saying?" asked Mo, staring with some curiosity at Max Pardon who had exhausted himself and stood with his back to a gilded statue, a small, neatly-wrapped figure wearing an English tweed cap. "You know what my French is like."

"His taxes are too high," said Jerry.

* * *

7. PUMP UP YOUR NETWORK

"Daran habe ich gar nicht gedacht!"
—Albert Einstein

"Now LOOK HERE, Mr. Cornelius, you can't come
in here with your insults and your threats. What
will happen to the poor beggars who depend on
their corps for their healthcare and their massive
mortgages? Would you care to have negative equity
and be unemployed?" Rupert Fox spread his
gnarled antipodean hands, and then mournfully fingered the folds of his face, leaning into the
mirror-cam. His new facelift had not taken as well
as he had hoped. He looked like a partially rehy-
drated peach. "Platitudes *are* news, old boy." He
exposed his expensive teeth to the view overlooking
Green Park. In the distance, the six flags of Texas
waved all the way up the Mall to Buckingham
Palace. "We give them reality in other ways. The
reality the public wants. Swelp me. I should know.
I've got God. What do you have? A bunch of
idols."

"I thought idolatory was your stock in trade."

"Trade makes the world go round."

"The great idolator, eh? All those beads swapped
with the natives."

"I don't have to listen to this crap." Rupert Fox
made a show of good humor. "You enjoy yourself
with your fantasies while I get on with my realities,
sport. You can't live in the past forever. The Empire
has to grow and change." He motioned towards his

office's outer door. "William will show you to the elevator."

8. IS HE THE GREATEST FANTASY PLAYER OF ALL TIME?

One of the keys to being seen as a great leader is to be seen as a commander-in-chief... My father had all this political capital built up when he drove the Iraqis out of Kuwait and he wasted it. If I have a chance to invade... if I had that much capital, I'm not going to waste it...

—George W. Bush to Mickey Herskowitz, 1999

BANNING NEVER REALLY changed. Jerry parked the Corniche in the disabled parking space and got out. A block to the east, I-10 roared and shook like a disturbed beast. A block to the west, and the town spread out to merge with the scrub of semi-desert, its single-storey houses decaying before his eyes. But here, outside Grandma's Kitchen, he knew he was home and dry. He was going to get some of the best country cooking between Santa Monica and Palm Springs. The restaurant was alone amongst the concessions and chains of Main Street. It might change owners now and again, but never its cooks or waitresses. Never its well-advertised politics, patriotism and faith. Grandma's was the only place worth eating in a thousand miles. He took off his wide-brimmed Panama and wiped his neck and forehead. It had to be a hundred and ten. The rain, roaring down from Canada and up from the Gulf of

Mexico had not yet reached California. When it did, it would not stop. Somewhere out there, in the heavily irrigated fields, wetbacks were desperately working to bring in the crops before they were swamped. From now on, they would probably be growing rice, like the rest of the country.

He pushed open the door and walked past the display of flags, crosses, fish, and Support Our Troops signs. There was a Christmas theme, too. Every sign and ikon had fake snow sprayed over it. Santa and his sleigh and reindeers swung from every available part of the roof. There was an artificial tree in the middle of the main dining room. Christmas songs were playing over the speakers. A few rednecks looked up at him and nodded a greeting. A woman in a red felt elf hat, who might have been Grandma herself, led him through the wealth of red and white checkered tablecloths and wheel-backed chairs to a table in a corner. "Can I get you a nice glass of iced tea, son?"

"Unsweetened. Thanks, ma'am. I'm waiting for a friend."

"I can recommend the Turkey Special," she said.

Twenty minutes went by before Max Pardon came in, removing his own hat and looking around him in delight. "Jerry! This is perfect. A cultural miracle." The natty Frenchman had shaved his moustache. He had been stationed out here for a couple of months. Banning had once owed a certain prosperity, or at least her existence, to oil. Now she was a dormitory extension for the casinos. You could have bought the whole place for the price of a mid-sized Pasadena apartment. M. Pardon had actually been thinking of doing just that. He ordered his food and gave the waitress one of his charming, sad smiles. She responded by calling him "Darling".

When their meals arrived, he picked up his knife and fork and shrugged. "Don't feel too sorry for me, Jerry. It's healthy enough, once you get back from the interstate aways." He spoke idiomatic American. He leaned forward over his turkey dinner to murmur. "I think I've found the guns."

Jerry grinned.

As if in response to M. Pardon's information, from somewhere out in the scrubland came the sound of rapid shooting. "That's not the Indians," he said. "The locals do that about this time every day."

"You'll manage to get them to the Diné on schedule?"

"Sure." Max raised his eyebrows as he tasted the fowl. "You bet."

Grandma brought them condiments. She turned up her hearing aid, cocking her head. "This'll put Banning on the map." She spoke with cheerful satisfaction. "Just in time to celebrate the season."

Jerry sipped his tea.

Max Pardon always knew how to make the most of Christmas. By the time the Diné arrived, Banning would be a serious bargain.

* * *

9. THEY WANT TO MAKE FIREARMS OWNERSHIP A BURDEN—NOT A FREEDOM!

In August most upscale Parisians head north for Deauville for the polo and the racing or to the cool woods of their country estates in the Loire or Bordeaux... Paris's most prestigious hotel at that time of the year is crawling with camera-toting tourists and rubberneckers.

—Tina Brown, *The Diana Chronicles*, 2007

"WELCOME TO THE Hotel California," Jerry sang into his Bluetooth. The beautiful violet light winked in time in his long, dark hair as the ruins sped past on either side of I-10—wounded houses, shops, shacks, filling stations, churches, all covered in Day-Glo blue PVC, stacks of fallen trunks, piles of reclaimed planks, leaning firehouses, collapsed trees lying where the hurricane had thrown them, over-turned cars and trucks, collapsed barns, flattened billboards, flooded strip malls, mountains of torn foliage, state and federal direction signs twisted into tattered scrap, smashed motels and roadside restaurants, mile upon mile of detritus growing more plentiful the closer they got to New Orleans.

In the identical midnight blue Corniche beside him, connected by her own Bluetooth, Cathy joined in the chorus. The twin cars headed over cypress swamps, bayous, and swollen rivers on the way to where the Mississippi met the city.

Standing in the still, swollen ponds on either side of the long bridges, egrets and storks regarded them with cool, incurious eyes. Crows hopped along the roadside, pecking at miscellaneous corpses; buzzards cruised overhead. It looked like rain again.

Here and there massive cracks and gaps in the concrete had been filled in with tar-like black holes in a flat gray vacuum. Hand-made signs offered the services of motel chains or burger concessions and every few miles they were told how much closer they were to Prejean's or Michaux's where the music was still good and the gumbo even tastier. The fish had been enjoying a more varied diet. Zydeco and cajun, crawfish and boudin. Oo-oo. Oo-oo. Still having fon on the bayou... Everything still for sale. The Louisiana heritage.

"Them Houston gals done got ma soul!" crooned Cathy. "Nearly home."

10. PIRATES OF THE UNDERSEAS

At places where two road networks cross, a vertical interchange of bridges and tunnels will separate the traffic systems, and Palestinians from Israelis.
—Eyal Weizman, *Hollow Land: Israel's Architecture of Occupation*, 2007

"Christmas won't be Christmas without presents," grumbled Mo, lying on the rug. He got up to sit down again at his keyboard. "Sorry, but that's my experience." He was writing about the authenticity of rules in the game of *Risk*. "I mean you have to give it a chance, don't you? Or you'll never know who you are." He cast an absent-minded glance about the lab. He was in a world of his own.

Miss Brunner came in wearing a white coat. "The kids called. They won't be here until Boxing Day."

"Bugger," said Mo. "Don't they want to finish this bloody game?" He was suspicious. Had her snobbery motivated her to dissuade them, perhaps subtly, from coming? He already had her down as a social climber. Still, a climber was a climber. "Why didn't you let them talk to me?"

"You were out of it," she said. "Or cycling or something. They thought you might be dead."

He shook his head. "There's days I wonder about you."

Catherine Cornelius decided to step in. He was clearly at the end of his rope. "Can I ask a question, Mo?"

He took a breath and began to comb his hair. "Be my guest."

"What's this word?" She had been looking at Jerry's notes. "Is this holes, hoes or holds?"

"I think it's ladies," said Mo.

"Oh, of course." She brightened. "Little women. Concord, yes? The dangers of the unexamined life?"

THE WHEELS OF CHANCE

1. GUNS IS GUNS

Everyone will be wealthy, living like a lord,
Getting plenty of things today they can't afford
But when's it going to happen? When? Just by
and by!

*Oh, everything will be lovely, when the pigs
begin to fly!*
—Charles Lambourne, EVERYTHING WILL BE
LOVELY c. 1860

"I ADMIRE A MAN who can look cool on a camel."
Bessy Burroughs presented Jerry with her perfectly
rounded vowels. Born in Kansas, she had been edu-
cated in Sussex. Regular vowels, her dad had always
said, were the key to success, no matter what your calling. "God! Is it always this hot in Cairo?"

"It used to be lovely in the winter." Jerry jumped
down from his kneeling beast and came to help Bessy
dismount. Only Karen von Krupp preferred to remain
in her saddle. Shielding her eyes against the rising sun,
she peered disdainfully at a distant clump of palms.

Bessy had none of her father's lean, lunatic wit.
Her full name was Timobeth, a combination of
those her parents had chosen for a girl or a boy.
Bunny believed that old-fashioned names were an
insult to the future. They pandered to history. Her
parents still hated history. A sense of the past was
but a step on the road to nostalgia and nostalgia, as
Bunny was fond of saying, was a vice which cor-
rupts and distorts.

Jerry remembered his lazy lunches at Rules.
Bunny had loved Rules. But he had come to hate the
heritage industry as 'a brothel disguised as a
church'. Jerry wasn't sure what he meant and had
never had a chance to find out. If he turned up, as
promised, by the Sphinx, perhaps this would be a
good time to ask him.

"Dad loves it out here." Pulling her veil down from her hat, Bessy began to follow him across the hard sand towards the big pyramid. "Apart from the old stuff. He hates the old stuff. But he loves the beach. The old stuff can crumble to dust for all he cares." She paused to wipe her massive cheeks and forehead. That last box of Turkish Delight was beginning to tell on her. She had been raised, by some trick of fate, by Bishop Beesley as his own daughter until Mitzi had finally objected and Bunny had been recalled from Tangier to perform his paternal duties.

"You don't like to be connected to the past?" asked Karen von Krupp, bringing up a lascivious lear and thwacking her "Charlie" on its rump with a curious-looking whip. "I love history. So romantic."

"Hate it. Loathe it. History disgusts me. Hello! Who's this type, I wonder?"

"Good god!" Suddenly fully awake, Jerry pushed back his hat. "Talk about history! It's Major Nye."

Major Nye, in the full uniform of Skinner's Horse, rode up at a clip and brought his gray to a skidding stop in the sand.

"Morning, major."

"Morning, Cornelius. Where's that hotel gone?"

"I gather it had its day, major. Demolished. I can't imagine what's going up in its place." His knees were crumping.

"I can." With a complacent hand Bessy patted a brochure she produced from a saddle bag. "It's going to be like The Pyramid. That's why I asked you all here. Only three times bigger. And in two buildings. You'll be able to get up in the morning and look down on all that." She waved vaguely in the direction of the pyramids. "It'll be a knockout. It will knock you unconscious! Really!" She nodded vigorously, inviting them, by her example, to smile.

"Gosh," said Jerry. Major Nye peered gravely down at his horse's mane.

"We are born unconscious and we die unconscious." Karen von Krupp gestured with her whip. "In between we suffer precisely because we are conscious, whereas the other creatures with whom we share this unhappy planet are unconscious forever, no? I was not. I am. I shall not be. Is this the past, present, and future? Is this what we desire from Time?"

"I must apologize, dear lady. I'm not following you, I fear."

"This hotel I'm talking about. Two big pyramids. Sheraton are interested already."

"Ah, but the security." Karen von Krupp laid her whip against her beautiful leg and arranged her pleated skirt. "These days. What can you guarantee?"

"No problem. Saudis."

"I prefer Nubians," said Jerry.

"These will be Saudis. That's non-negotiable."

Jerry looked up. From the far horizon came the steady thump of helicopter engines, then the sharper thwacking of their blades. He had a feeling about this. "Nubians or nothing," he said. And began to run back towards his camel.

* * *

2. THE BRANDY AND SELTZER BOYS

According to quantum theory, a card perfectly balanced on its edge will fall down in what is known as a "superposition"—the card really is in two places at once. If a gambler bets money on the queen landing face up, the gambler's own state changes to become a superposition of two possible outcomes—winning or losing the bet in either of these parallel worlds, the gambler is unaware of the other outcome and feels as if the card fell randomly.

—NATURE, 5 July 2007

"WE NEED RITUALS, Jerry. We need repetition. We need music and mythology and the constant reassurance that at certain times of the day we can visit the waterhole in safety. Without ritual, we are worthless. That's what the torturer knows when he takes away even the consistent repetition of our torment." Bunny Burroughs ordered another beer. There were still a few minutes to Curtain Up. This was to be the first time Gloria Cornish and Una Persson had appeared on the same stage. A revival. *The Arcadians.*

"These are on me." Jerry signed for the bill. "Repetition is a kind of death. It's what hopeless people do—what loonies do—sitting and rocking and muttering the same meaningless mantras over and over again. That's not conscious life."

"We don't *want* conscious life." Miss Brunner, coming in late, gave her coat to Bishop Beesley to take to the cloakroom. "Have I got time for a quick G&T? We don't want real variety. From the catch-phrase of the comedian to the reiteration of familiar opinions, they're the beating of a mother's heart, the breathing of a sleeping father."

"Maybe we've at last dispossessed ourselves of the past. We name our children after bathroom products, fantasy characters, drugs, diseases, and candy bars. We used to name them after saints or popular politicians..." Jerry finished his beer. A bell began to ring.

"That's just a different kind of continuity. The trusted brand has taken over from the trusted saint." Miss B. picked up her programme. "We're still desperate for the familiar. We try to discard it in favor of novelty, but it isn't really novelty, it's just another kind of familiarity. We tell ourselves of our self-expression and self-assertion. When I was a girl, my days were counted in terms of food. Sunday was a hot joint. Tuesday was cold sliced meat, potatoes, and a vegetable. Wednesday was shepherd's pie. Thursday was cauliflower cheese. Friday was fish. Saturday, we had a mixed grill. Just as lessons came and went at school, we attended the Saturday matinee, Sunday at a museum. Something uplifting, anyway, on Sunday. We move forward by means of rituals. We just try to find the means of keeping the carousel turning. We sing worksongs as we build roads. Music allows a semblance of progression, but it isn't real progression. Real progress leads where? To the grave, if we're lucky? Our stories are the same, with minor variations. We're comfortable, with minor variations, in the same clothes. The sun comes up and sets at the same time and we welcome the rise and fall of the workman's hammer, the beat of the drum. If we really wanted to cut our ties with the past we would do the only logical thing. We would kill ourselves."

"Isn't that just as boring?"

"Oh, I guess so, Mr. Cornelius." Bunny petted at his face and put down his empty glass.

As they walked towards their box, the overture was striking up.

3. FROM CLUE TO CLUE

The theme of the Wandering Jew has a history of centuries behind it, and many are the romances which that sinister and melancholy figure has flitted through. In this story you will see how the coming of the mythical Wanderer was a direct threat to the existence of our Empire, and how, when he, as the figurehead of revolt faded out of the picture, Sexton Blake tackled the real causes behind it.

—THE CASE OF THE WANDERING JEW,
Sexton Blake Annual, 1940

"I'M RUNNING OUT of memory." Jerry put his head on one side, like a parrot. "Or at best storage. I'm forgetting things. I think I might have something."

"Oh, god, don't give it to us." Miss Brunner became contemplative. "Is it catching? Like Alzheimer's?"

"I don't remember." Jerry took an A to Z from the pocket of his black car coat. "It depends if it's the past or the present. Or the future. I remember where Berwick Street is in Soho and I could locate Decatur Street. I'm not losing my bearings any worse than usual. Why is everyone trying to forget?"

"It wasn't part of the plan. I'm a bit new to this."
Bunny Burroughs glanced hopefully at Miss Brunner. "I think."

Now Jerry really was baffled. "Plan?"

"The plan for America. Remember Reagan?"

"Vaguely," said Jerry. He pointed ahead of him.
"If that's not a mirage, we've found an oasis."

4. THE NEW XJ—LUXURY TRANSFORMED BY DESIGN

Freighter captains avoid them as potential catastrophes; climate scientists see them as a bellwether of global warming. But now marine biologists have a more positive take on the thousands of icebergs that have broken free from Antarctica in recent years. These frigid, starkly beautiful mountains of floating ice turn out to be bubbling hot spots of biological activity. And in theory at least they could help counteract the buildup of greenhouse gases that are heating the planet.

—Michael D. Lemonick, TIME MAGAZINE,
6 August 2007 ·

"THEY'VE BEEN IN Trinity churchyard digging up the famous. I can't tell you how much they got for Audubon." Jerry sipped his chicory and coffee. The Café du Monde wasn't what it had been but they'd taken the worst of the rust off the chairs and the joss sticks helped. From somewhere down by the river came the broken sound of a riverboat bell. Then he began to smile at his friend across the table. "That was you, wasn't it?"

Max Pardon shrugged. "We were downsized. What can I say? We have to make a living as best we can. The bottom dropped out of real estate. I'm a bone broker these days, Mr. Cornelius. It's an honest job. Some of us still have an interest in our heritage. Monsieur Audubon was a very great man. He made his living, you could say, as a resurrectionist. Mostly. He killed that poor, mad golden eagle. Do I do anything worse?"

Jerry took a deep breath and regretted it.

5. THE FLOODS THAT REALLY MATTER ARE COMPOSED OF MIGRANT LABOUR

Intimate talk about loving your age, finding true joy, and the three words that can change your life.
—GOOD HOUSEKEEPING, June 2005

IN ISLAMABAD, JERRY traded his Banning for an antique Lee-Enfield .303 with a telescopic sight. He had come all the way by aerial cruiser, the guest of Major Nye, with the intention of seeing, if he could do it secretly, his natural son Hussein, who was almost ten. Slipping the beautifully embellished rifle into his cricket bag, he made for an address on Kabul Street, ridding himself of two sets of "shadows". The most recent Islamic government were highly suspicious of all Europeans, even though Jerry's Turkish passport gave his religion as Moslem. He wore a beautifully cut coat in two shades of light blue silk, with a set of silver buttons and a turban in darker blue. To the casual eye he resembled a prosperous young stockbroker, perhaps from Singapore.

Arriving at Number Eight, Jerry made his way through a beautiful courtyard to a shaded staircase which he climbed rapidly after a glance behind him to see if he was followed. On the third floor at the door furthest along the landing he stopped and knocked. Almost immediately the recently painted door was opened and Bunny Burroughs let him in, his thin lips twisting as he recognized the cricket bag.

"Your fifth attempt, I understand, Jerry. Did you have a safe trip? And will you be playing your usual game this Sunday?"

"If I can find some whites." Jerry set the bag down and removed his rifle. With his silk handkerchief he dabbed at his sleeve. "Oil. Virgin. Is the boy over there?"

"With his nanny. The mother, as I told you, is visiting her uncle."

Jerry peered through the slats of a blind. Across the courtyard, at a tall window, a young woman in a sari was mixing a glass of diluted lemon juice and sugar. Behind her the blue screen of a TV was showing an old Humphrey Bogart movie.

"*Casablanca*," murmured Bunny.

"*The Big Sleep*." Jerry lifted the rifle to his shoulder and put his eye close to the sight.

He would never know another sound like that which followed his pulling the trigger and the bang the gun made.

He had done the best he could. That at least he understood.

* * *

6. THE PHANTOM OF THE TOWERS

International trade in great white sharks now will be regulated, which is especially important for fish that range far beyond the shelter of regional protection. The humphead or Napoleon wrasse—worth tens of thousands of dollars on the market—also received protections, in turn saving coral reefs from the cyanide used to capture them.

—ANIMAL UPDATE, Winter 2005

HUBERT LANE AND Violet Elizabeth Bott were waiting on the corner for Jerry as soon as he reached the outskirts of the village. He had driven over from Hadley to see old Mr. Brown. Hubert smirked when he saw Jerry's Phantom IV. "You've done a lot better for yourself than anyone would have guessed a few years ago."

Jerry ignored him.

"Hewwo, Jewwy," lisped Violet Elizabeth, rather grotesquely coy for her age. "Wovely to see you."

Jerry scowled. He was already regretting his decision but he opened the gate and began to walk up the surprisingly overgrown path. The Browns clearly hadn't kept their gardener on. Things had deteriorated rather a lot since 1978. The front door of the double fronted Tudor-style detached house could do with a lick of paint. The brass needed a polish, too. He lifted the knocker.

The door was opened by a woman in uniform.

"Mr. 'Cornelius?'"

"That's right."

"Mr. Brown said you were coming. He's upstairs. I'm the District Nurse. I hung on specially. This way."

She moved her full lips in a thin, professionaal smile and took him straight upstairs. The house smelled familiar and the wallpaper hadn't changed since his last visit. Mrs. Brown had been alive then. The older children, Ethel and Robert, had been home from America and Australia respectively.

"They're expected any time," said the nurse when he asked. She opened the bedroom door. Now the medicinal smell overwhelmed everything else. Old Mr. Brown was completely bald. His face was much thinner. Jerry no longer had any idea of his age. He looked a hundred.

"Hello, boy." Mr. Brown's voice was surprisingly vibrant. "Nice of you to drop in." His smile broadened. "Hoping for a tip were you?"

"Crumbs!" said Jerry.

7. A GAME OF PATIENCE

For ten years South Park has tackled America's idiocies through violence, swearing, and song. But two academic studies miss the joke.

—NEW STATESMAN, 25 June 2007

BANNING BEHIND HIM, Mo put the Humvee in gear and set off across a desert which reminded him of Marilyn Monroe, Charles Manson, and Clark Gable. Tumbleweed, red dust, the occasional cactus, yucca, jasper trees. He was heading west and south, trying to avoid the highways. Eventually he saw mountains.

A couple of days later, he woke Jerry, who had been asleep in the back since Banning.

"Here we are, Mr. C."

Jerry stretched out on the old rug covering the floor of the vehicle. "Christmas should be Christmas now we've presents," he blinked out of the window at a butte. There were faces in every rock. This was the South West as he preferred it. Mo was dragging his gun behind him as he squeezed into a narrow fissure, one of several in the massive rockface. According to legend, some hunted Indian army had made this their last retreat. Somewhere within, there was water, grass, even corn. The countless variegated shades of red and brown offered some hint of logic, at least symmetry, swirling across the outcrops and natural walls as if painted by a New York expressionist. They reminded Jerry of the Martian dead sea bottoms he had loved in his youth. He had been born in London, but he had been raised on Mars. He could imagine the steady movement of waves overhead. He looked up.

Zuni knifewings had been carved at intervals around the entrance of the canyon; between each one was a swastika.

"I wonder what they had against the Jews," said Mo. He paused to take a swig from his canteen.

Jerry shrugged. "You'd have thought there was a lot in common."

Now Mo disappeared into the fissure. His voice echoed. "It's huge in here. Amazing. I'll start placing the charges, shall I?"

Jerry began to have second thoughts. "This doesn't feel like Christmas any more."

Behind them, on the horizon, a Diné or Apaché warband sat on ponies so still they might have been carved from the same ancient rock.

Jerry sighed. "Or bloody Kansas!" He started to set up his Banning.

8. A CITY SLICKER EMAILED IN THE STICKS

Tony Blair claims that one of his many achievements in office was not to repeal the employment laws passed by Margaret Thatcher's government to weaken trade union power. But Blair, as a young and politically ambitious barrister, was a staunch supporter of trade union rights.

—NEW STATESMAN, 25 June 2007

"I KNOW WHERE you're coming from, Jerry." Bunny Burroughs closed his laptop. Of course he didn't. He had only the vaguest idea. Jerry didn't even bother to tell him about *The Magnet*, Sexton Blake, or George Formby. They certainly had some memories in common, but even those were filtered through such a mix of singular cultural references they changed the simplest meaning. Bunny's baseball and Cornelius's cricket: the list was endless. Yet somehow exile brought out the best in them. They would always have Paris.

Jerry sniffed. "Are you still selling that stuff?"

"Virtual vapour? It's very popular. While thousands die in Rwanda, millions watch TV and concern themselves with the fate of the mountain gorilla whose time in the world is actually less

limited. Assuming zoos continue to do their stuff."
He held up a can. "Want a sniff?" He peered round
at the others. "Anybody?"

"If I had a shilling for every year I've thought
about the future, I'd be a rich man today." Bishop
Beesley hesitated before slipping a Heath Bar
between his lips and breathing in the soft scent of
chocolate and burned sugar. "Sweet!" He let a sentimental smile drift across his lips. "I know it's a
weakness, but which of us isn't weak somewhere? I
live to forget. I mean forgive. I've a parish in South
London now. Did you know?"

"I think you told me."

"No," said Bill.

"No? It's only across the river. We could."

"No." Jerry continued to look for a channel. "I
don't cross running water if I can help it. And I
don't do snow."

"It's really not as cold as people say it is. Even
Norbury's warmer than you'd guess. Kingsley Amis
grew up there. And Edwy Searles Brooks. Brooks
was the most famous person to come from Norbury. St. Franks? Waldo the Wonderman?"

Jerry shuddered. He'd be hearing about the wonders of Wimbledon next. Tactfully he asked if
Beesley knew a second-hand tyre shop easily
reached.

"There's even a beach of sorts." The bishop
breathed impatience. "Where Tooting Common
used to be. Though they haven't axed the chestnut
trees."

"They must be borders," suggested Bill.

"Still plenty for the little 'uns."

"Plenty?"

"Conkers." The bishop put a knowing hand on Jerry's arm. "Don't worry. No ward of mine has ever come to harm."

"Conkers? No, you're barmy. Bonkers." Jerry shook him off, swiftly walking to the outside door.

"Pop in. Any time. You've not forgotten how to pray?"

The bishop's voice was muffled, full of half-masticated Mars.

Jerry paused, trying to think of a retort.

Bunny Burroughs stood up, his thin body awkward beneath the cloth of his loose, charcoal gray suit. "I am a gloomy man, Mr. Cornelius. I have a vision. Follow me. Of the appalling filth of this world, I am frequently unobservant. Once I revelled in it, you could fairly say. Now it disgusts me. I am no longer a lover of shit. I came on the streetcar. That's what I like about Europe. Are the streetcars. Environment friendly and everything. They have a narrative value you don't run into much any more. Certainly not in America. My mother was German. Studied eugenics, I think. On the evidence. But I'm English on my father's side. I fought on my father's side."

He turned to look out of the window. "The slave-ships threw over the dead and dying. *Typhoon coming on.*" He picked up the laptop. "Trained octopi drove those trams, they say."

Jerry said. "OK. I give up. When can you get me connected?"

"It depends." Burroughs frowned, either making a calculation or pretending to make one. "It depends how much memory you want. Four to seven days?" His long, sad face contemplated some invisible chart. His thin fingers played air computer. "Any options?"

Jerry had become impatient. "Only connect," he said. God, how he yearned for a taste of the real world. The world he had been sure he knew. Even Norbury.

9. THE MOST FUEL EFFICIENT AUTO COMPANY IN AMERICA

Britain's got talent, Simon Cowell has tried to prove over the past few weeks, but is it really in the stick-twirling, octogenerian tap-dancing toddler music hall turns, or transvestite singing acts we've seen on TV.
—New Statesman, 25 June 2007

"What I can't understand about you, Mr. Cornelius," Miss Brunner opened a cornflower blue sunshade only slightly wider than her royal blue Gainsborough hat, "is why so many of your mentors are gay. Or Catholic. Or both."

"Or Jewish," said Jerry. "You can't forget the Jews. It's probably the guilt."

"You? Guilt? Have you ever felt guilt?"

"That's not the point." He found himself thinking again of Alexander, his unborn son. Invisibly, he collected himself. "I reflect it."

"That's gilt. Not guilt."

"Oh, believe me. They're often the same thing."

From somewhere beyond the crowd a gun cracked.

She brightened, quickening her high-heeled trot. "They're off!"

Jerry tripped behind her. There was something about Surrey he was never going to like.

10. THE SLEEP YOU'VE BEEN DREAMING OF

Swaths of regulation on an industry of "feat entrepreneurs" have fuelled a climate of timidity about the dangers of every day life. If lawsuits replace the concept of a simple no-fault accident, this will damage not only our national resilience, but also the economy.

—NEW STATESMAN, 30 July 2007

BACK IN ISLAMABAD, Jerry read the news from New Orleans. He wondered if the French were going to regret their decision to buy it back. Of course, it did give them the refineries and a means of getting their tankers up to Memphis, but how would the American public take to the reintroduction of the minstrels on the showboats?

"People who are free, who live in a real republic, are never offended, Jerry. At best they are a little irritated. They should be able to take a joke by now. In context."

"Wait till they burn *your* bloody car." Jerry was still upset about what had happened in Marseilles.

"They are citizens. They have the same rights and responsibilities as me." Max Pardon swung his legs on his stool. He had rewaxed his moustache. Possibly with cocoa butter.

Jerry lit a long, black Sherman. "At least you've brought back smoking."

"That's the Republic, Jerry."

Max Pardon raised his hat to a passing Bedouin. "God bless the man who discovered sand-power." Overhead the last of the great aerial steamers made its stately way into the sunrise just as the muezzin began to call the faithful to prayer. Monsieur Pardon unrolled his mat and kneeled. "If you'll forgive me."

11. WHY I LOVE METAL

It's what you've been craving. Peaceful sleep without a struggle. That's what LUNESTA© is all about: helping most people fall asleep quickly, and stay asleep all through the night. It's not only non-narcotic; it's approved for long-term use.

—Ad for eszopiclone in TIME MAGAZINE,
6 August 2007

"I AM SICK of people who can't distinguish the taste of sugar from the taste of fruit, who can't tell salt from cheese, who think watching CNN makes them into intellectuals and believe that Big Brother and The Batchelor is real life. The richest, most powerful country in the world is about as removed from reality as Oz is from Kansas or Kansas is from Kabul." Major Nye was in a rare mood as he leaned over the rail of *The Empress of India* searching with his binoculars for his old station.

From somehwere among the bleak, rolling downs puffs of smoke showed the positions of the Pashtoon.

"I remember all the times the British tried to invade and hold Afghanistan. What surprises me is why these Yanks think they are somehow better at it, when they've never won a war by themselves since the Mexicans decided to let them have California. Every few years they start another bloody campaign and refuse to listen to their own military chaps and go swaggering in to get their bottoms kicked for the umpteenth time. They learned an unfortunate lesson from their successes against the Indians, such as they were. If you ask me they would have done better to have taken a leaf from Custer's book."

"Education's never been their strength." Holding her hat with her left hand, Miss Brunner waved and smiled at someone in the observation gallery. "It's windy out here, don't you think?"

"Better than that fug in there." Major Nye indicated the Smoking Room. With a gesture close to impatience, he threw his cigarette over the side.

As if in answer, another rifle spoke from below.

Miss Brunner looked down disapprovingly. "There should be more school shootings, if you ask me. They should just be more selective." She looked up, directing a frigid smile at Mitzi Beesley, who came out to join them. Mitzi was wearing a borrowed flying helmet, a short, pink divided skirt, a flounced white blouse, a knitted bolero jacket.

Jerry remembered her closing the gate of her Hampstead Garden Village bijou cottage, as she left him in charge for a week. That had been the last time they had met. She was no longer speaking to him. He went back into the bar and closed the door. It seemed almost silent here; just the soft hum of the giant electric motors. He accepted a pint of Black Velvet. He had a rat buttoned inside his coat. Its nose tickled his chest and he gave an involuntary twitch. Mitzi still didn't know he had rescued "Sweety" from the fire. He had grown attached to the little animal and felt Mitzi was an imperfect owner. The Bengali barman polished a glass. "Life's a bloody tragedy, isn't it sir? Same again?"

Outside, the rain began to drum on the canopy. Major Nye and the women came running in. "I for one will be glad to get back to Casablanca," said Miss Brunner.

12. WILL BROWN BE BUSH'S NEW POODLE?

Until recently, criticisms of the BBC were helpful, and attacks upon it harmless; indeed it provided, among other blessings, a happy grumbling ground for the sedentary, where they could release their superfluous force... and if not much good was done there was anyhow no harm... Unfortunately, [the BBC's] dignity is only superficial. It does yield to criticism, and to bad criticism, and it yields in advance—the most pernicious of surrenders.

—E.M.Forster NEW STATESMAN,
4 April 1931

JERRY HAD SHOWERED and was getting into his regular clothes when Professor Hira came into the changing rooms.

"You were superb today, Mr. Cornelius. Especially under the circumstances.

Jerry accepted his handshake. "Oh, you know, it's not as if they got the whole of London."

"Hampstead, Islington, Camden! The Heath is a pit of ash. We saw the cloud on TV. Red and black. The blood! The smoke. Of course, we know that our bombs, for instance, are much more powerful. But Hampstead Garden Village! My home was there for over four years. The Beesley's, too. And so many other dear neighbours."

"You think it was their target?"

"No doubt about it. And next time it will be Hyde Park or Wimbledon Common. Even Victoria Park. They are easy to home in on, you see."

"Another park is where they'll strike next?"

"Or, heaven forbid, Lords. Or the Oval."

"Good god. They'll keep the ashes forever!"

"Our fear exactly." Professor Hira took Jerry's other hand. "You plan, I hope, to stay in Mombai for a bit? We could do with a good all-rounder."

Jerry considered this. It was quite a while since he'd been to the pictures. "It depends what's on, I suppose." He bent and picked up his cricket bag. "And I'm sure it's still possible to get a game or two in before things become too hot."

"Oh, at least. And, Mr. Cornelius, it will never be too hot for you in India. Pakistan has far too many distractions, what with the Americans and their own religeuses."

Jerry scratched his head. Reluctant as he was to leave, he thought it was time he got back home again.

13. BETRAYAL IN IRAQ

MEN LOVE POWER. Why? Ever see what happens when something gets in the way of a tornado? Exactly. That's the thinking behind the Chevy Vortec™ Max powertrain—create a ferocious vortex inside the combustion chamber, along with a high compression ratio, to generate formidable power. And the 345-hp Vortec™ Max, available on the 2006 Silverado, is no exception... **CHEVY SILVERADO: AN AMERICAN REVOLUTION.**

—Chevrolet Ad, Texas Monthly,
December 2005

CHRISTMAS 1962, SNOW still falling just after dawn when Jerry sprung the gate into Ladbroke Grove/Elgin Gardens and walked onto the path leaving black pointed prints and tiny heel marks. He had never made a cooler trail. Slipping between the gaps in the netting, he crossed the tennis court and stopped to look back. The marks might have been those of an exotic animal. Nobody coming behind him would know a human had made them. Yet they were already filling up again.

He would never be sure he had deceived anyone. He darted into the nearest back garden. From the French windows came the sound of a Schoenberg piano roll. The snow was a foot deep on the brick wall, on the small lawn. Yellow light fell from the window above. He heard a woman's voice not unlike his mother's. "Go back to bed, love. It's not time yet." He recognized Mrs. Pash. Her grandchildren were up early, pedalling the piano. He caught a glimpse of the tree through the half-drawn curtains.

Jerry stepped softly out of the little garden. A blind moved on the first floor in the corner house. The colonel and his wife were looking at him. Another minute and they'd call the police. Their hangovers always made them doubly suspicious. He bowed and returned the way he had come, back into Ladbroke Grove, back across to Blenheim Crescent, past the Convent of the Poor Clares, on his left, to 51, where his mother still lived.

Humming to himself, Jerry went down the slippery area steps to let himself in with his key. Nobody was up. He unshipped the sack from his shoulder and checked out the row of stockings hanging over the black, greasy kitchen range from which a few whisps of smoke escaped. He opened the stove's top and shovelled in more coke. His mum had put the turkey in to cook overnight. There wasn't a tastier smell in the whole world. Then, carefully, he began to fill the stockings from his sack.

Upstairs, he thought he heard someone stirring. He could imagine what the tree looked like, how delighted Catherine and Frank would be when they came down to see their presents.

Outside, the snow still fell, softening the morning. He found the radio set and turned it on. Christmas carols began to sound. The noises upstairs grew louder.

Travel certainly made you appreciate the simple things of life, he thought. His eyes filled with happy tears. He went to the kitchen cupboard and took out the bottle of Heine he had put there the night before. Frank hadn't found it. The seal was unbroken. Jerry helped himself to a little nip.

Mrs. Cornelius came thumping downstairs in her old carpet slippers. She wore a bright red and green dressing gown, her hair still in curlers, last night's make-up still smeared across her face. She rubbed her eyes, staring with approval at the lumpy stockings hanging over the stove.

"Cor," she said. "Merry Christmas, love."

"Merry Christmas, mum." He leaned to kiss her. "God bless us, every one."

THE END

Parts of this story originally appeared in NATURE, PLANET STORIES, THE NEW STATESMAN, TIME MAGAZINE, THE SPECTATOR, FANTASY SPORTS, PC WORLD, WIRED, TWO SCIENCE ADVENTURE BOOKS, THE HAPPY MAG, BOY'S FRIEND LIBRARY, SCHOOLBOY'S OWN LIBRARY, THE MAGNET, NELSON LEE LIBRARY, SEXTON BLAKE LIBRARY, UNION JACK LIBRARY, GOOD HOUSEHEEPING, SPORTS ILLUSTRATED, TEXAS MONTHLY, HARPERS, THE NEW YORKER, THE NEW YORK TIMES, THE GUARDIAN, NOVAE TERRAE and others.

Point of Contact

Dan Abnett

THEY WERE NOT a highly advanced civilization. They had not been looking for us, nor were they particularly surprised to find us.

Their spacecraft were not monolithic slabs of techno-organic wonder hanging in the thin reaches of our upper atmosphere, neither were they saucer-, helix-, or cigar-shaped objects.

Though a frisson of existential panic briefly trembled across our world, as we coped with the profound implications for society, biology, and, most of all, religion that their arrival heralded, they did not seem especially exercised by the whole thing. They had not encountered other life before, but they had always accepted that its existence was a given. We were not the conclusive evidence their culture had been yearning for.

For our part, there was some sporadic faith-based rioting and a temporary rise in the basal suicide rate, but things soon settled down. The fundamental tenets of our global civilizations did not collapse overnight. The sky did not catch fire. The world did not stand still. There was no panic in the streets. Cats and dogs did not start living together. There was no ontologically triggered apocalypse, though global sales of science fiction slumped a little.

They were not invaders, which was generally regarded as a good thing. They did not have ray guns or robots. They were not armed in any way we could spot. They had no antigravity devices or force fields, no matter transporter systems or warp drives. They were not traders or slavers, nor possessed of some malign agenda inimical to man. They were not even, it had to be said, especially motivated explorers, cartographers or discoverers. They did not plant a flag, or similar totem, in our planet's crust upon arrival, and they did not claim our world in the name of some distant stellar hegemony, empire, or overlord.

They did not possess a universal translator. Open discourse between species took three years to really get beyond the basics, and even then it was of a level equivalent to the "useful expressions" one might find in a tourist phrase book. The inter-translation work was not accomplished with computers, because our computers were not in any way compatible with theirs. The whole business was rather more a case of pointing to objects and repeating their names in a loud voice. They did not seem particularly disposed to learn our speech, or our customs and habits, and never really mastered the subjunctive.

They could not breathe our air, or suffer any part of our climate or atmosphere directly. They could not automatically adjust their biology to suit the prevailing conditions or, presumably, alter ours. Their space suits were not really very sleek or impressive. They were slightly grubby and had valves, which seemed to require a great deal of cleaning and adjustment. They were always wiping condensation off their visors.

They were only slightly impressed to meet our heads of state, and not at all taken with the parades and celebrations we threw for them. They liked to stay together, and point at things, and whisper.

Biologically they were not like us, and shared none of our symmetries or evolutionary traits. They were not gold-skinned and beautiful. They were not hideous and fear-inspiring. They were not visually identical to humans except for some cosmetic differences around the eyebrow ridge. They were not shape-changers or mimics, telepaths or telekinetics. They were not, in any way, cybernetically enhanced. They could not possess us or control our minds. They were not derived from any identifiable evolutionary origin, such as cats, or wolves, or jellyfish, or lizards. They were not green, or gray.

They were not even curious as specimens. In general, we found they were rather unremarkable and slightly, very slightly, unattractive, like a boorish neighbor or an oaf in a pub. They allowed us to study them, but we did not learn anything to our particular advantage. They did not render up secrets that paved the way to breakthroughs in our medicine or sciences. They did not have a cure for cancer. They did not have cancer. They could not live forever, nor had they devised a means to artificially prolong their natural life spans. They had no wish to do so.

In the course of the contact period, we did manage to learn certain things. They had little or no sense of humor. They were not inflamed with a desire to respect and preserve a bioverse's ecology, and they knew no salutary warning stories or species parables concerning races that had thoughtlessly despoiled their homeworlds and suffered as a consequence. They did not much care about solutions for global warming.

They most certainly had not seeded us here in the first place, and they didn't know of anyone who might have been responsible. They did not think it likely at all. They had not picked up our decades of indiscriminately scattered television and radio signals and thus formed an opinion about what sort of people we were. They had not built, or over seen the construction of, Stonehenge, the Pyramids, or Nazca, nor had they been involved in the demolition of Atlantis (which, in any case, they could not locate on a map). They had not visited us before, in some antediluvian era, and taught us everything they knew. They had never lost anything in New Mexico.

They had not come very far. They told us about their world. It did not sound very edifying. They had no mile-high spires, or crystal habitat domes, or hive cities. They did not live underground, or underwater, or in gently drifting cloud cities. They did not have a single towering repository containing their accumulated knowledge. They did not worship a vast and mysterious techno-logical artifact that pre-dated the rise of their own species. They had not survived a terrible atomic war in their history, and this had not given rise to widespread genetic mutation, or divergent strands in their species. They were not ruled over, or even benevolently administered to, by an artificial sentience. They did not believe in god, and they knew neither the secrets of the uni-verse, nor the meaning of life. They did not, as has already been remarked, possess a technology sufficiently advanced that it might be indistin-guishable from magic.

On the plus side, they did not require any portion or portions of our anatomy as food, or even delica-cy. Our souls were also not an essential part of their diet. They did not wish to mate with our females. Or our males. Or our whales.

They implied, diplomatically, that news of the contact would not be a particularly big deal back home, and tended to play down the idea that more of them might come, even for a brief visit. There was not, they added, a galactic council, federation, coalition, or other similar body that we might join, be recognized by, or send envoys to.

They showed us some of their art and literature. It was not especially engaging, sublime, or metaphysically profound to our tastes. There were paintings and sculptures and lyrical works, which were not all that dissimilar to our own, to be fair, but without a proper context, they seemed rather flat and pedestrian: like our art and literature, really, but just not quite so good. We, naturally, shared with them our artistic legacy, and their response did not extend much beyond "meh".

Though they were not hostile, they had not come in friendship. They were, it seemed, passing through, and they were not particularly forthcoming as to where "through" might lead them. They did not invite us to accompany them on their voyage. They did not invite us to visit their world either. Addresses were exchanged, as with holiday acquaintances, for appearance sake, but there was no real expectation of an actual follow up made by either party. They did not stay long. They did not say goodbye.

We did not wish them godspeed. We did not stand en masse and watch them ascend into the night sky with tears in our eyes. We did not raise our hands in a last farewell and think, with lumps in our throats, that things would never, ever be the same again.

We were right.

They did not change the world. We considered, for a short time, initiating a space flight program to send a mission to their system, but in the end we decided not to spend the trillion trillion dollars required. We did not, having saved that money, spend it wisely elsewhere.

Aside from a little more of the sporadic faith-based rioting and another temporary rise in the basal suicide rate, we got over their departure. Our culture did not change. We did not mend our ways, or feel enlightened. We did not appreciate our place in the cosmos differently. We did not enter a new, positive age of understanding. And we did not especially care.

They did not come back. We have not heard from them again.

About the Authors

Paul Di Filippo is one of the most prolific—and unclassifiable—authors working in the genre today. His short stories have won him much critical acclaim and he has been a finalist for the Hugo, Nebula, BSFA, Philip K. Dick, and World Fantasy awards. His short story collections include: *The Steampunk Trilogy*, *Ribofunk*, *Little Doors*, *Lost Pages*, and *Harsh Oases* (to name but a few). His novels include: *Ciphers*, *Joe's Liver*, *Fuzzy Dice*, *A Mouthful of Tongues*, *Spondulix*, and *Cosmocopia*. He lives in Providence, Rhode Island.

Kay Kenyon's seventh SF novel, *Bright of the Sky*, received high critical acclaim upon publication, including a starred review in *Publishers Weekly*. Forthcoming (March 2008) is book two of this series, *A World Too Near*. Her novels *Maximum Ice* and *The Braided World* were short-listed for the Philip K. Dick and John W. Campbell awards, respectively. Her novels and short stories have been variously anthologized, podcast, and translated into French and Russian. Kay is the president of the

Write on the River conference in eastern Washington. She publishes "Still Writing," a newsletter on writing fiction. Her website is *www.kaykenyon.com*.

Chris Roberson's novels include *Set the Seas on Fire*, *Here, There & Everywhere*, *The Voyage of Night Shining White*, *Paragaea: A Planetary Romance*, and *The Dragon's Nine Sons*, and he is the editor of the anthology *Adventure Vol. 1*. Roberson has been a finalist for the World Fantasy Award for Short Fiction, twice for the John W. Campbell Award for Best New Writer, and twice for the Sidewise Award for Best Alternate History Short Form (winning in 2004 with his story "O One"). He runs the independent press MonkeyBrain Books with his wife Allison Baker. his website is *www.chrisroberson.net*.

Robert Reed is the ridiculously prolific author of more than 160 published stories and nearly a dozen novels. He has been nominated for multiple Hugos, a Nebula, and a World Fantasy Award. Robert lives in Lincoln, Nebraska with his wife, Leslie, and their six year-old daughter, Jessie. When asked what her father does for a living, Jessie proudly exclaims, "He lies!"

Neal Asher's *Polity* universe is one of the most dark, dangerous, and downright fun settings in modern science fiction. It includes the novels *Gridlinked*, *The Skinner*, *The Line of Polity*, *Brass*

Man, *The Voyage of the Sable Keech*, *Polity Agent*, *Prador Moon,* and *Hilldiggers*. His short fiction has been published in a wide variety of locations, from Asimov's to the British small press and most places in-between. He lives in Essex, England.

Brenda Cooper is a futurist, a writer, and a technology professional. Her short fiction has appeared in Analog, Asimov's, Strange Horizons, Nature, and in multiple anthologies. She writes and blogs at *www.futurist.com* and can sometimes be found talking to business audiences about the future. Her latest novel is *The Silver Ship and the Sea*.

Peter Watts is a one-time marine biologist who is actually far more personable than his fiction might lead one to believe. His various novels and short stories deal with such issues as *The Healing Power of Revenge*, *Genocide—the Silver Lining*, and *What Do We Really Need The Environment For Anyway?* His latest novel, *Blindsight*, a rumination on the nature and evolutionary function of Human consciousness (with space vampires), has been nominated for several prestigious awards; as of this writing, it has won exactly none of them.

Eric Brown has written over twenty-five books and almost a hundred short stories. He is twice winner of the BSFA award for short fiction. His recent books include the novel *Helix* and the novella *Starship Summer*. Forthcoming is the novel *Kéthani*.

His monthly SF review column appears in *The Guardian*. He remains one of the most important British writers working in the field today and his humane, character-driven fiction continues to receive critical acclaim. He lives in Cambridge, England, with his wife and daughter. His website is at: *http://ericbrown.co.uk*

Mary Robinette Kowal is a professional puppeteer who moonlights as a writer. Originally from North Carolina, Mrs. Kowal lives in New York or Iceland. Her short fiction appears in *Strange Horizons*, *Cosmos,* and *CICADA*.

Dominic Green was born. Breathes oxygen just like you do. An attempt to educate him was made, in vain, by St Catharine's College, Cambridge. Learned to program computers in COBOL. Spent the next ten years not programming computers in COBOL. Works for a large and vengeful credit card issuer and acquirer. Was formerly a martial arts instructor. Was married to a super lady in 2005. Is owned by a cat. He bleeds. You can kill him.

Karl Schroeder is a science fiction writer and foresight analyst. He has published seven novels, including the award-winning *Permanence*, *Lady of Mazes*, and the acclaimed Virga series which includes *Sun of Suns*. In addition to his writing, Karl consults on foresight issues and is a regular contributor to the world's leading "bright green" weblog, *www.worldchanging.com*. He lives in Toronto, Canada with his wife and daughter.

David Louis Edelman is the author of *Infoquake*, which was nominated for the John W. Campbell Award for Best Novel. Barnes & Noble also listed the book as its Top SF Novel of 2006, calling it "the love child of Donald Trump and Vernor Vinge." Over the past ten years, Edelman has programmed websites for the U.S. Army and the FBI, taught software to the U.S. Congress and the World Bank, written articles for the Washington Post and Baltimore Sun, and directed the marketing departments of biometric and e-commerce companies. His next novel, *MultiReal*, will be released in Summer 2008.

Born at the end of 1939, **Michael Moorcock** published his first fanzine at the age of nine, his first professional work at 15, and edited various national magazines including New Worlds before he was 24. As a musician he worked with The Deep Fix, Hawkwind, Blue Oyster Cult, Robert Calvert, and others. He's won most SF and fantasy awards, has been nominated for both Booker and Whitbread, and won The Guardian Fiction Prize for Cornelius Quartet. He writes for *Daily Telegraph*, *Spectator*, *New Statesman*, *Nature*, *The Guardian* etc. He lives in Austin, Texas, and Paris, France.

Dan Abnett is a novelist and an award-winning comic book writer. He has written twenty-five novels for the Black Library, including the acclaimed

Gaunt's Ghosts series and the Inquisitor Eisenhorn trilogy. His Black Library novel *Horus Rising* and his Torchwood novel *Border Princes* (for the BBC) were both national bestsellers. He lives and works in Maidstone, Kent.

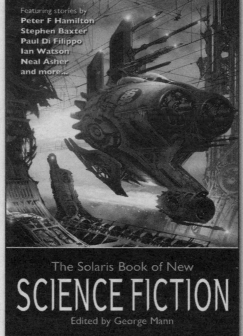